Emmanuel Guibert

ARIOL

Thunder

PAPERCUTZ™

ARiOL Graphic Novels available from PAPERCUTZ™

Emmanuel Guibert
Marc Boutavant
ARiOL
Just a Donkey Like You and Me
PAPERCUTZ™

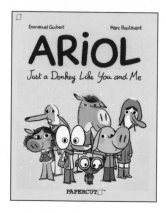

Graphic Novel #1
"Just a Donkey Like
You and Me"

Emmanuel Guibert
Marc Boutavant
ARiOL
Thunder Horse
PAPERCUTZ™

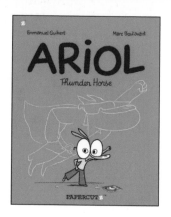

Graphic Novel #2
"Thunder Horse"

Emmanuel Guibert
Marc Boutavant
ARiOL
Happy as a Pig...
PAPERCUTZ™

Coming Soon!
Graphic Novel #3
"Happy as a Pig..."

ARiOL graphic novels are available for $12.99 only in paperback. Available from booksellers everywhere. You can also order online from www.papercutz.com. Or call 1-800-886-1223, Monday through Friday, 9-5 EST. MC, Visa and AmEx accepted. To order by mail, please add $4.00 for postage and handling for first book ordered, $1.00 for each additional book and make check payable to NBM Publishing. Send to: Papercutz, 160 Broadway, Suite 700, East Wing, New York, NY 10038.

ARiOL graphic novels are also available digitally wherever e-books are sold.

papercutz.com

Thunder Horse

Stickers, *page 5*

Chocolate Éclairs, *page 15*

Vaccine Reaction, *page 25*

Karaté, *page 35*

We're Going to Have Fun, *page 45*

Hide and Break, *page 55*

ARiOL's Secrets, *page 65*

ARiOL Plants a Tree, *page 75*

Summer Vacation, *page 85*

In the Train, *page 95*

OH! THE SEA!, *page 105*

A Good Book, *page 115*

To Madame Gassin,
– Emmanuel Guibert

ARIOL

#2 Thunder Horse

Emmanuel Guibert – Writer

Marc Boutavant – Artist

Joe Johnson – Translation

Michael Petranek – Lettering

Beth Scorzato – Production Coordinator

Michael Petranek – Associate Editor

Jim Salicrup

Editor-in-Chief

Volume 2: Le CHEVALiER CHEVAL © Bayard Editions –– 2007

ISBN: 978-1-59707-412-4

Printed in China
June 2013 by New Era Printing, LTD.
Unit C. 8/F Worldwide Centre
123 Chung Tau, Kowloon
Hong Kong

Papercutz books may be purchased for business or promotional use. For information on bulk purchases please contact Macmillan Corporate and Premium Sales Department at (800) 221-7945 x5442.

Distributed by Macmillan
First Papercutz Printing

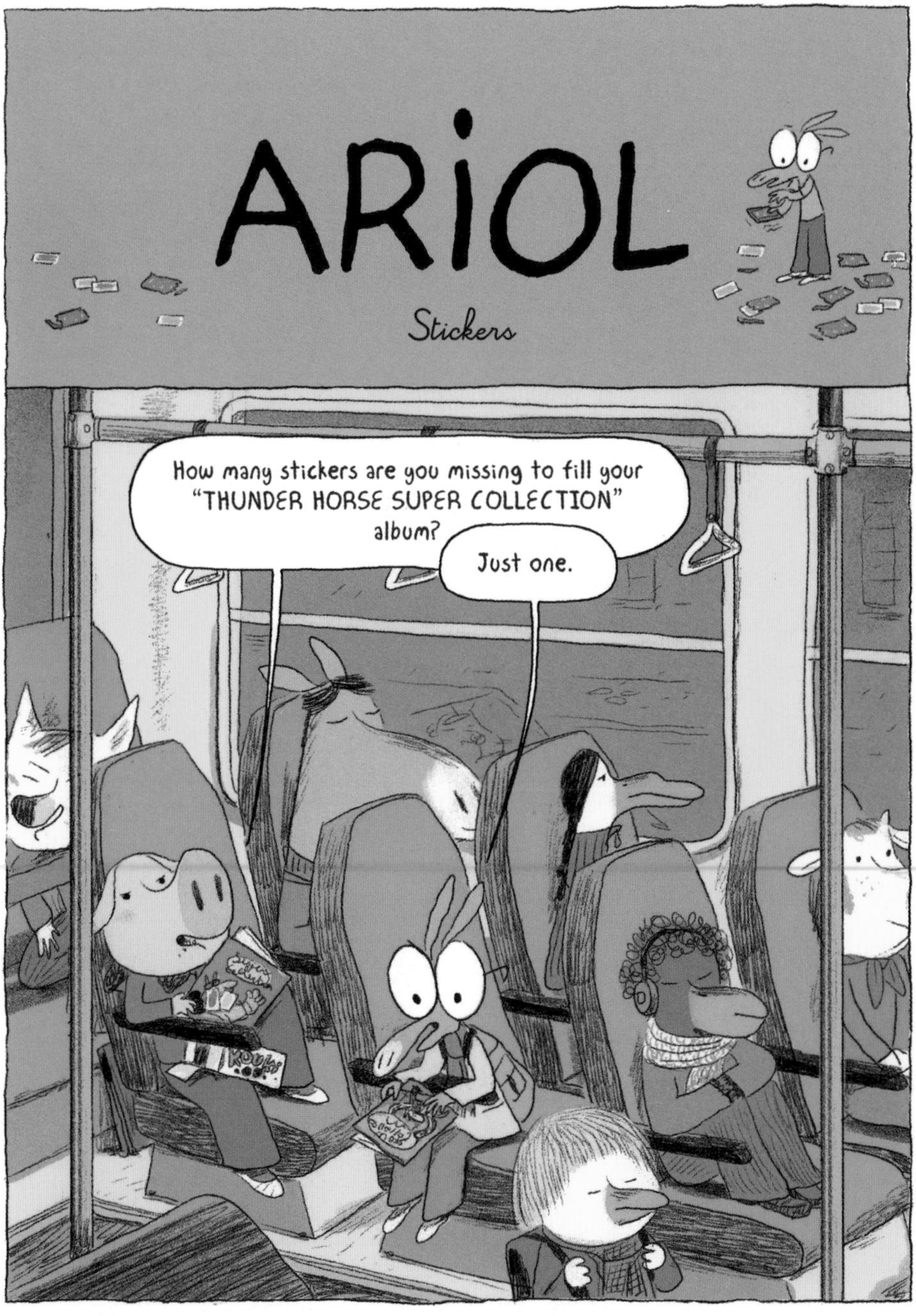
ARiOL
Stickers
How many stickers are you missing to fill your "THUNDER HORSE SUPER COLLECTION" album?
Just one.

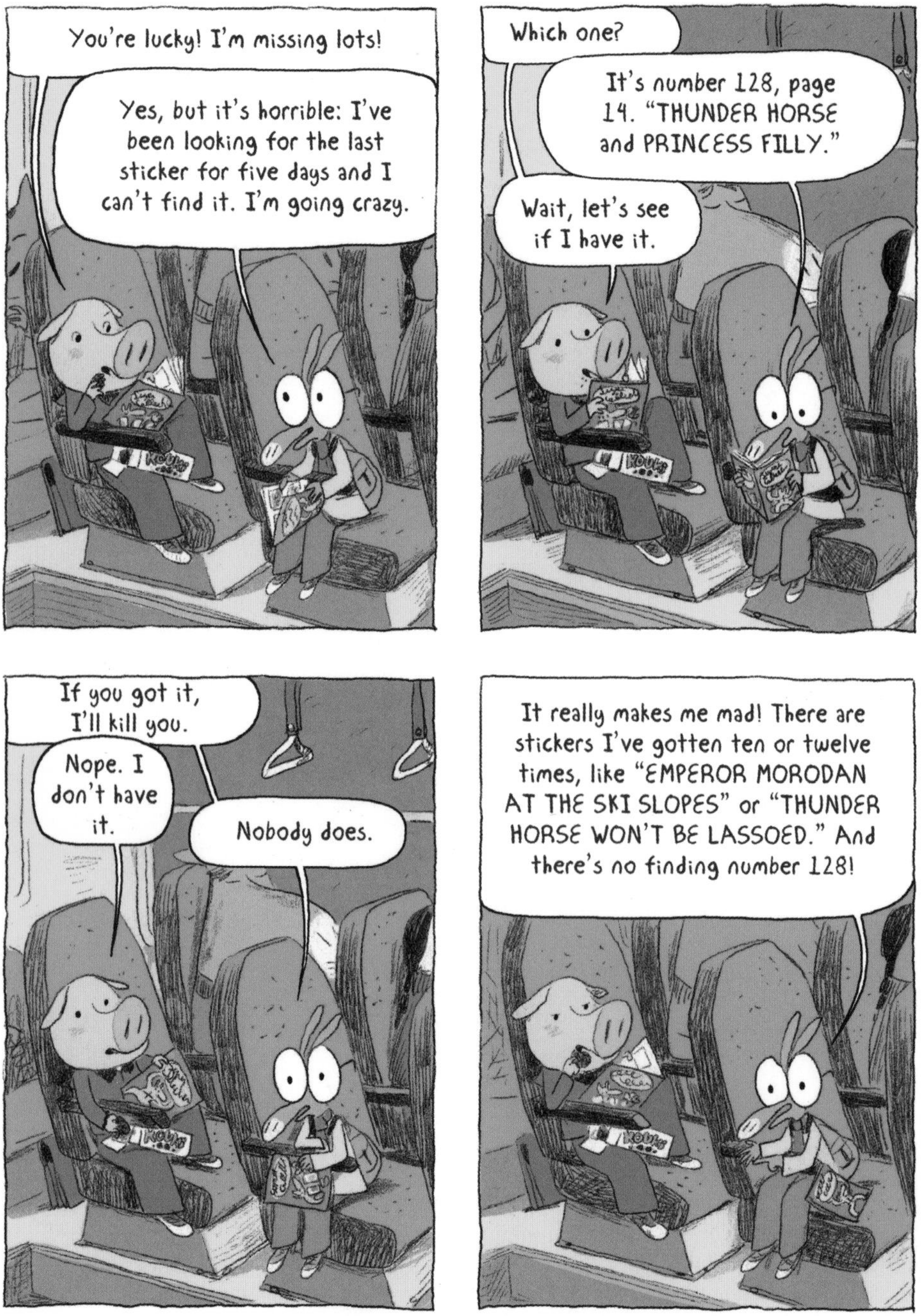
You're lucky! I'm missing lots!
Yes, but it's horrible: I've been looking for the last sticker for five days and I can't find it. I'm going crazy.
Which one?
It's number 128, page 14. "THUNDER HORSE and PRINCESS FILLY."
Wait, let's see if I have it.
If you got it, I'll kill you.
Nope. I don't have it.
Nobody does.
It really makes me mad! There are stickers I've gotten ten or twelve times, like "EMPEROR MORODAN AT THE SKI SLOPES" or "THUNDER HORSE WON'T BE LASSOED." And there's no finding number 128!

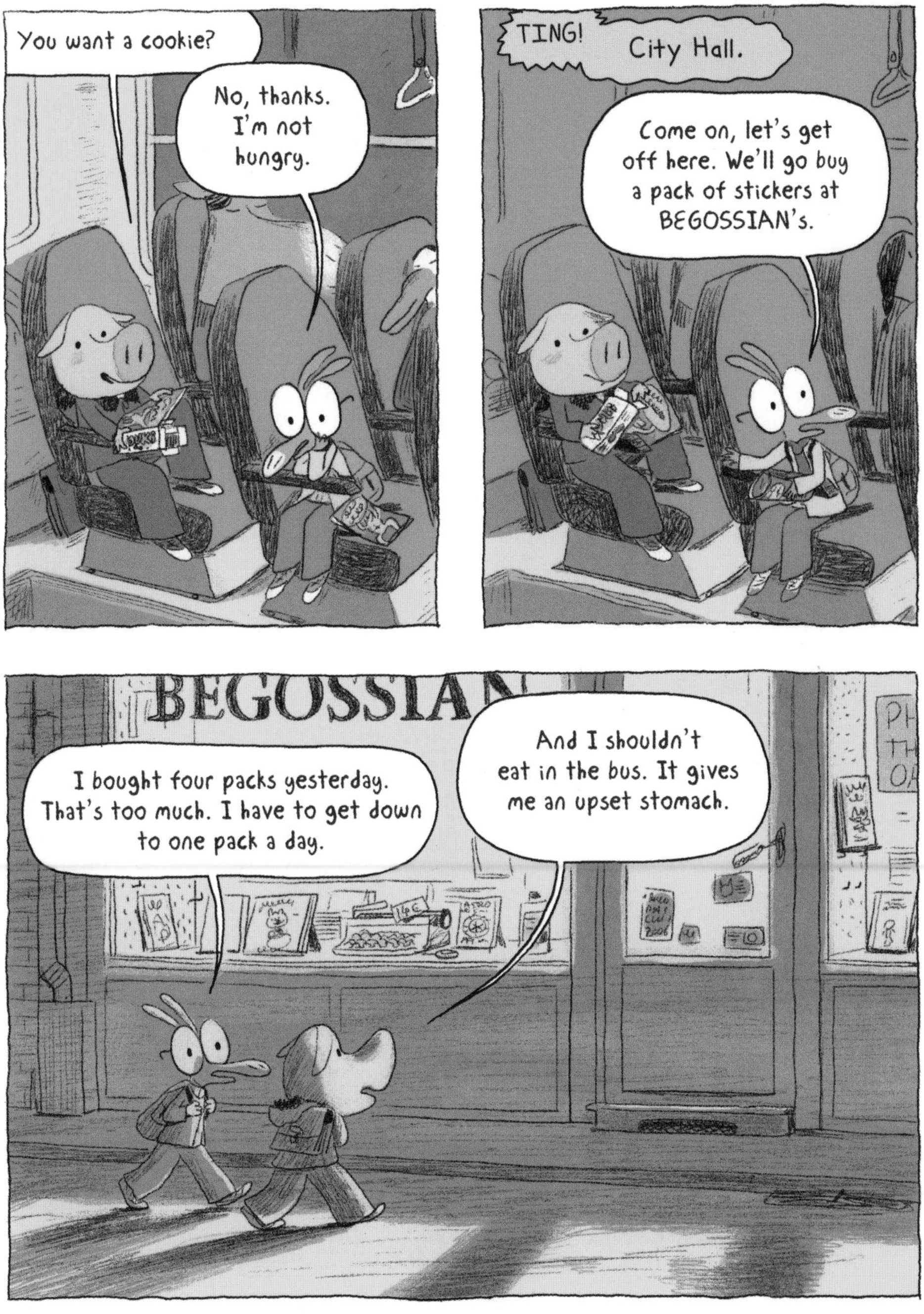
You want a cookie?
No, thanks. I'm not hungry.
TING!
City Hall.
Come on, let's get off here. We'll go buy a pack of stickers at BEGOSSIAN's.
BEGOSSIAN
I bought four packs yesterday. That's too much. I have to get down to one pack a day.
And I shouldn't eat in the bus. It gives me an upset stomach.

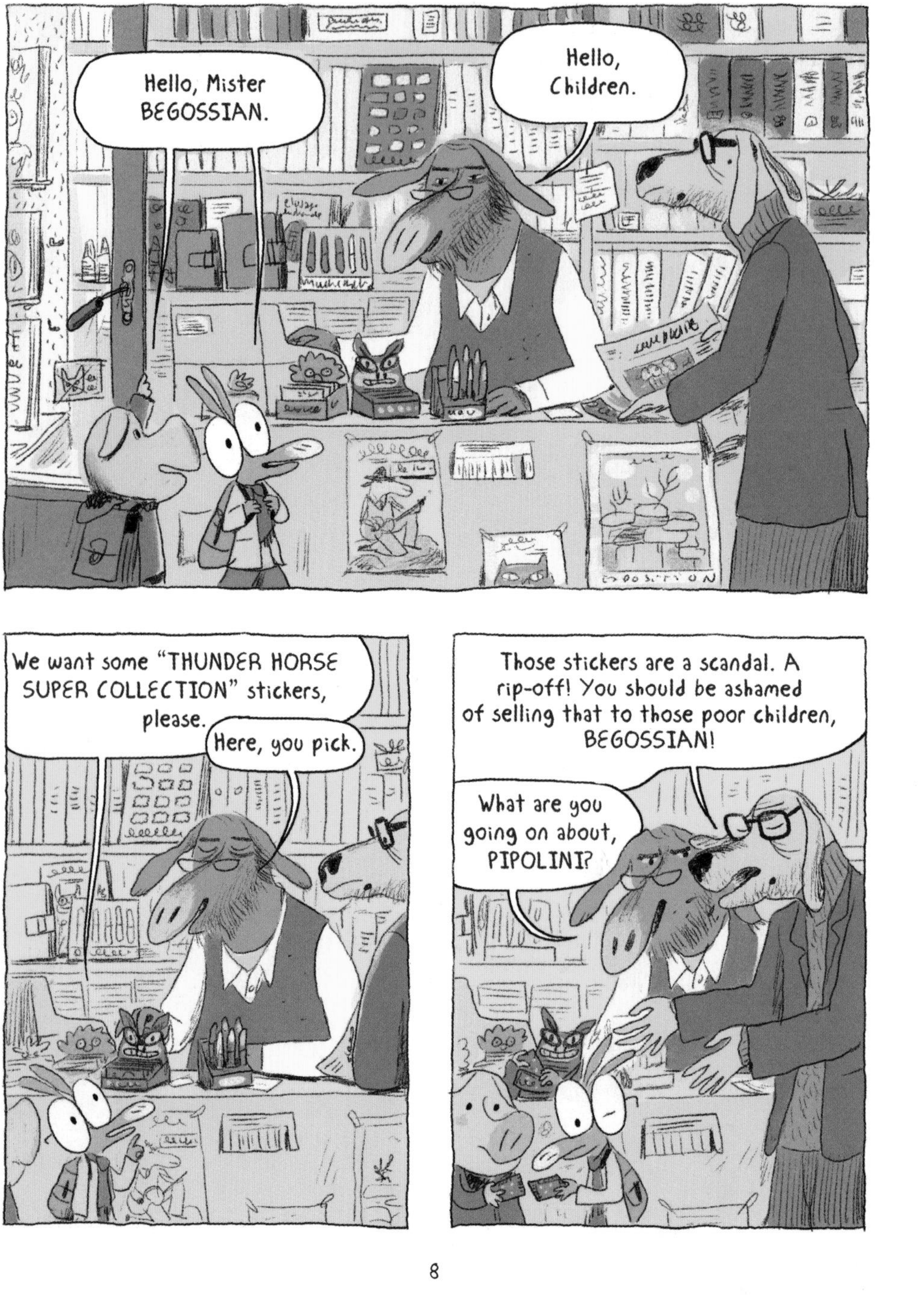
Hello, Mister BEGOSSIAN.
Hello, Children.
We want some "THUNDER HORSE SUPER COLLECTION" stickers, please.
Here, you pick.
Those stickers are a scandal. A rip-off! You should be ashamed of selling that to those poor children, BEGOSSIAN!
What are you going on about, PIPOLINI?

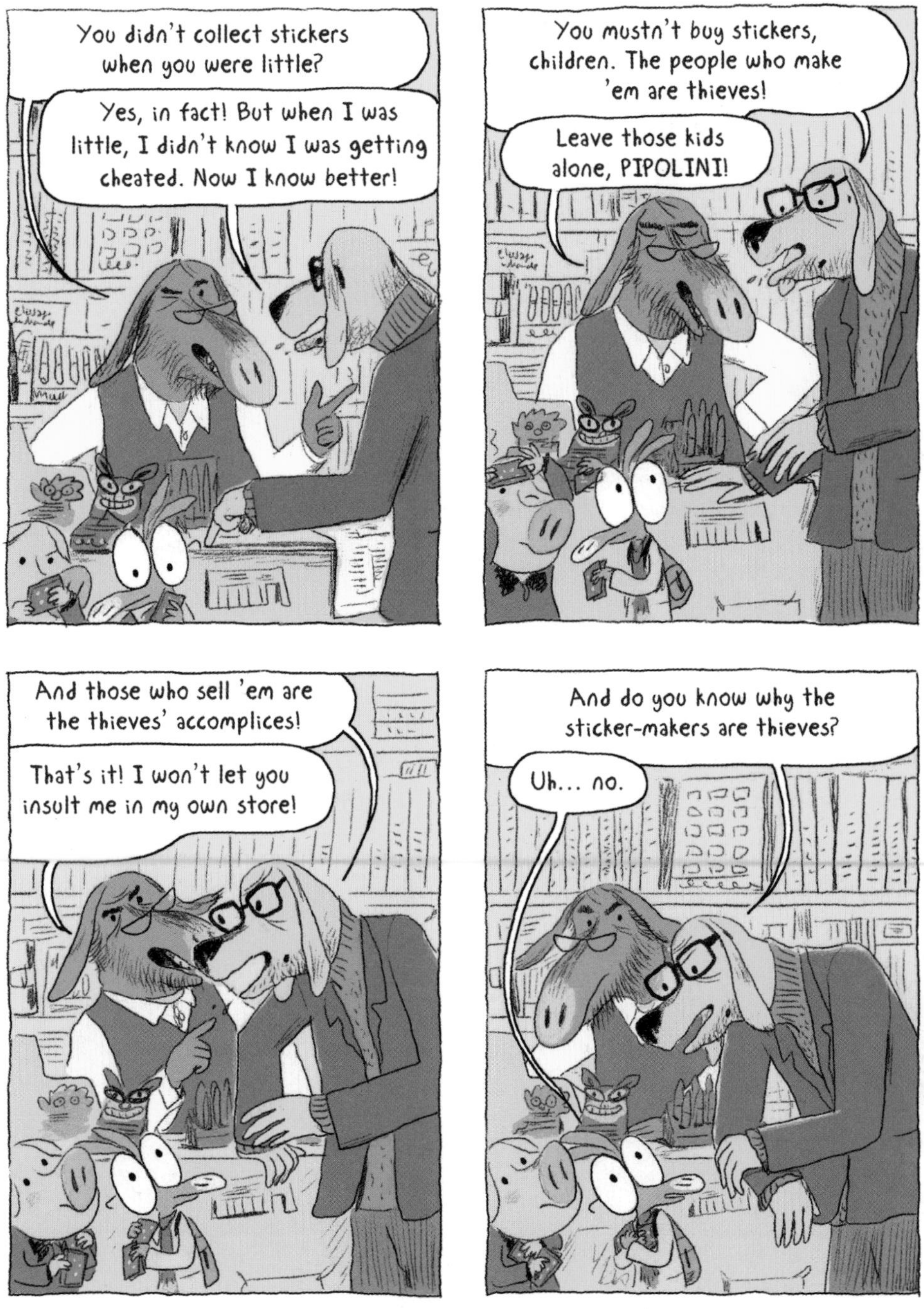
You didn't collect stickers when you were little?
Yes, in fact! But when I was little, I didn't know I was getting cheated. Now I know better!
You mustn't buy stickers, children. The people who make 'em are thieves!
Leave those kids alone, PIPOLINI!
And those who sell 'em are the thieves' accomplices!
That's it! I won't let you insult me in my own store!
And do you know why the sticker-makers are thieves?
Uh... no.

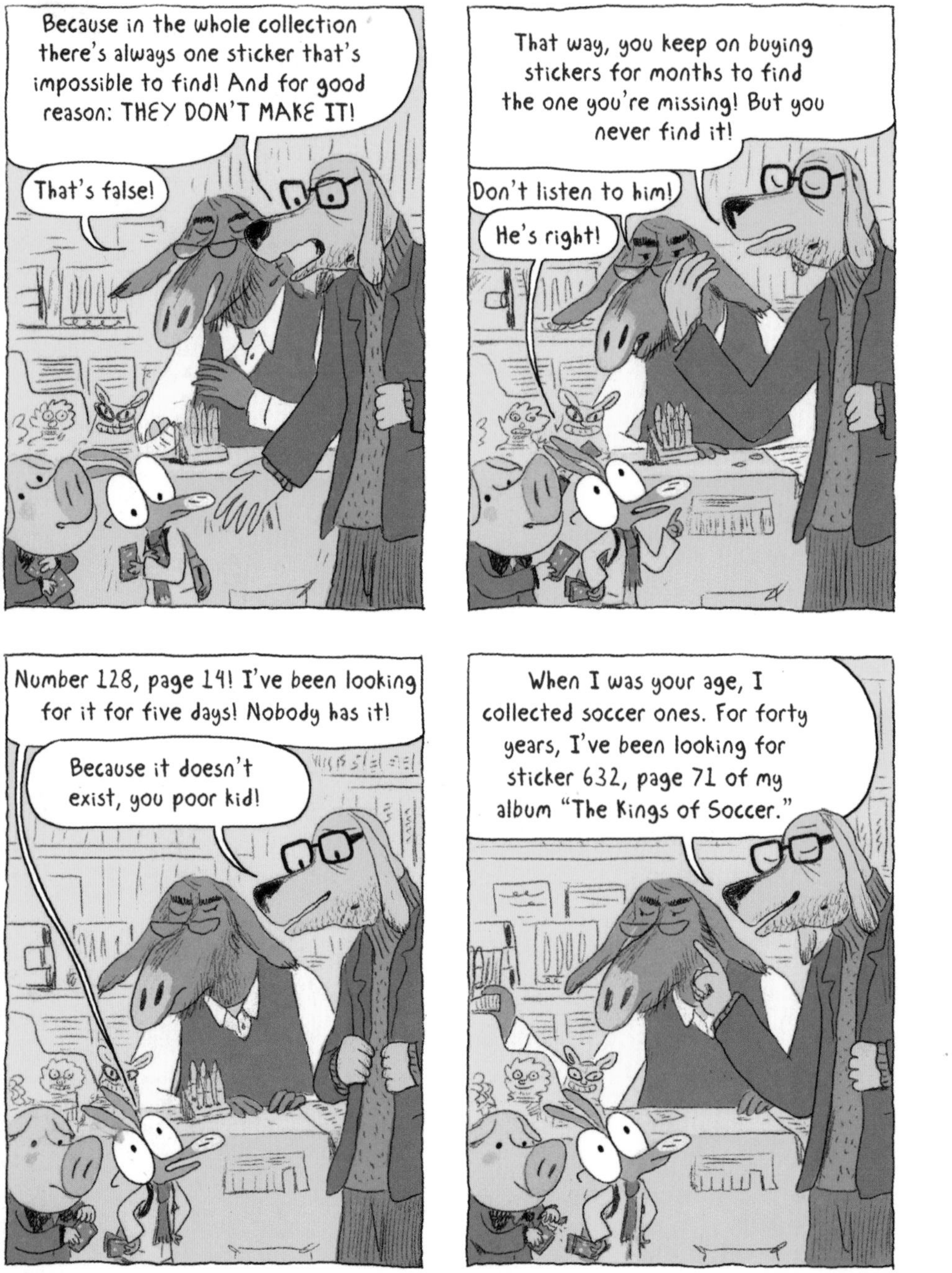
Because in the whole collection there's always one sticker that's impossible to find! And for good reason: THEY DON'T MAKE IT!
That's false!
That way, you keep on buying stickers for months to find the one you're missing! But you never find it!
Don't listen to him!
He's right!
Number 128, page 14! I've been looking for it for five days! Nobody has it!
Because it doesn't exist, you poor kid!
When I was your age, I collected soccer ones. For forty years, I've been looking for sticker 632, page 71 of my album "The Kings of Soccer."

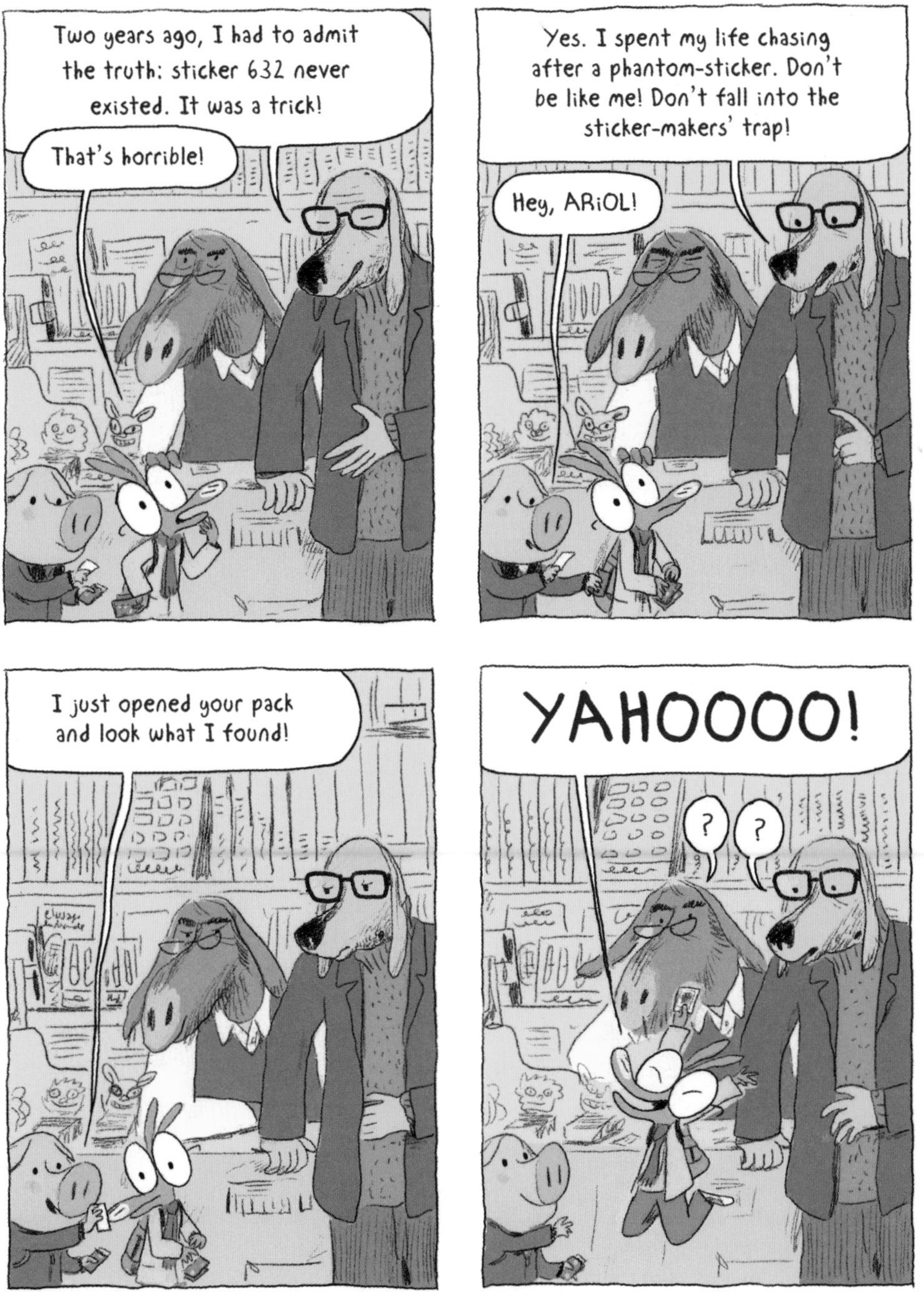
Two years ago, I had to admit the truth: sticker 632 never existed. It was a trick!
That's horrible!
Yes. I spent my life chasing after a phantom-sticker. Don't be like me! Don't fall into the sticker-makers' trap!
Hey, ARiOL!
I just opened your pack and look what I found!
YAHOOOO!
?
?

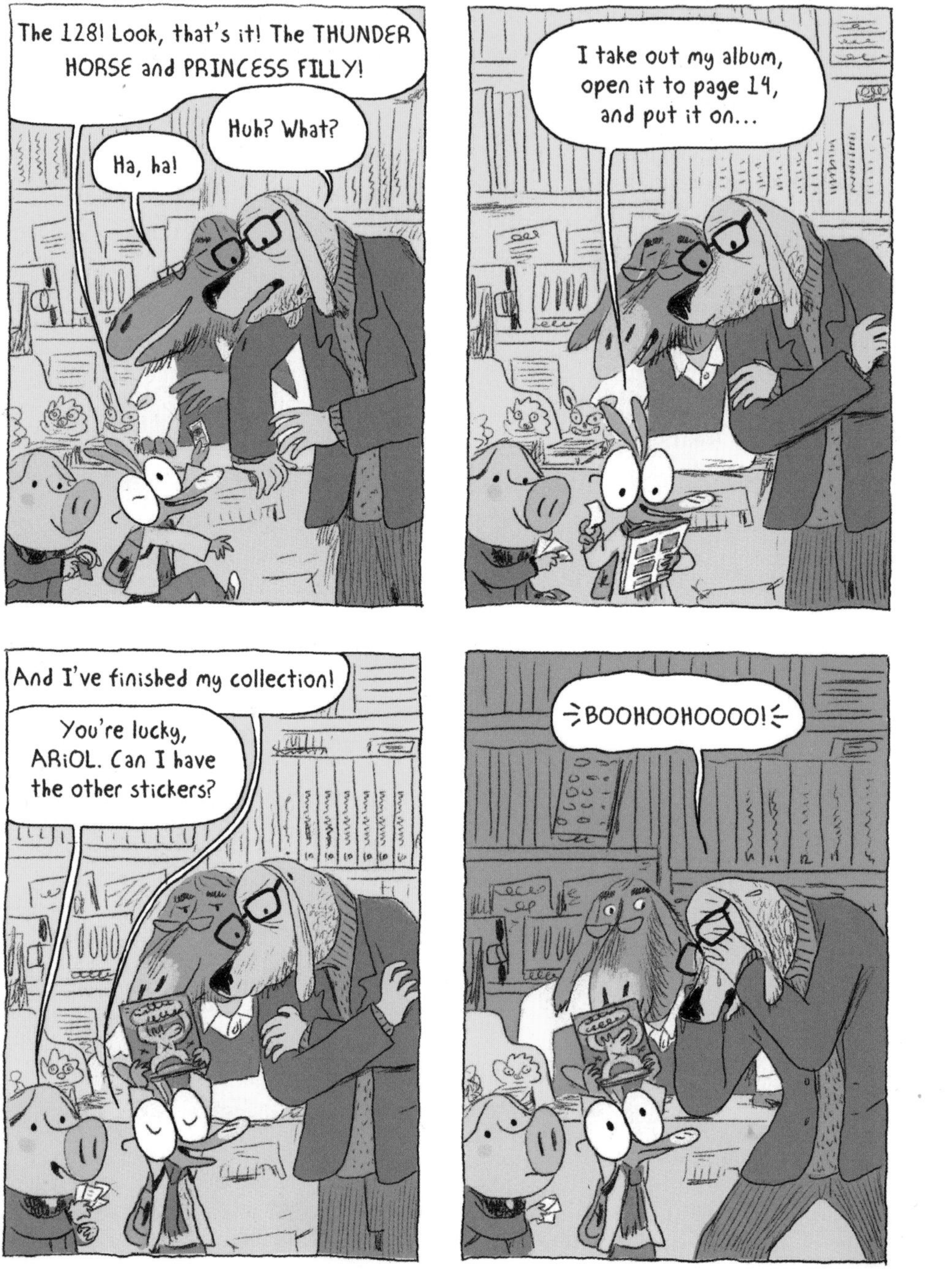
The 128! Look, that's it! The THUNDER HORSE and PRINCESS FILLY!
Ha, ha!
Huh? What?
I take out my album, open it to page 14, and put it on...
And I've finished my collection!
You're lucky, ARiOL. Can I have the other stickers?
BOOHOOHOOOO!

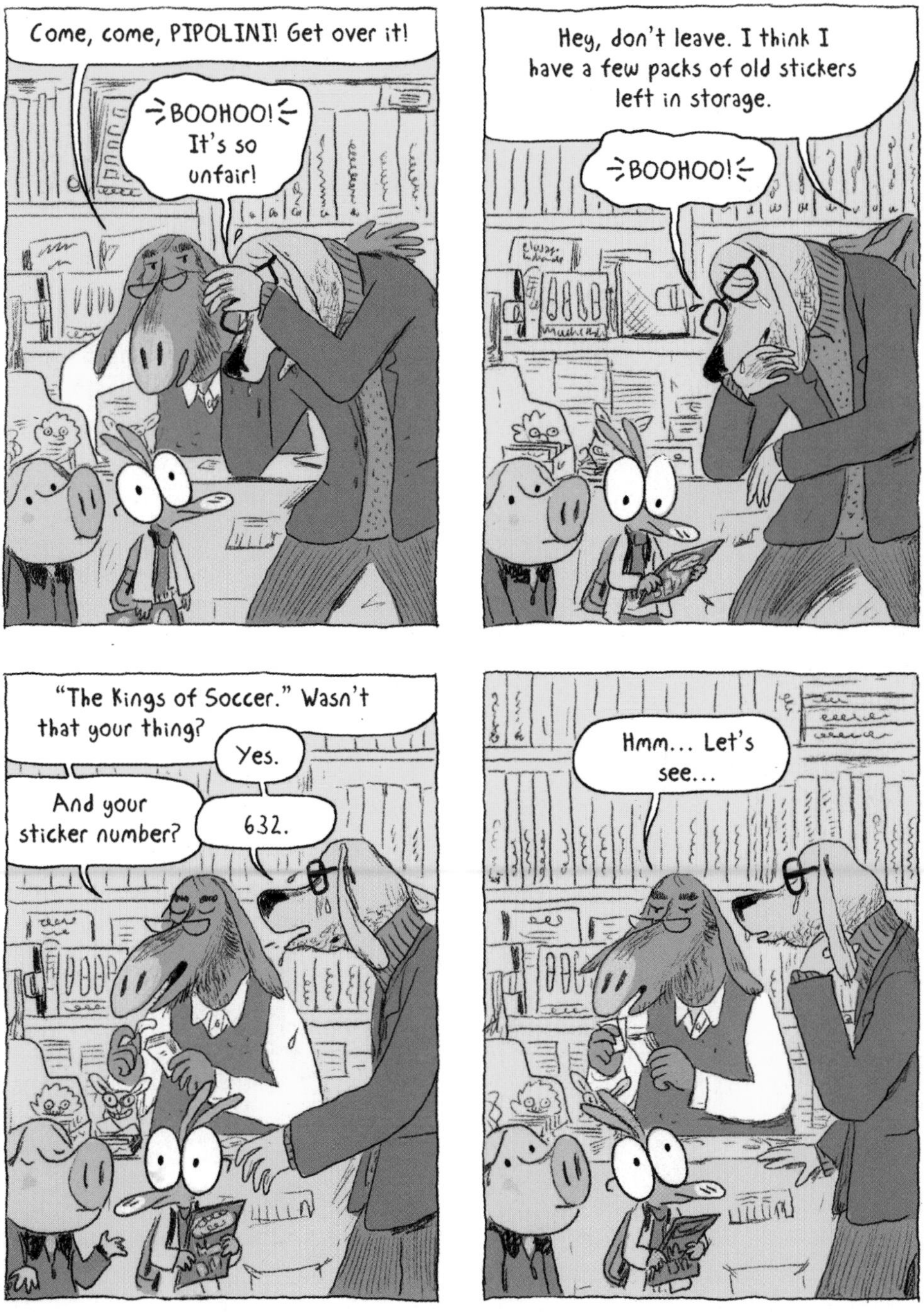
Come, come, PIPOLINI! Get over it!
BOOHOO! It's so unfair!
Hey, don't leave. I think I have a few packs of old stickers left in storage.
BOOHOO!
"The Kings of Soccer." Wasn't that your thing?
Yes.
And your sticker number?
632.
Hmm... Let's see...

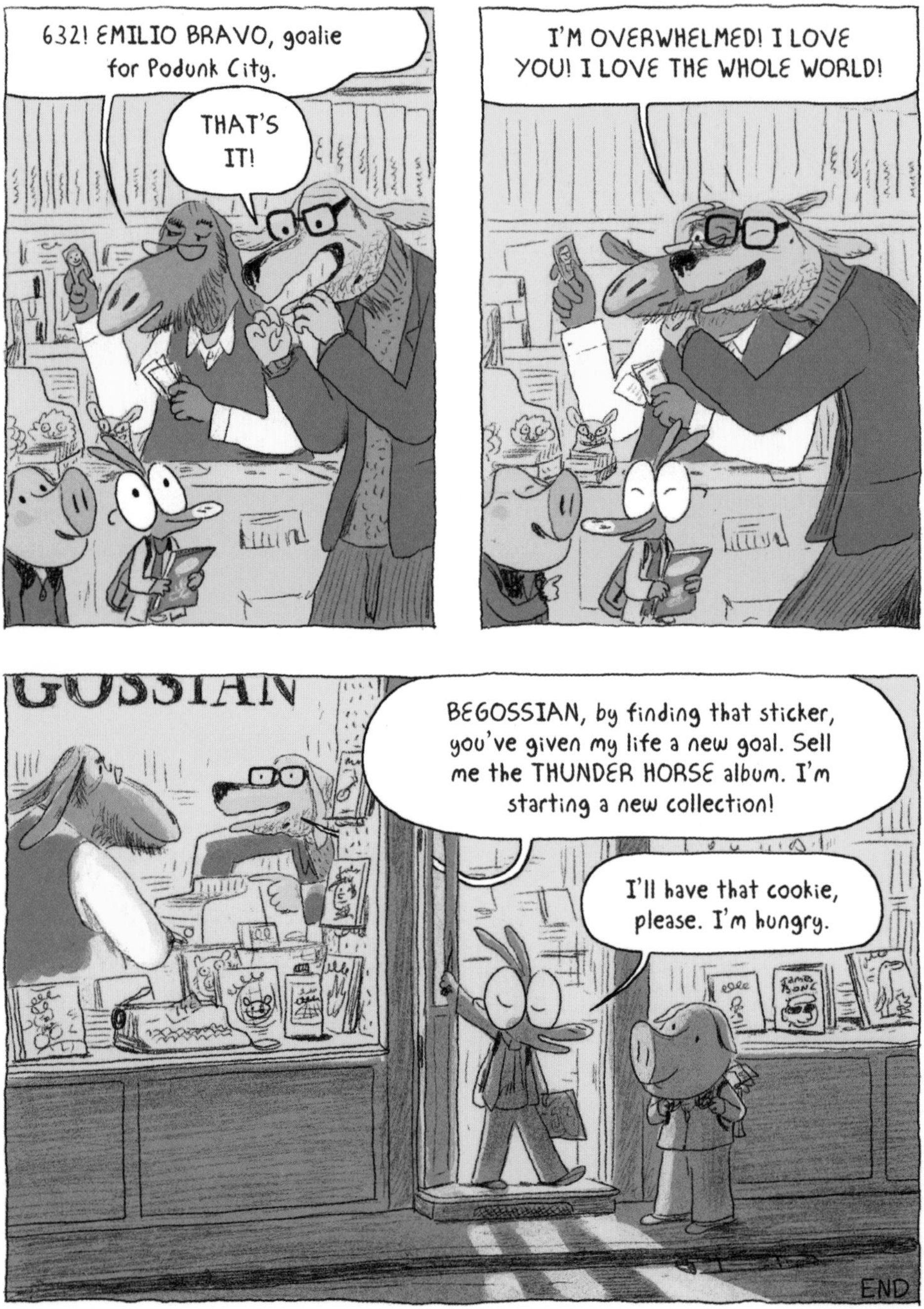
632! EMILIO BRAVO, goalie for Podunk City.
THAT'S IT!
I'M OVERWHELMED! I LOVE YOU! I LOVE THE WHOLE WORLD!
GOSSIAN
BEGOSSIAN, by finding that sticker, you've given my life a new goal. Sell me the THUNDER HORSE album. I'm starting a new collection!
I'll have that cookie, please. I'm hungry.
END

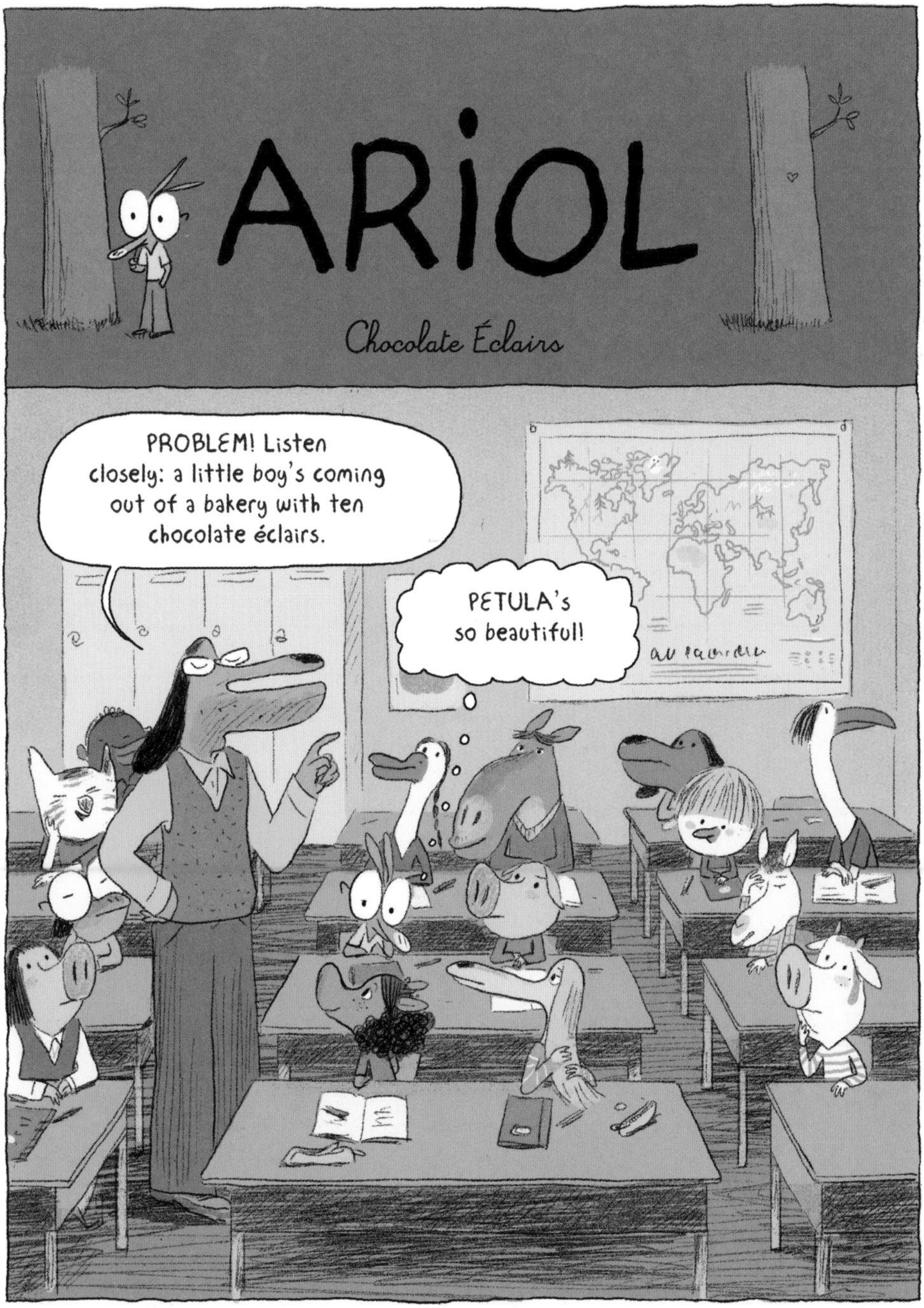
ARiOL
Chocolate Éclairs
PROBLEM! Listen closely: a little boy's coming out of a bakery with ten chocolate éclairs.
PETULA's so beautiful!

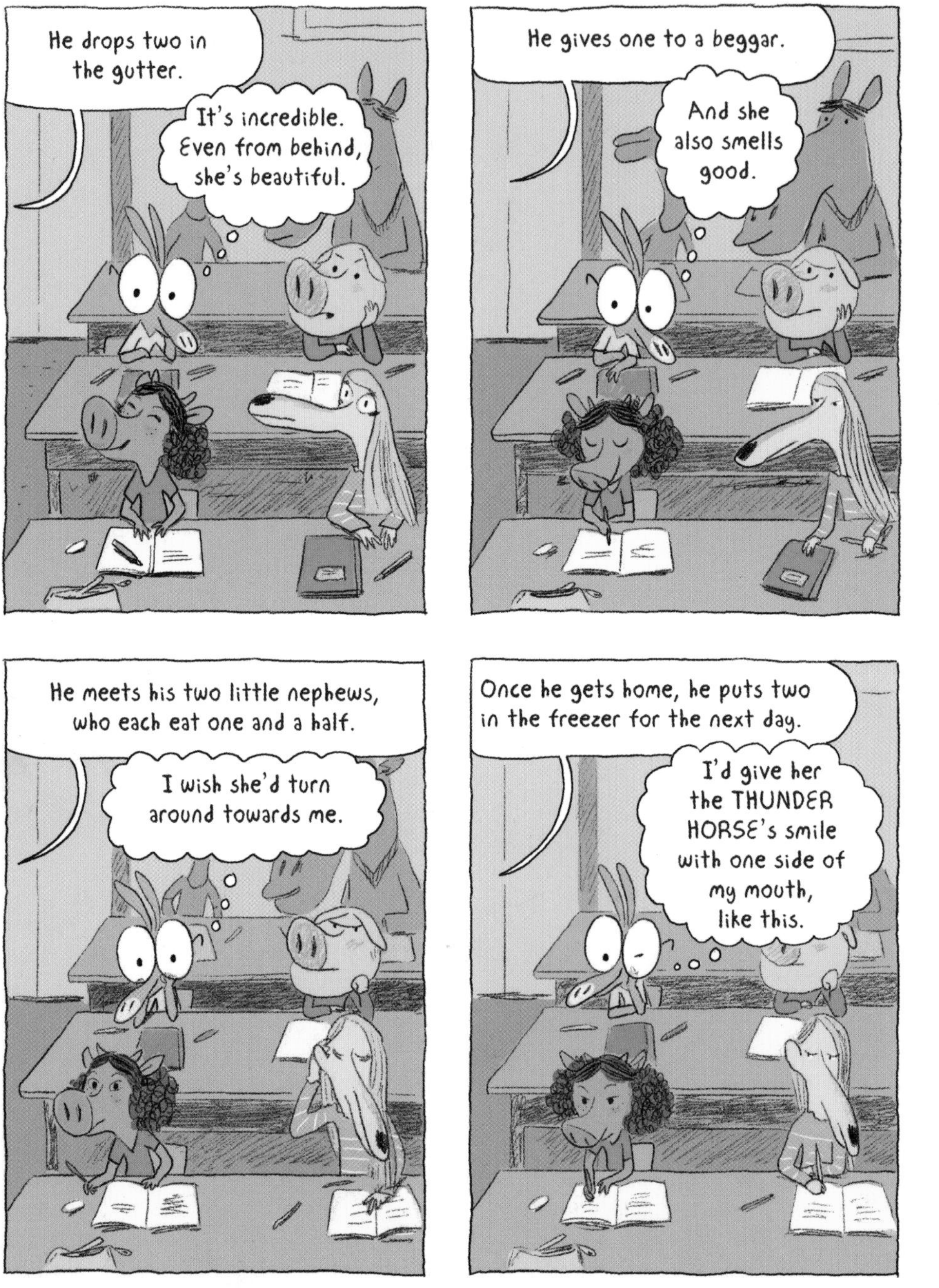
He drops two in the gutter.
It's incredible. Even from behind, she's beautiful.
He gives one to a beggar.
And she also smells good.
He meets his two little nephews, who each eat one and a half.
I wish she'd turn around towards me.
Once he gets home, he puts two in the freezer for the next day.
I'd give her the THUNDER HORSE's smile with one side of my mouth, like this.

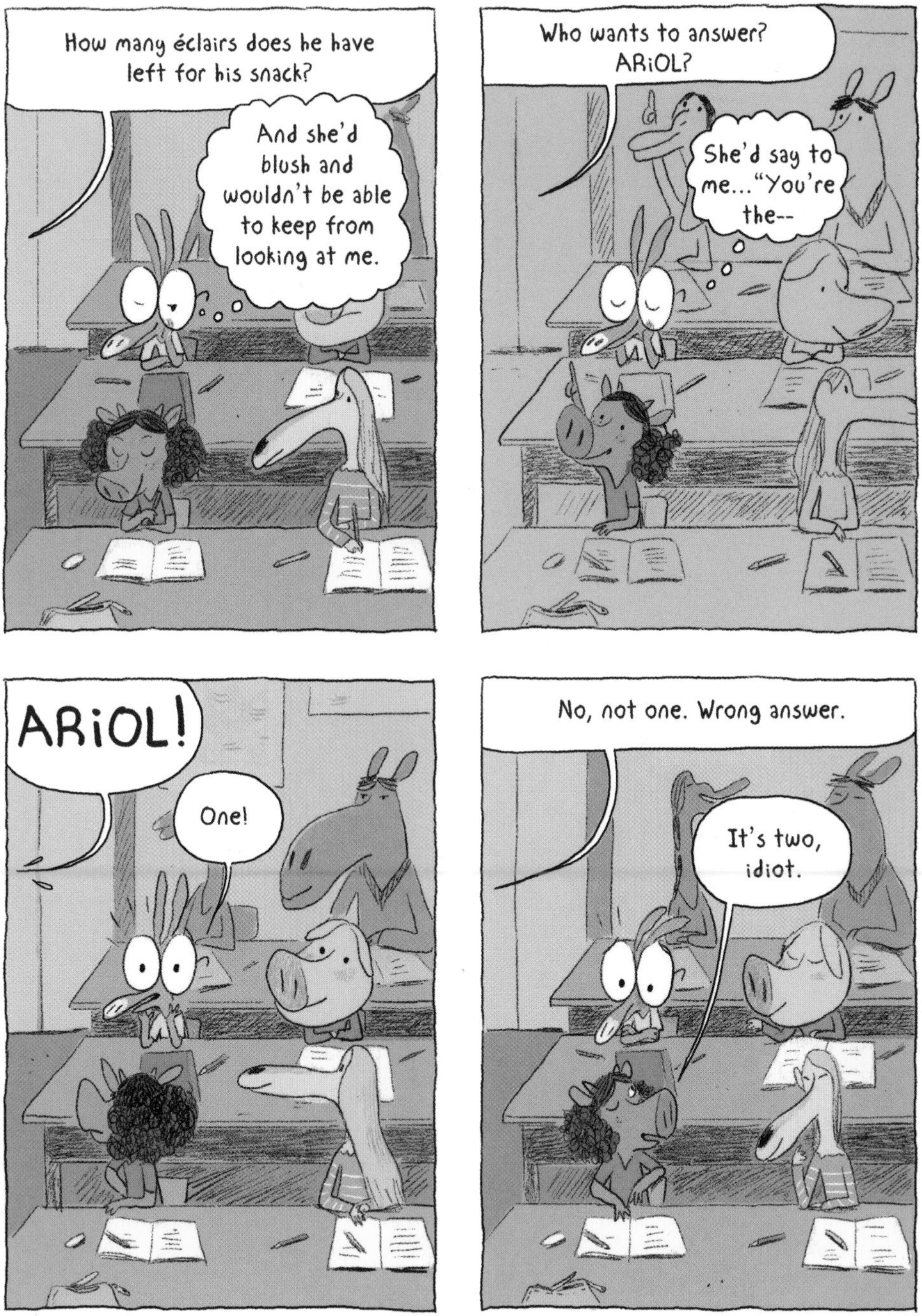
How many éclairs does he have left for his snack?
And she'd blush and wouldn't be able to keep from looking at me.
Who wants to answer? ARiOL?
She'd say to me..."You're the--
ARiOL!
One!
No, not one. Wrong answer.
It's two, idiot.

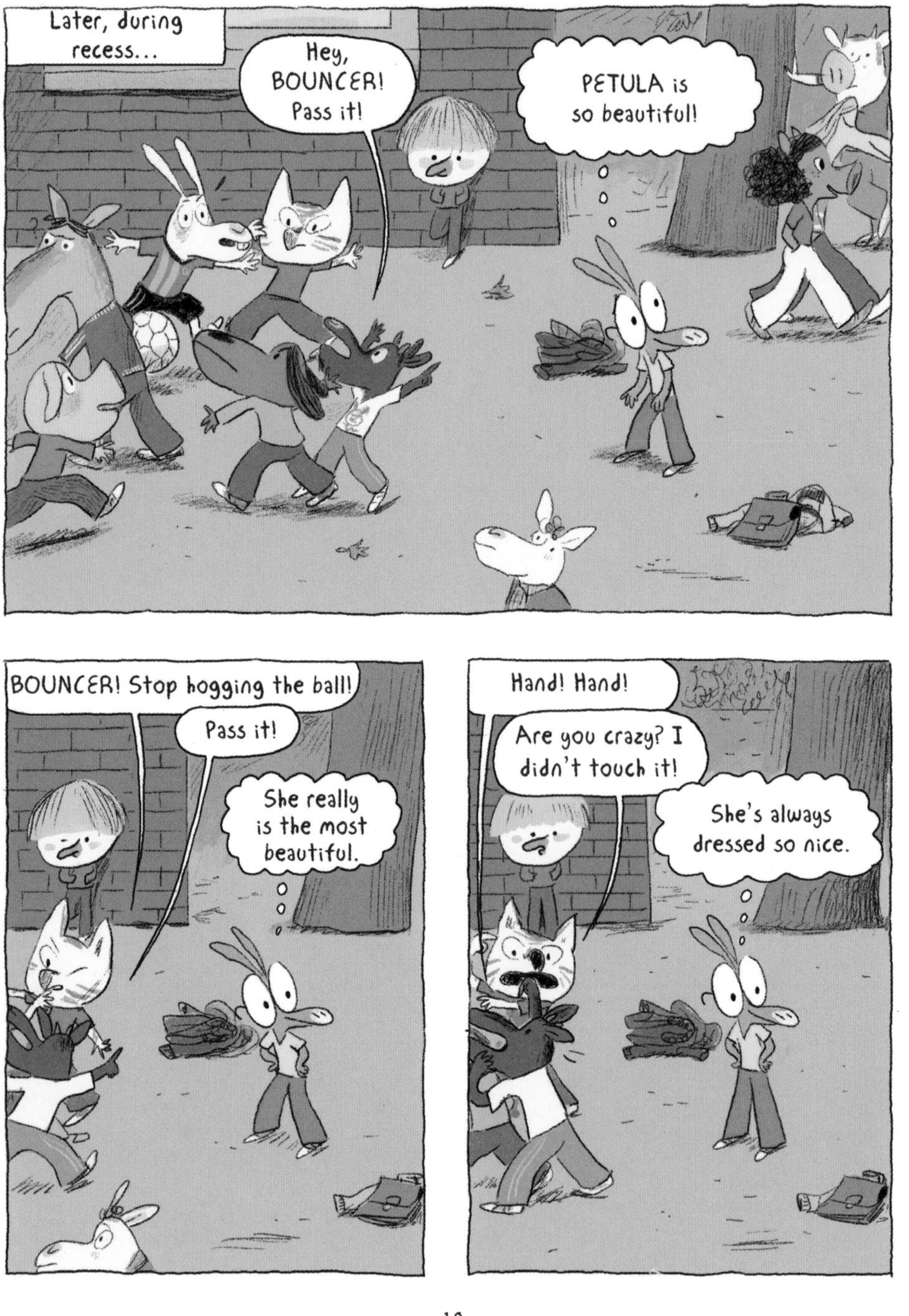
Later, during recess...
Hey, BOUNCER! Pass it!
PETULA is so beautiful!
BOUNCER! Stop hogging the ball!
Pass it!
She really is the most beautiful.
Hand! Hand!
Are you crazy? I didn't touch it!
She's always dressed so nice.

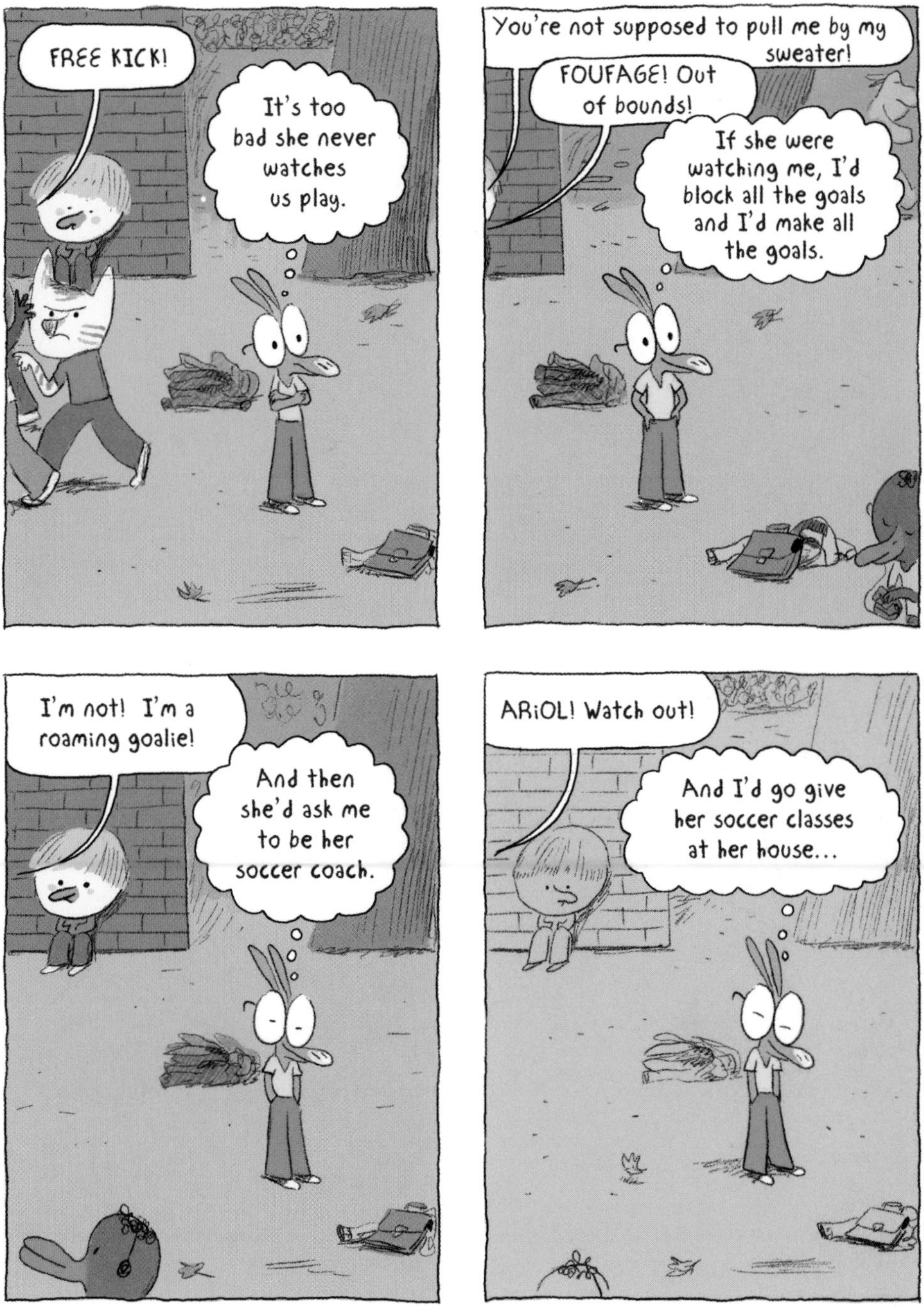
FREE KICK!
It's too bad she never watches us play.
You're not supposed to pull me by my sweater!
FOUFAGE! Out of bounds!
If she were watching me, I'd block all the goals and I'd make all the goals.
I'm not! I'm a roaming goalie!
And then she'd ask me to be her soccer coach.
ARiOL! Watch out!
And I'd go give her soccer classes at her house...

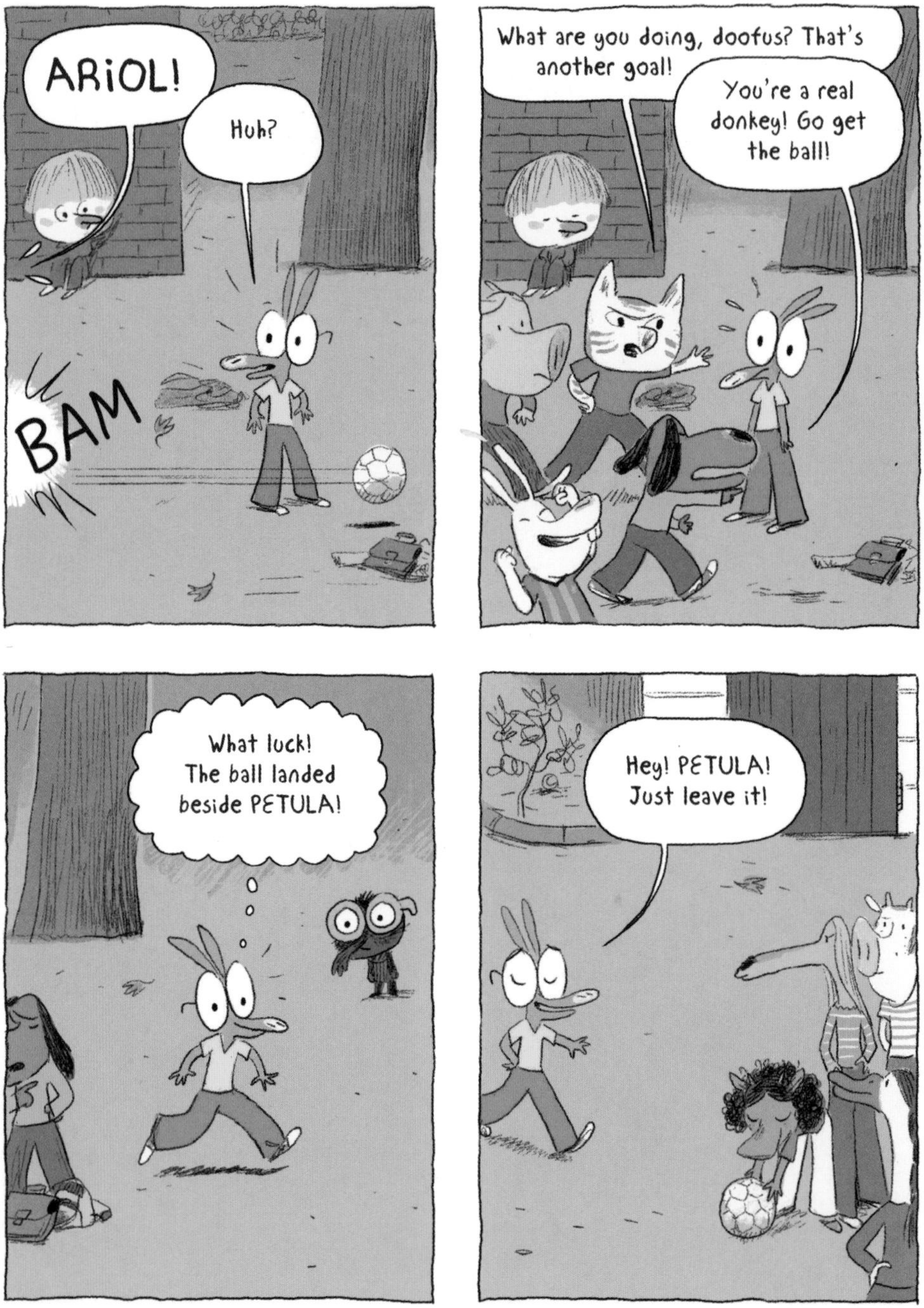
ARiOL!
Huh?
BAM
What are you doing, doofus? That's another goal!
You're a real donkey! Go get the ball!
What luck! The ball landed beside PETULA!
Hey! PETULA! Just leave it!

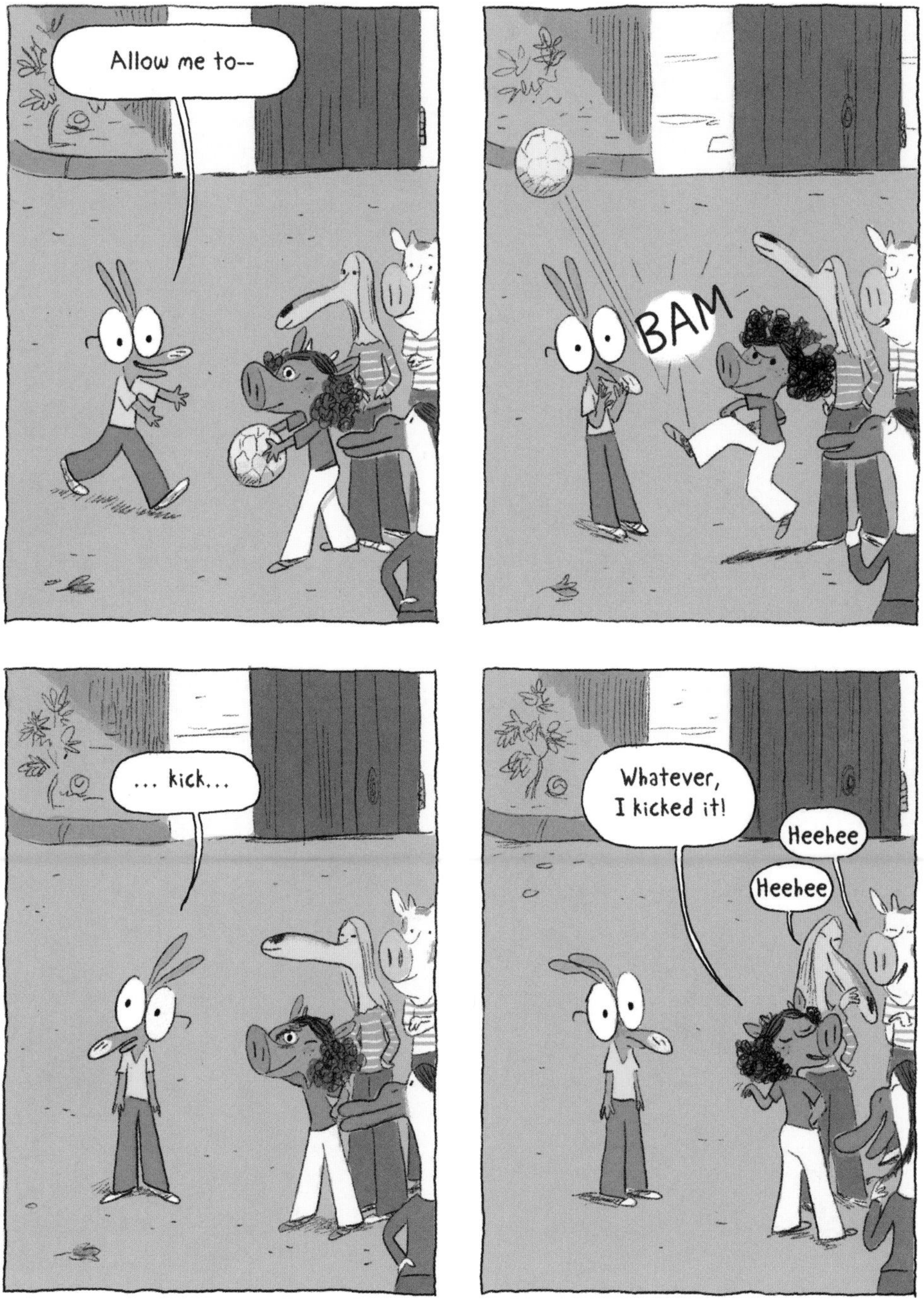
Allow me to--
BAM
... kick...
Whatever, I kicked it!
Heehee
Heehee

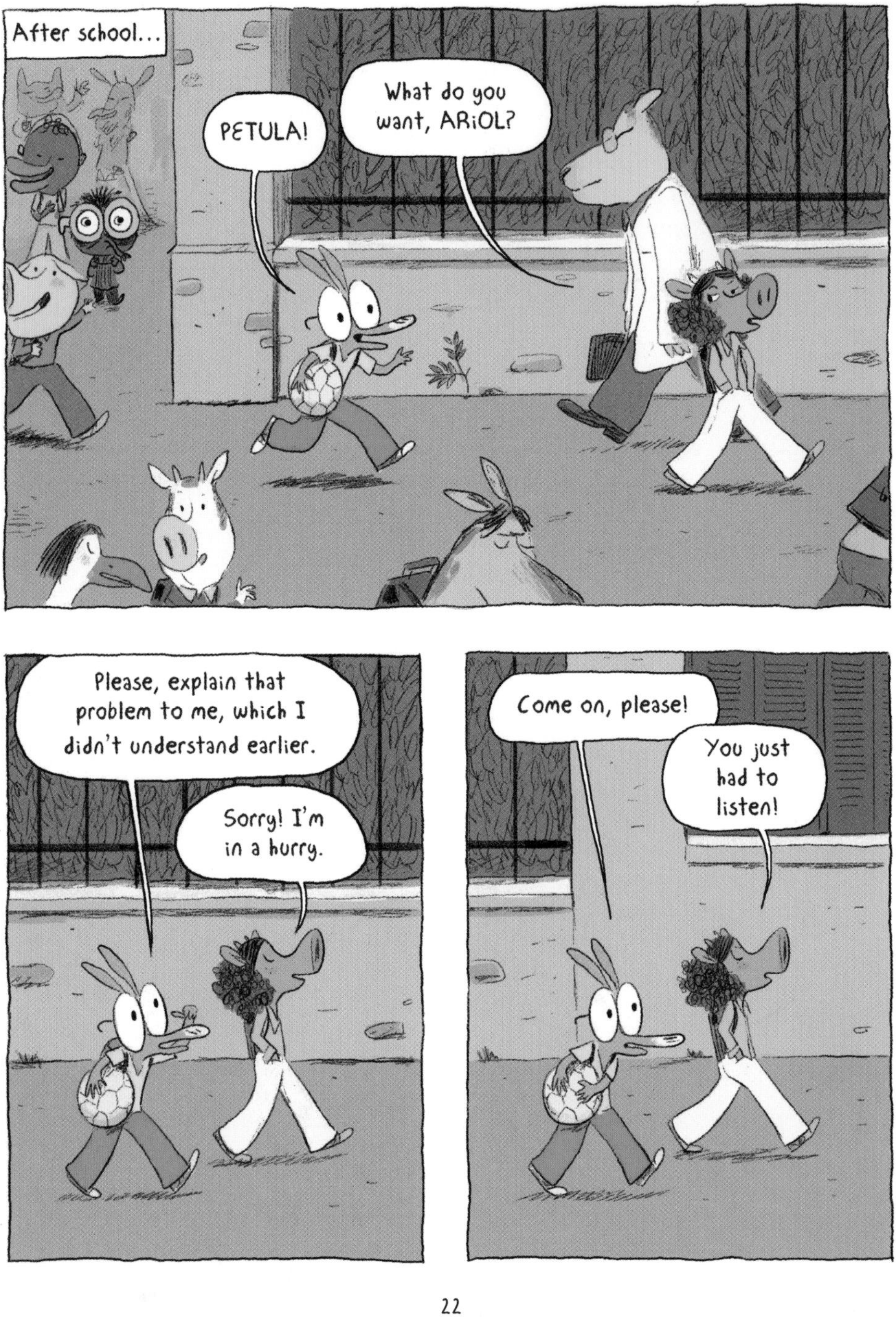
After school...
PETULA!
What do you want, ARiOL?
Please, explain that problem to me, which I didn't understand earlier.
Sorry! I'm in a hurry.
Come on, please!
You just had to listen!

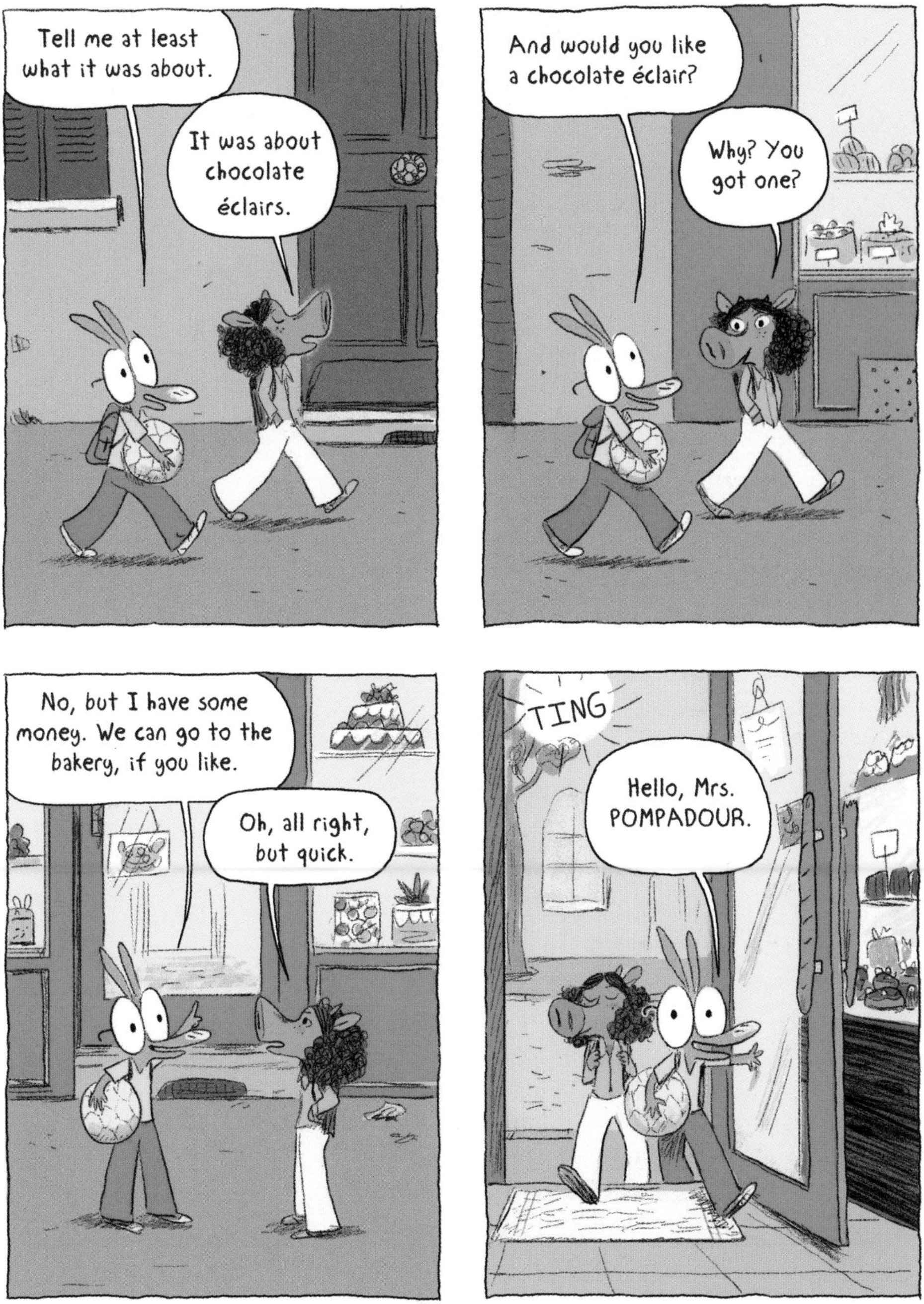
Tell me at least what it was about.
It was about chocolate éclairs.
And would you like a chocolate éclair?
Why? You got one?
No, but I have some money. We can go to the bakery, if you like.
Oh, all right, but quick.
TING
Hello, Mrs. POMPADOUR.

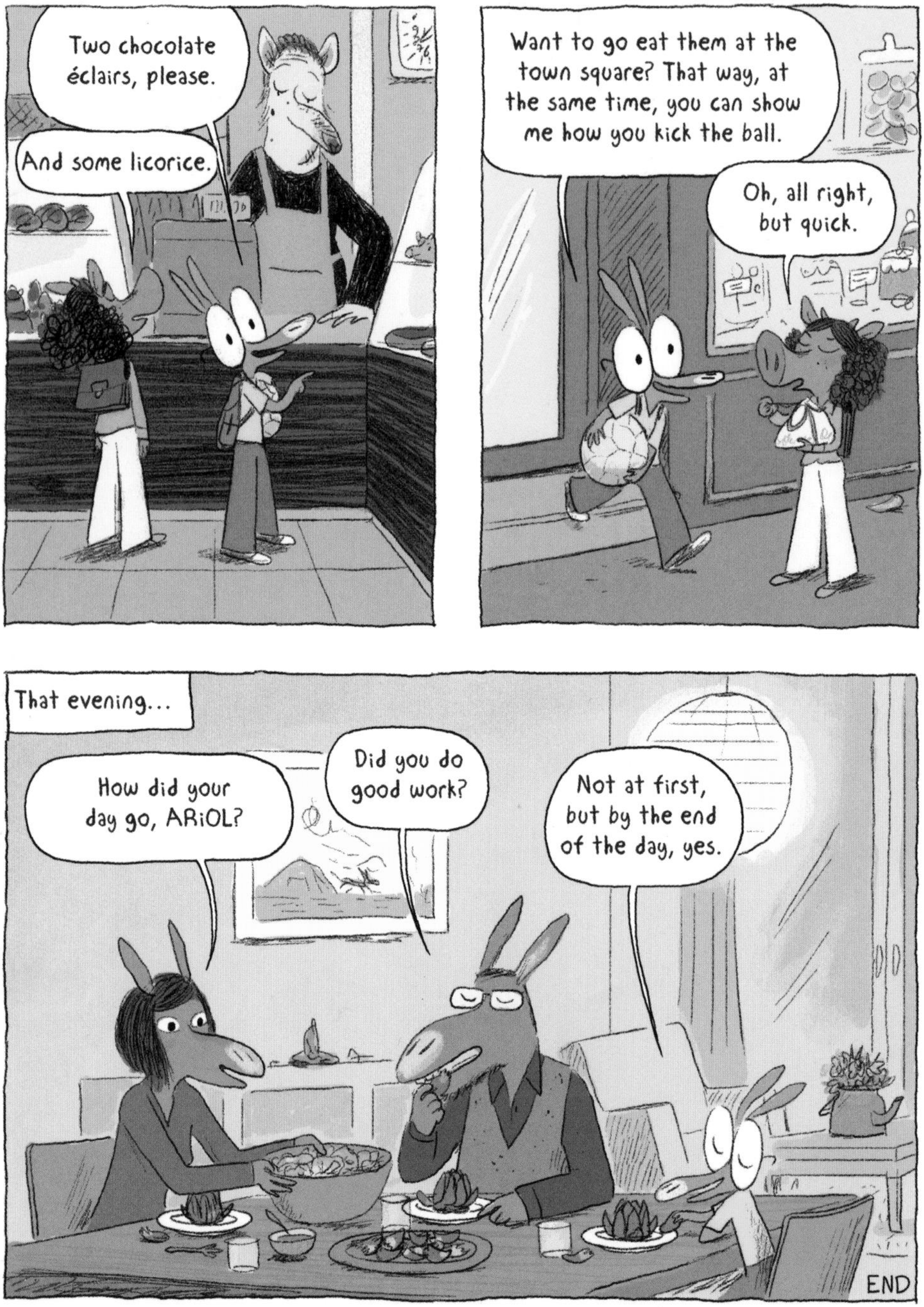
Two chocolate éclairs, please.
And some licorice.
Want to go eat them at the town square? That way, at the same time, you can show me how you kick the ball.
Oh, all right, but quick.
That evening...
How did your day go, ARiOL?
Did you do good work?
Not at first, but by the end of the day, yes.
END

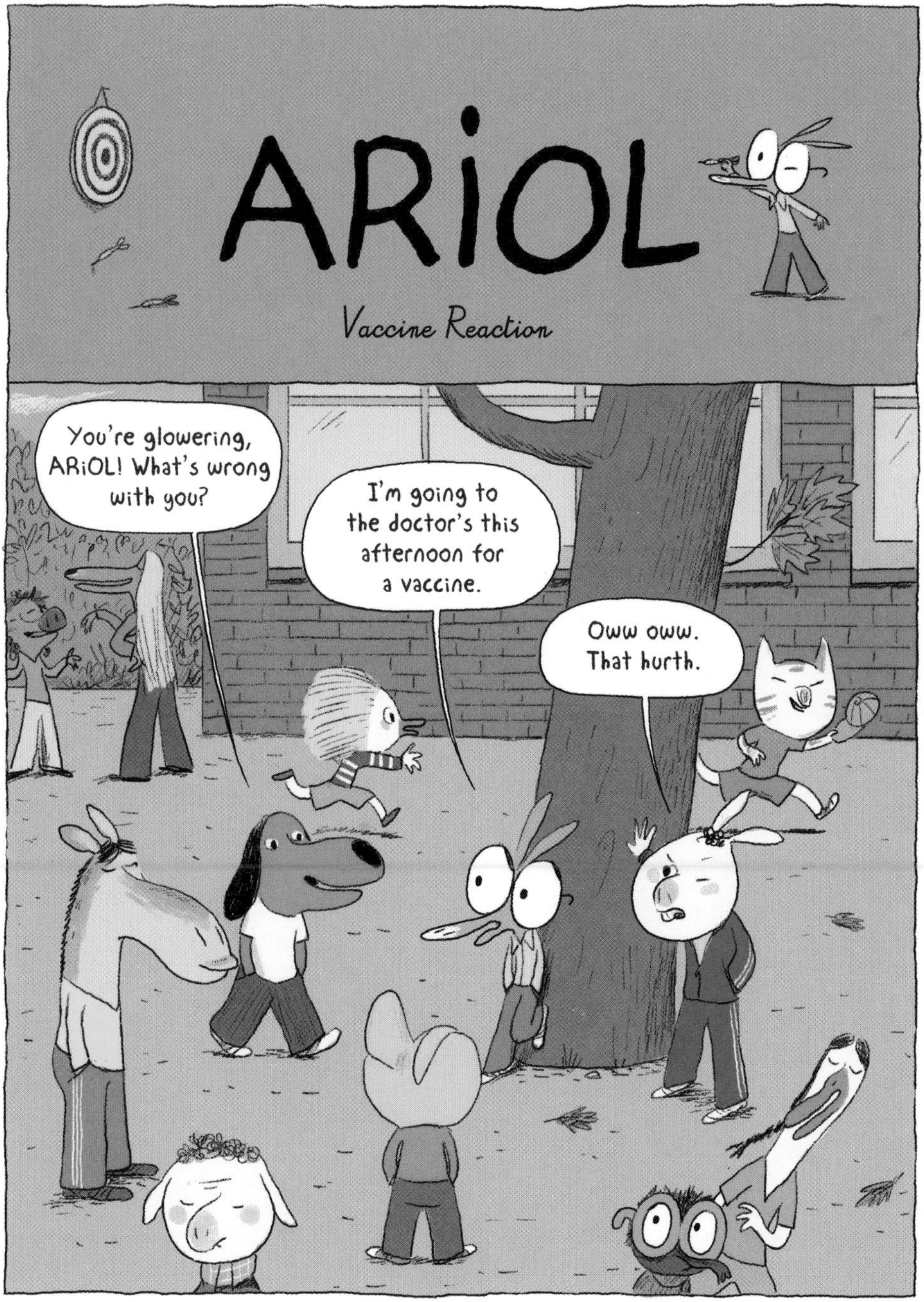

ARiOL
Vaccine Reaction
You're glowering, ARiOL! What's wrong with you?
I'm going to the doctor's this afternoon for a vaccine.
Oww oww. That hurth.

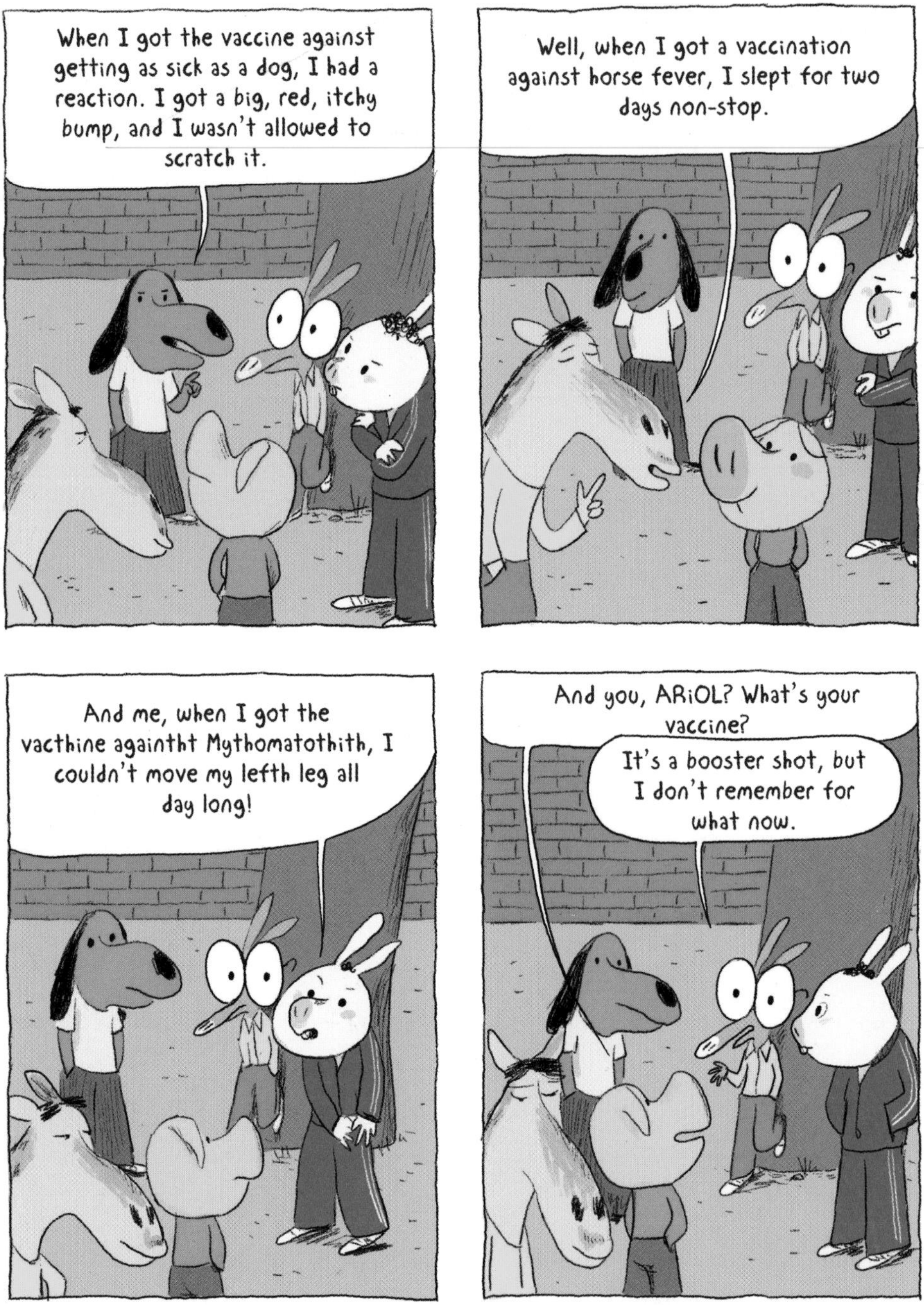
When I got the vaccine against getting as sick as a dog, I had a reaction. I got a big, red, itchy bump, and I wasn't allowed to scratch it.
Well, when I got a vaccination against horse fever, I slept for two days non-stop.
And me, when I got the vacthine againtht Mythomatothith, I couldn't move my lefth leg all day long!
And you, ARiOL? What's your vaccine?
It's a booster shot, but I don't remember for what now.

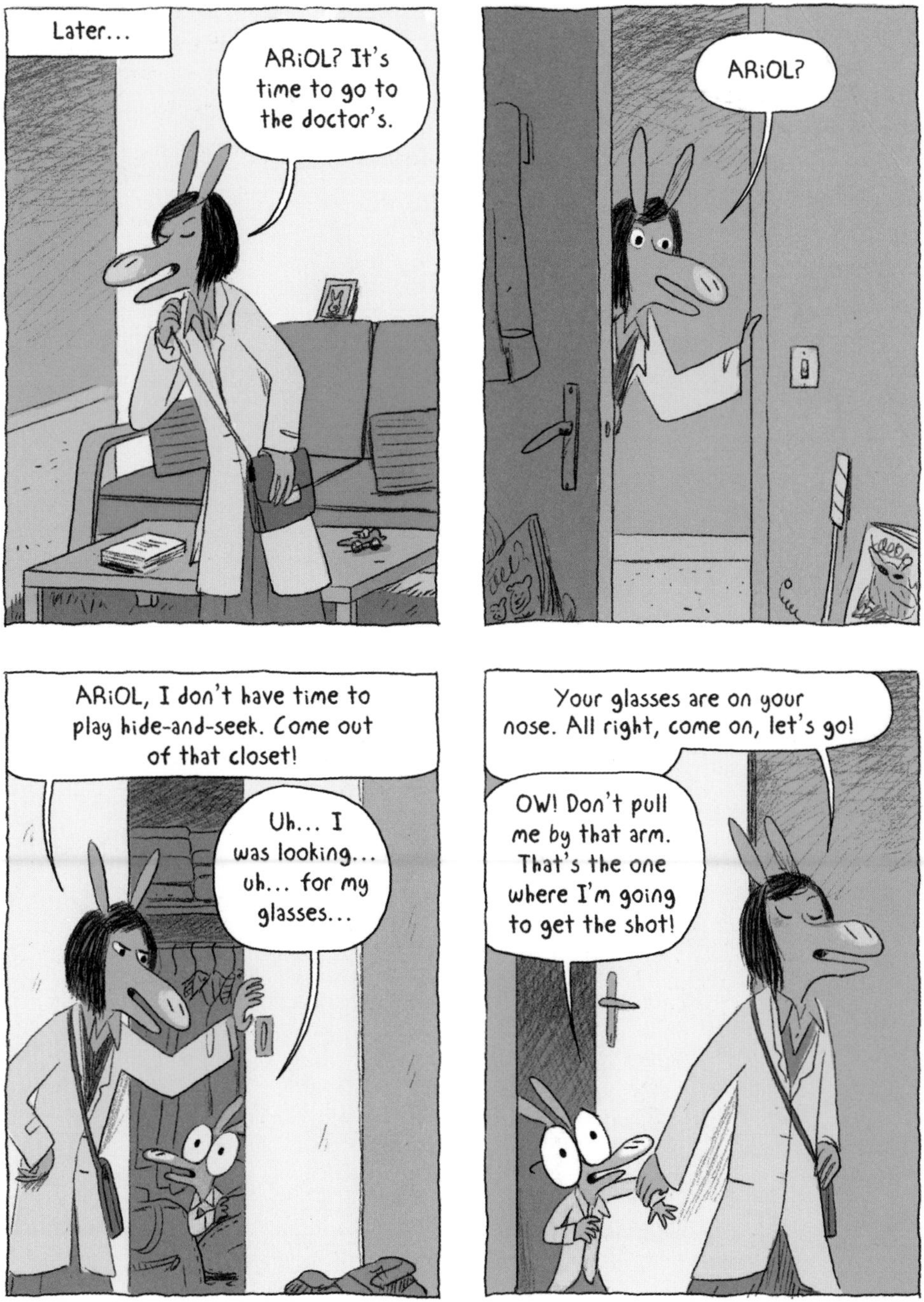
Later...
ARiOL? It's time to go to the doctor's.
ARiOL?
ARiOL, I don't have time to play hide-and-seek. Come out of that closet!
Uh... I was looking... uh... for my glasses...
Your glasses are on your nose. All right, come on, let's go!
OW! Don't pull me by that arm. That's the one where I'm going to get the shot!

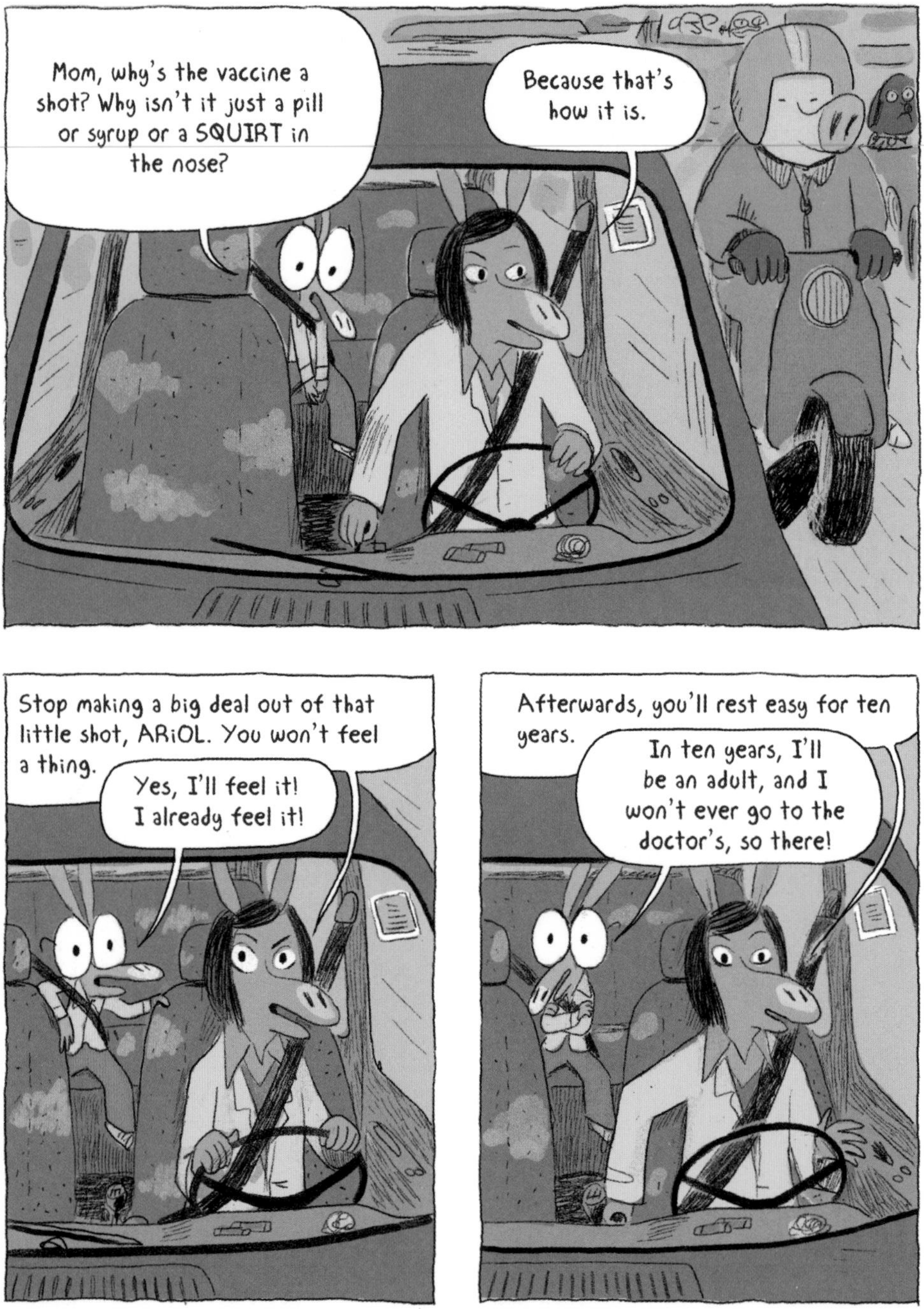
Mom, why's the vaccine a shot? Why isn't it just a pill or syrup or a SQUIRT in the nose?
Because that's how it is.
Stop making a big deal out of that little shot, ARiOL. You won't feel a thing.
Yes, I'll feel it! I already feel it!
Afterwards, you'll rest easy for ten years.
In ten years, I'll be an adult, and I won't ever go to the doctor's, so there!

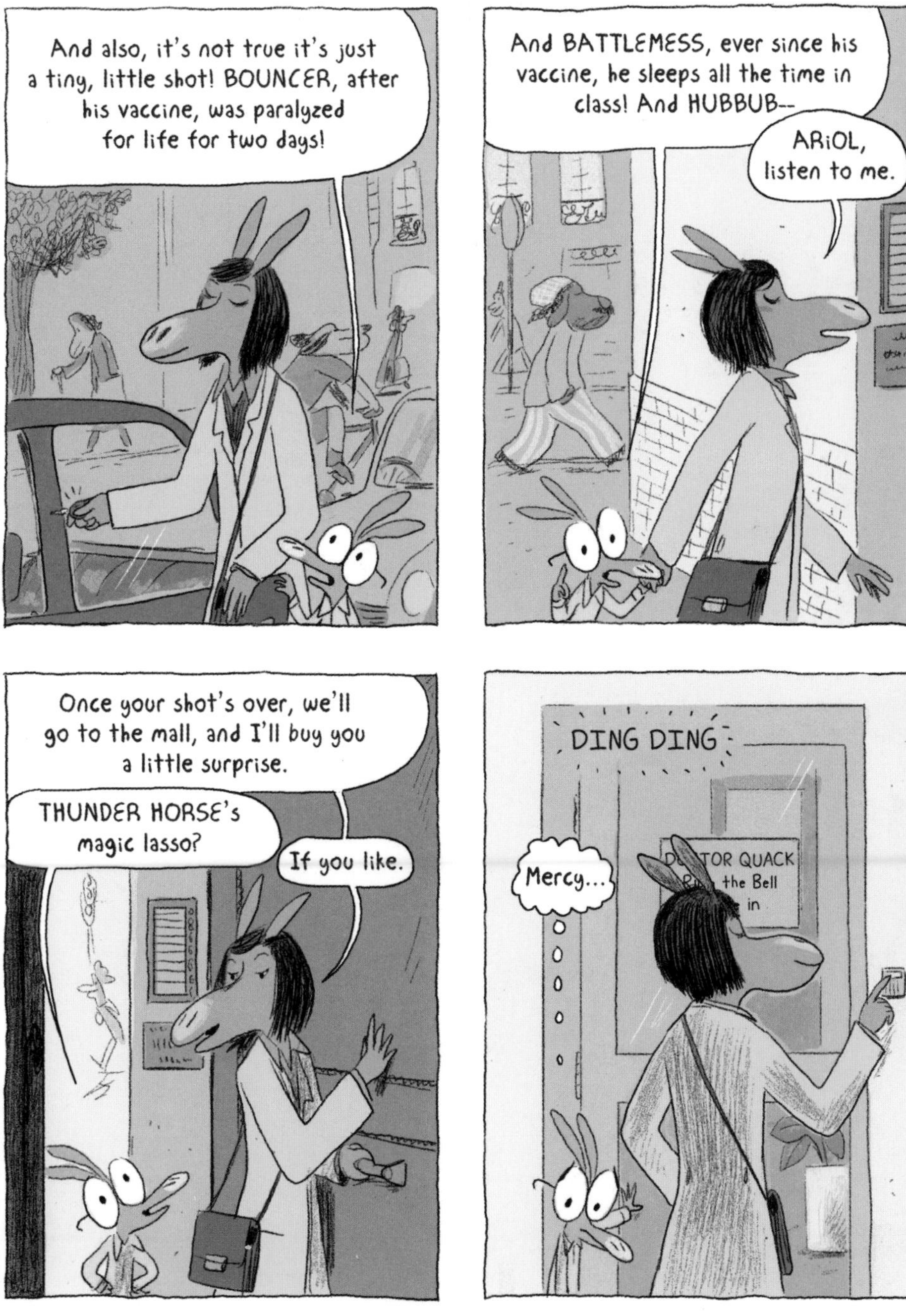
And also, it's not true it's just a tiny, little shot! BOUNCER, after his vaccine, was paralyzed for life for two days!
And BATTLEMESS, ever since his vaccine, he sleeps all the time in class! And HUBBUB--
ARiOL, listen to me.
Once your shot's over, we'll go to the mall, and I'll buy you a little surprise.
THUNDER HORSE's magic lasso?
If you like.
DING DING
Mercy...
the Bell
in

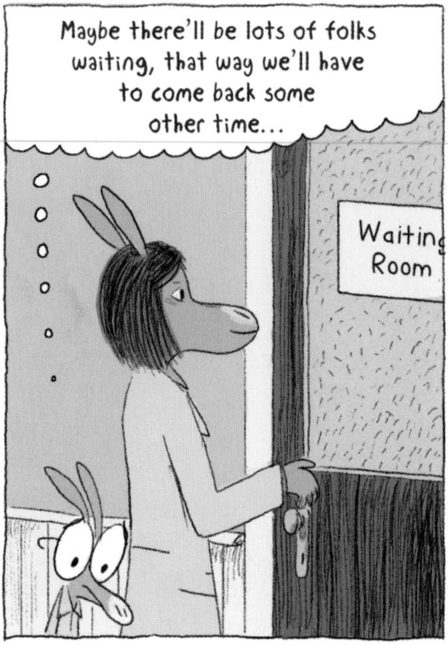
Maybe there'll be lots of folks waiting, that way we'll have to come back some other time...
Waiting Room

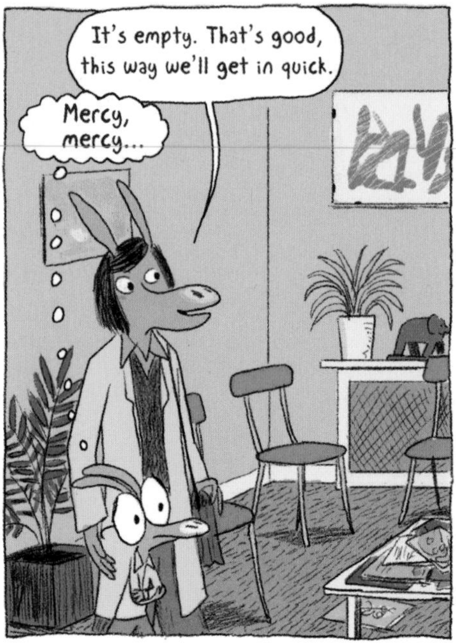
It's empty. That's good, this way we'll get in quick.
Mercy, mercy...

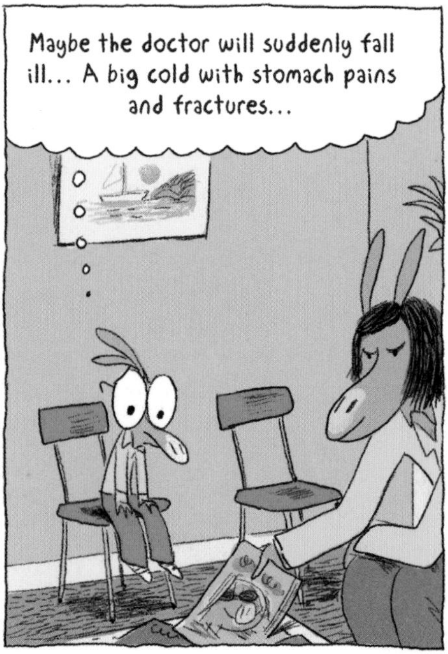
Maybe the doctor will suddenly fall ill... A big cold with stomach pains and fractures...

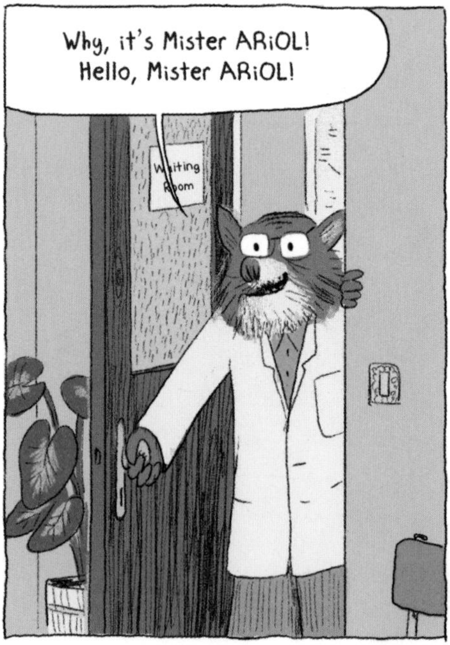
Why, it's Mister ARiOL! Hello, Mister ARiOL!
Waiting Room

So, Mister ARiOL, you've brought your pretty mom along to see me? I'm lucky! Hello, ma'am.

Hello, doctor.

So, Mister ARiOL, strip down to your t-shirt, so I can make you suffer.

Mercy mercy mercy...

Is this Mister ARiOL eating right? Is he sleeping well? Is he fidgety?

Oh, that! He's a fidgety one, all right!

Very good, very good.

And tell me, Mister ARiOL, are you still a fan of your... what's his name? Your hero? You told me about him the last time.

Thu— THUNDER HORSE...

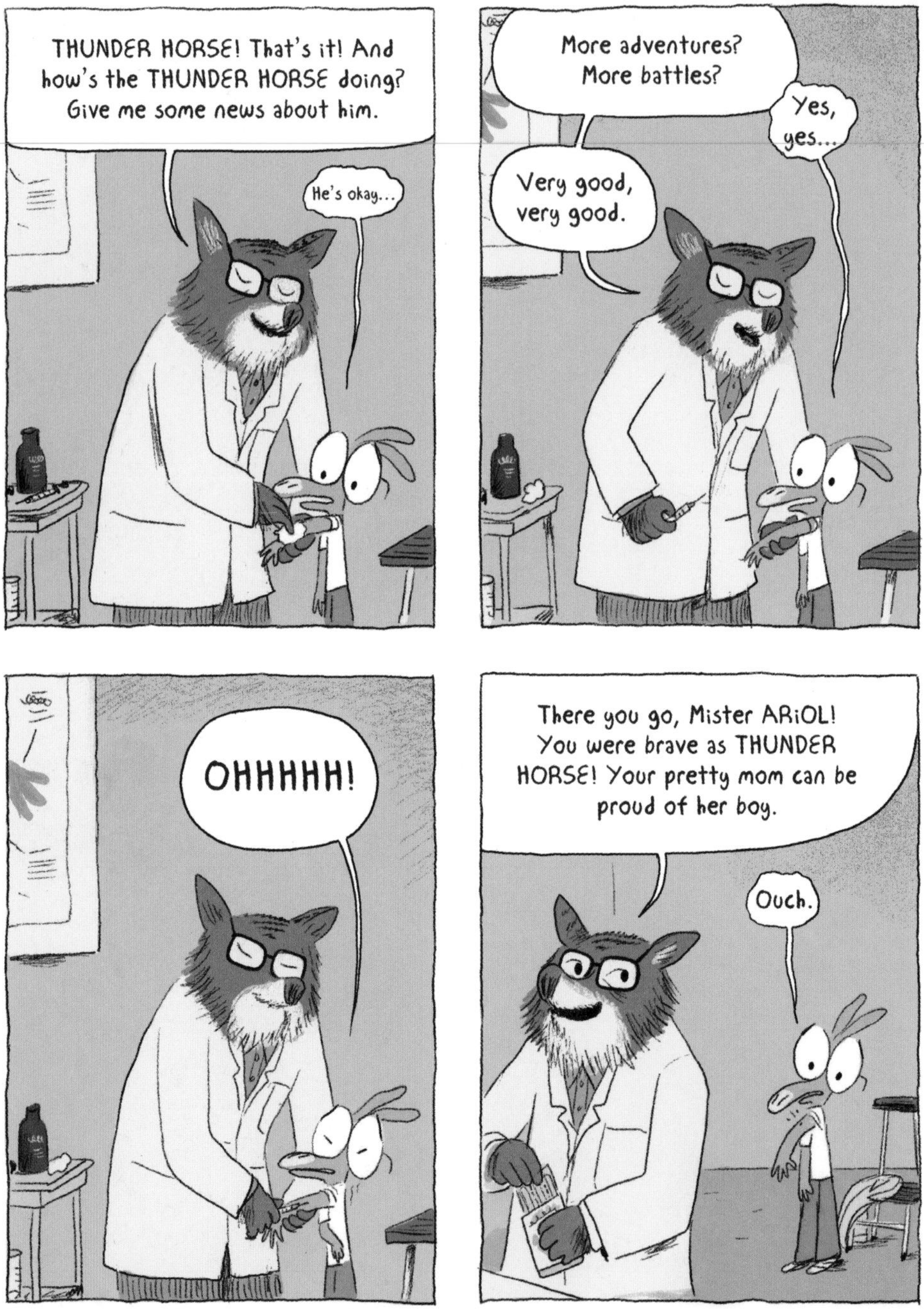
THUNDER HORSE! That's it! And how's the THUNDER HORSE doing? Give me some news about him.
He's okay...
More adventures? More battles?
Yes, yes...
Very good, very good.
OHHHHH!
There you go, Mister ARiOL! You were brave as THUNDER HORSE! Your pretty mom can be proud of her boy.
Ouch.

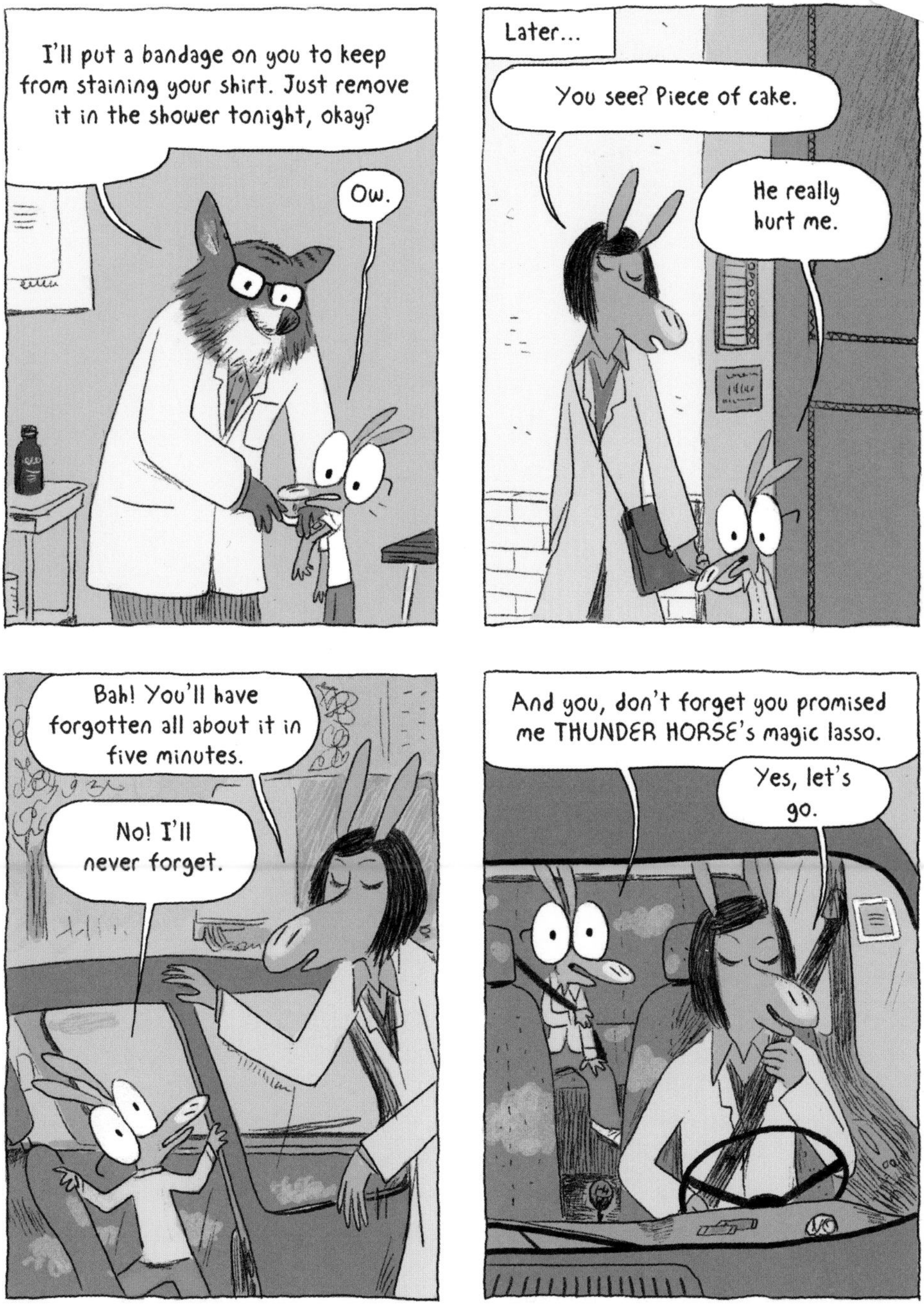
I'll put a bandage on you to keep from staining your shirt. Just remove it in the shower tonight, okay?
Ow.
Later...
You see? Piece of cake.
He really hurt me.
Bah! You'll have forgotten all about it in five minutes.
No! I'll never forget.
And you, don't forget you promised me THUNDER HORSE's magic lasso.
Yes, let's go.

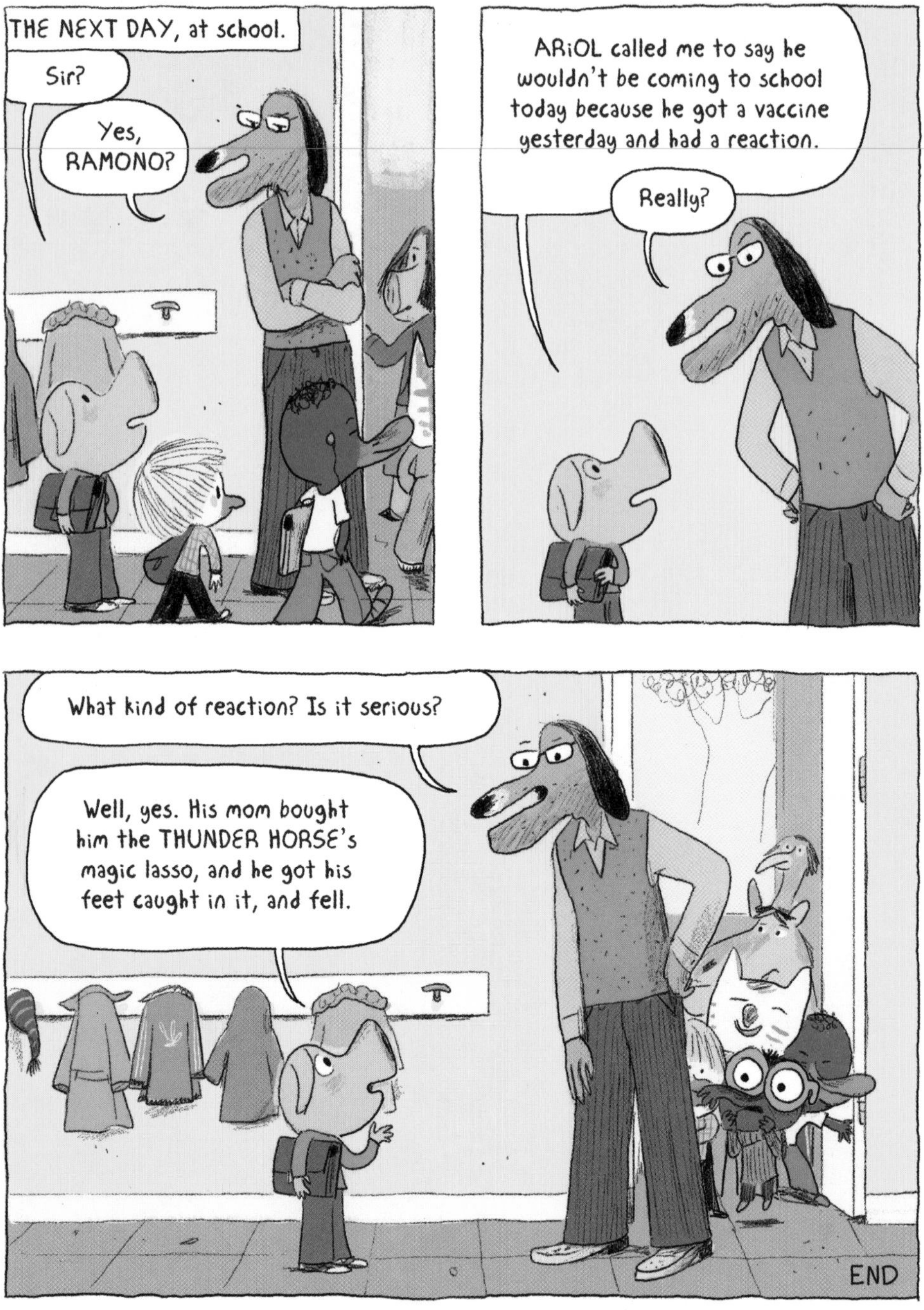
THE NEXT DAY, at school.
Sir?
Yes, RAMONO?
ARiOL called me to say he wouldn't be coming to school today because he got a vaccine yesterday and had a reaction.
Really?
What kind of reaction? Is it serious?
Well, yes. His mom bought him the THUNDER HORSE's magic lasso, and he got his feet caught in it, and fell.
END

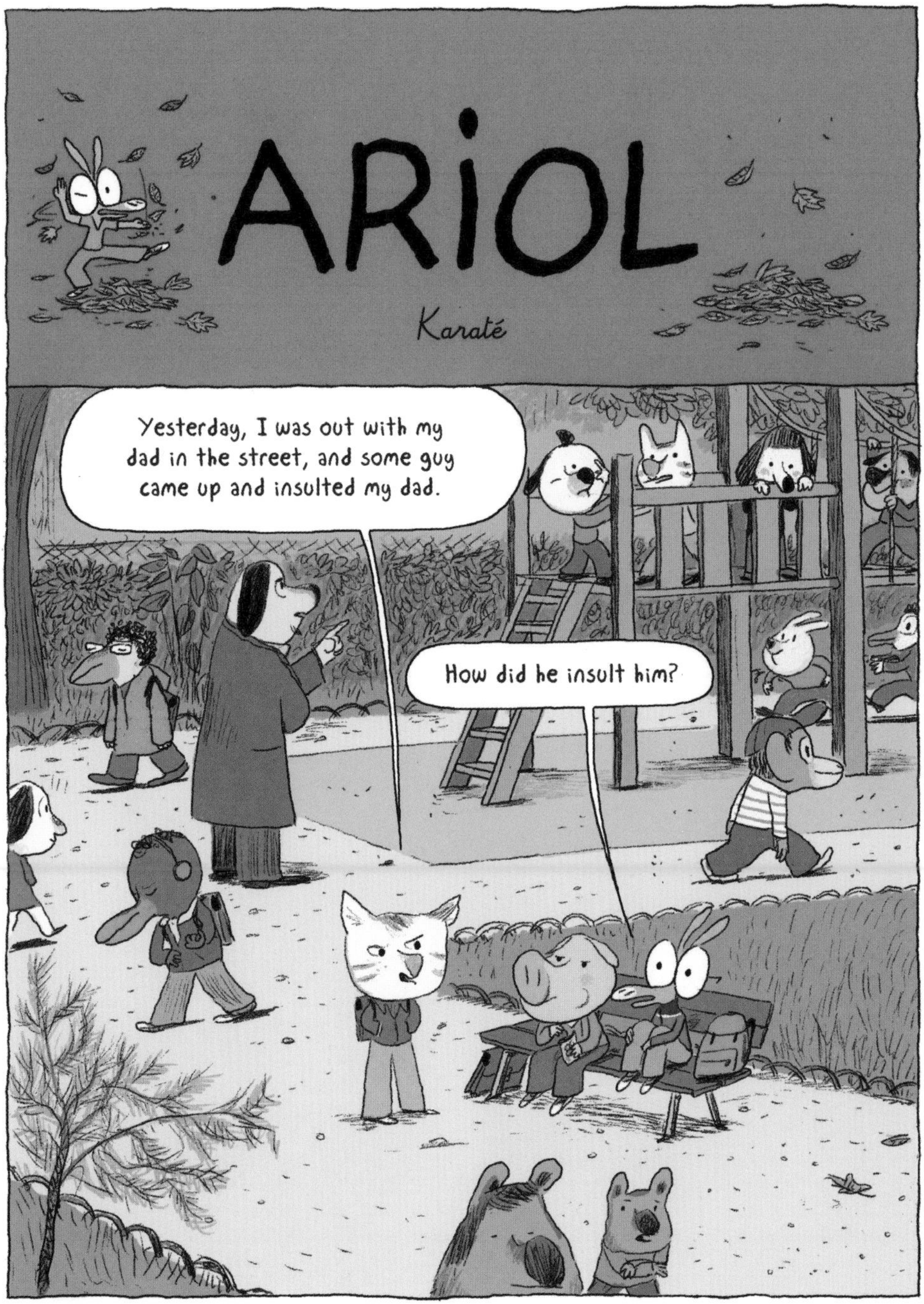
ARiOL
Karaté
Yesterday, I was out with my dad in the street, and some guy came up and insulted my dad.
How did he insult him?

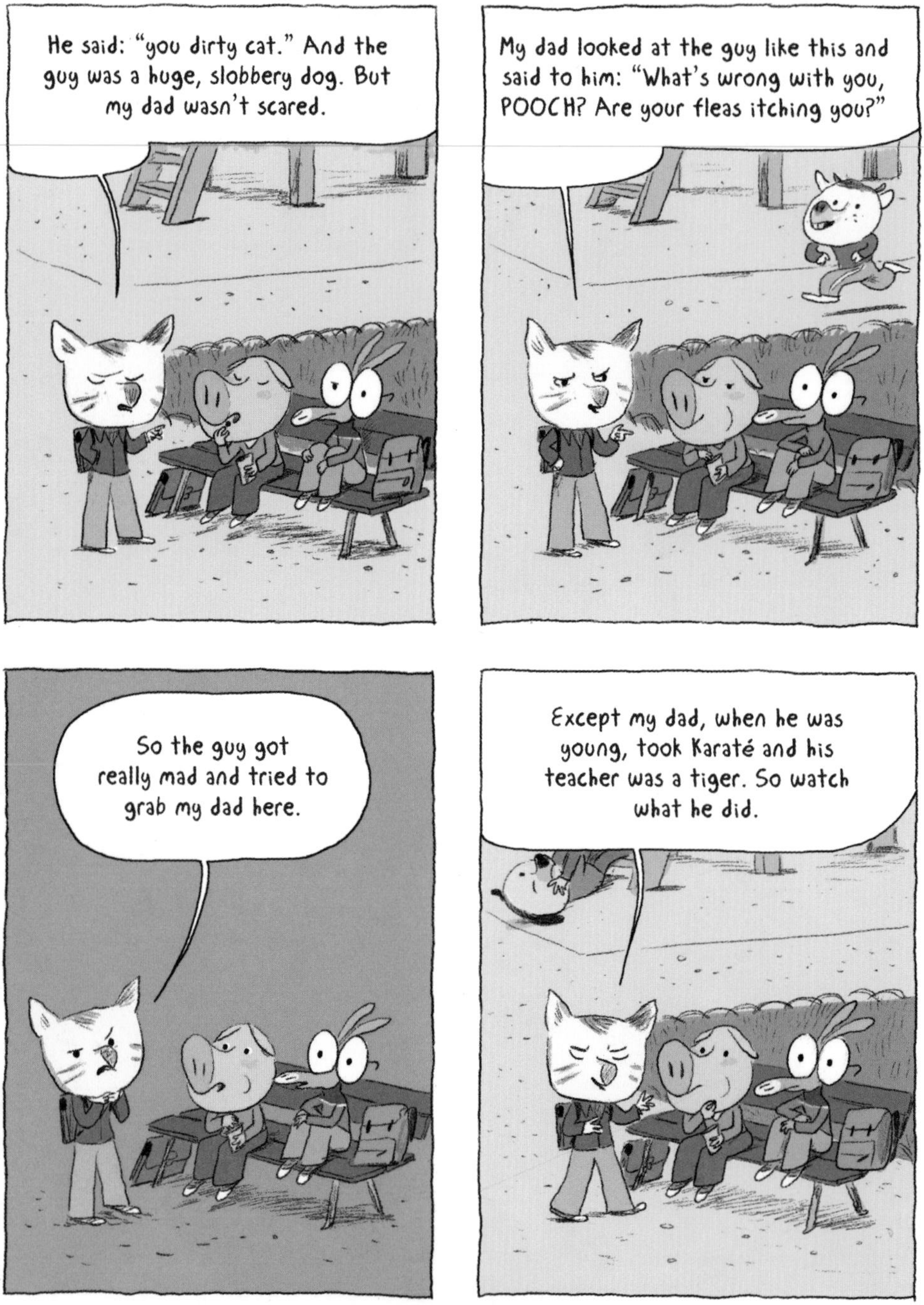
He said: "you dirty cat." And the guy was a huge, slobbery dog. But my dad wasn't scared.
My dad looked at the guy like this and said to him: "What's wrong with you, POOCH? Are your fleas itching you?"
So the guy got really mad and tried to grab my dad here.
Except my dad, when he was young, took Karaté and his teacher was a tiger. So watch what he did.

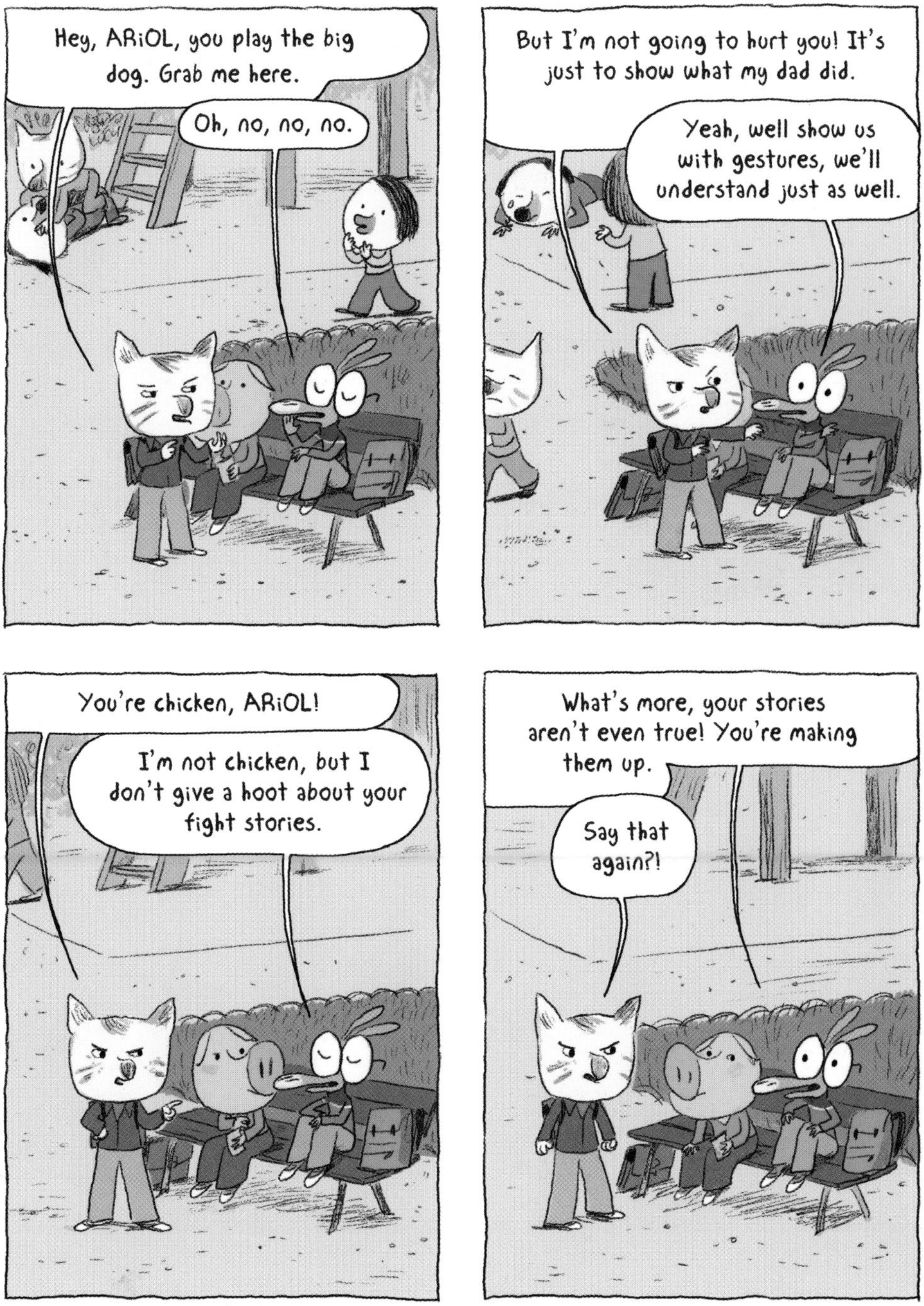
Hey, ARiOL, you play the big dog. Grab me here.
Oh, no, no, no.
But I'm not going to hurt you! It's just to show what my dad did.
Yeah, well show us with gestures, we'll understand just as well.
You're chicken, ARiOL!
I'm not chicken, but I don't give a hoot about your fight stories.
What's more, your stories aren't even true! You're making them up.
Say that again?!

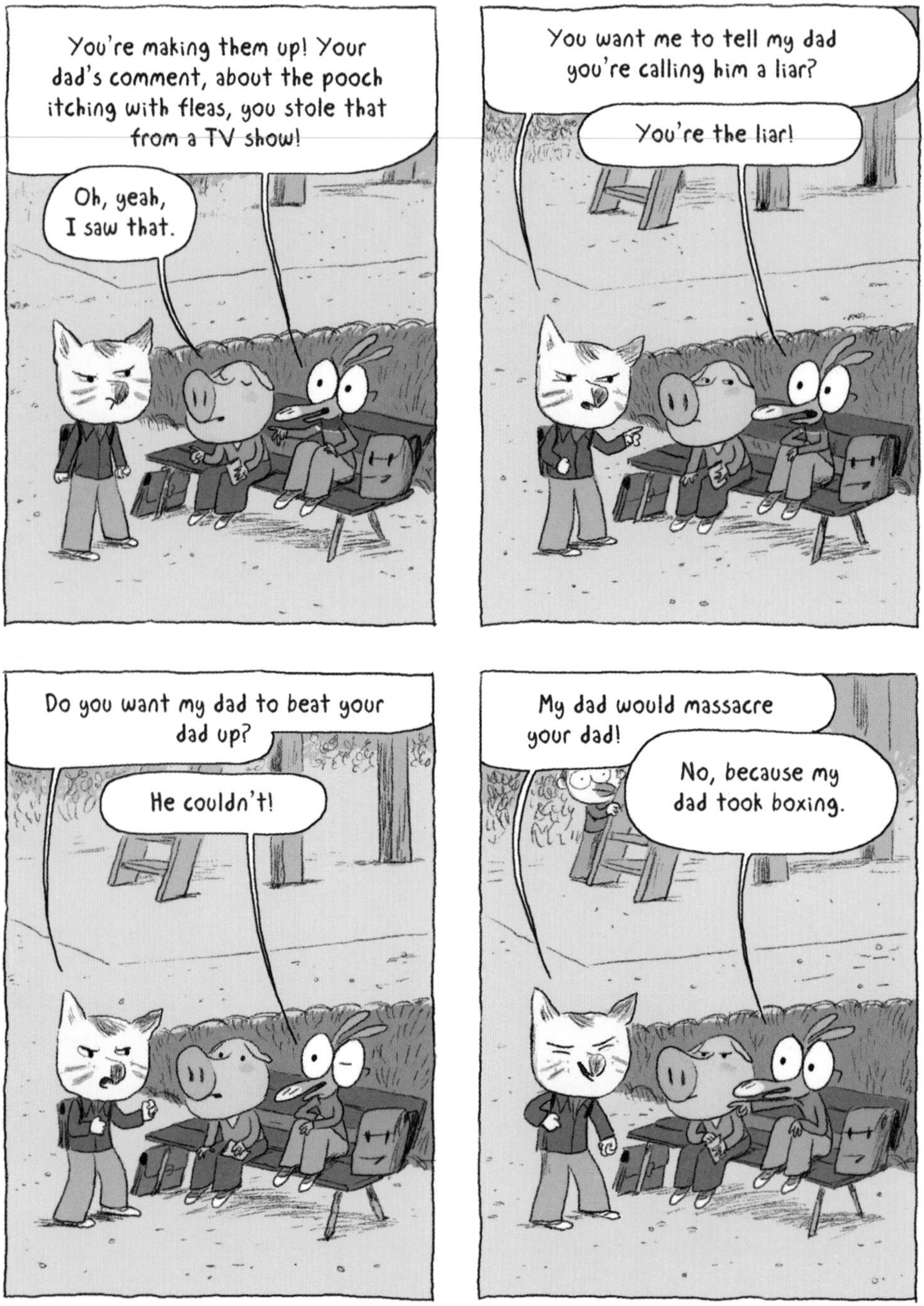
You're making them up! Your dad's comment, about the pooch itching with fleas, you stole that from a TV show!
Oh, yeah, I saw that.
You want me to tell my dad you're calling him a liar?
You're the liar!
Do you want my dad to beat your dad up?
He couldn't!
My dad would massacre your dad!
No, because my dad took boxing.

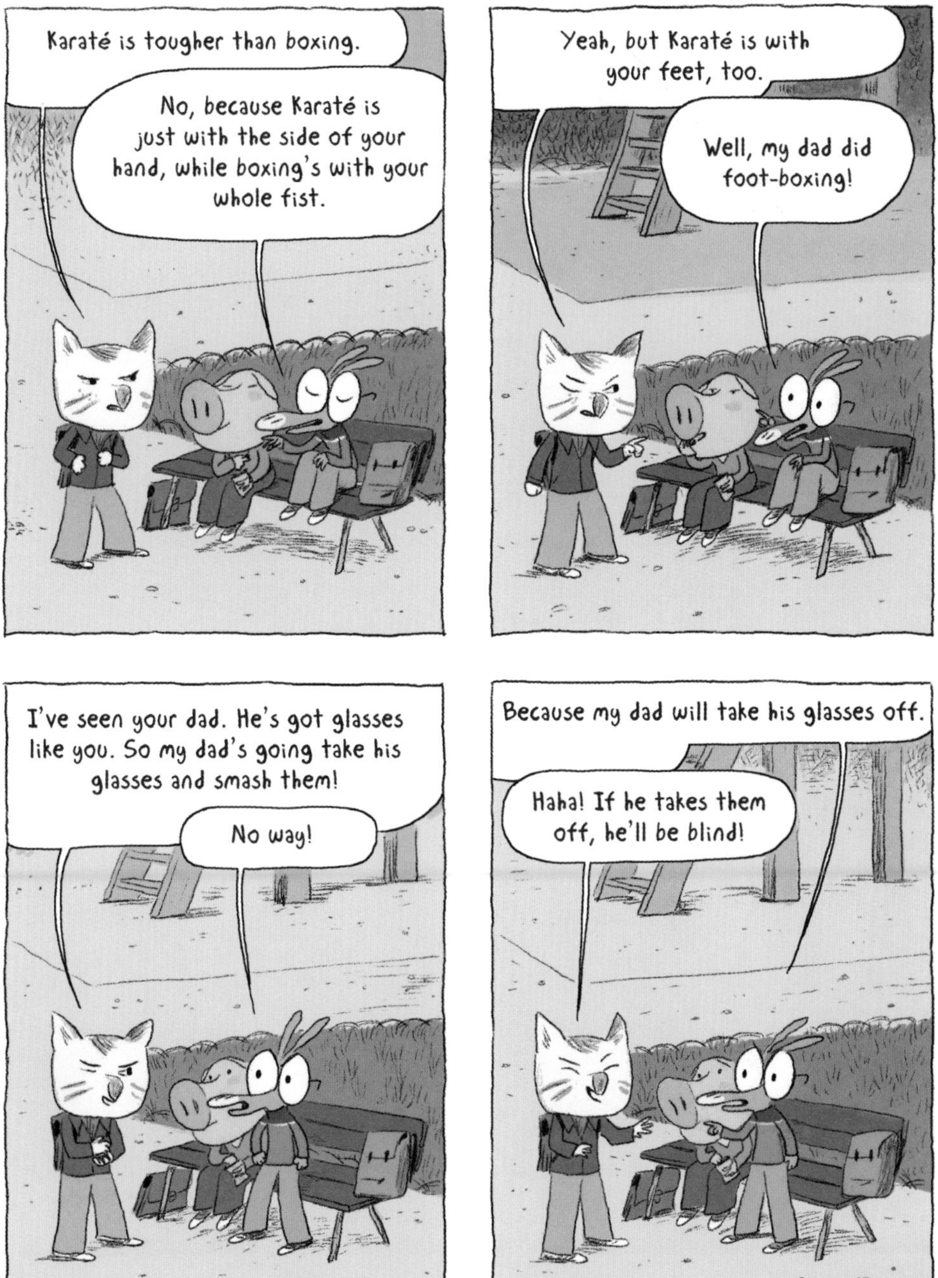
Karaté is tougher than boxing.
No, because Karaté is just with the side of your hand, while boxing's with your whole fist.
Yeah, but Karaté is with your feet, too.
Well, my dad did foot-boxing!
I've seen your dad. He's got glasses like you. So my dad's going take his glasses and smash them!
No way!
Because my dad will take his glasses off.
Haha! If he takes them off, he'll be blind!

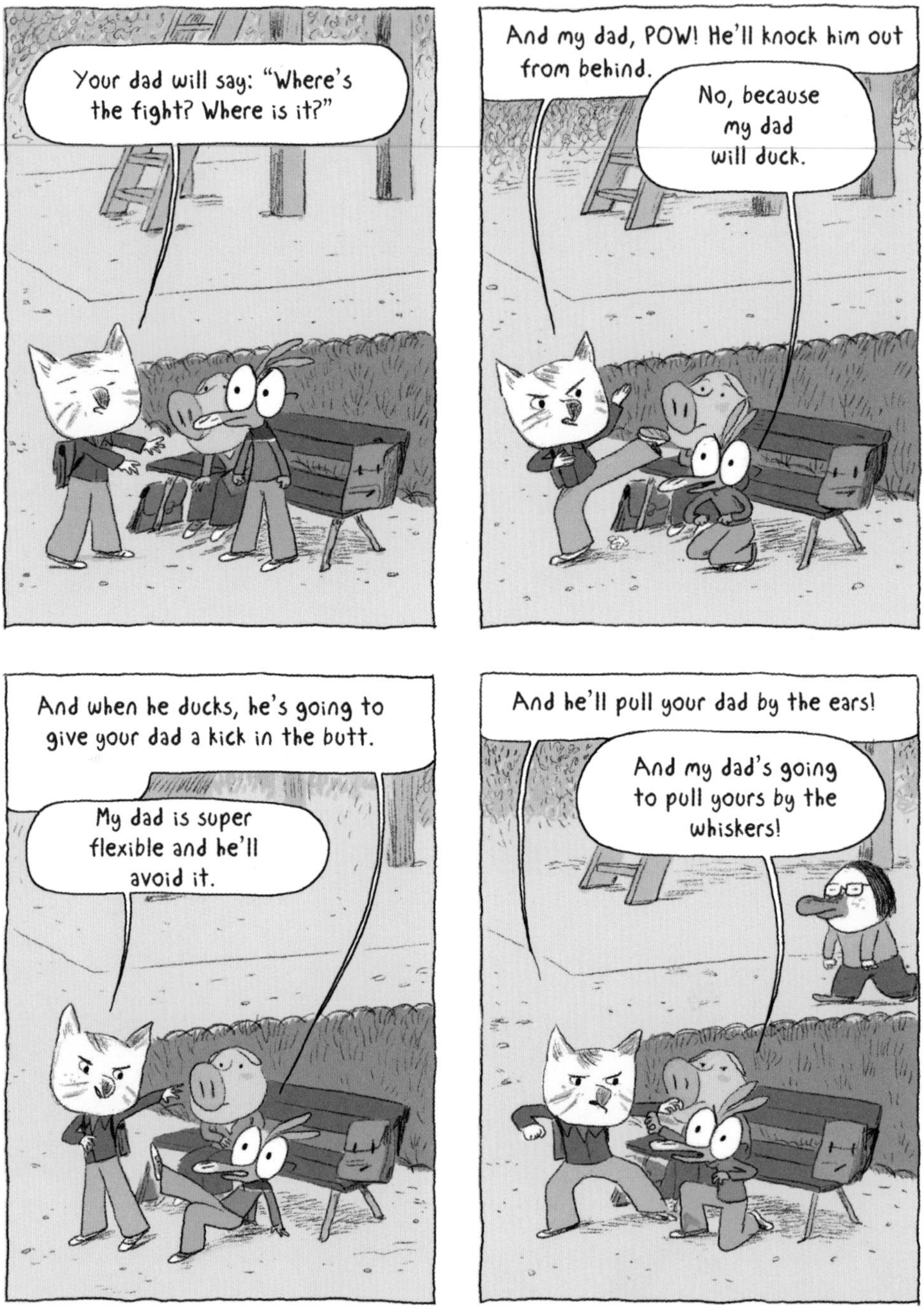
Your dad will say: "Where's the fight? Where is it?"
And my dad, POW! He'll knock him out from behind.
No, because my dad will duck.
And when he ducks, he's going to give your dad a kick in the butt.
My dad is super flexible and he'll avoid it.
And he'll pull your dad by the ears!
And my dad's going to pull yours by the whiskers!

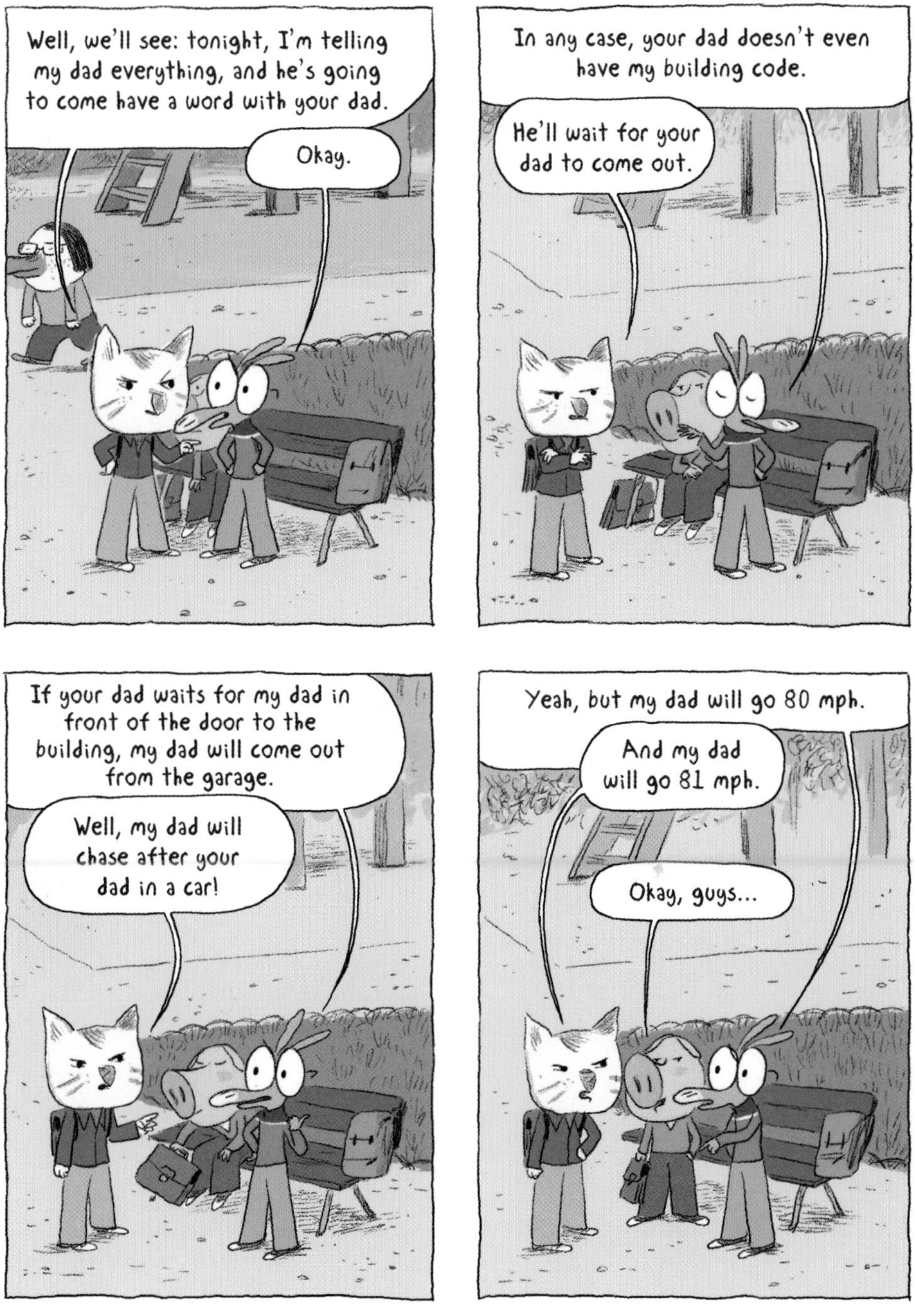
Well, we'll see: tonight, I'm telling my dad everything, and he's going to come have a word with your dad.
Okay.
In any case, your dad doesn't even have my building code.
He'll wait for your dad to come out.
If your dad waits for my dad in front of the door to the building, my dad will come out from the garage.
Well, my dad will chase after your dad in a car!
Yeah, but my dad will go 80 mph.
And my dad will go 81 mph.
Okay, guys...

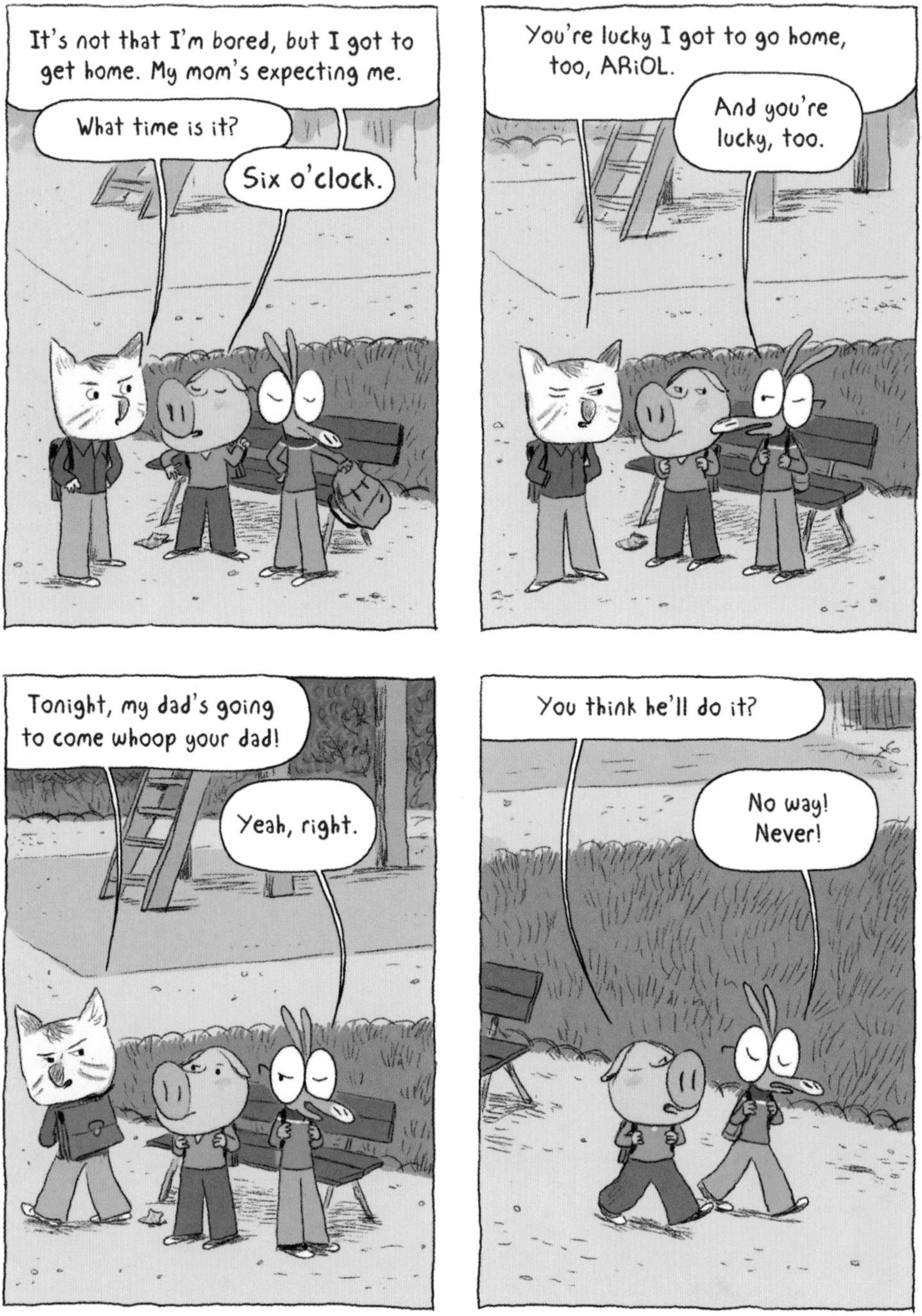
It's not that I'm bored, but I got to get home. My mom's expecting me.
What time is it?
Six o'clock.
You're lucky I got to go home, too, ARiOL.
And you're lucky, too.
Tonight, my dad's going to come whoop your dad!
Yeah, right.
You think he'll do it?
No way! Never!

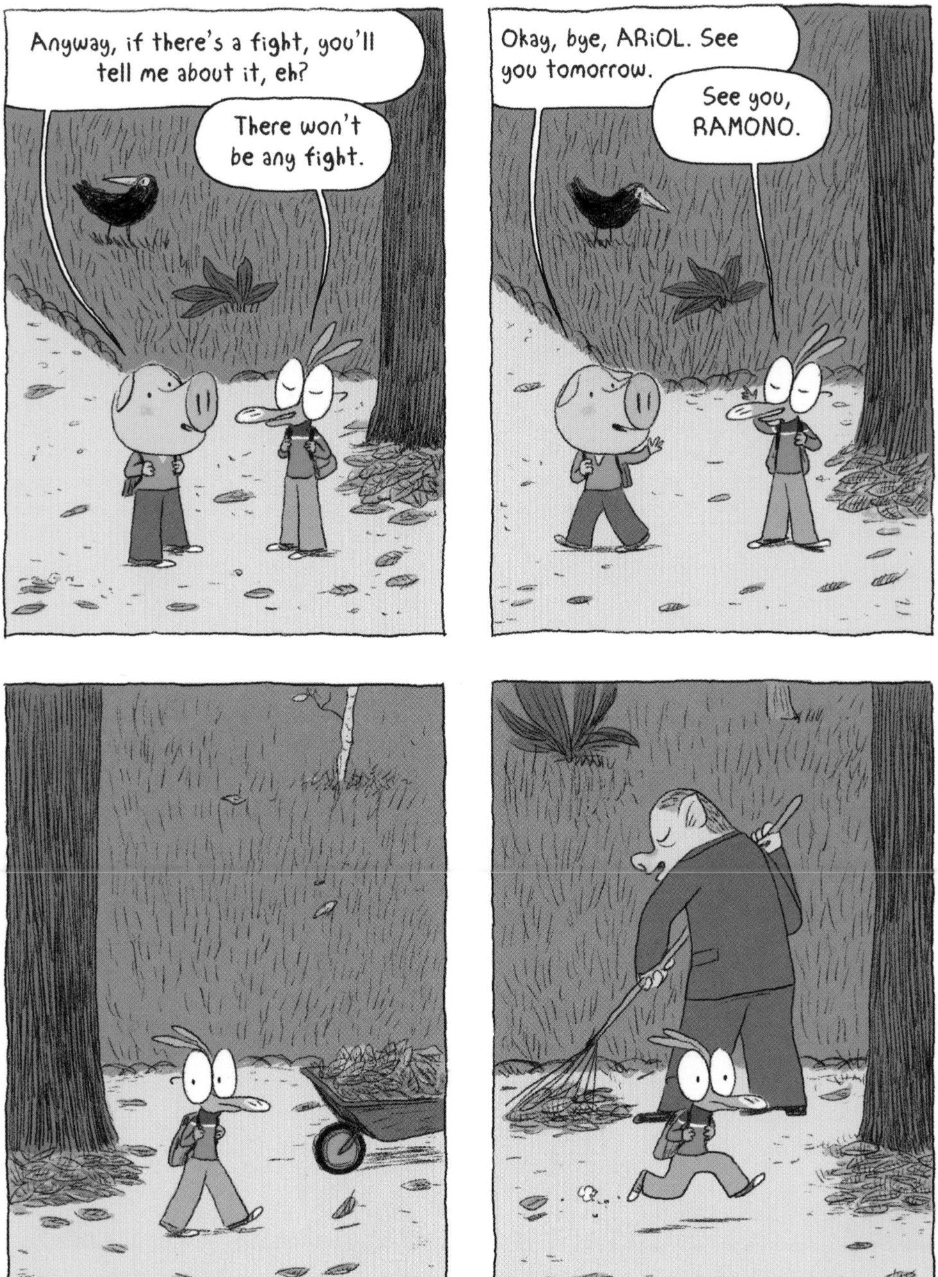

Anyway, if there's a fight, you'll tell me about it, eh?
There won't be any fight.
Okay, bye, ARiOL. See you tomorrow.
See you, RAMONO.

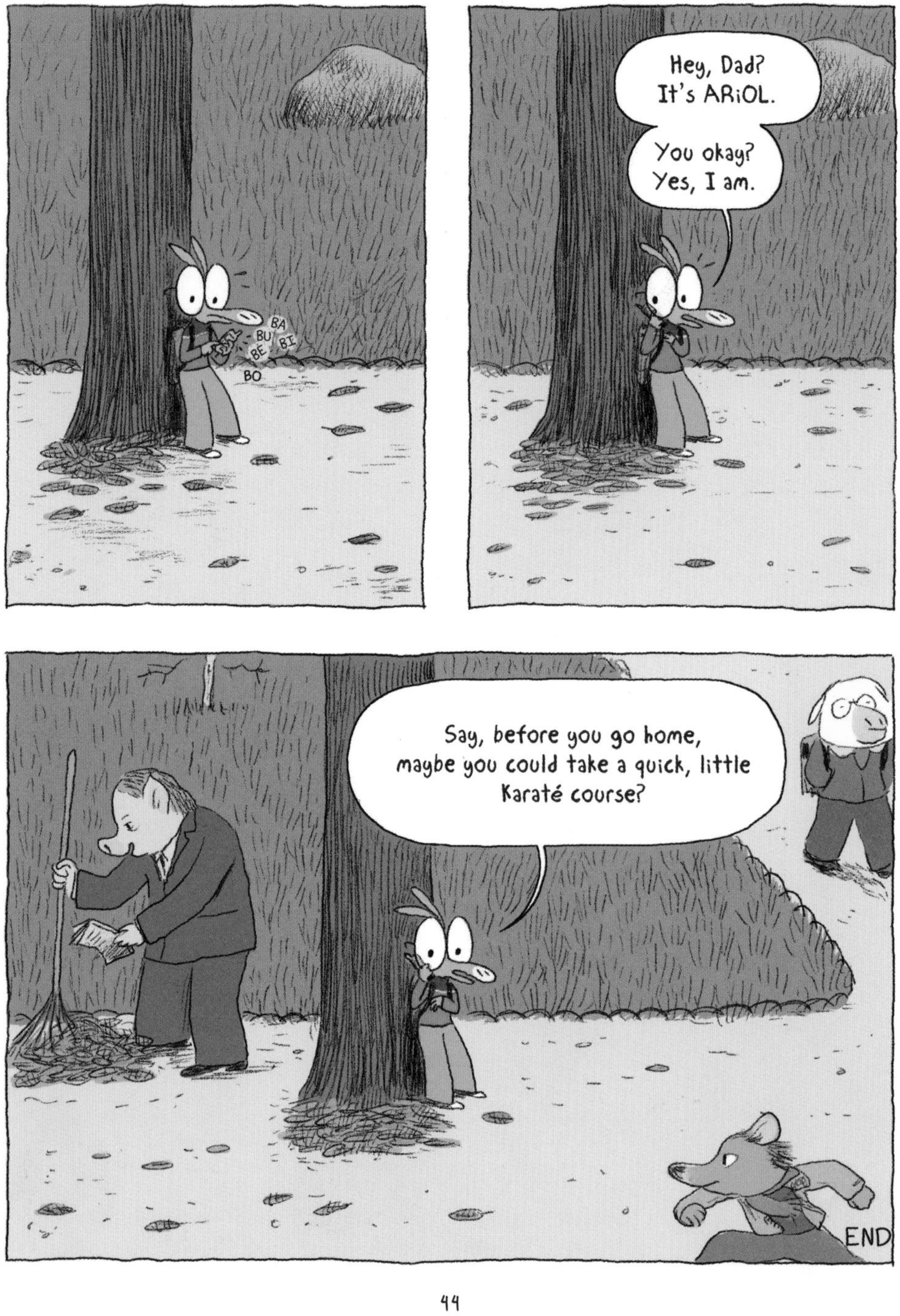

BA
BU
BE
BI
BO
Hey, Dad? It's ARiOL.
You okay? Yes, I am.
Say, before you go home, maybe you could take a quick, little Karaté course?
END

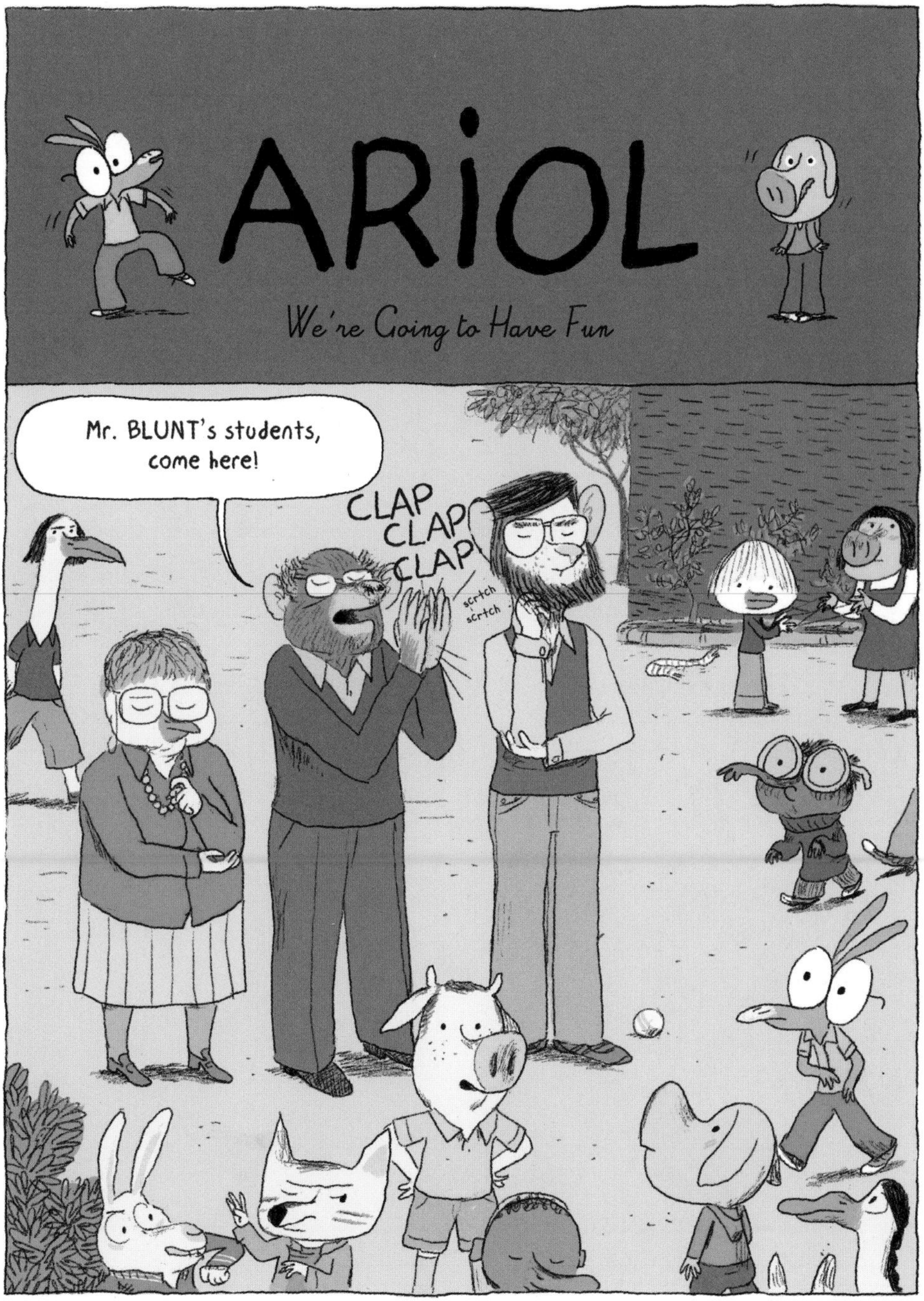
ARiOL
We're Going to Have Fun
Mr. BLUNT's students, come here!
CLAP CLAP CLAP
scrtch scrtch

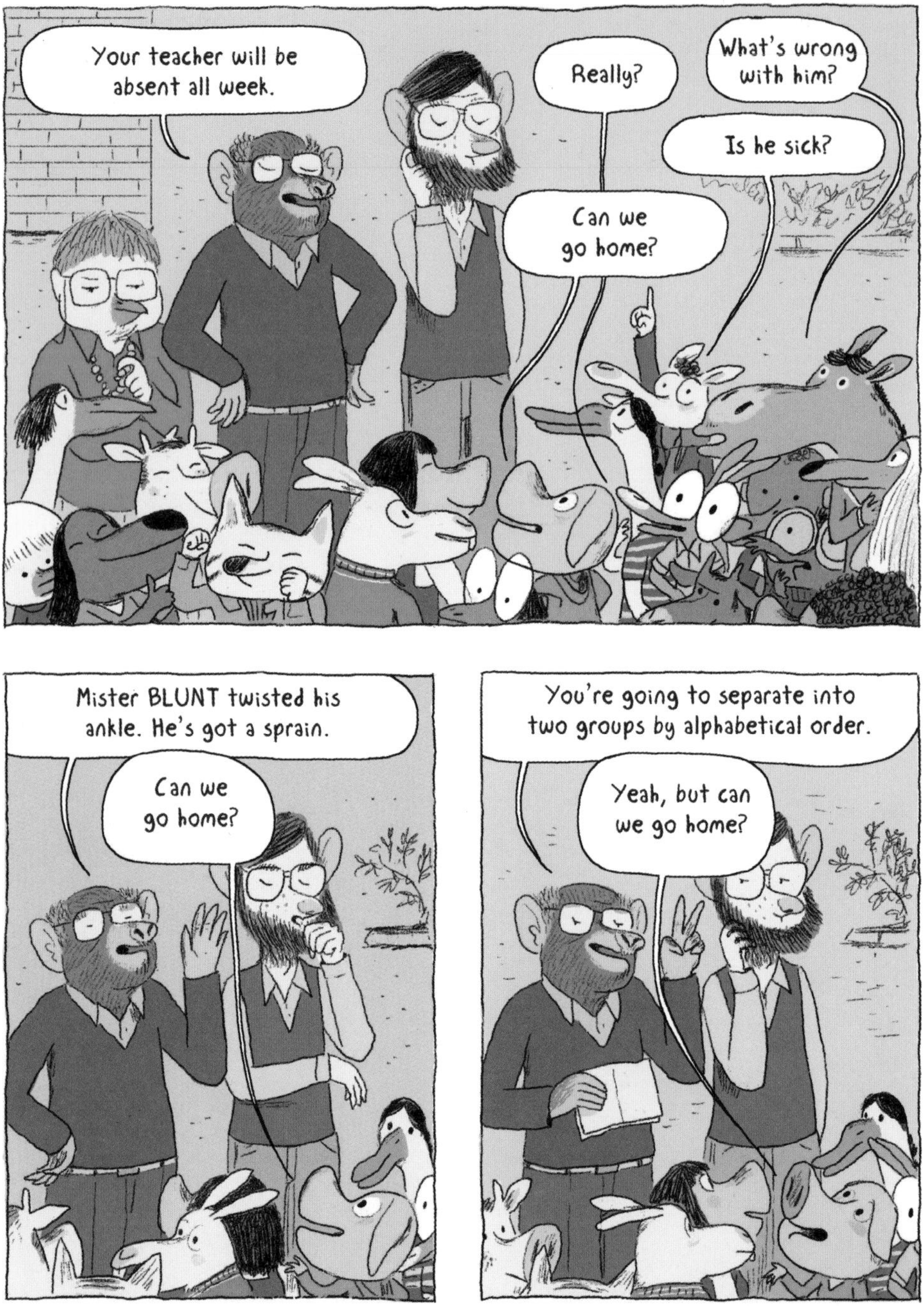

Your teacher will be absent all week.
Really?
What's wrong with him?
Is he sick?
Can we go home?
Mister BLUNT twisted his ankle. He's got a sprain.
Can we go home?
You're going to separate into two groups by alphabetical order.
Yeah, but can we go home?

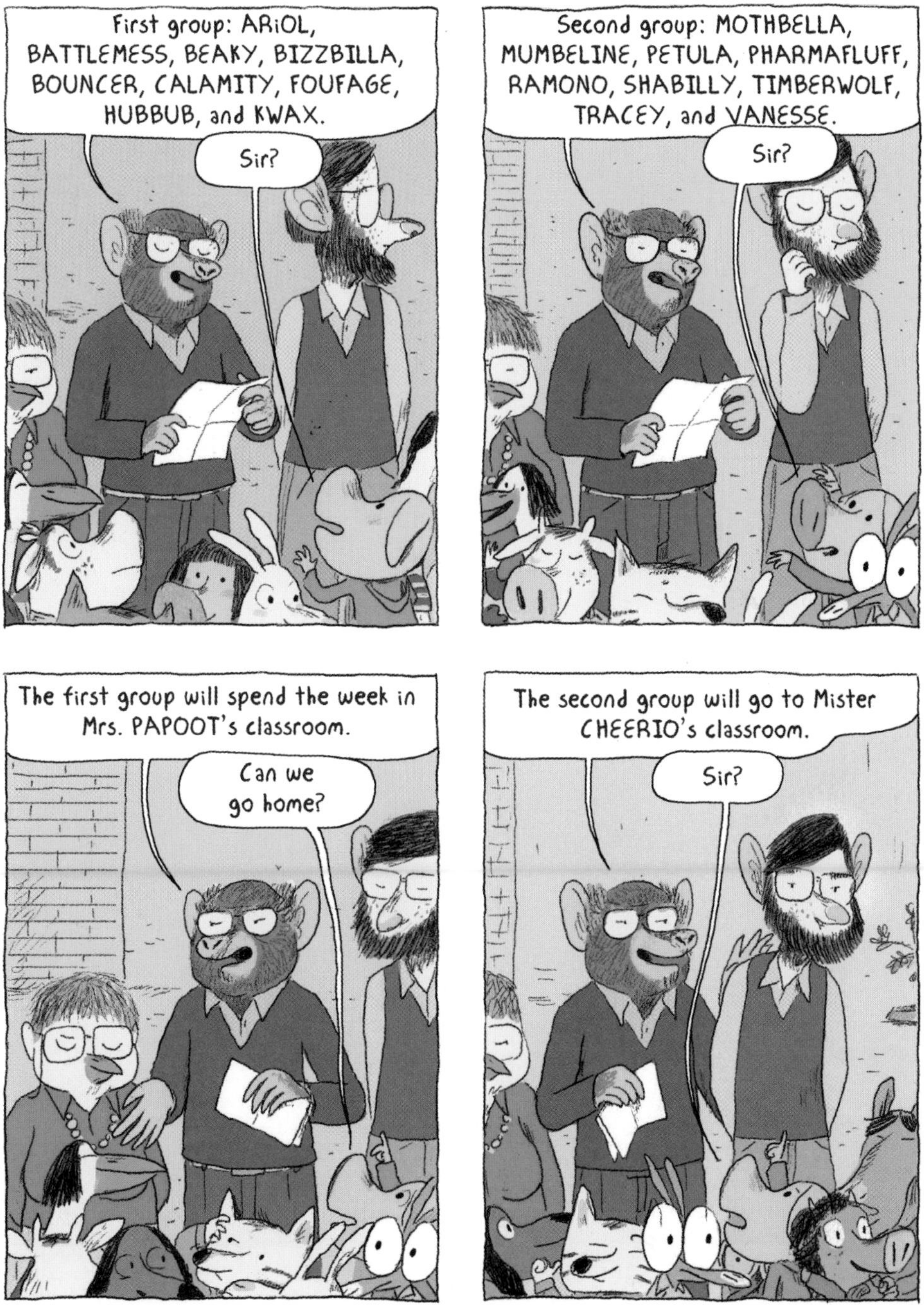
First group: ARiOL, BATTLEMESS, BEAKY, BIZZBILLA, BOUNCER, CALAMITY, FOUFAGE, HUBBUB, and KWAX.
Sir?
Second group: MOTHBELLA, MUMBELINE, PETULA, PHARMAFLUFF, RAMONO, SHABILLY, TIMBERWOLF, TRACEY, and VANESSE.
Sir?
The first group will spend the week in Mrs. PAPOOT's classroom.
Can we go home?
The second group will go to Mister CHEERIO's classroom.
Sir?

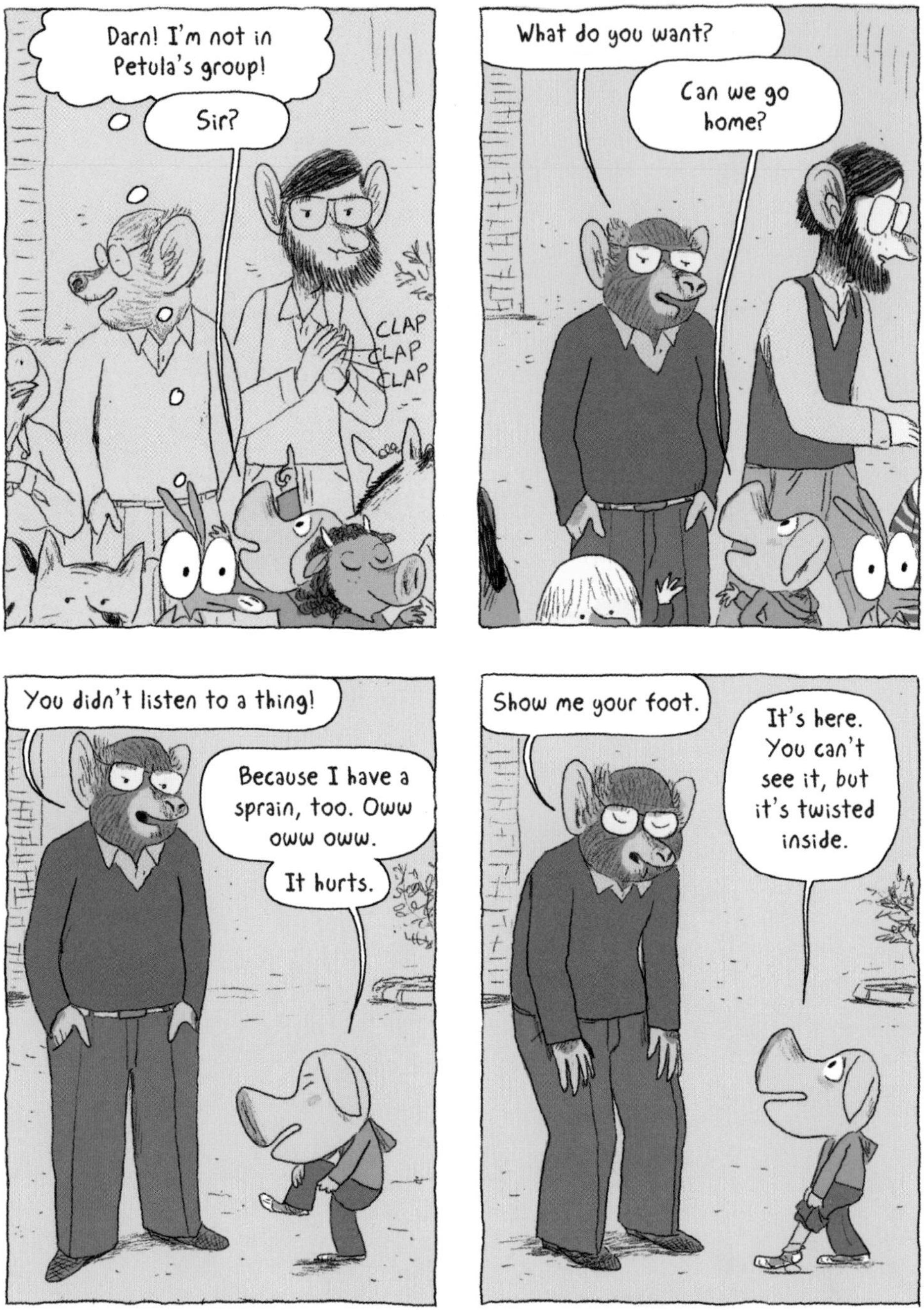
Darn! I'm not in Petula's group!
Sir?
CLAP CLAP CLAP
What do you want?
Can we go home?
You didn't listen to a thing!
Because I have a sprain, too. Oww oww oww.
It hurts.
Show me your foot.
It's here. You can't see it, but it's twisted inside.

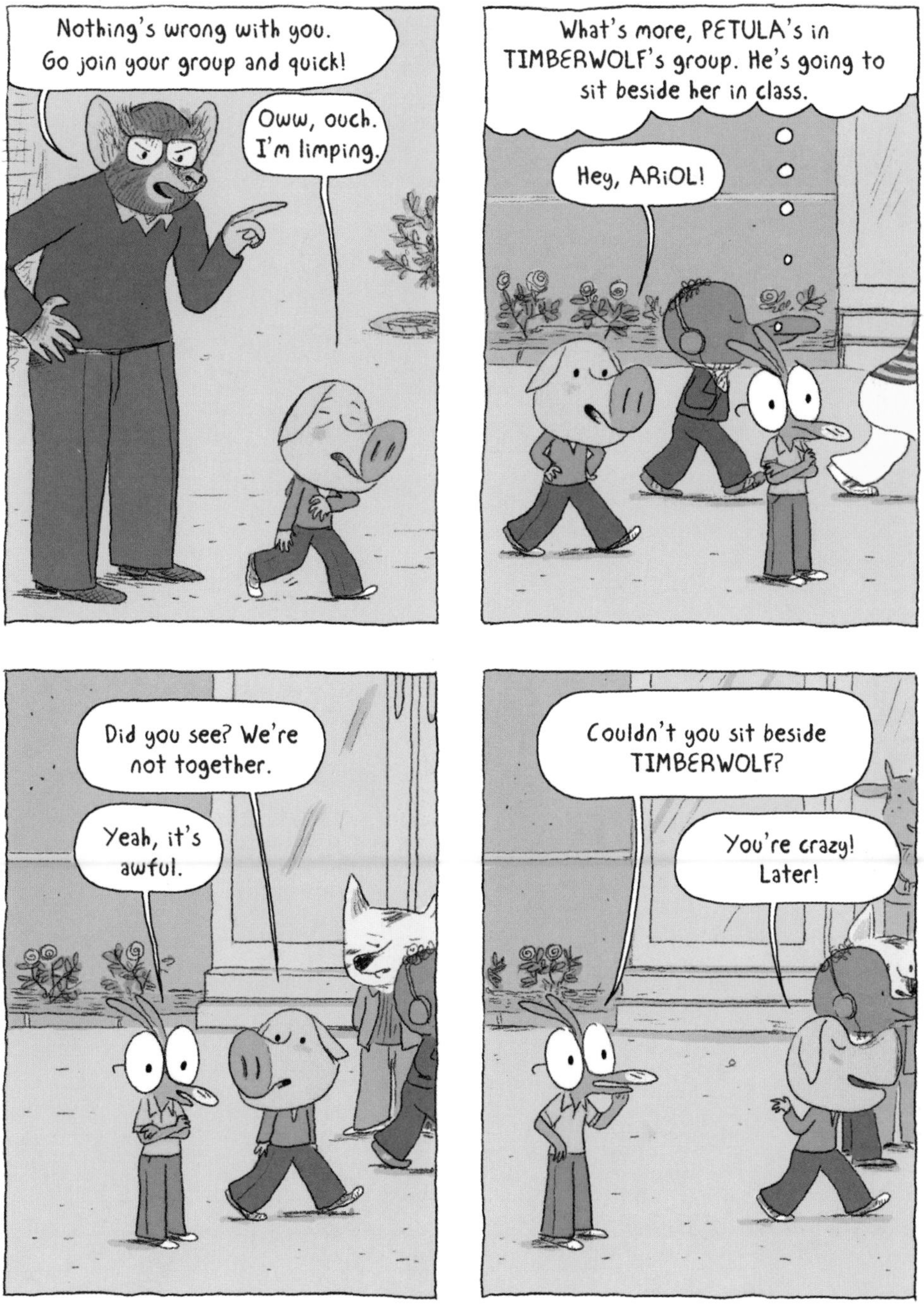

Nothing's wrong with you. Go join your group and quick!
Oww, ouch. I'm limping.
What's more, PETULA's in TIMBERWOLF's group. He's going to sit beside her in class.
Hey, ARiOL!
Did you see? We're not together.
Yeah, it's awful.
Couldn't you sit beside TIMBERWOLF?
You're crazy! Later!

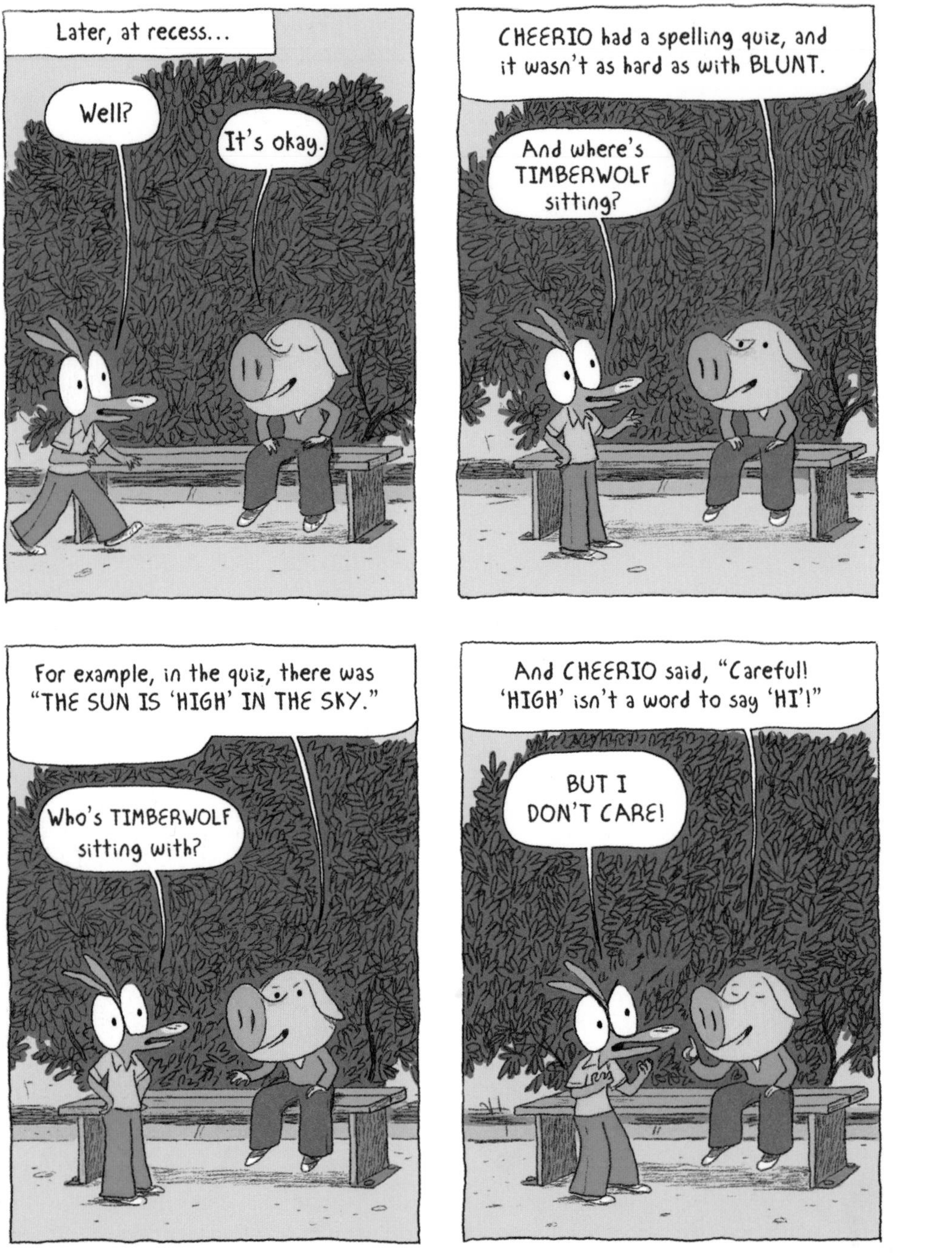
Later, at recess...
Well?
It's okay.
CHEERIO had a spelling quiz, and it wasn't as hard as with BLUNT.
And where's TIMBERWOLF sitting?
For example, in the quiz, there was "THE SUN IS 'HIGH' IN THE SKY."
Who's TIMBERWOLF sitting with?
And CHEERIO said, "Careful! 'HIGH' isn't a word to say 'HI'!"
BUT I DON'T CARE!

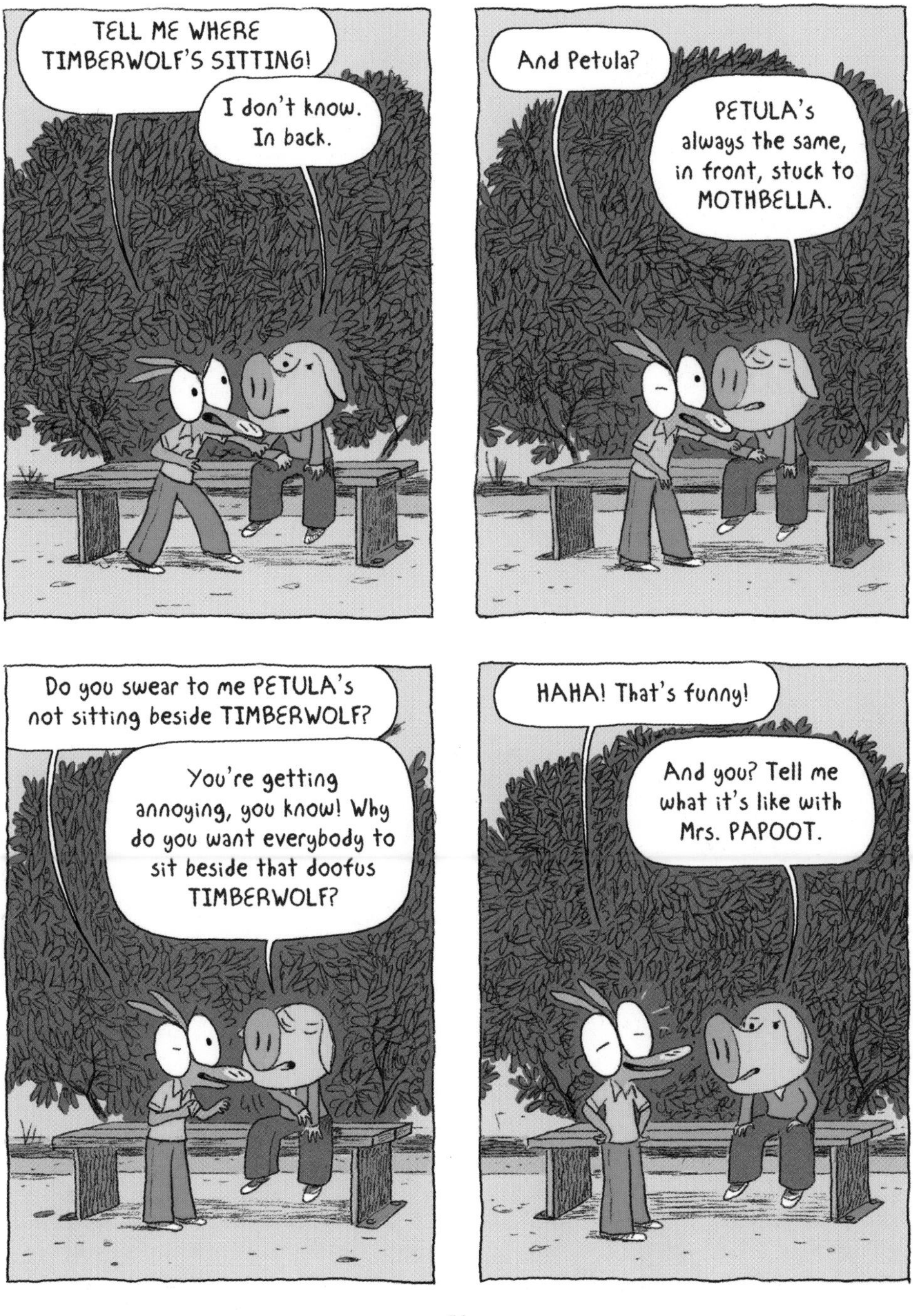
TELL ME WHERE TIMBERWOLF'S SITTING!
I don't know. In back.
And Petula?
PETULA's always the same, in front, stuck to MOTHBELLA.
Do you swear to me PETULA's not sitting beside TIMBERWOLF?
You're getting annoying, you know! Why do you want everybody to sit beside that doofus TIMBERWOLF?
HAHA! That's funny!
And you? Tell me what it's like with Mrs. PAPOOT.

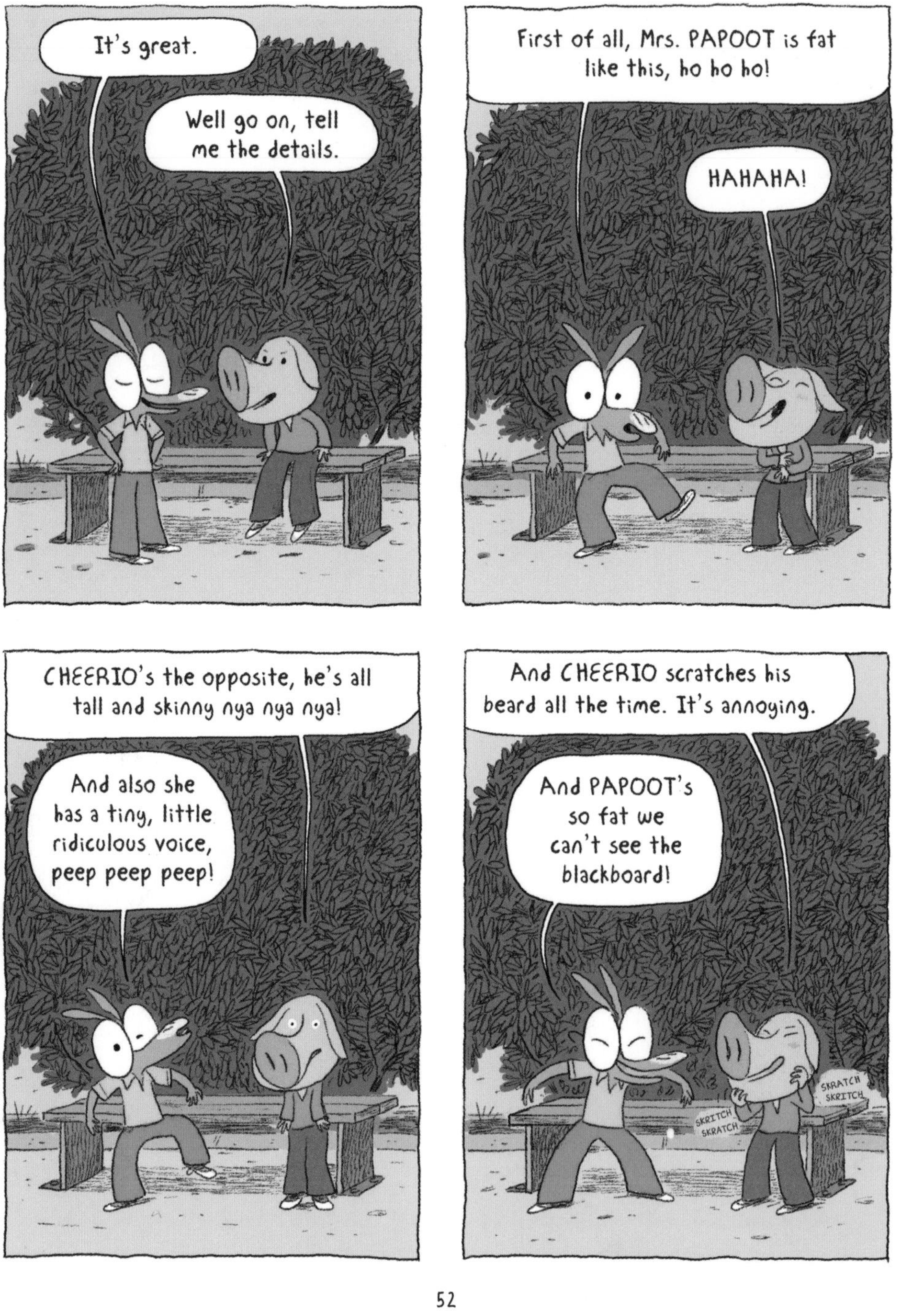
It's great.
Well go on, tell me the details.
First of all, Mrs. PAPOOT is fat like this, ho ho ho!
HAHAHA!
CHEERIO's the opposite, he's all tall and skinny nya nya nya!
And also she has a tiny, little ridiculous voice, peep peep peep!
And CHEERIO scratches his beard all the time. It's annoying.
And PAPOOT's so fat we can't see the blackboard!
SKRITCH SKRATCH
SKRATCH SKRITCH

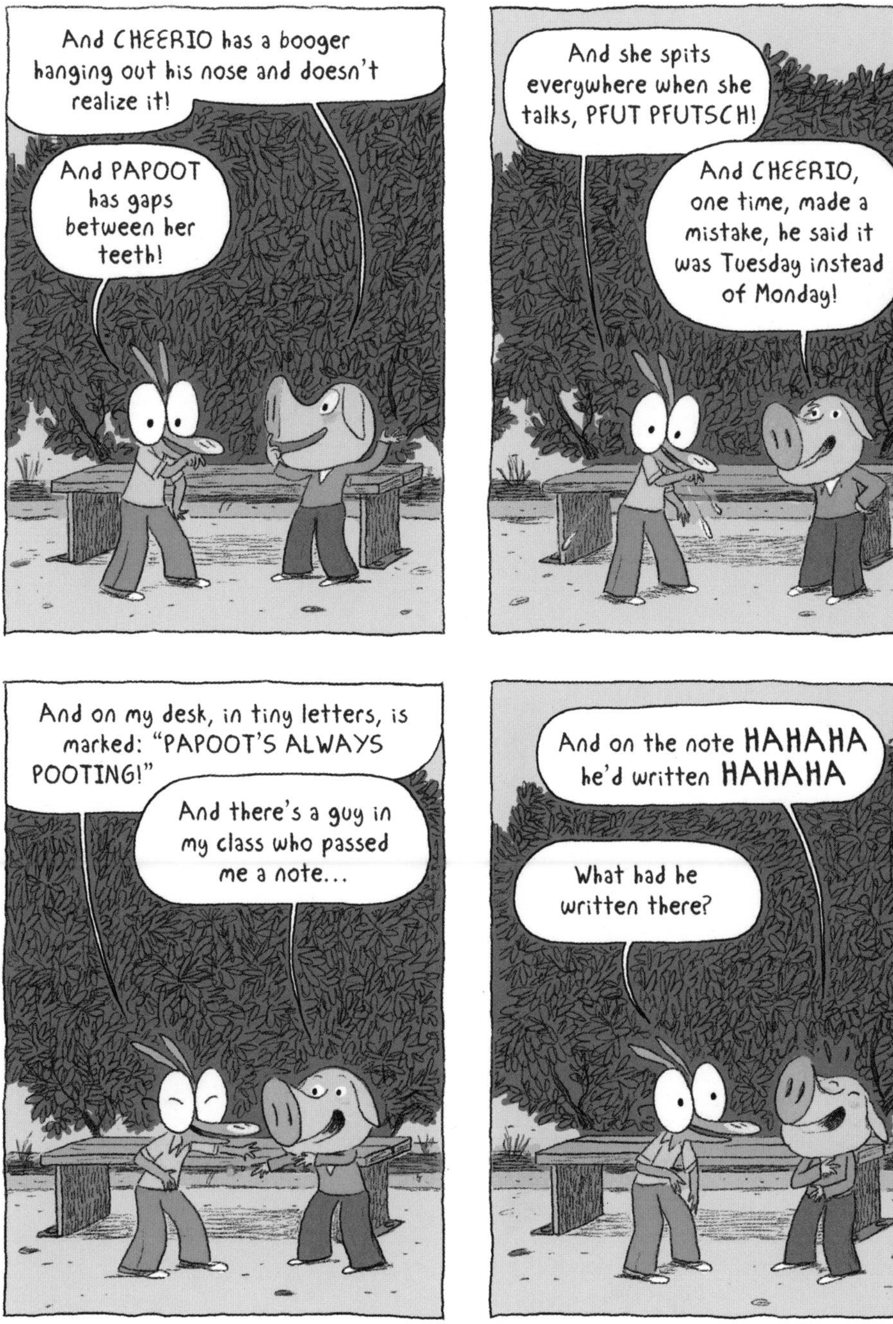
And CHEERIO has a booger hanging out his nose and doesn't realize it!
And PAPOOT has gaps between her teeth!
And she spits everywhere when she talks, PFUT PFUTSCH!
And CHEERIO, one time, made a mistake, he said it was Tuesday instead of Monday!
And on my desk, in tiny letters, is marked: "PAPOOT'S ALWAYS POOTING!"
And there's a guy in my class who passed me a note...
And on the note HAHAHA he'd written HAHAHA
What had he written there?

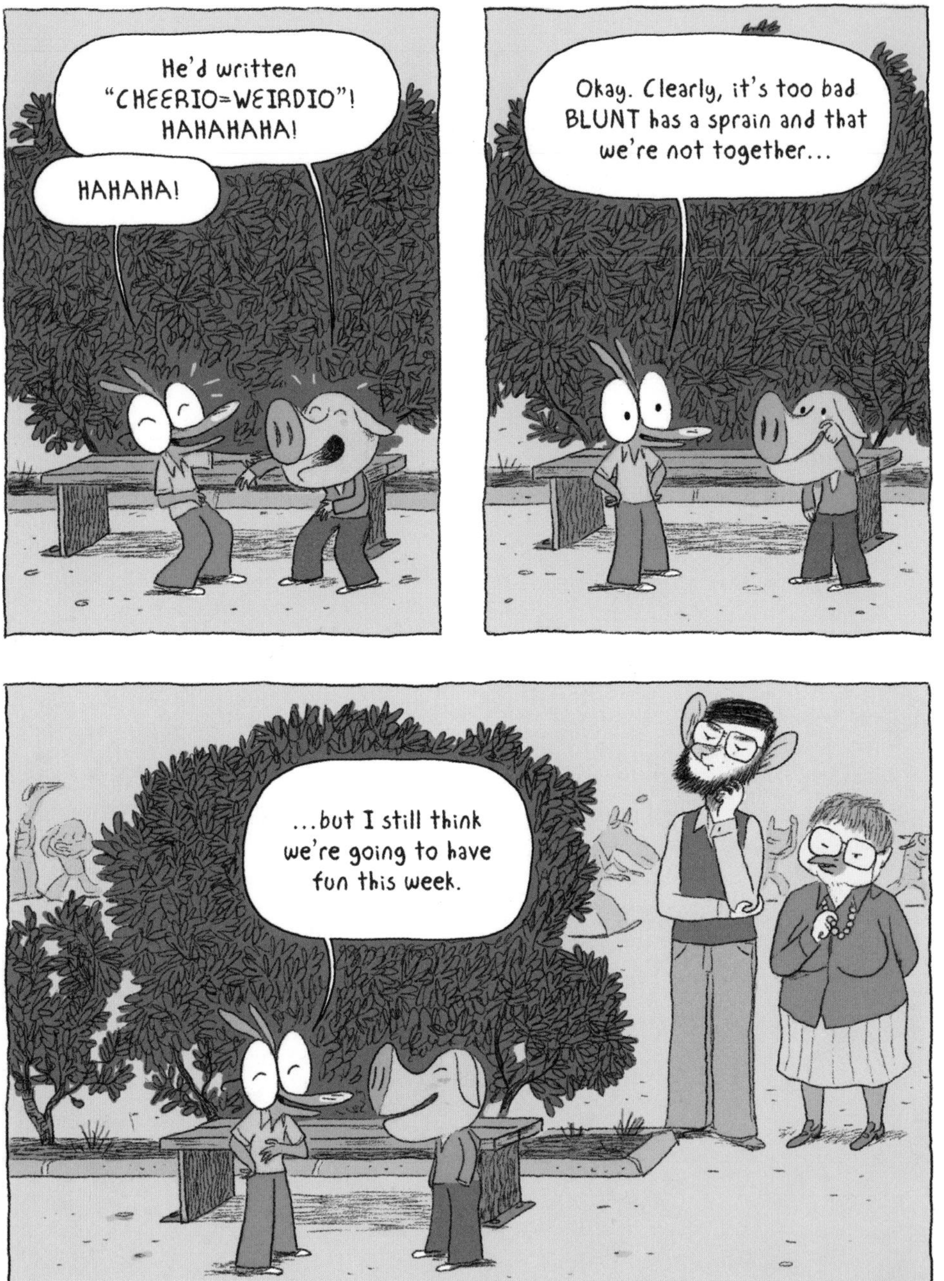
He'd written "CHEERIO=WEIRDIO"! HAHAHAHA!
HAHAHA!
Okay. Clearly, it's too bad BLUNT has a sprain and that we're not together...
...but I still think we're going to have fun this week.
END

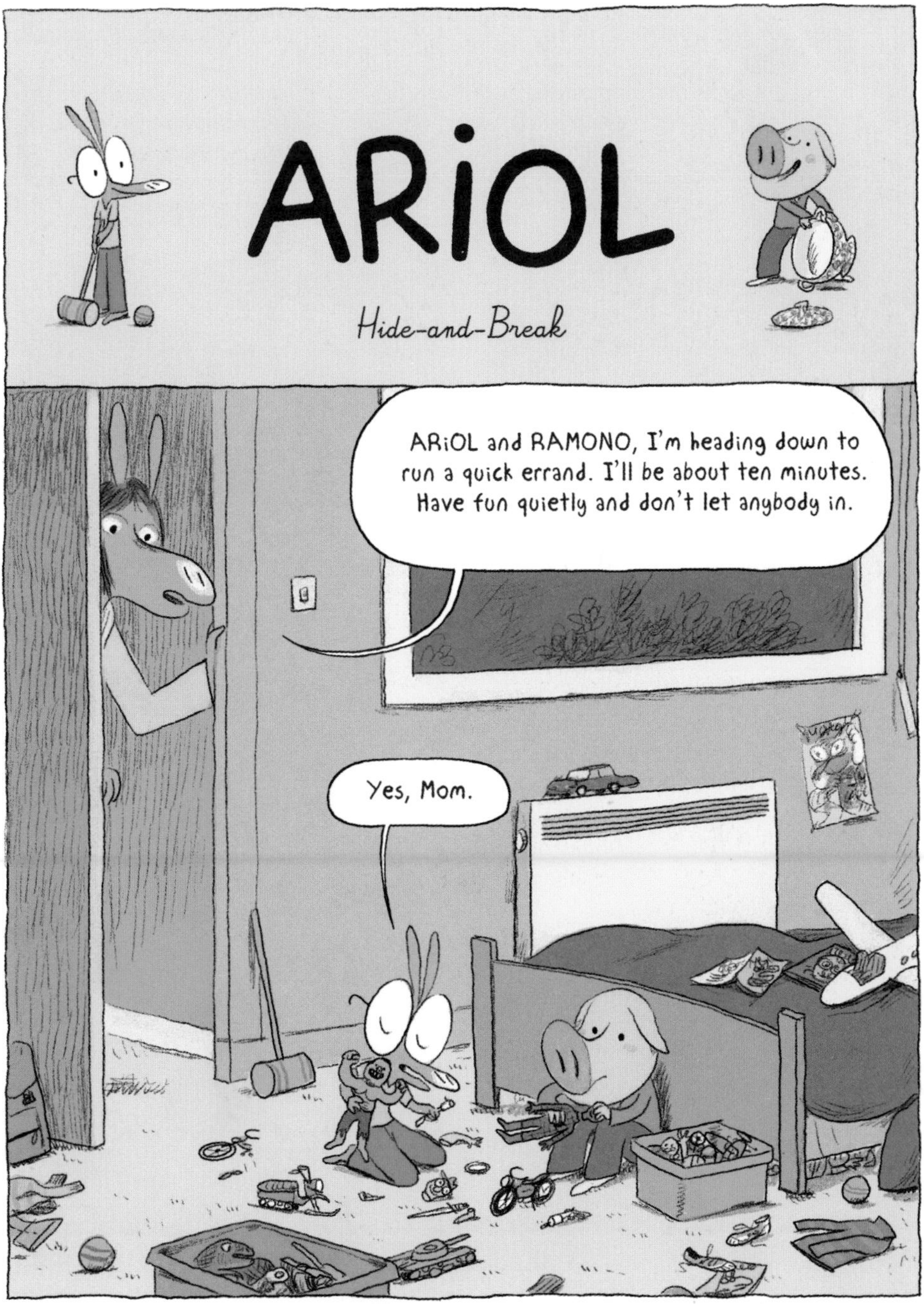
ARiOL
Hide-and-Break
ARiOL and RAMONO, I'm heading down to run a quick errand. I'll be about ten minutes. Have fun quietly and don't let anybody in.
Yes, Mom.

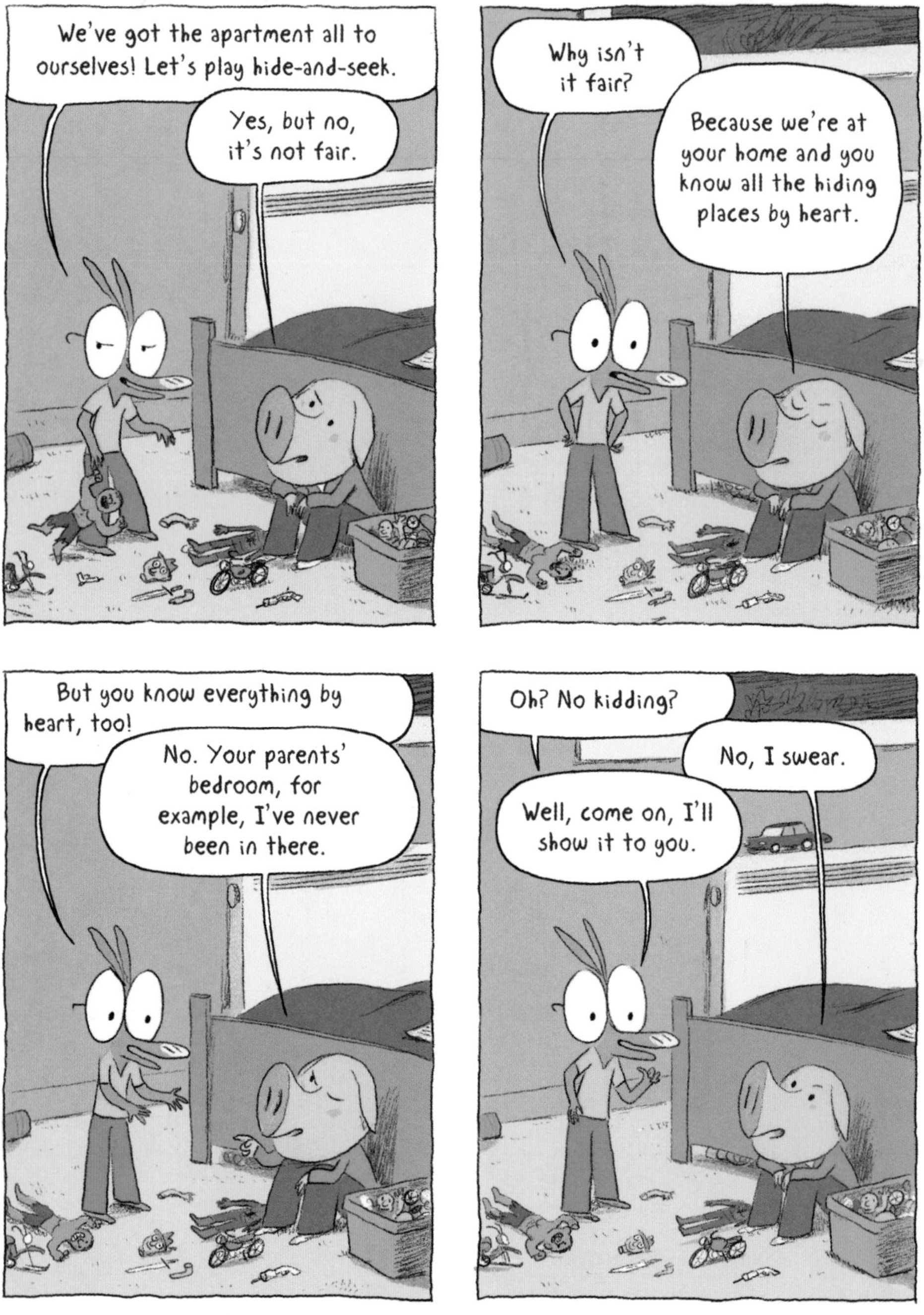
We've got the apartment all to ourselves! Let's play hide-and-seek.
Yes, but no, it's not fair.
Why isn't it fair?
Because we're at your home and you know all the hiding places by heart.
But you know everything by heart, too!
No. Your parents' bedroom, for example, I've never been in there.
Oh? No kidding?
No, I swear.
Well, come on, I'll show it to you.

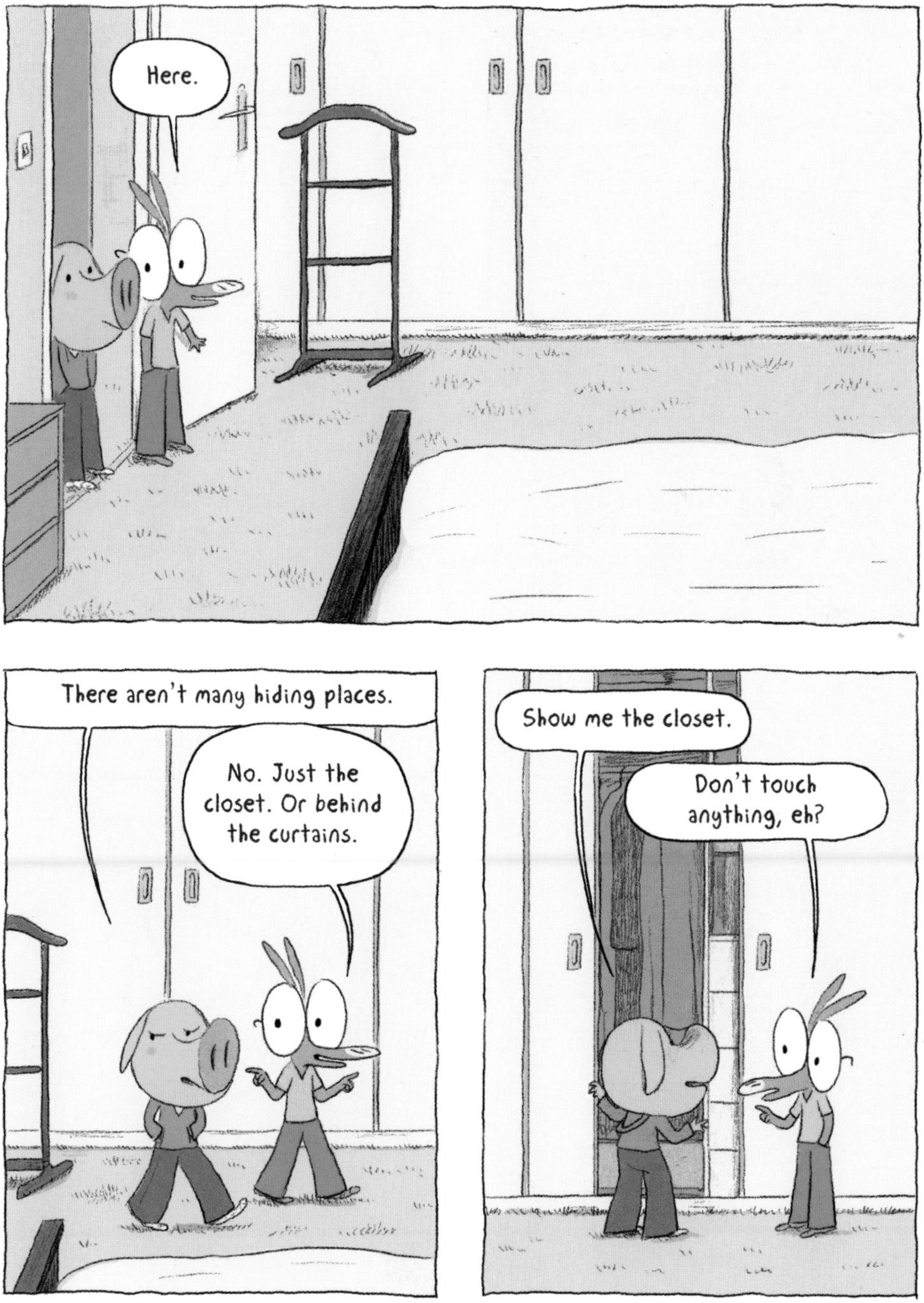
Here.
There aren't many hiding places.
No. Just the closet. Or behind the curtains.
Show me the closet.
Don't touch anything, eh?

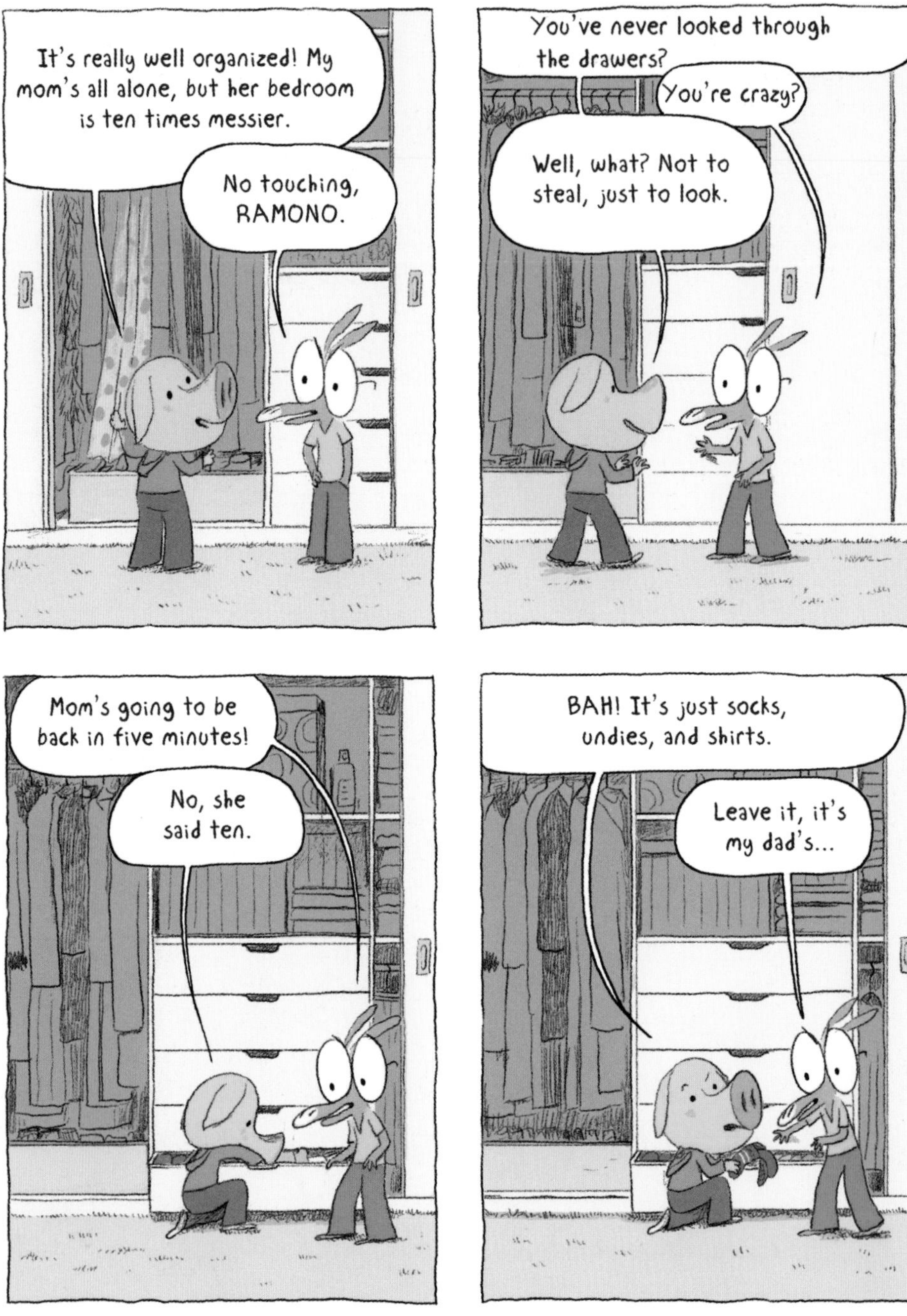

It's really well organized! My mom's all alone, but her bedroom is ten times messier.
No touching, RAMONO.
You've never looked through the drawers?
You're crazy?
Well, what? Not to steal, just to look.
Mom's going to be back in five minutes!
No, she said ten.
BAH! It's just socks, undies, and shirts.
Leave it, it's my dad's...

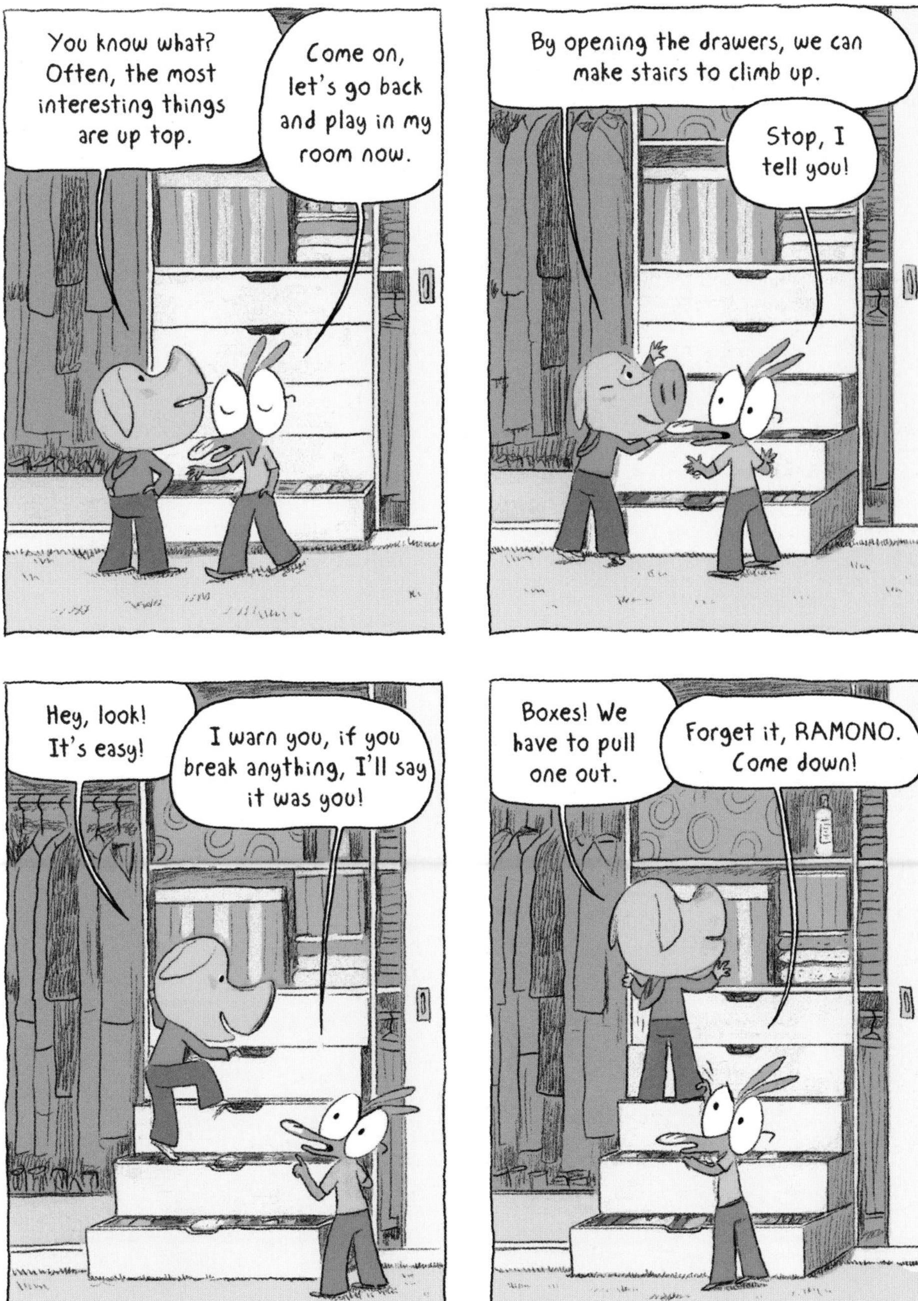
You know what? Often, the most interesting things are up top.
Come on, let's go back and play in my room now.
By opening the drawers, we can make stairs to climb up.
Stop, I tell you!
Hey, look! It's easy!
I warn you, if you break anything, I'll say it was you!
Boxes! We have to pull one out.
Forget it, RAMONO. Come down!

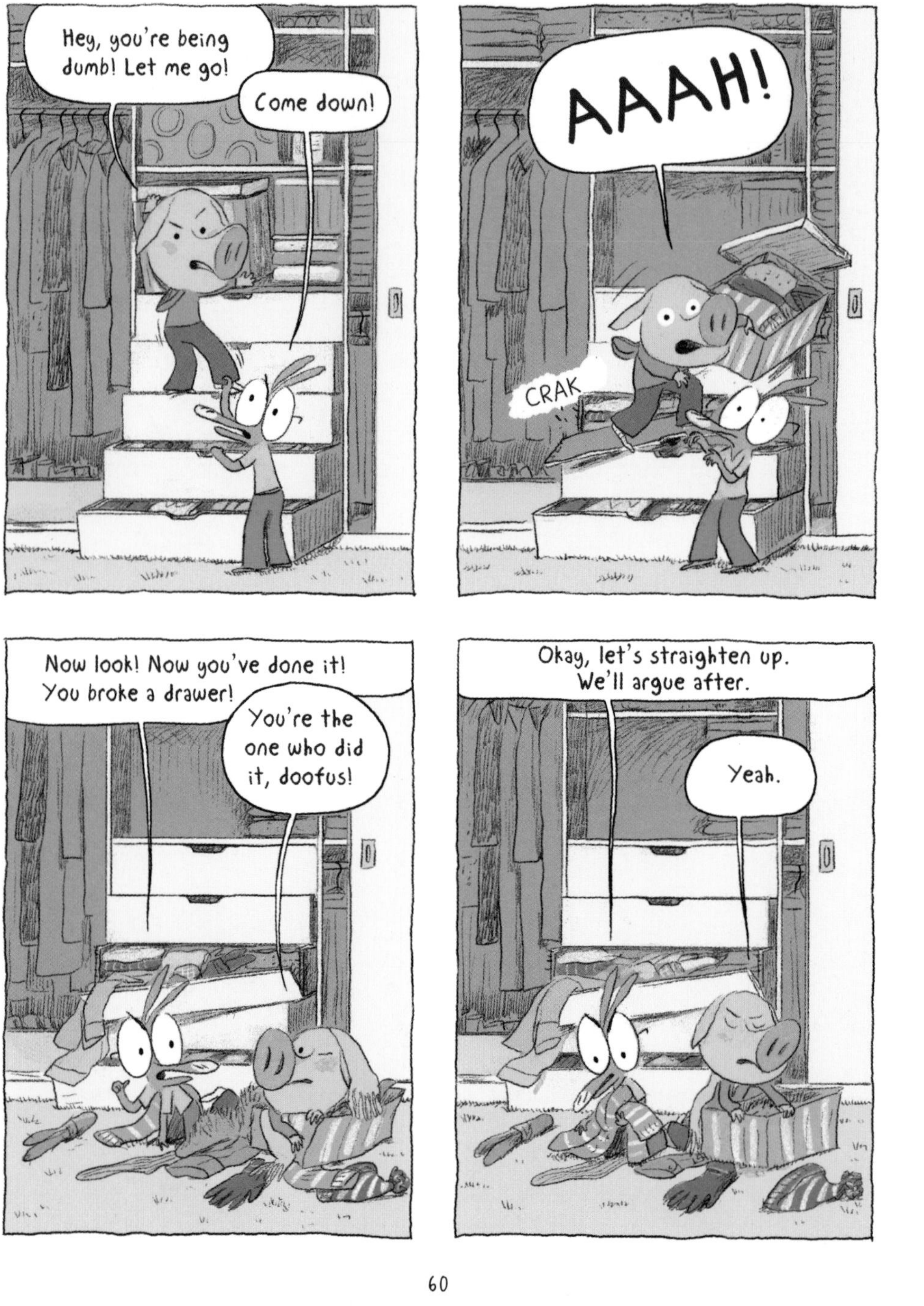
Hey, you're being dumb! Let me go!
Come down!
AAAH!
CRAK
Now look! Now you've done it! You broke a drawer!
You're the one who did it, doofus!
Okay, let's straighten up. We'll argue after.
Yeah.

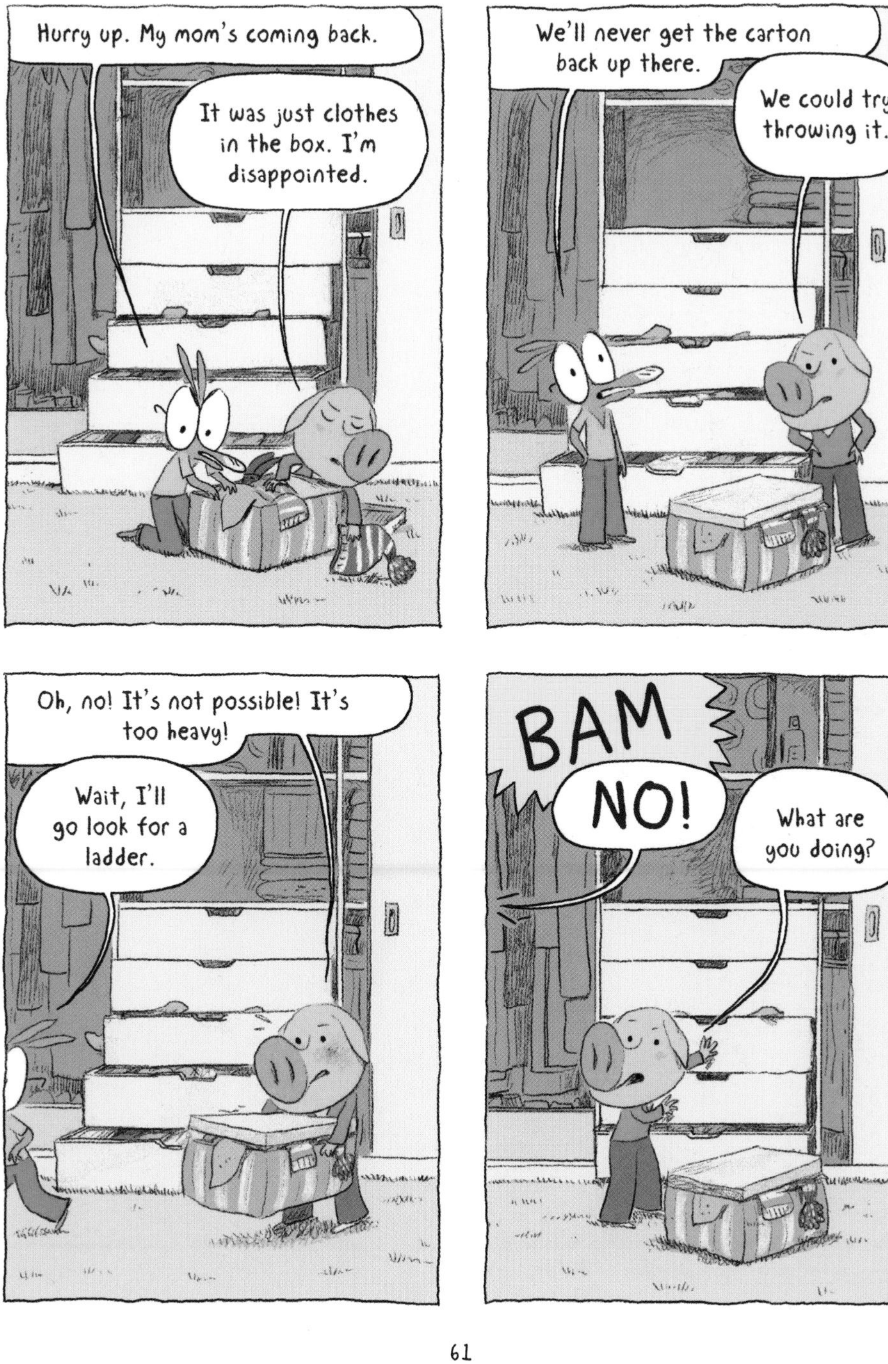
Hurry up. My mom's coming back.
It was just clothes in the box. I'm disappointed.
We'll never get the carton back up there.
We could try throwing it.
Oh, no! It's not possible! It's too heavy!
Wait, I'll go look for a ladder.
BAM
NO!
What are you doing?

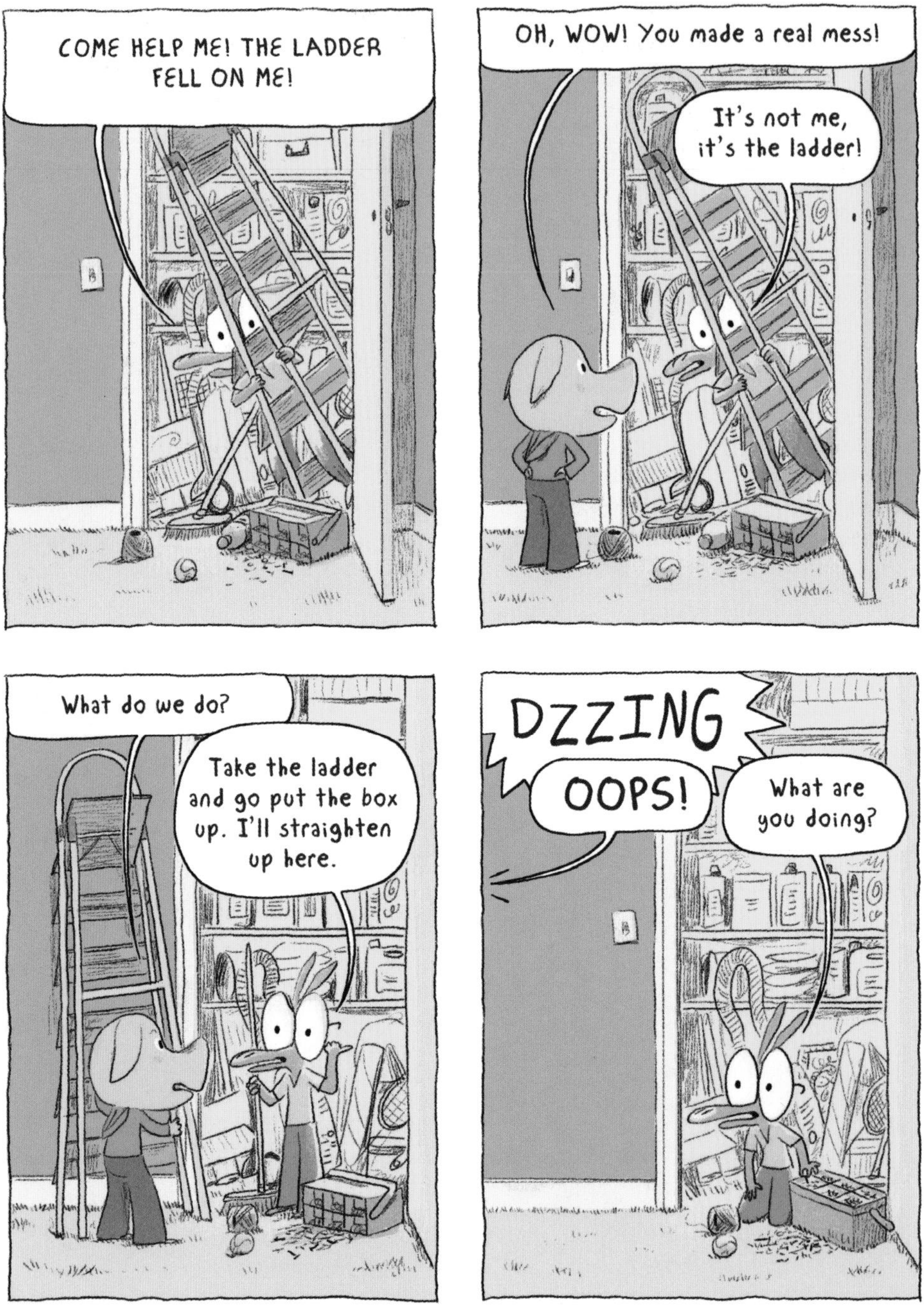
COME HELP ME! THE LADDER FELL ON ME!
OH, WOW! You made a real mess!
It's not me, it's the ladder!
What do we do?
Take the ladder and go put the box up. I'll straighten up here.
DZZING
OOPS!
What are you doing?

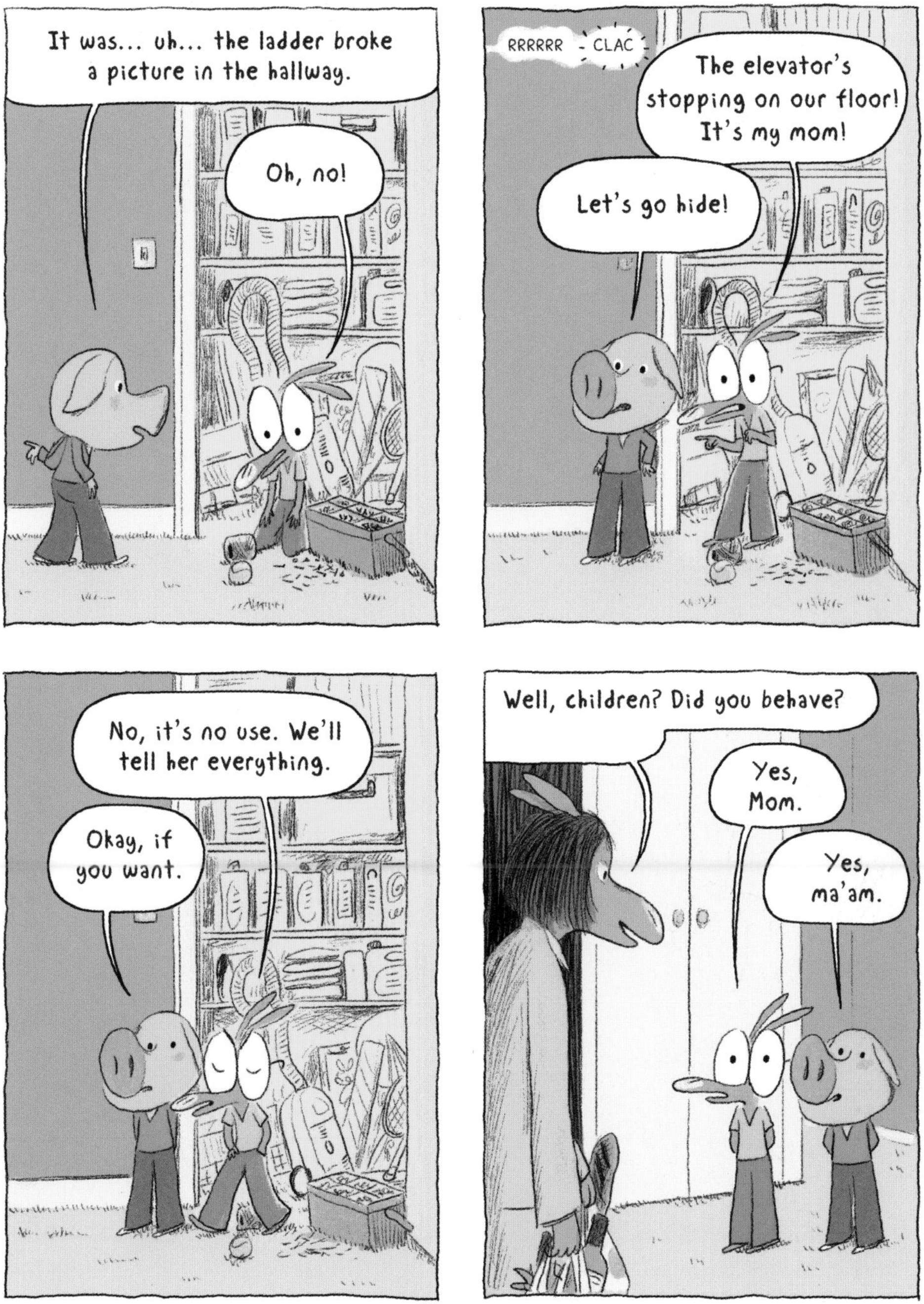
It was... uh... the ladder broke a picture in the hallway.
Oh, no!
RRRRRR
CLAC
The elevator's stopping on our floor! It's my mom!
Let's go hide!
No, it's no use. We'll tell her everything.
Okay, if you want.
Well, children? Did you behave?
Yes, Mom.
Yes, ma'am.

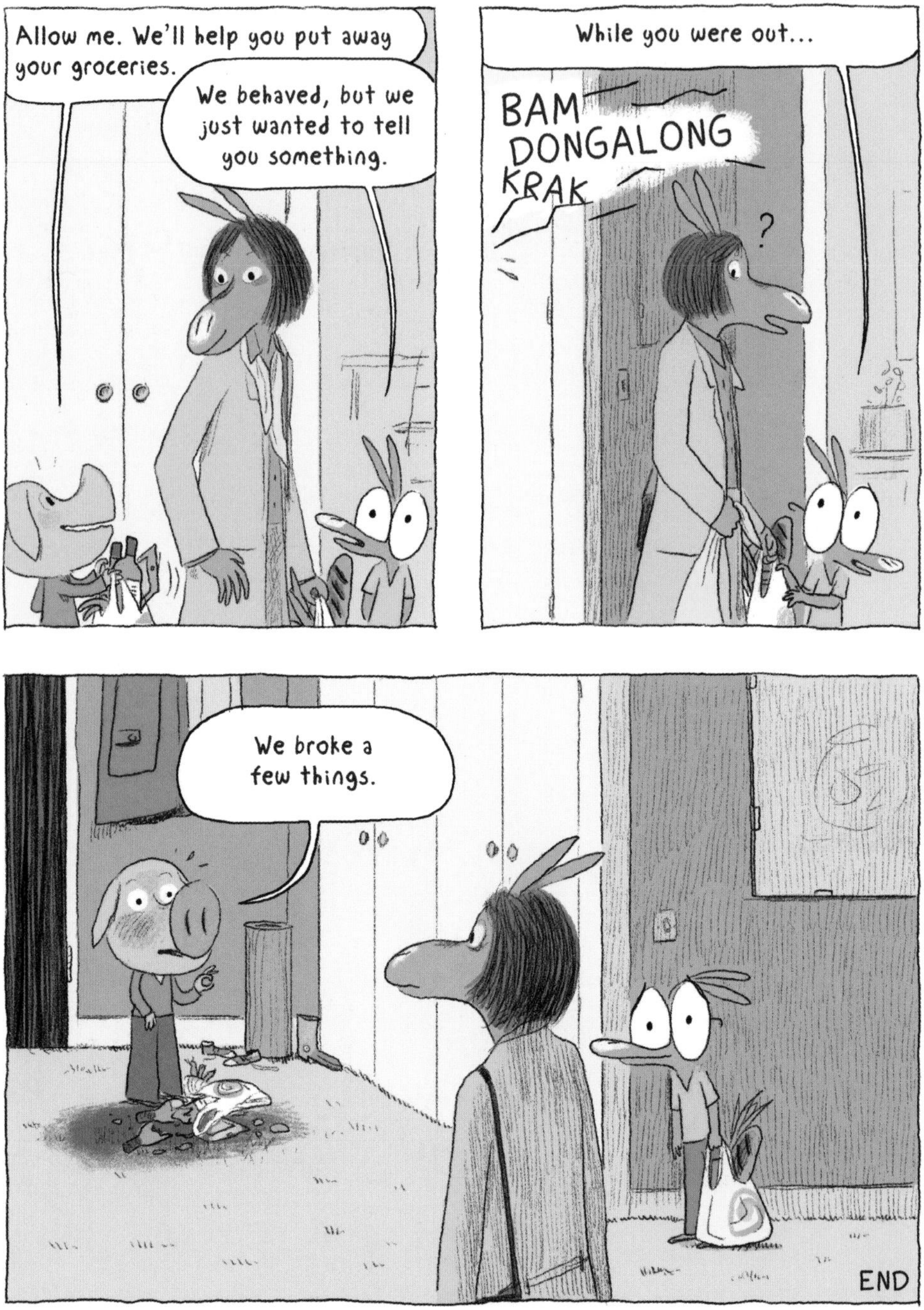
Allow me. We'll help you put away your groceries.
We behaved, but we just wanted to tell you something.
While you were out...
BAM
DONGALONG
KRAK
?
We broke a few things.
END

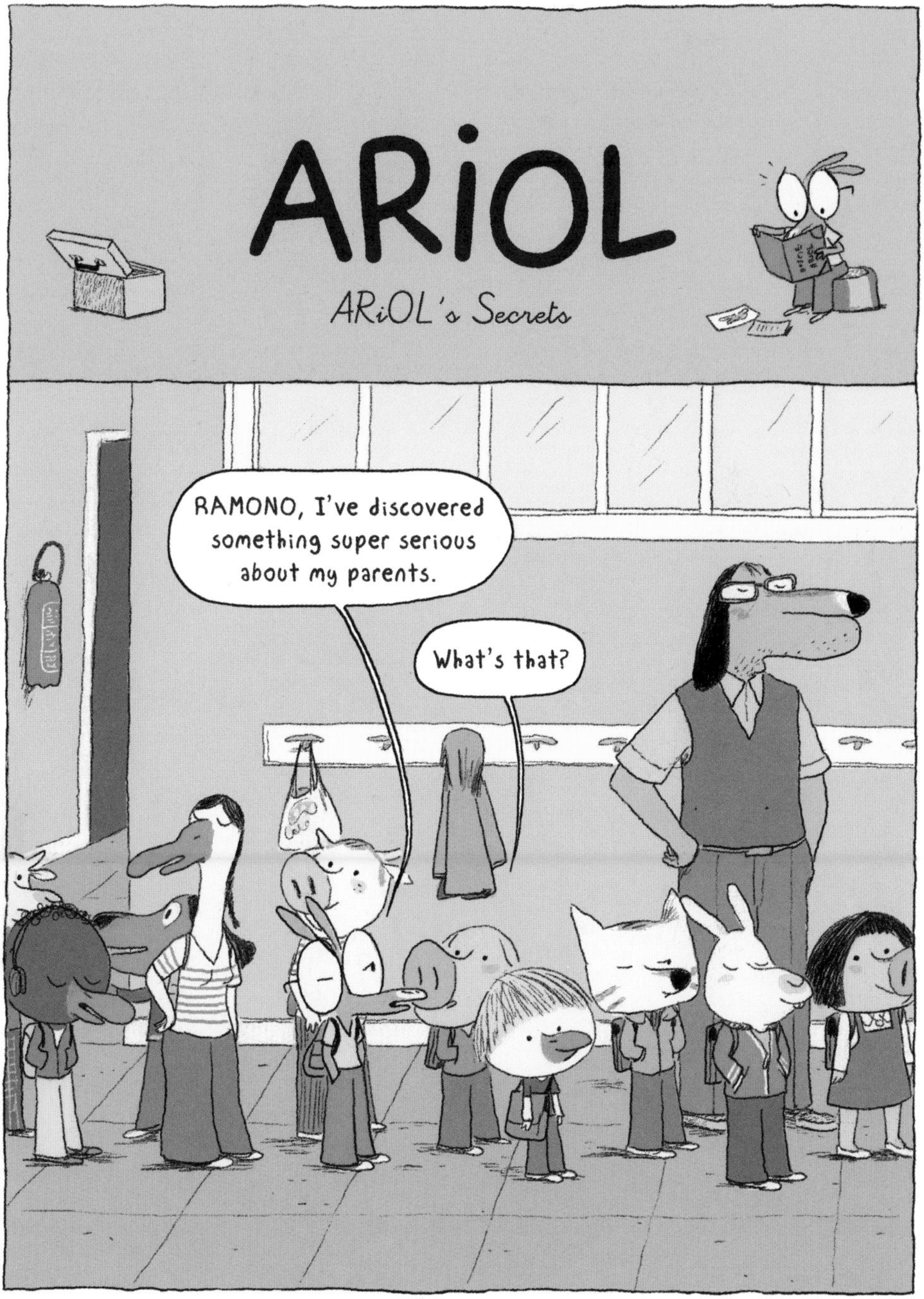
ARiOL
ARiOL's Secrets
RAMONO, I've discovered something super serious about my parents.
What's that?

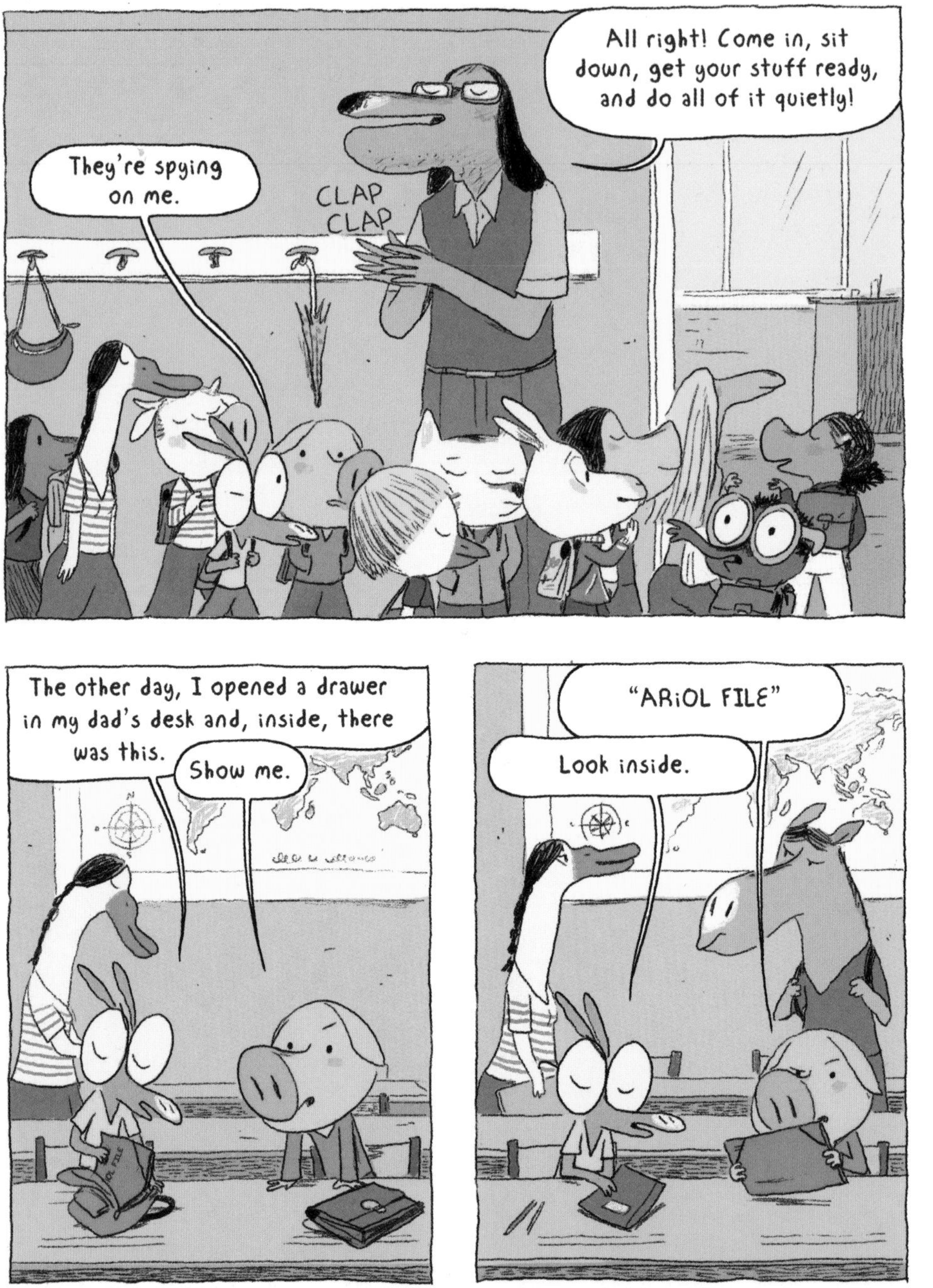

They're spying on me.
CLAP
CLAP
All right! Come in, sit down, get your stuff ready, and do all of it quietly!
The other day, I opened a drawer in my dad's desk and, inside, there was this.
Show me.
"ARiOL FILE"
Look inside.

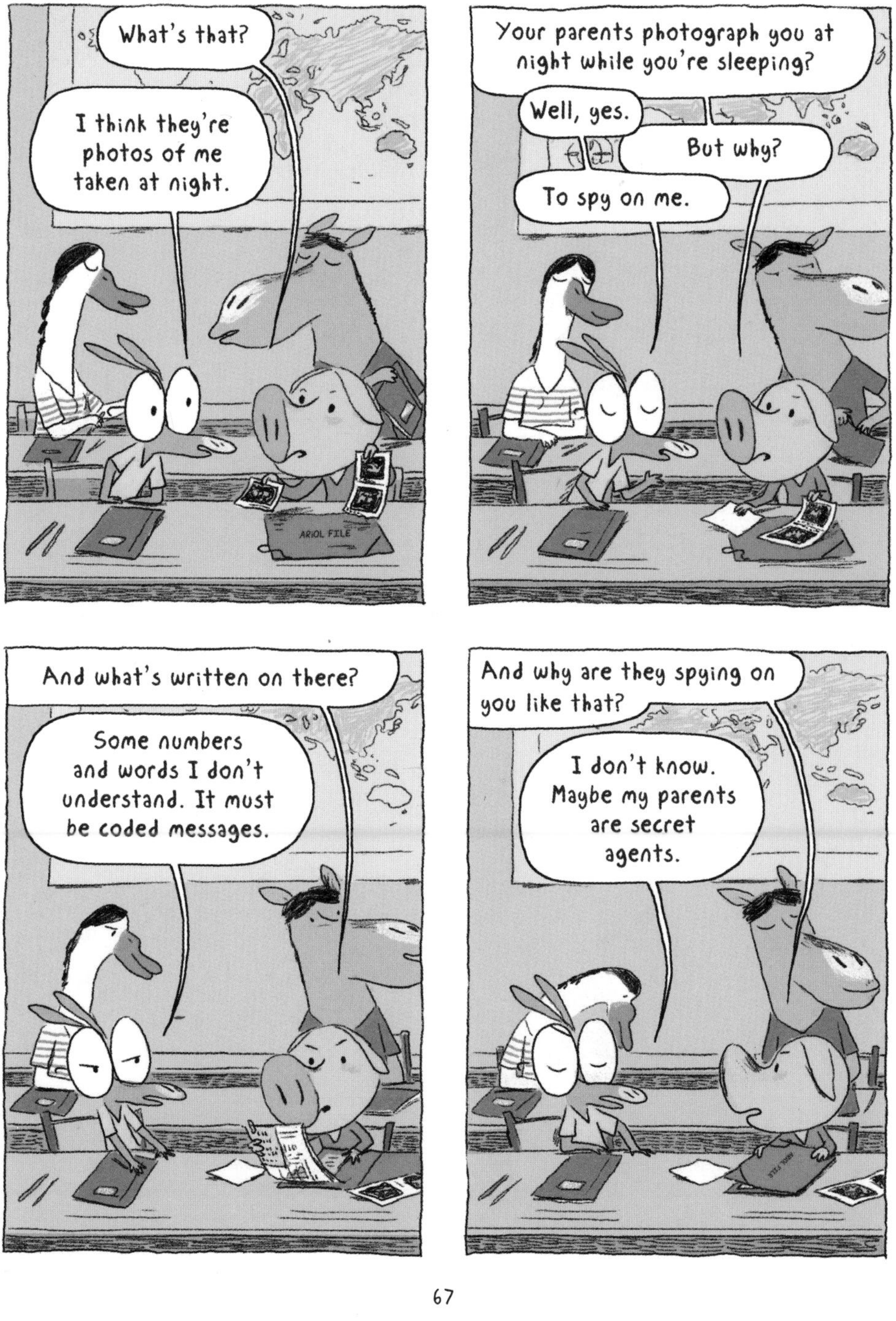
What's that?
I think they're photos of me taken at night.
ARIOL FILE
Your parents photograph you at night while you're sleeping?
Well, yes.
But why?
To spy on me.
And what's written on there?
Some numbers and words I don't understand. It must be coded messages.
And why are they spying on you like that?
I don't know. Maybe my parents are secret agents.

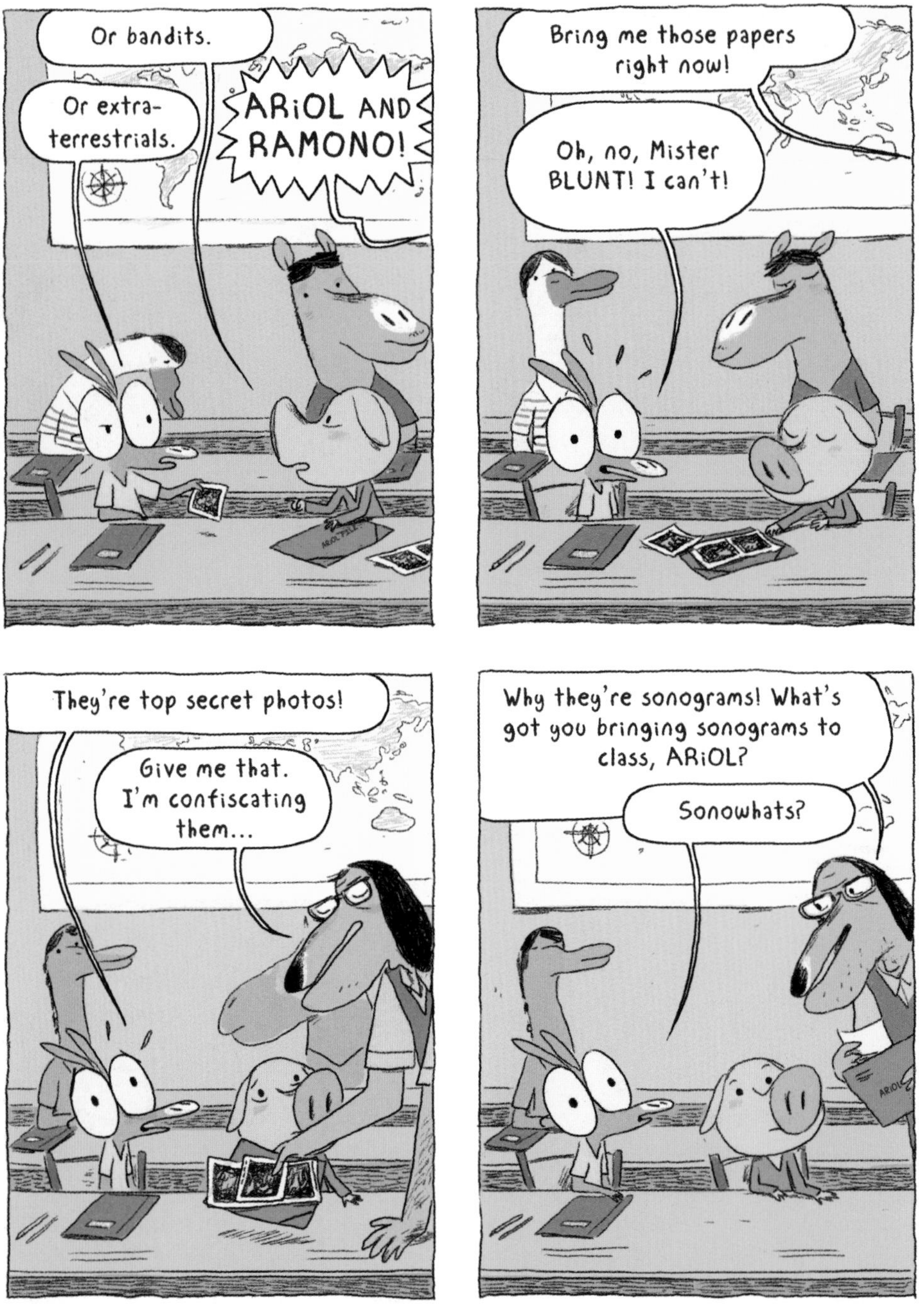
Or bandits.
Or extra-terrestrials.
ARiOL AND RAMONO!
Bring me those papers right now!
Oh, no, Mister BLUNT! I can't!
They're top secret photos!
Give me that. I'm confiscating them...
Why they're sonograms! What's got you bringing sonograms to class, ARiOL?
Sonowhats?
ARiOL

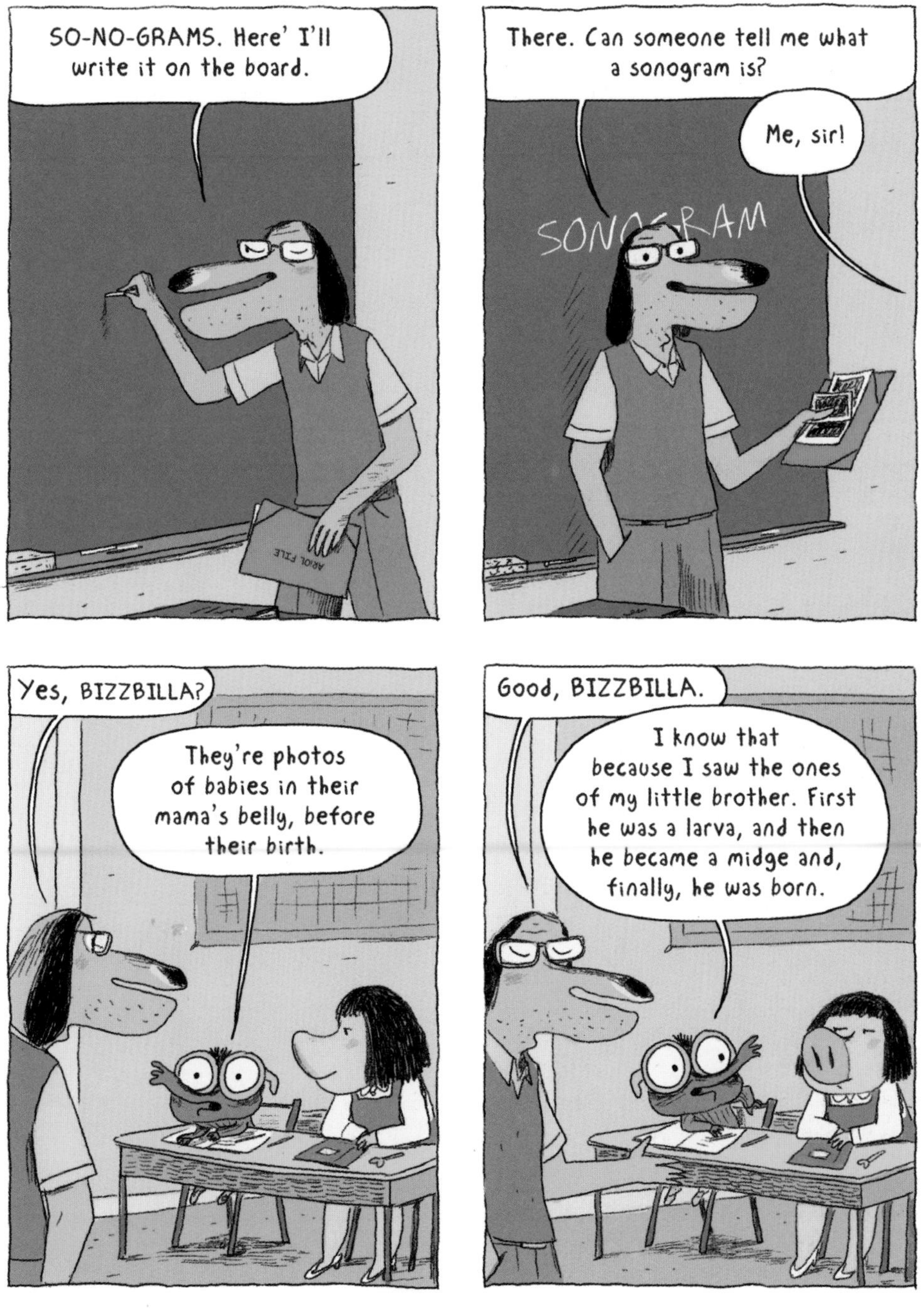
SO-NO-GRAMS. Here' I'll write it on the board.
ARIOL FILE
There. Can someone tell me what a sonogram is?
SONOGRAM
Me, sir!
Yes, BIZZBILLA?
They're photos of babies in their mama's belly, before their birth.
Good, BIZZBILLA.
I know that because I saw the ones of my little brother. First he was a larva, and then he became a midge and, finally, he was born.

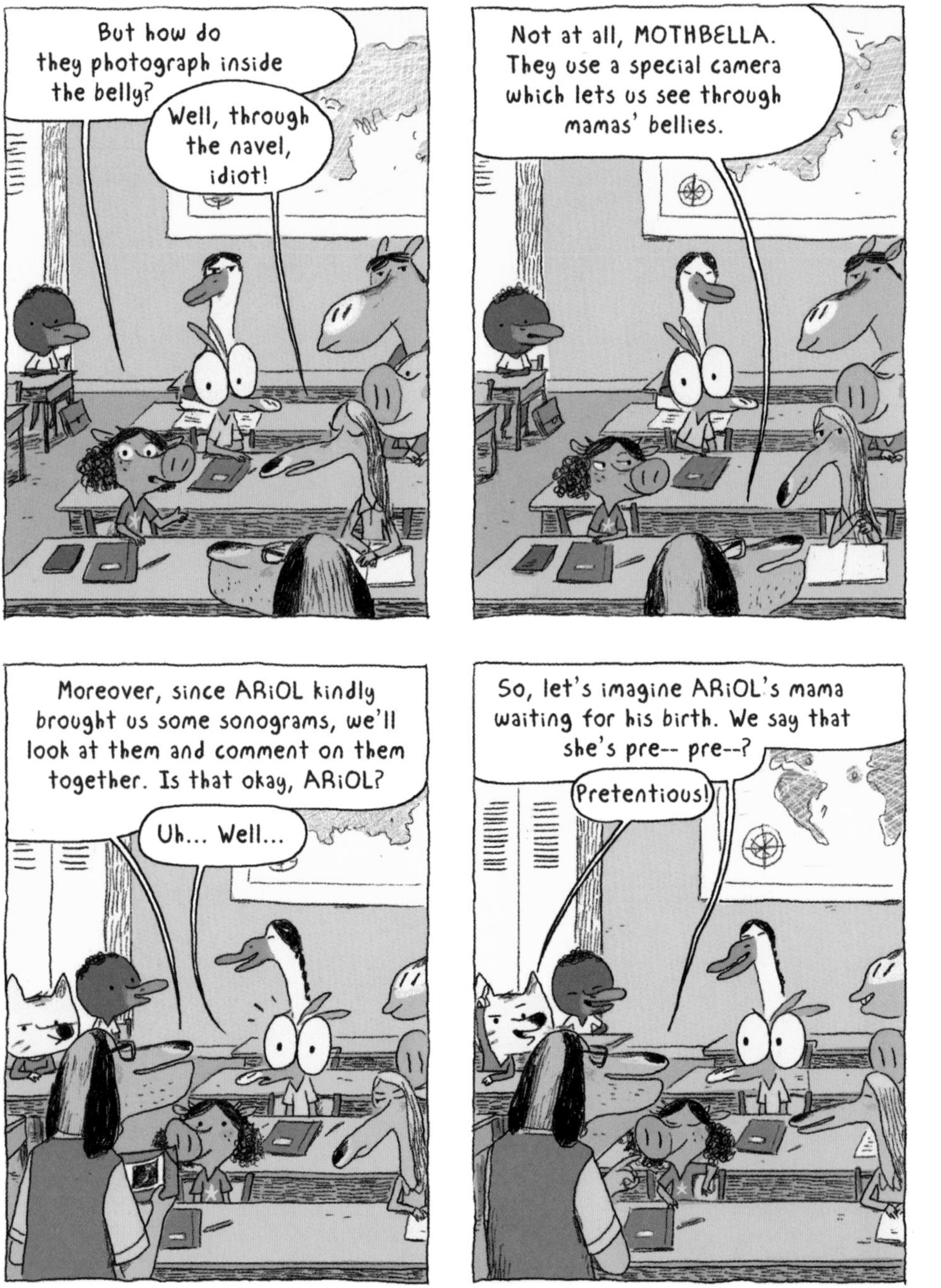
But how do they photograph inside the belly?
Well, through the navel, idiot!
Not at all, MOTHBELLA. They use a special camera which lets us see through mamas' bellies.
Moreover, since ARiOL kindly brought us some sonograms, we'll look at them and comment on them together. Is that okay, ARiOL?
Uh... Well...
So, let's imagine ARiOL's mama waiting for his birth. We say that she's pre-- pre--?
Pretentious!

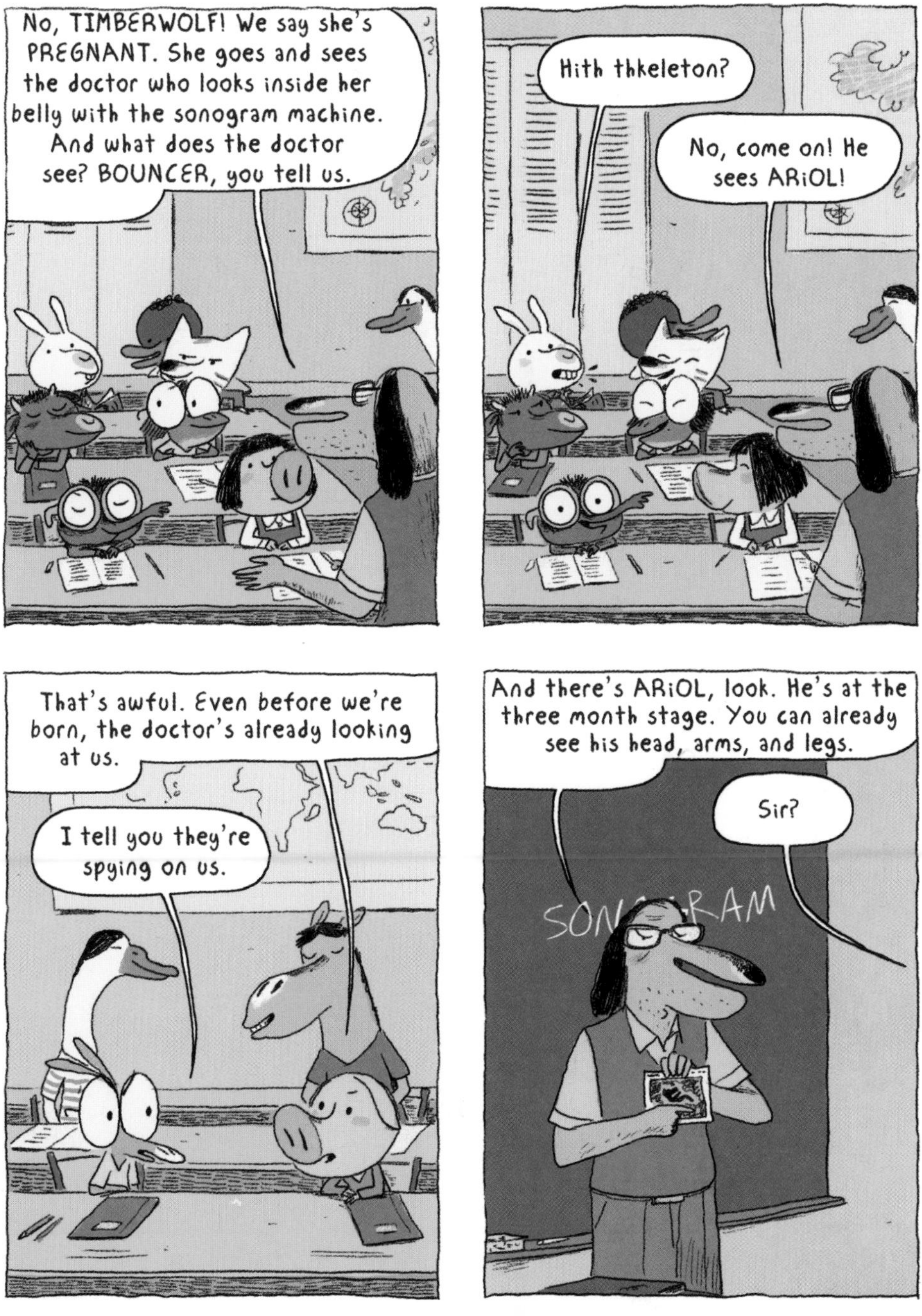
No, TIMBERWOLF! We say she's PREGNANT. She goes and sees the doctor who looks inside her belly with the sonogram machine. And what does the doctor see? BOUNCER, you tell us.
Hith thkeleton?
No, come on! He sees ARiOL!
That's awful. Even before we're born, the doctor's already looking at us.
I tell you they're spying on us.
And there's ARiOL, look. He's at the three month stage. You can already see his head, arms, and legs.
Sir?

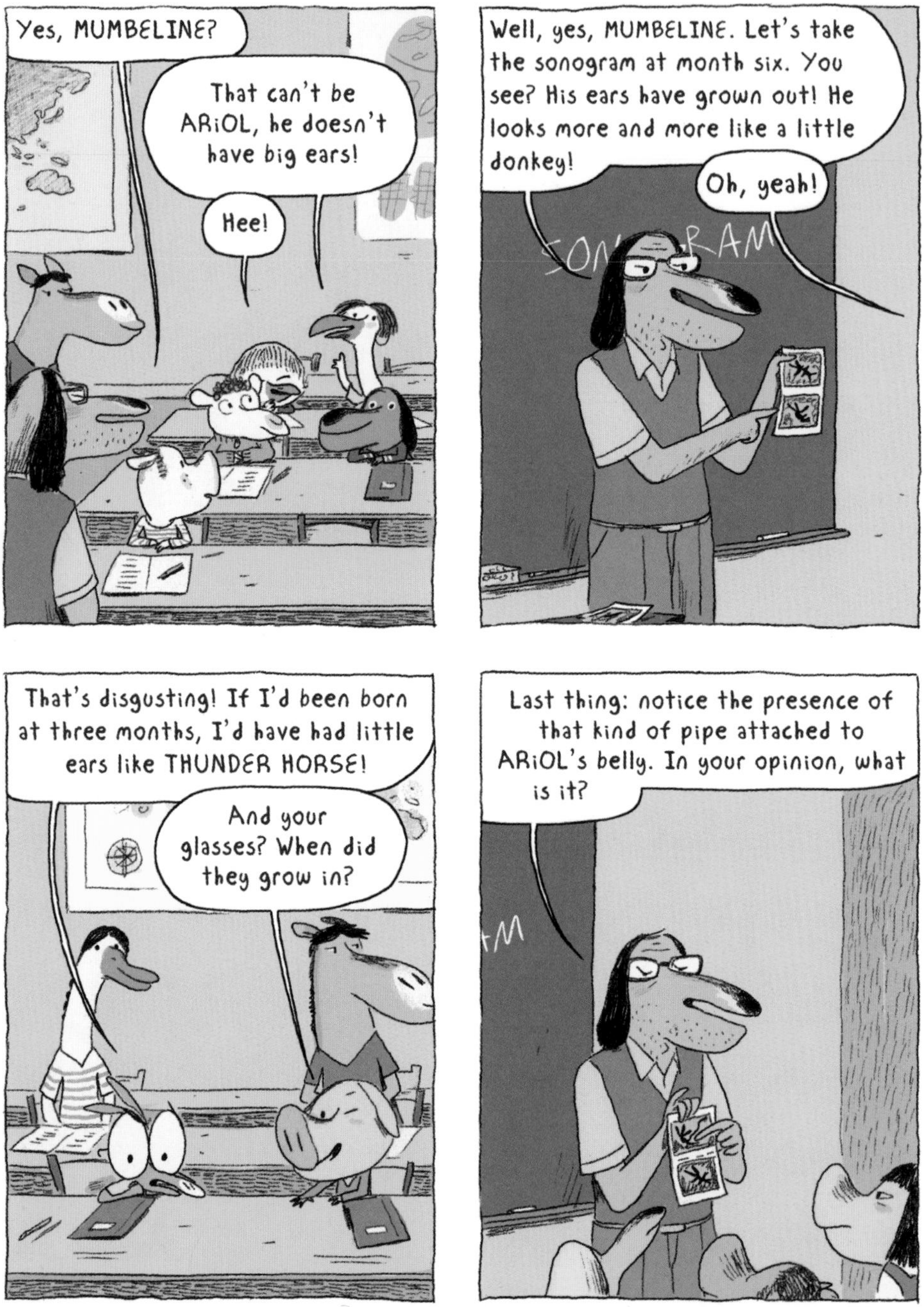
Yes, MUMBELINE?
That can't be ARiOL, he doesn't have big ears!
Hee!
Well, yes, MUMBELINE. Let's take the sonogram at month six. You see? His ears have grown out! He looks more and more like a little donkey!
Oh, yeah!
That's disgusting! If I'd been born at three months, I'd have had little ears like THUNDER HORSE!
And your glasses? When did they grow in?
Last thing: notice the presence of that kind of pipe attached to ARiOL's belly. In your opinion, what is it?

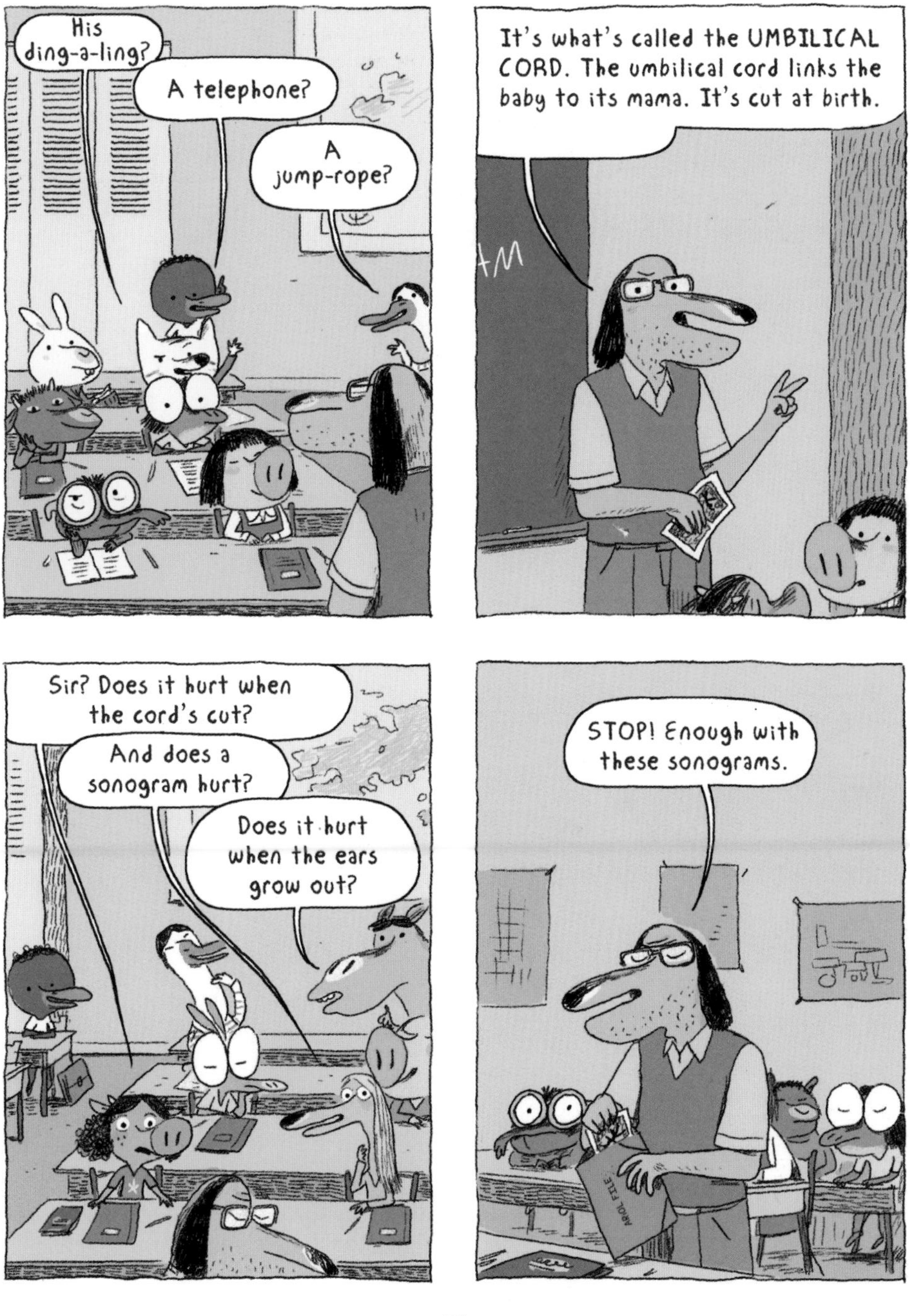
His ding-a-ling?
A telephone?
A jump-rope?
It's what's called the UMBILICAL CORD. The umbilical cord links the baby to its mama. It's cut at birth.
Sir? Does it hurt when the cord's cut?
And does a sonogram hurt?
Does it hurt when the ears grow out?
STOP! Enough with these sonograms.
ARDI FILE

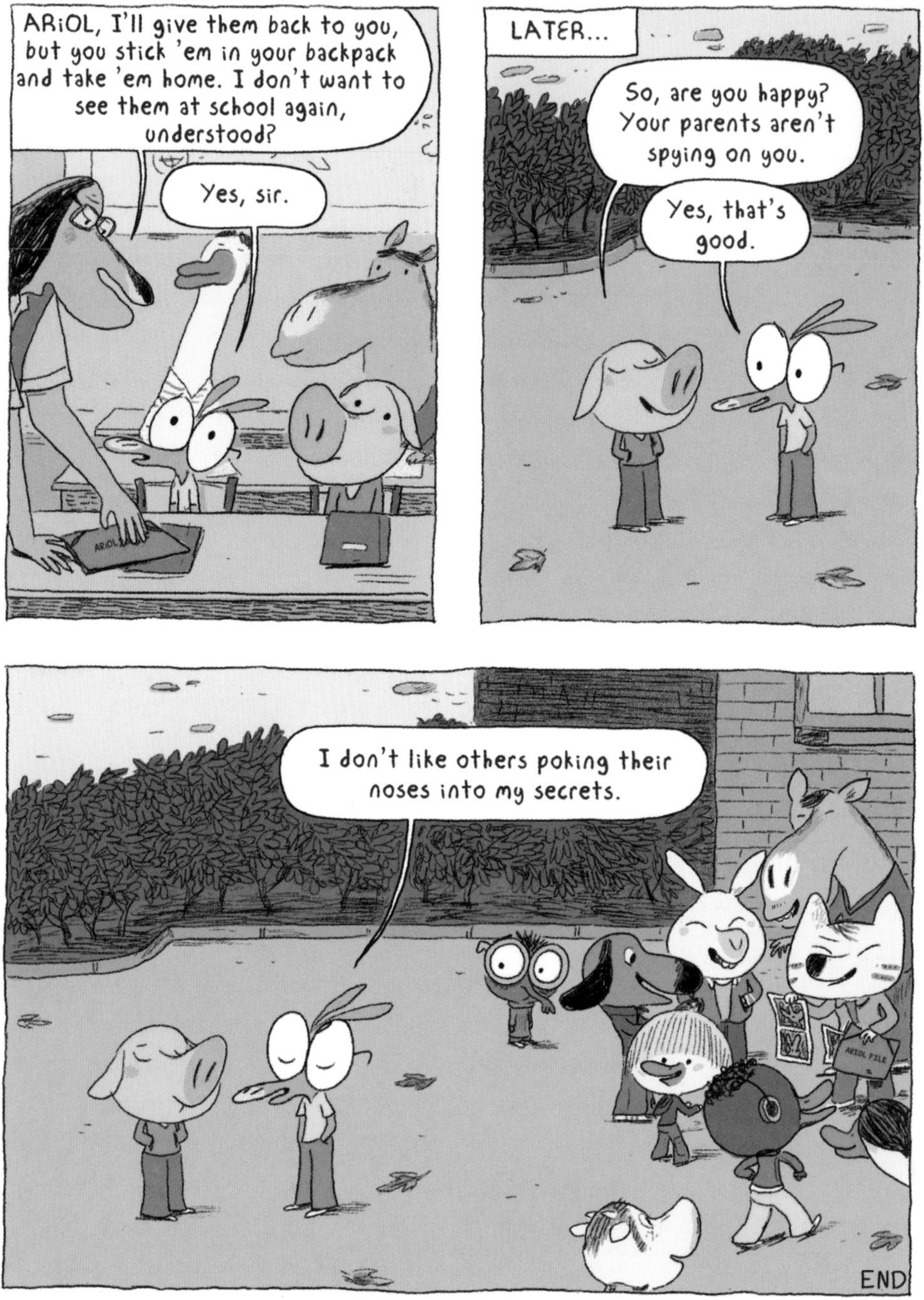
ARiOL, I'll give them back to you, but you stick 'em in your backpack and take 'em home. I don't want to see them at school again, understood?
Yes, sir.
ARiOL
LATER...
So, are you happy? Your parents aren't spying on you.
Yes, that's good.
I don't like others poking their noses into my secrets.
ARiOL FILE
END

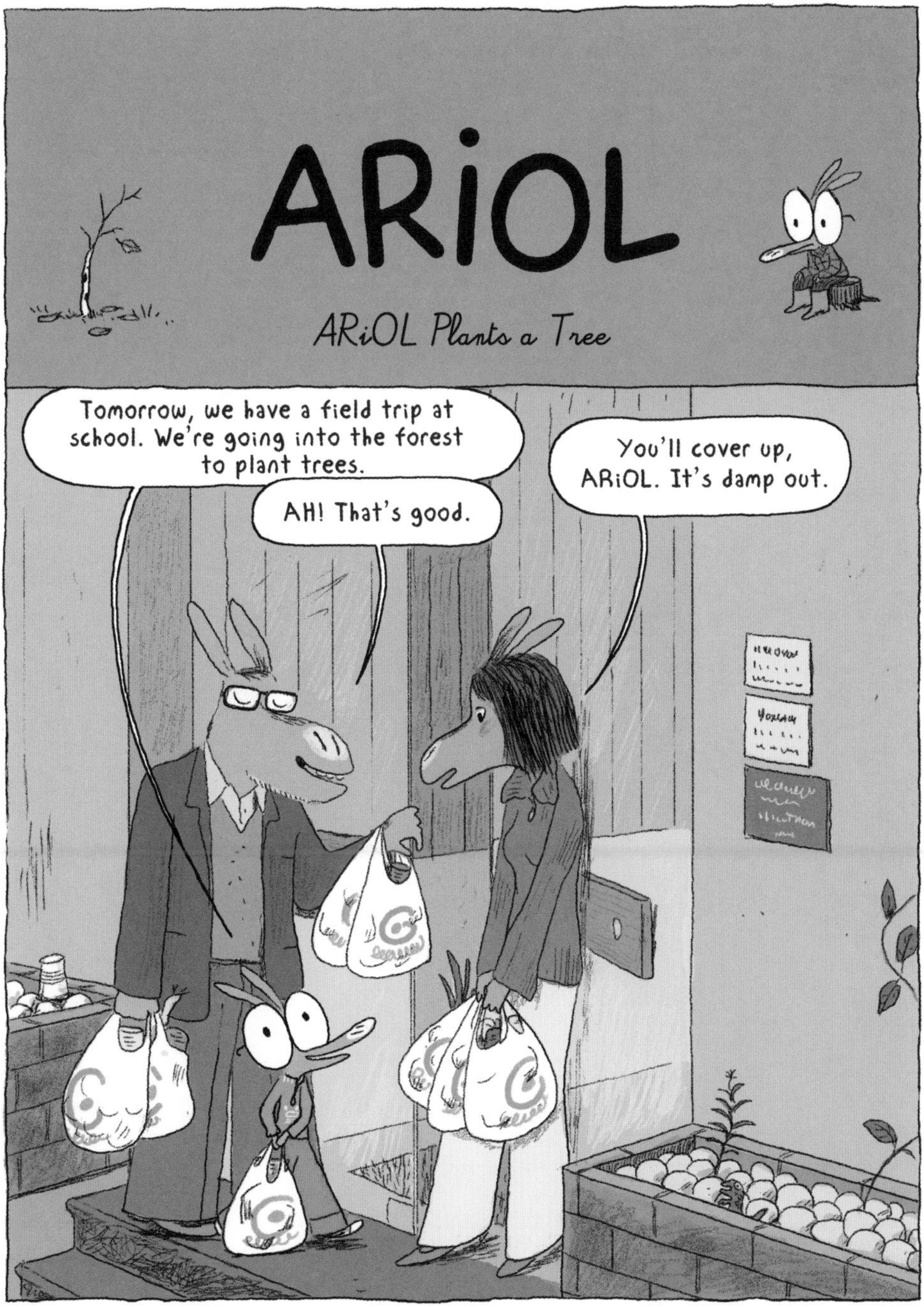
ARiOL
ARiOL Plants a Tree
Tomorrow, we have a field trip at school. We're going into the forest to plant trees.
AH! That's good.
You'll cover up, ARiOL. It's damp out.

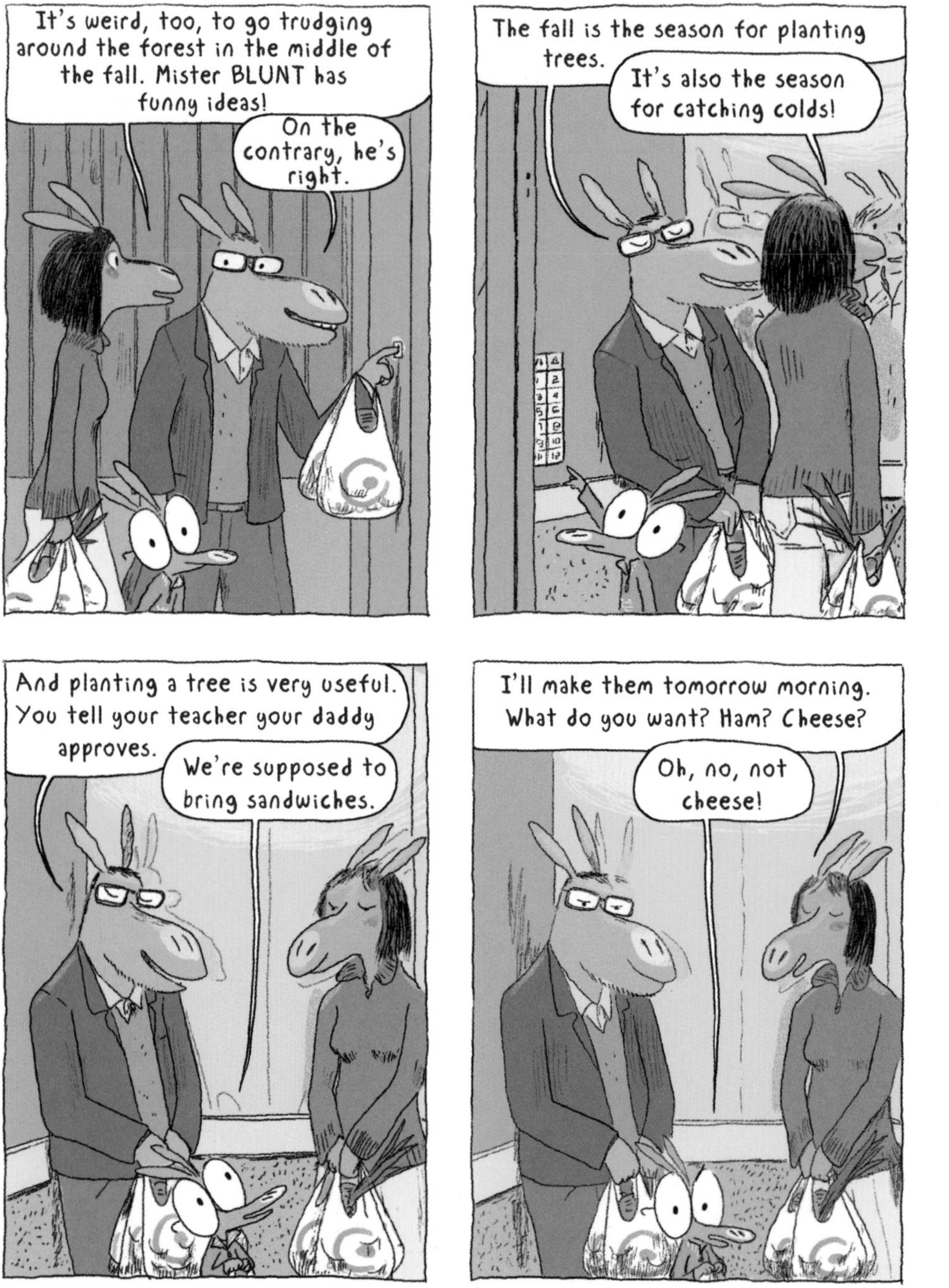
It's weird, too, to go trudging around the forest in the middle of the fall. Mister BLUNT has funny ideas!
On the contrary, he's right.
The fall is the season for planting trees.
It's also the season for catching colds!
And planting a tree is very useful. You tell your teacher your daddy approves.
We're supposed to bring sandwiches.
I'll make them tomorrow morning. What do you want? Ham? Cheese?
Oh, no, not cheese!

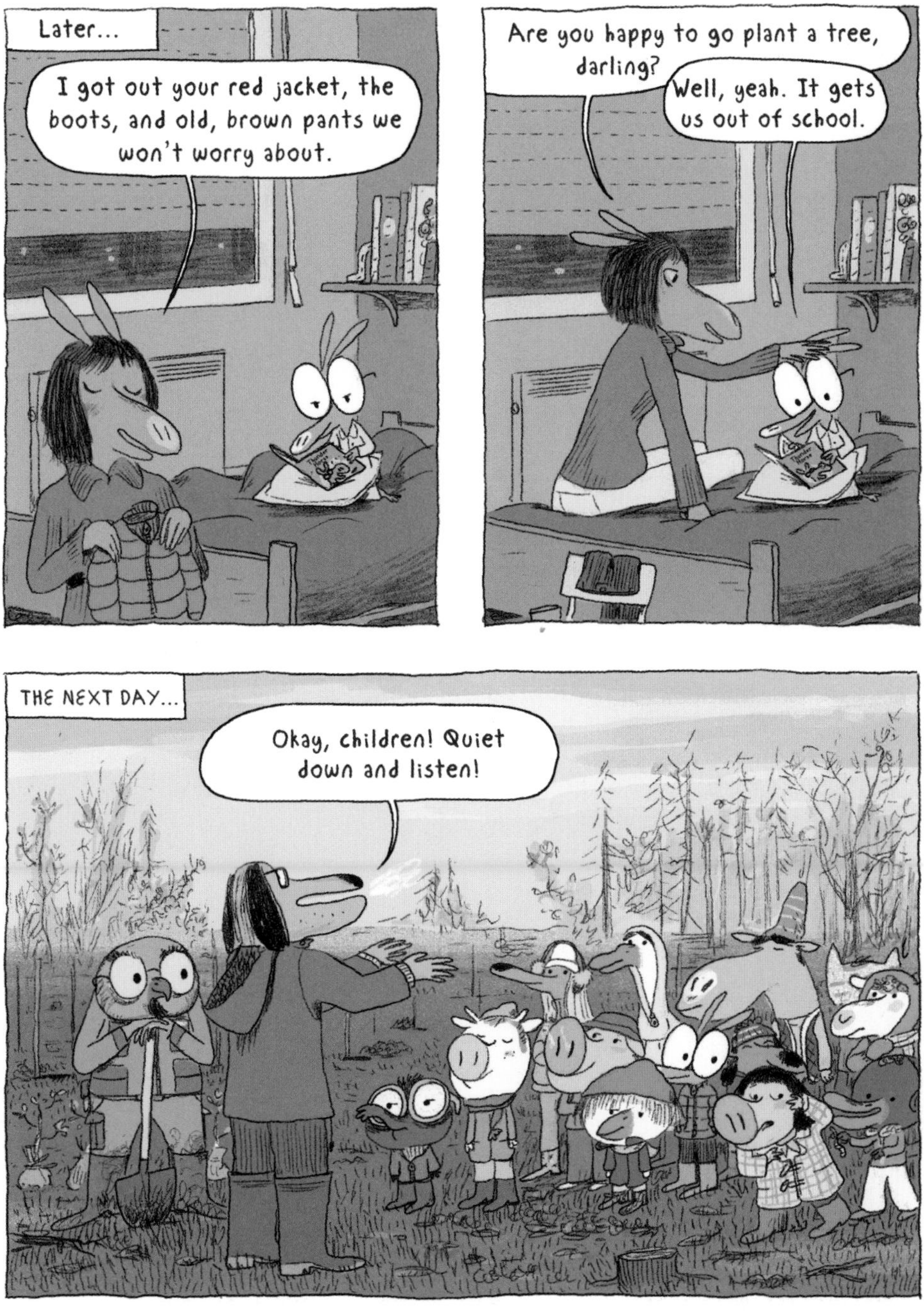

Later...
I got out your red jacket, the boots, and old, brown pants we won't worry about.
Are you happy to go plant a tree, darling?
Well, yeah. It gets us out of school.
THE NEXT DAY...
Okay, children! Quiet down and listen!

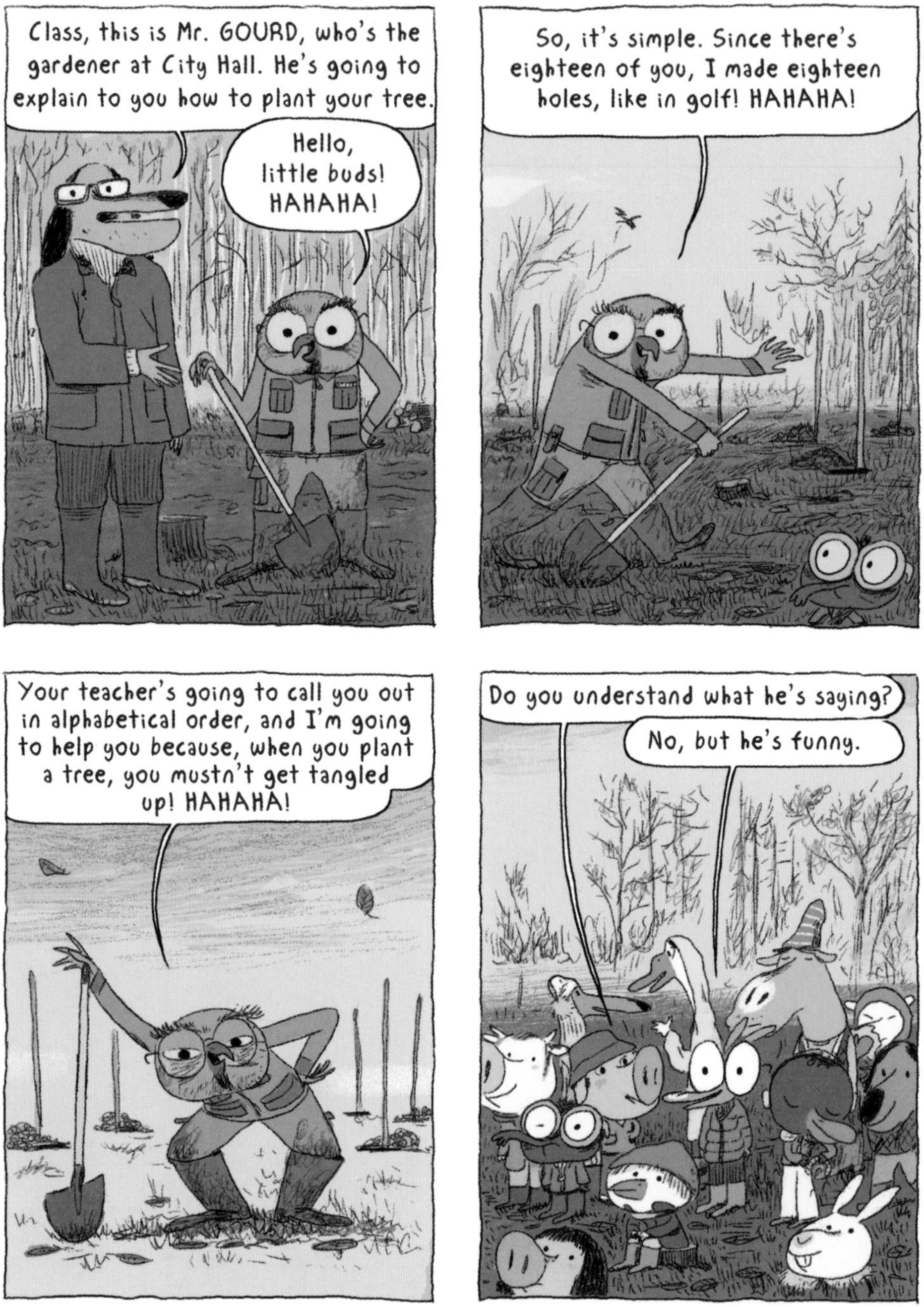
Class, this is Mr. GOURD, who's the gardener at City Hall. He's going to explain to you how to plant your tree.
Hello, little buds! HAHAHA!
So, it's simple. Since there's eighteen of you, I made eighteen holes, like in golf! HAHAHA!
Your teacher's going to call you out in alphabetical order, and I'm going to help you because, when you plant a tree, you mustn't get tangled up! HAHAHA!
Do you understand what he's saying?
No, but he's funny.

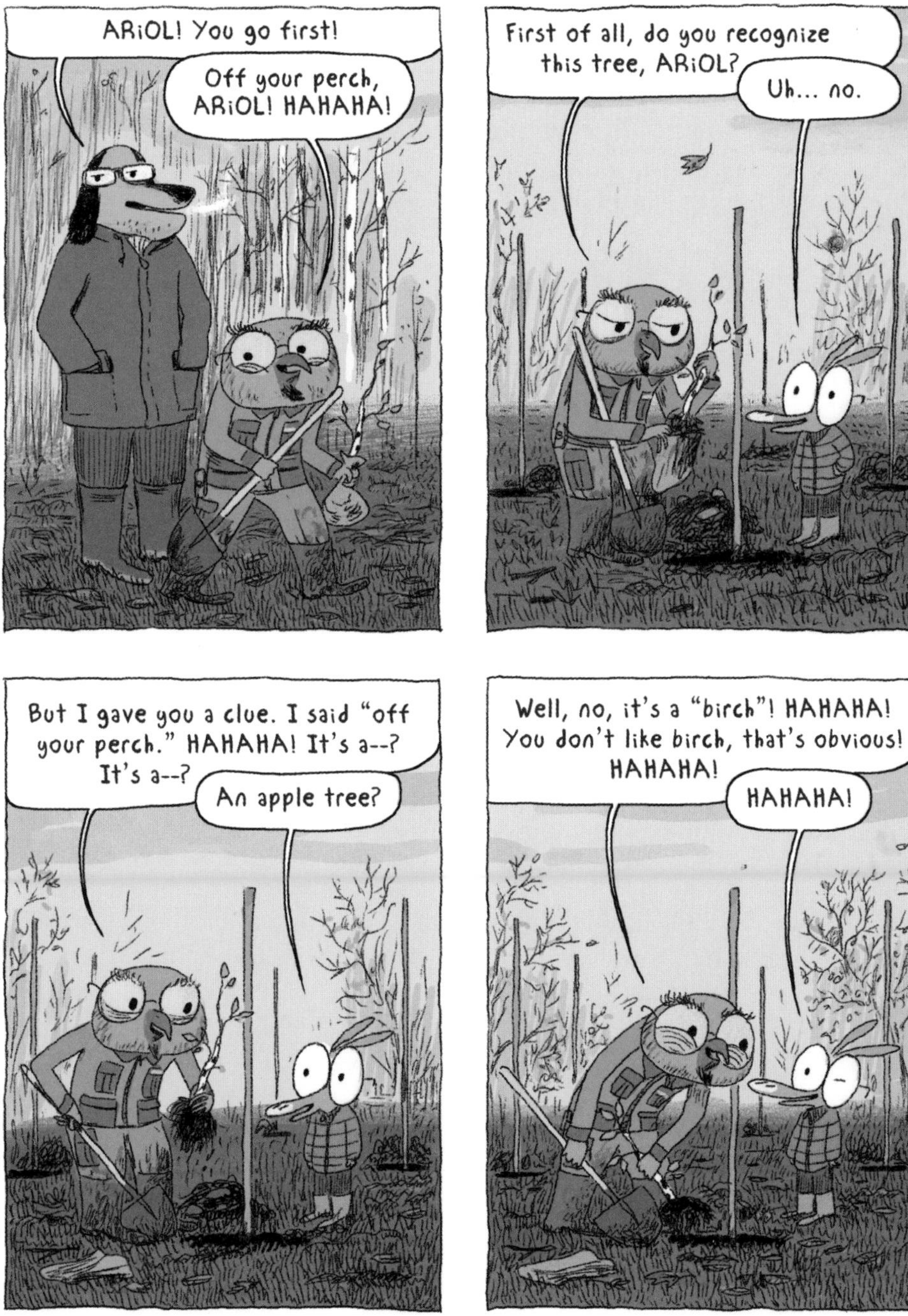
ARiOL! You go first!
Off your perch, ARiOL! HAHAHA!
First of all, do you recognize this tree, ARiOL?
Uh... no.
But I gave you a clue. I said "off your perch." HAHAHA! It's a--? It's a--?
An apple tree?
Well, no, it's a "birch"! HAHAHA! You don't like birch, that's obvious! HAHAHA!
HAHAHA!

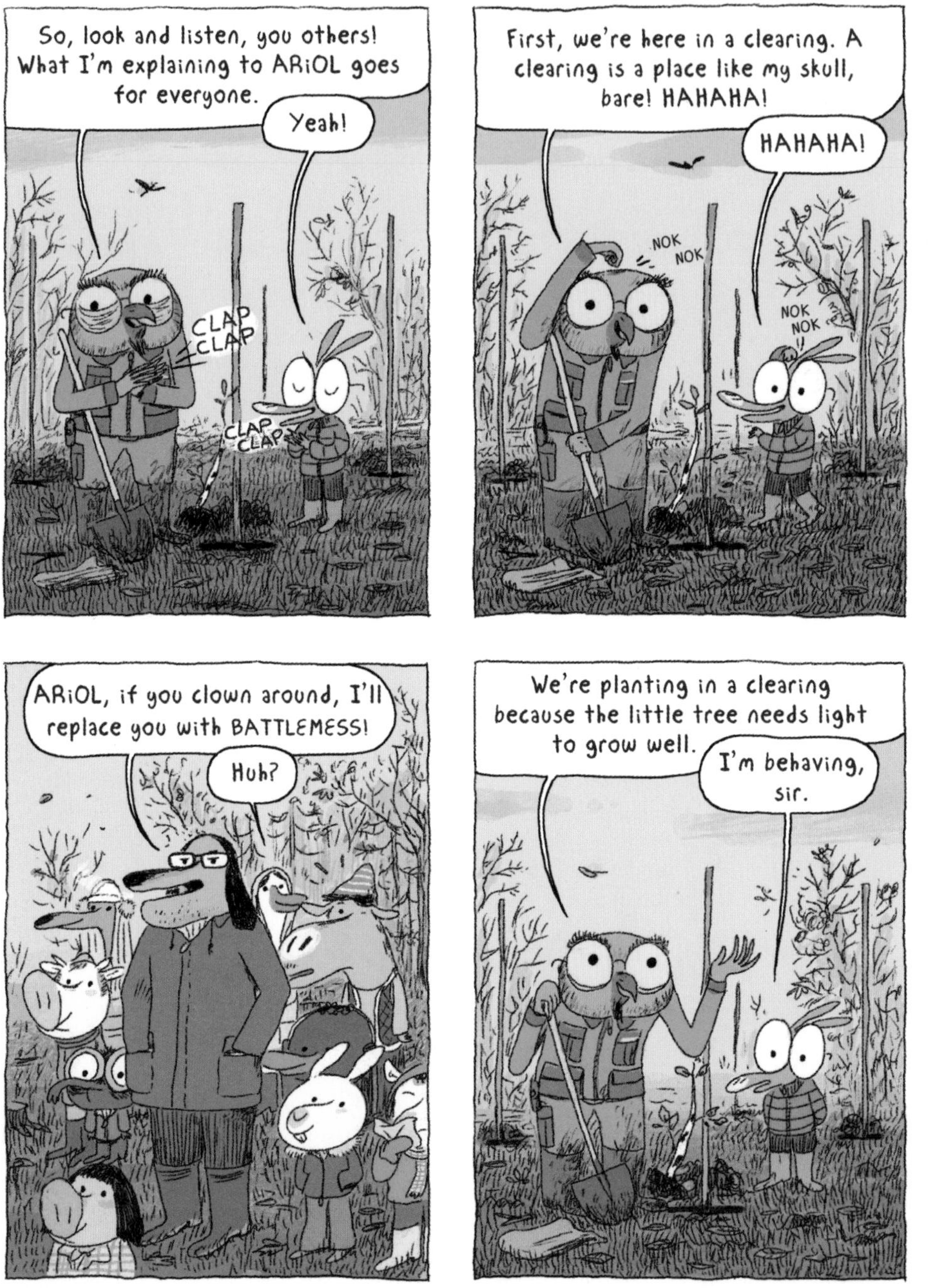
So, look and listen, you others! What I'm explaining to ARiOL goes for everyone.
Yeah!
CLAP CLAP
CLAP CLAP
First, we're here in a clearing. A clearing is a place like my skull, bare! HAHAHA!
HAHAHA!
NOK NOK
NOK NOK
ARiOL, if you clown around, I'll replace you with BATTLEMESS!
Huh?
We're planting in a clearing because the little tree needs light to grow well.
I'm behaving, sir.

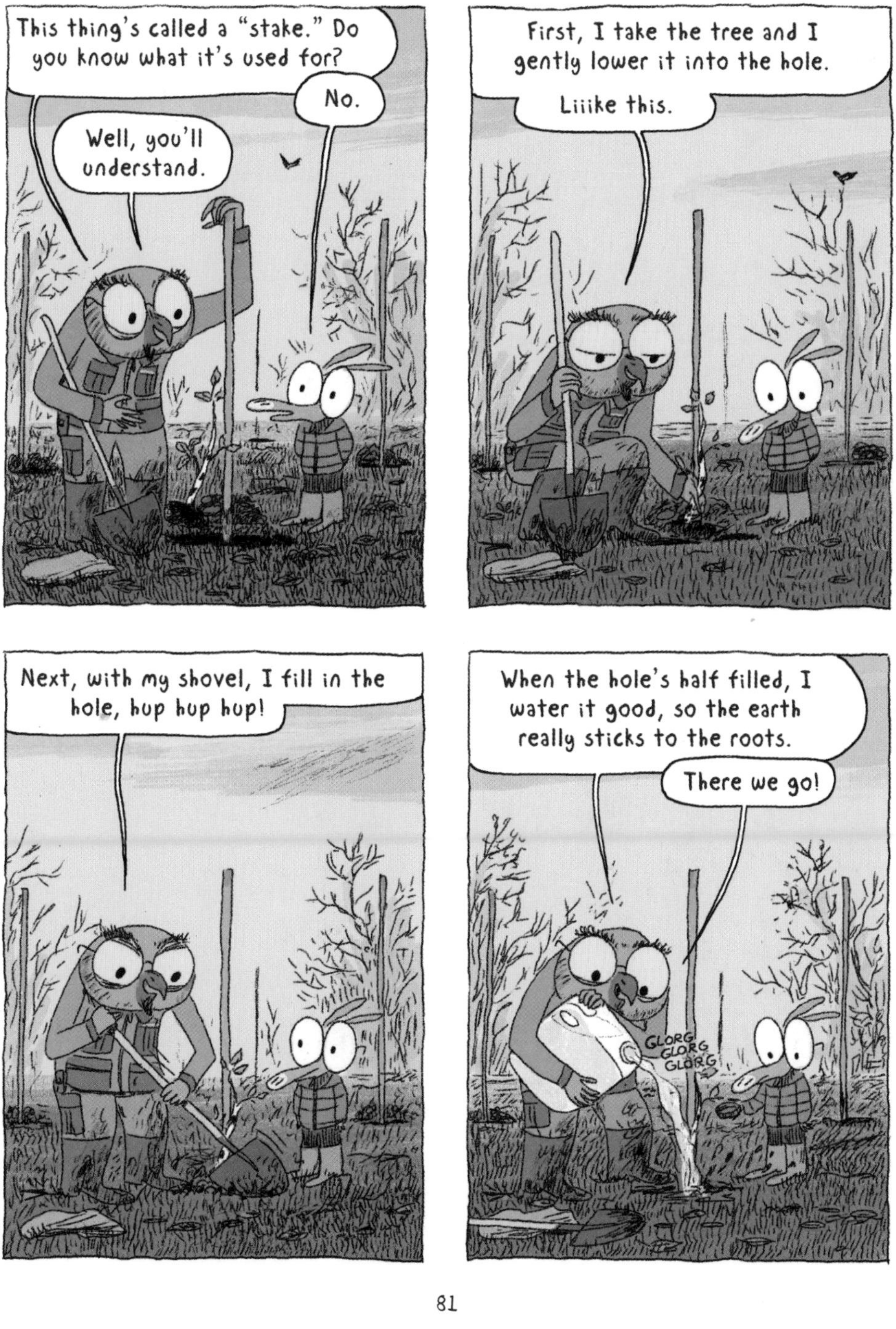
This thing's called a "stake." Do you know what it's used for?
No.
Well, you'll understand.
First, I take the tree and I gently lower it into the hole.
Liiike this.
Next, with my shovel, I fill in the hole, hup hup hup!
When the hole's half filled, I water it good, so the earth really sticks to the roots.
There we go!
GLORG GLORG GLORG

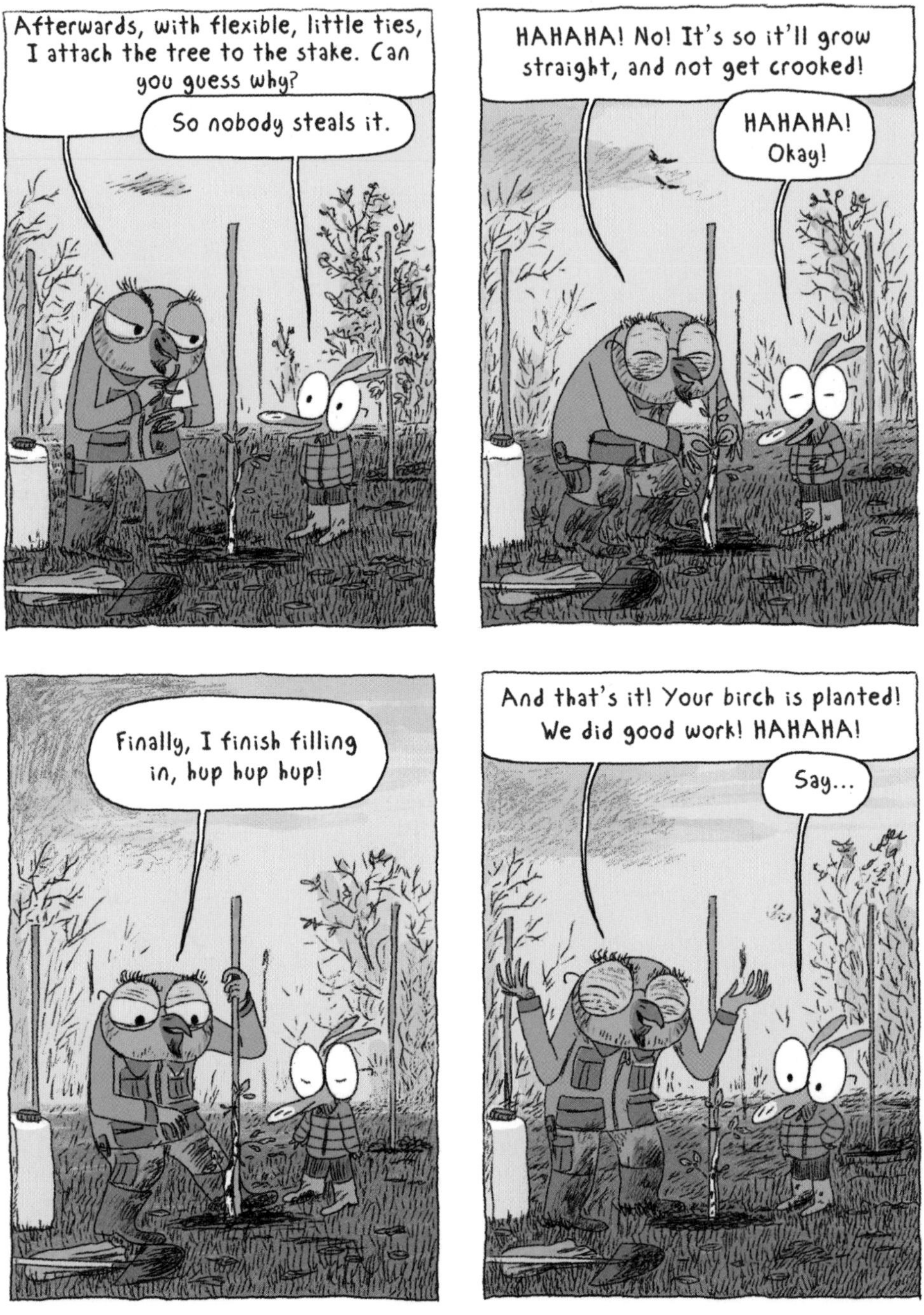
Afterwards, with flexible, little ties, I attach the tree to the stake. Can you guess why?
So nobody steals it.
HAHAHA! No! It's so it'll grow straight, and not get crooked!
HAHAHA! Okay!
Finally, I finish filling in, hup hup hup!
And that's it! Your birch is planted! We did good work! HAHAHA!
Say...

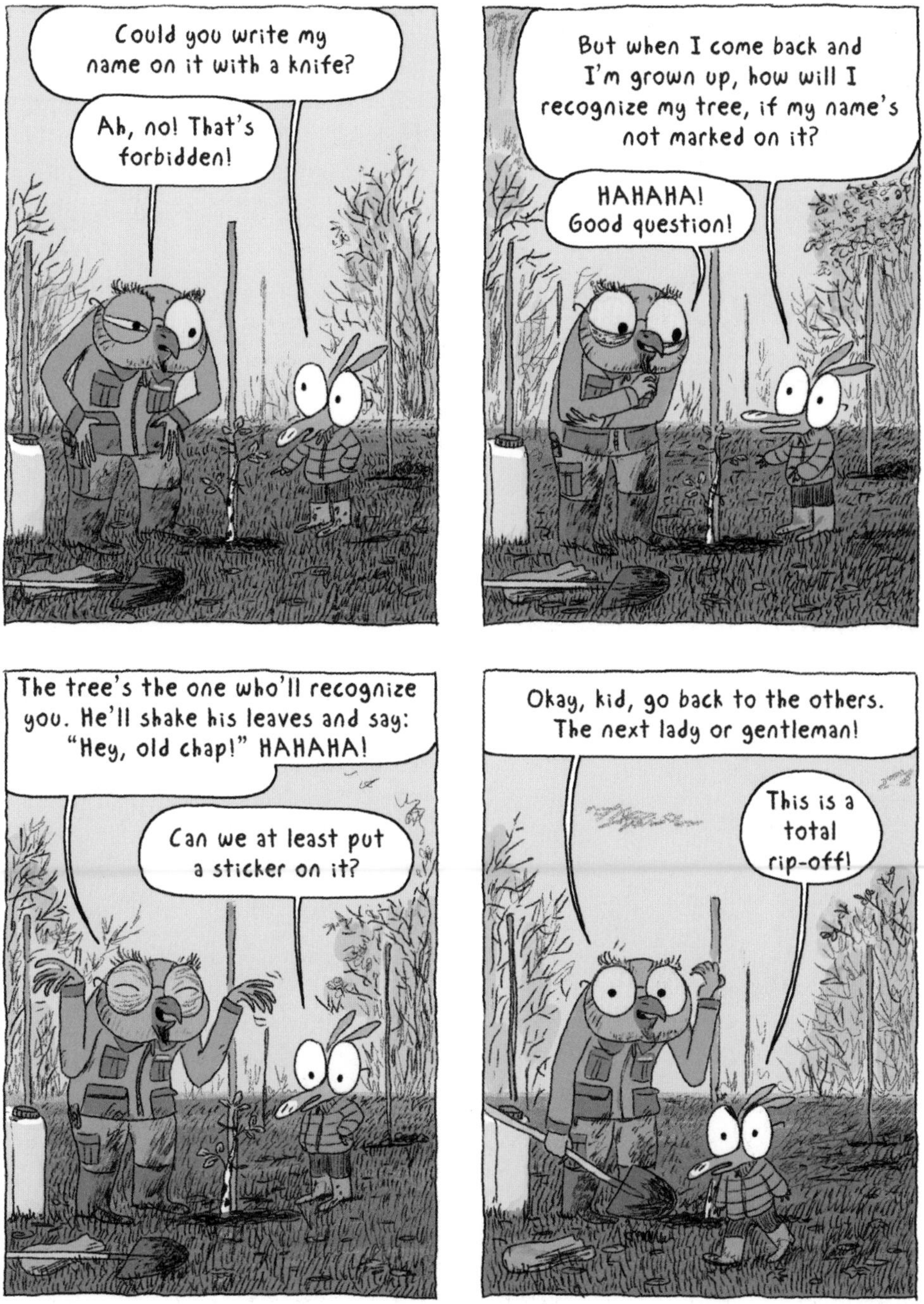

Could you write my name on it with a knife?
Ah, no! That's forbidden!
But when I come back and I'm grown up, how will I recognize my tree, if my name's not marked on it?
HAHAHA! Good question!
The tree's the one who'll recognize you. He'll shake his leaves and say: "Hey, old chap!" HAHAHA!
Can we at least put a sticker on it?
Okay, kid, go back to the others. The next lady or gentleman!
This is a total rip-off!

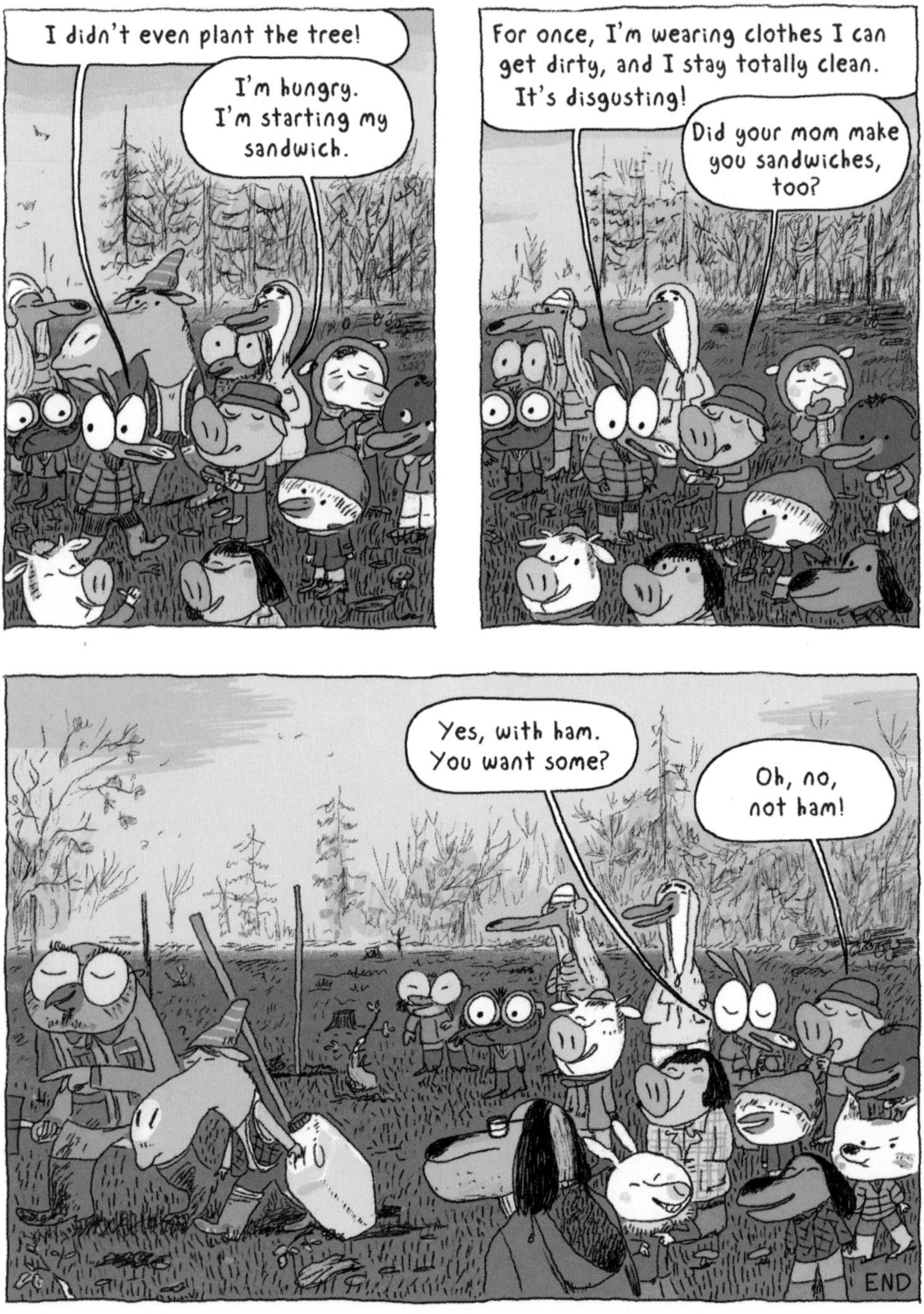
I didn't even plant the tree!
I'm hungry. I'm starting my sandwich.
For once, I'm wearing clothes I can get dirty, and I stay totally clean. It's disgusting!
Did your mom make you sandwiches, too?
Yes, with ham. You want some?
Oh, no, not ham!
END

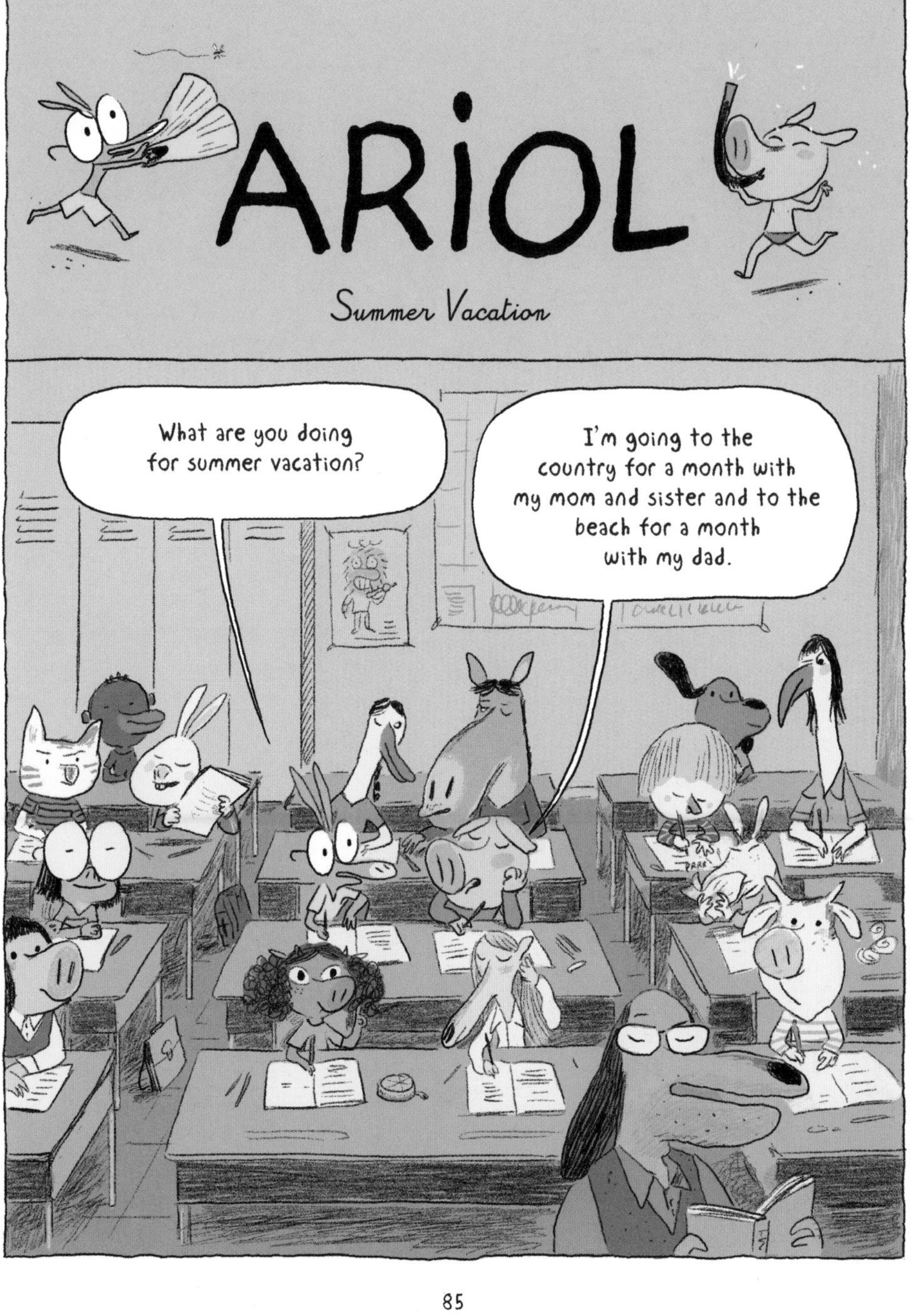
ARiOL
Summer Vacation
What are you doing for summer vacation?
I'm going to the country for a month with my mom and sister and to the beach for a month with my dad.

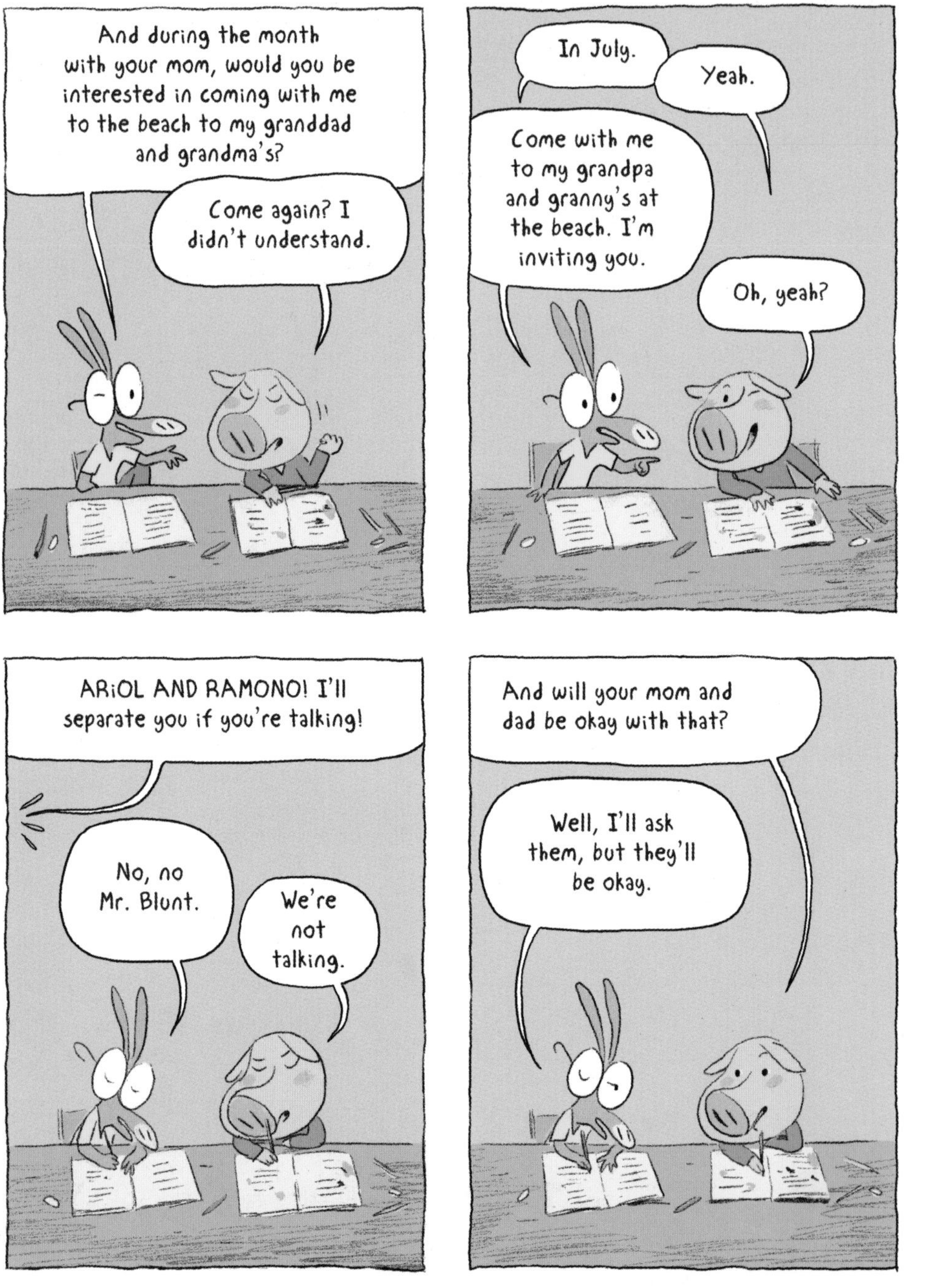

And during the month with your mom, would you be interested in coming with me to the beach to my granddad and grandma's?
Come again? I didn't understand.
In July.
Yeah.
Come with me to my grandpa and granny's at the beach. I'm inviting you.
Oh, yeah?
ARiOL AND RAMONO! I'll separate you if you're talking!
No, no Mr. Blunt.
We're not talking.
And will your mom and dad be okay with that?
Well, I'll ask them, but they'll be okay.

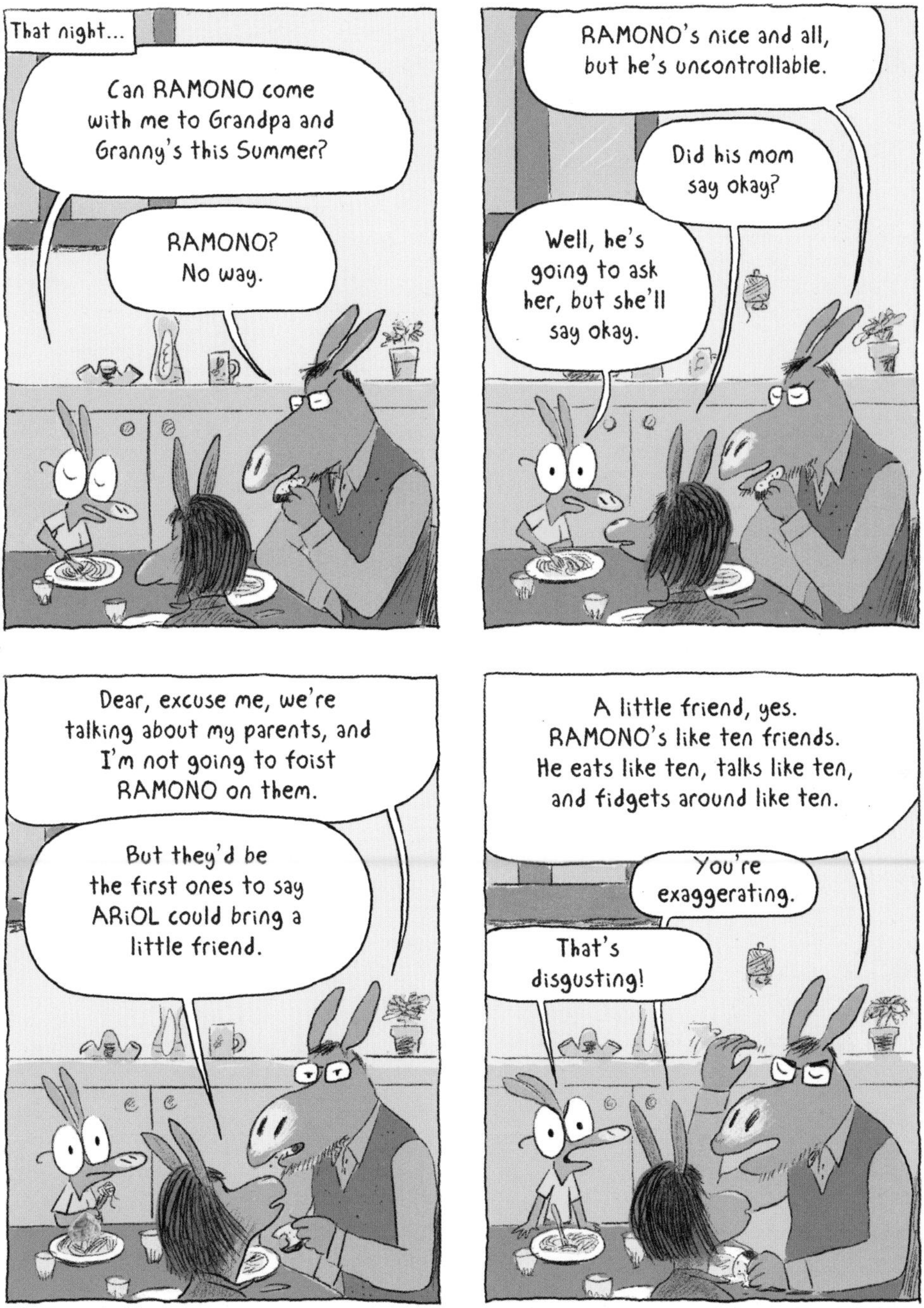
That night...
Can RAMONO come with me to Grandpa and Granny's this Summer?
RAMONO? No way.
RAMONO's nice and all, but he's uncontrollable.
Did his mom say okay?
Well, he's going to ask her, but she'll say okay.
Dear, excuse me, we're talking about my parents, and I'm not going to foist RAMONO on them.
But they'd be the first ones to say ARiOL could bring a little friend.
A little friend, yes. RAMONO's like ten friends. He eats like ten, talks like ten, and fidgets around like ten.
You're exaggerating.
That's disgusting!

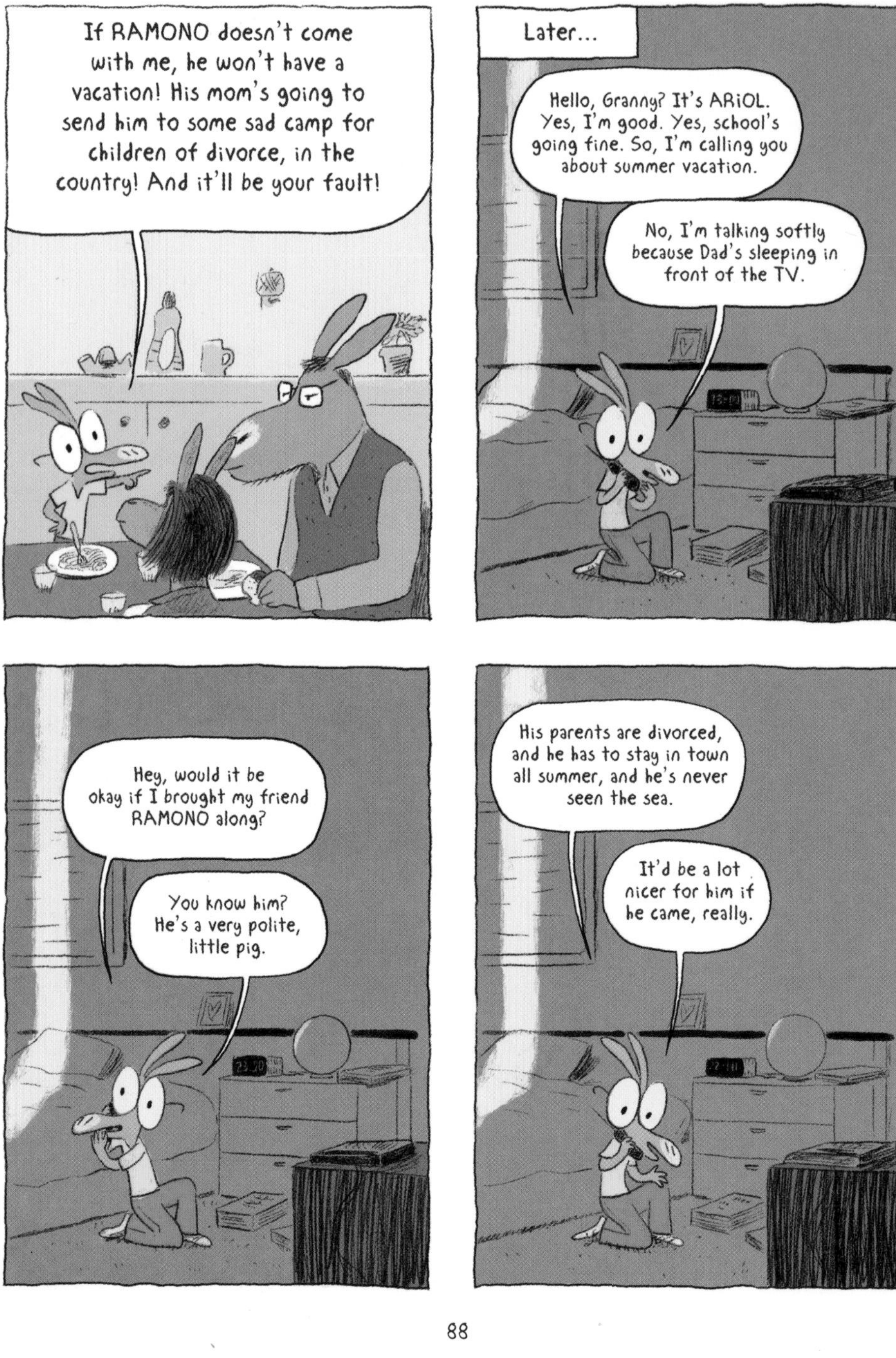
If RAMONO doesn't come with me, he won't have a vacation! His mom's going to send him to some sad camp for children of divorce, in the country! And it'll be your fault!
Later...
Hello, Granny? It's ARiOL. Yes, I'm good. Yes, school's going fine. So, I'm calling you about summer vacation.
No, I'm talking softly because Dad's sleeping in front of the TV.
Hey, would it be okay if I brought my friend RAMONO along?
You know him? He's a very polite, little pig.
His parents are divorced, and he has to stay in town all summer, and he's never seen the sea.
It'd be a lot nicer for him if he came, really.

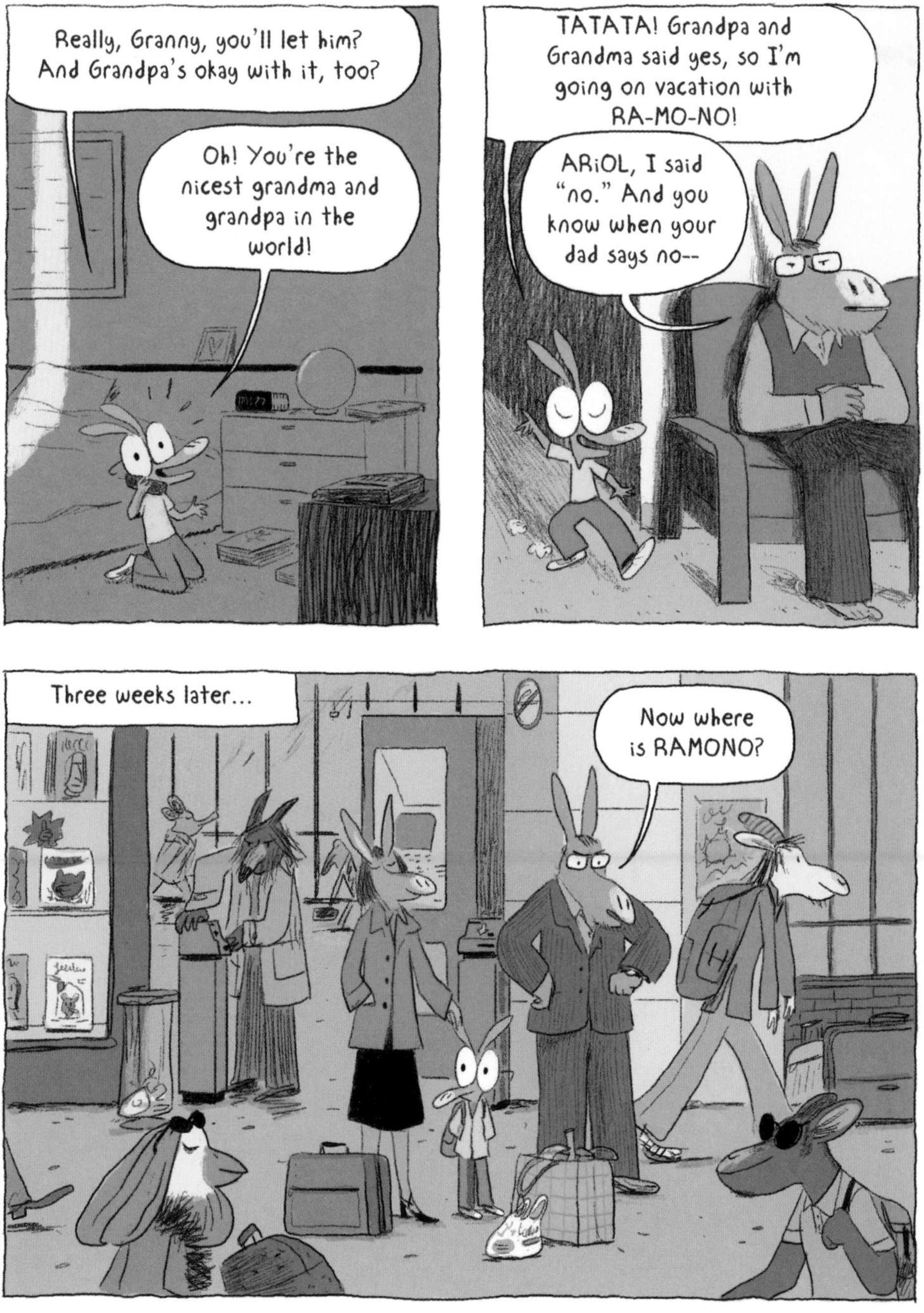
Really, Granny, you'll let him? And Grandpa's okay with it, too?
Oh! You're the nicest grandma and grandpa in the world!
TATATA! Grandpa and Grandma said yes, so I'm going on vacation with RA-MO-NO!
ARiOL, I said "no." And you know when your dad says no--
Three weeks later...
Now where is RAMONO?

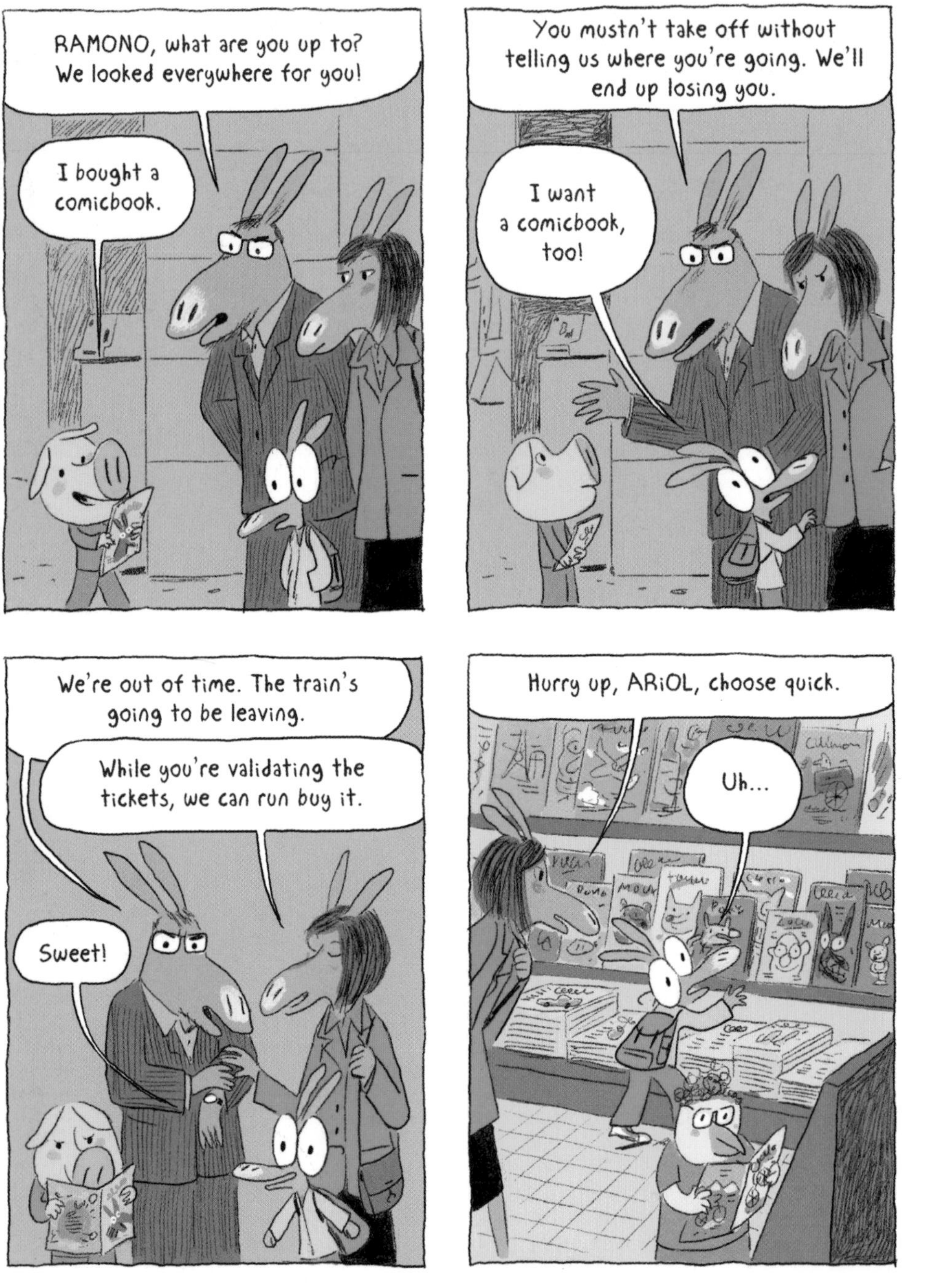
RAMONO, what are you up to? We looked everywhere for you!
I bought a comicbook.
You mustn't take off without telling us where you're going. We'll end up losing you.
I want a comicbook, too!
We're out of time. The train's going to be leaving.
While you're validating the tickets, we can run buy it.
Sweet!
Hurry up, ARiOL, choose quick.
Uh...

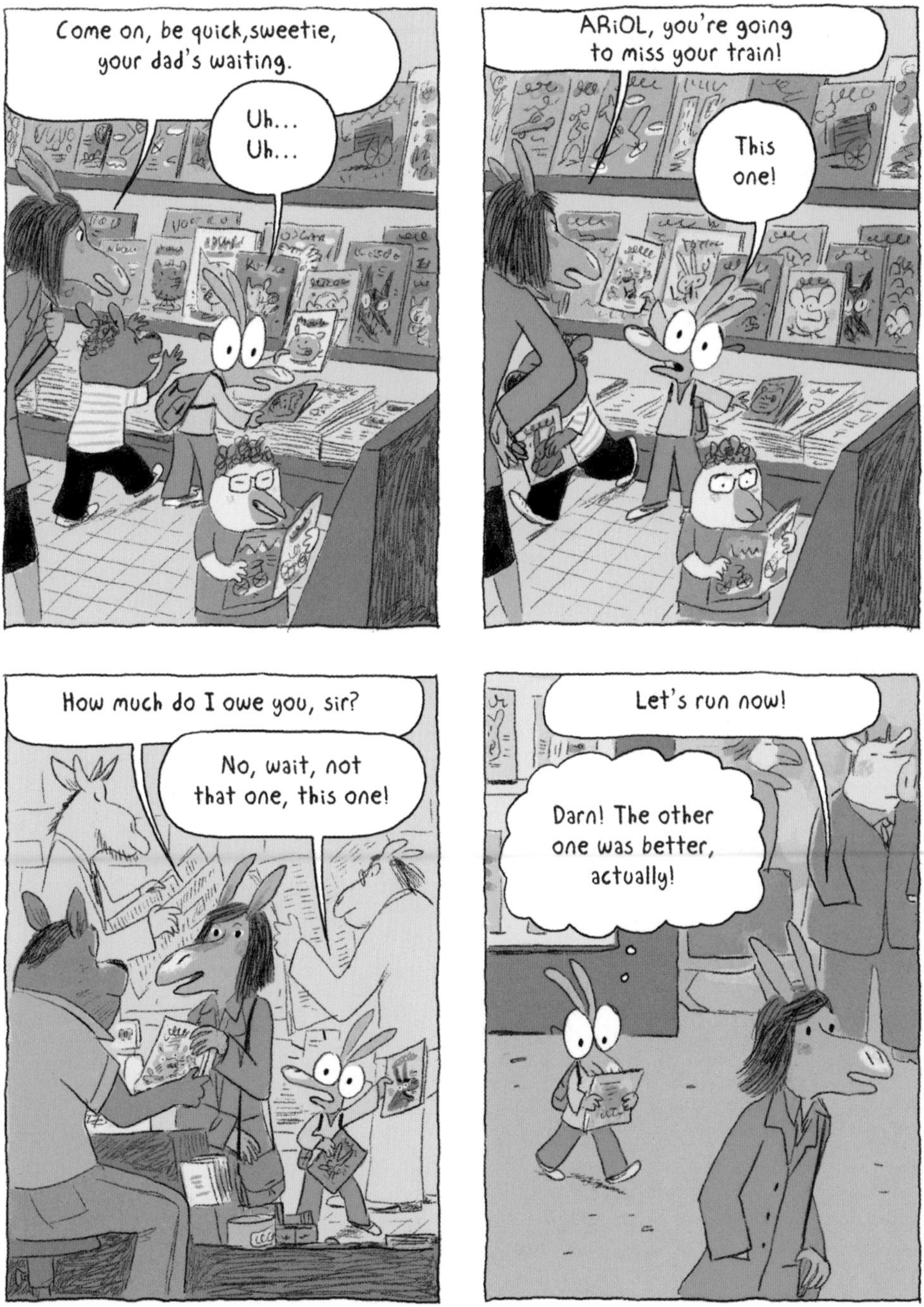
Come on, be quick,sweetie, your dad's waiting.
Uh... Uh...
ARiOL, you're going to miss your train!
This one!
How much do I owe you, sir?
No, wait, not that one, this one!
Let's run now!
Darn! The other one was better, actually!

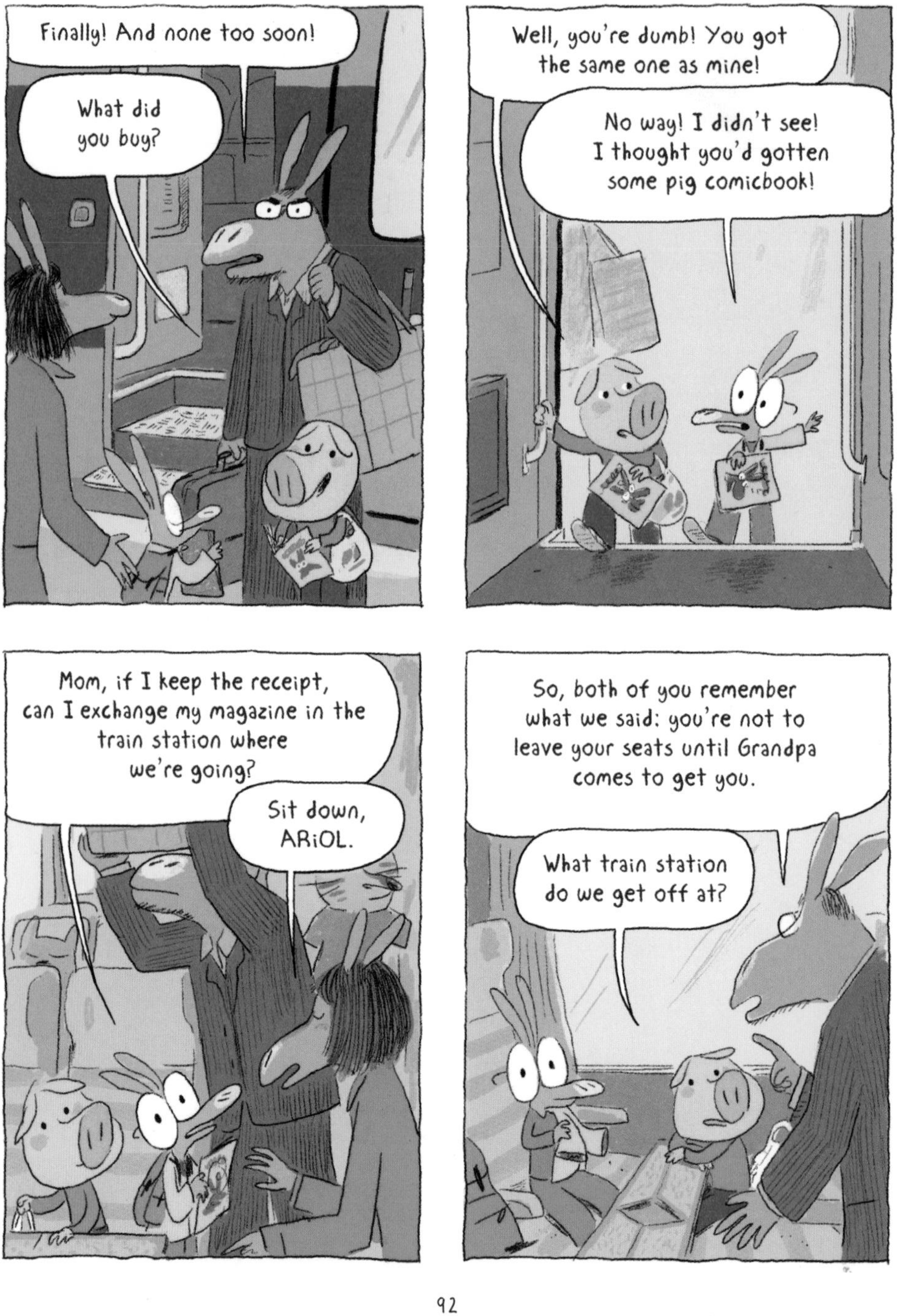
Finally! And none too soon!
What did you buy?
Well, you're dumb! You got the same one as mine!
No way! I didn't see! I thought you'd gotten some pig comicbook!
Mom, if I keep the receipt, can I exchange my magazine in the train station where we're going?
Sit down, ARiOL.
So, both of you remember what we said: you're not to leave your seats until Grandpa comes to get you.
What train station do we get off at?

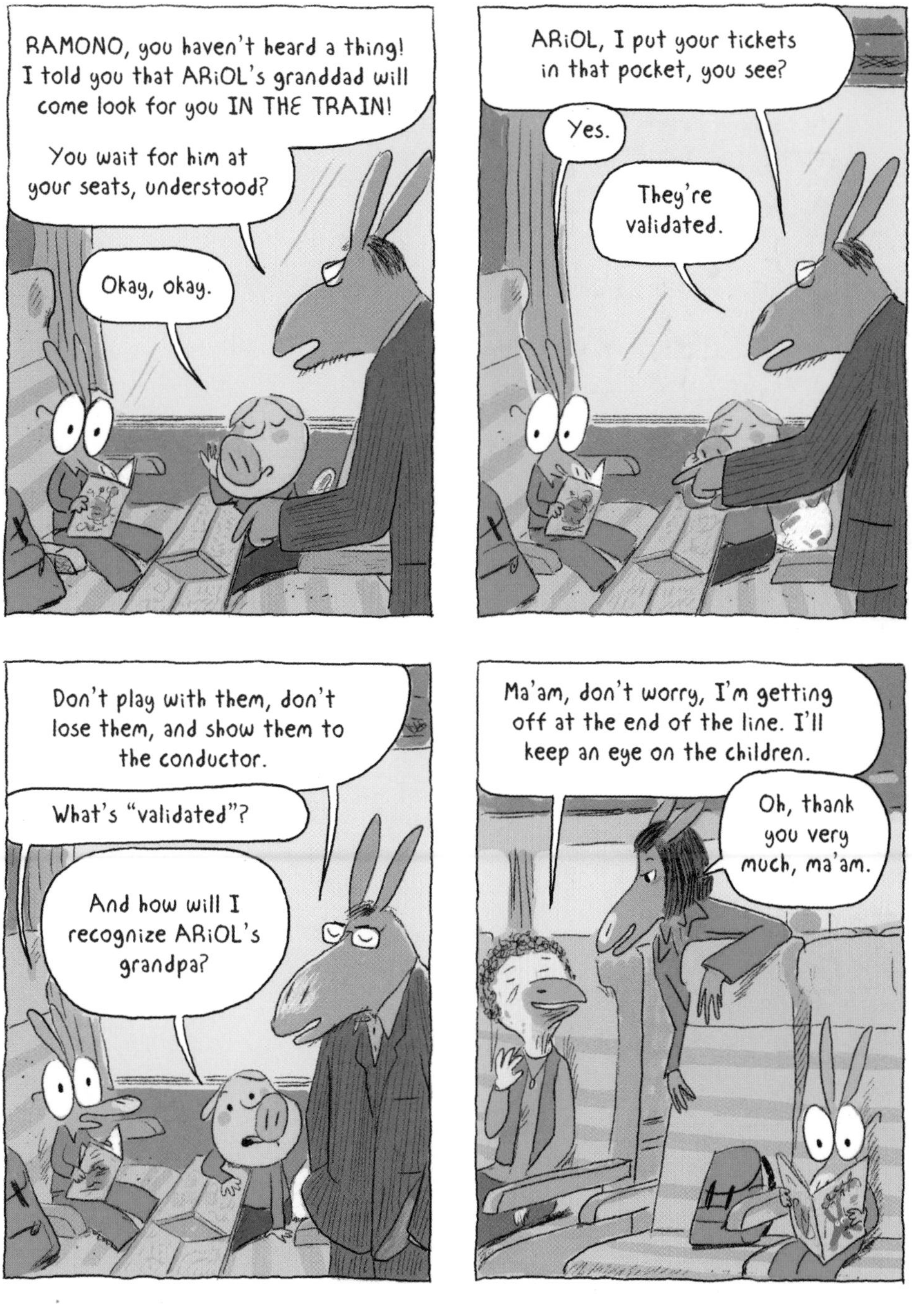
RAMONO, you haven't heard a thing! I told you that ARiOL's granddad will come look for you IN THE TRAIN!
You wait for him at your seats, understood?
Okay, okay.
ARiOL, I put your tickets in that pocket, you see?
Yes.
They're validated.
Don't play with them, don't lose them, and show them to the conductor.
What's "validated"?
And how will I recognize ARiOL's grandpa?
Ma'am, don't worry, I'm getting off at the end of the line. I'll keep an eye on the children.
Oh, thank you very much, ma'am.

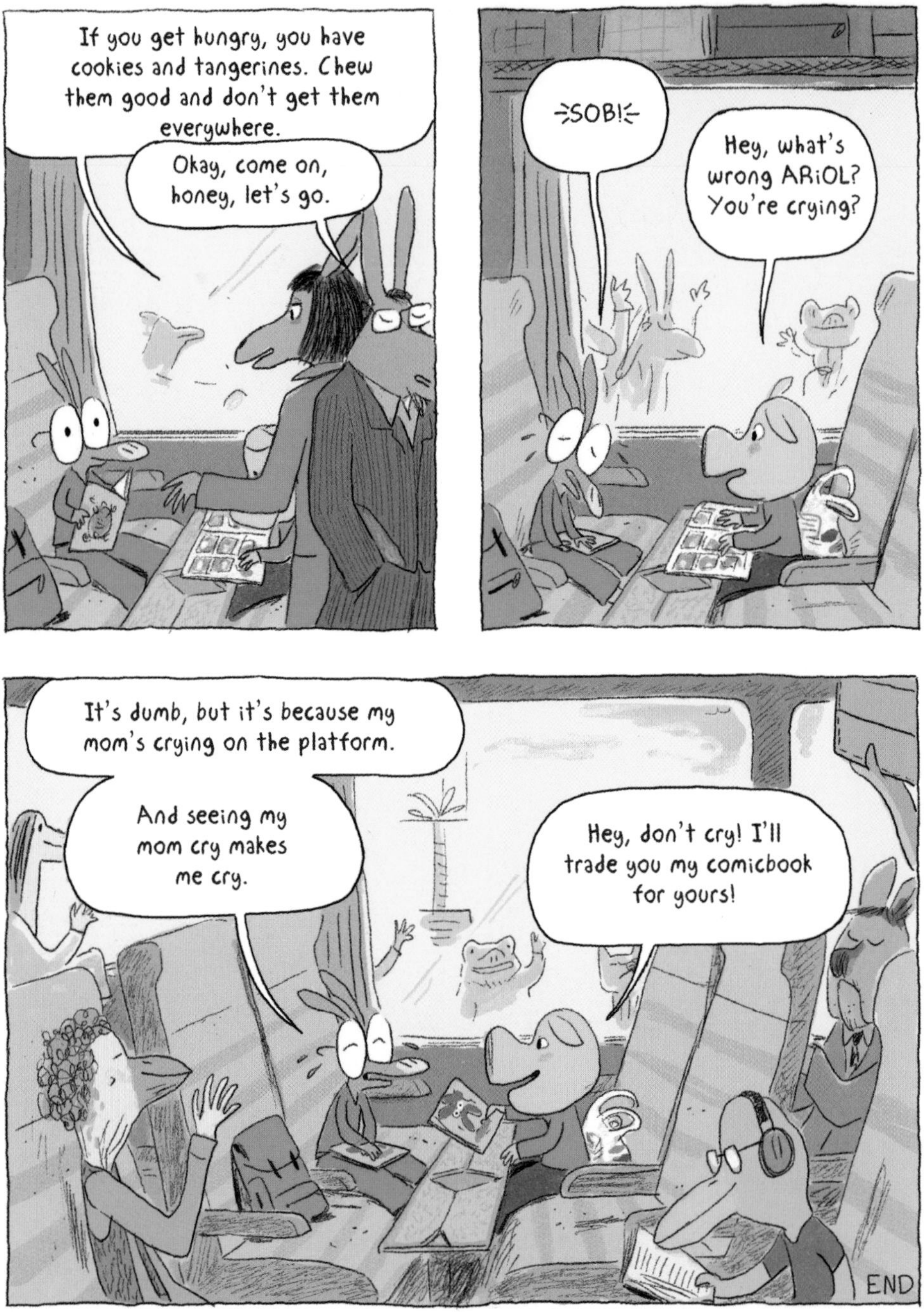
If you get hungry, you have cookies and tangerines. Chew them good and don't get them everywhere.
Okay, come on, honey, let's go.
SOB!
Hey, what's wrong ARiOL? You're crying?
It's dumb, but it's because my mom's crying on the platform.
And seeing my mom cry makes me cry.
Hey, don't cry! I'll trade you my comicbook for yours!
END

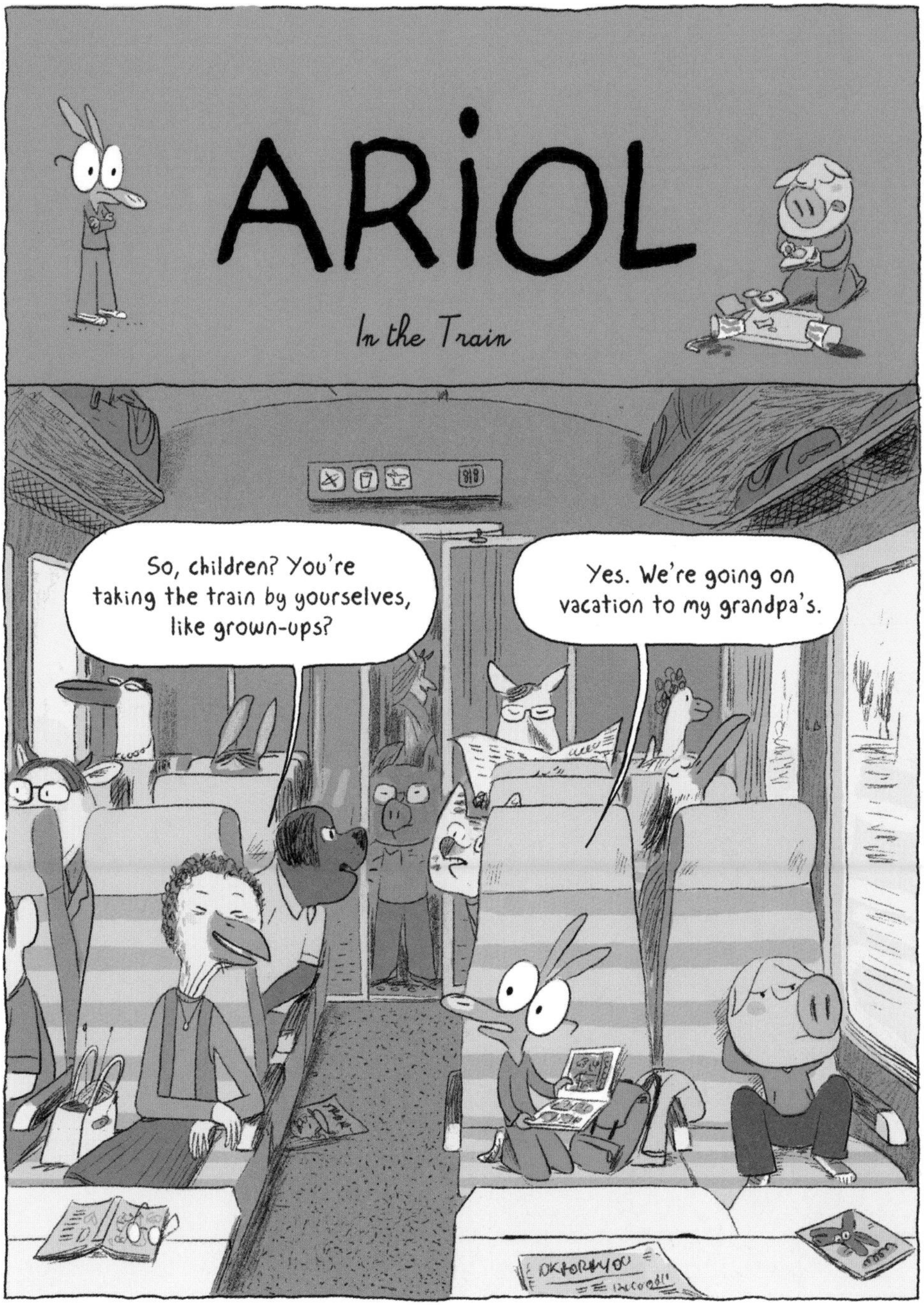
ARIOL
In the Train
So, children? You're taking the train by yourselves, like grown-ups?
Yes. We're going on vacation to my grandpa's.

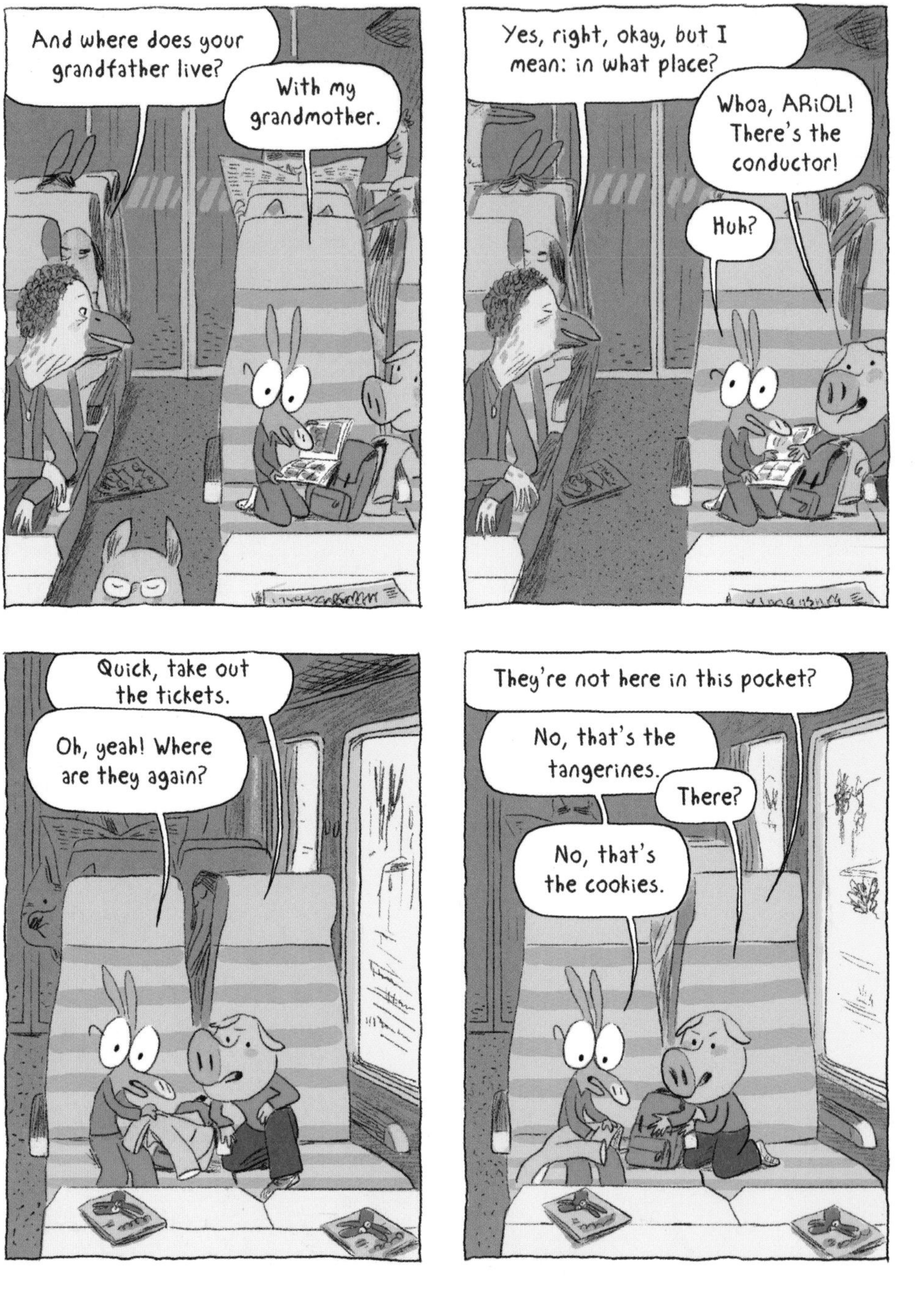
And where does your grandfather live?
With my grandmother.
Yes, right, okay, but I mean: in what place?
Whoa, ARiOL! There's the conductor!
Huh?
Quick, take out the tickets.
Oh, yeah! Where are they again?
They're not here in this pocket?
No, that's the tangerines.
There?
No, that's the cookies.

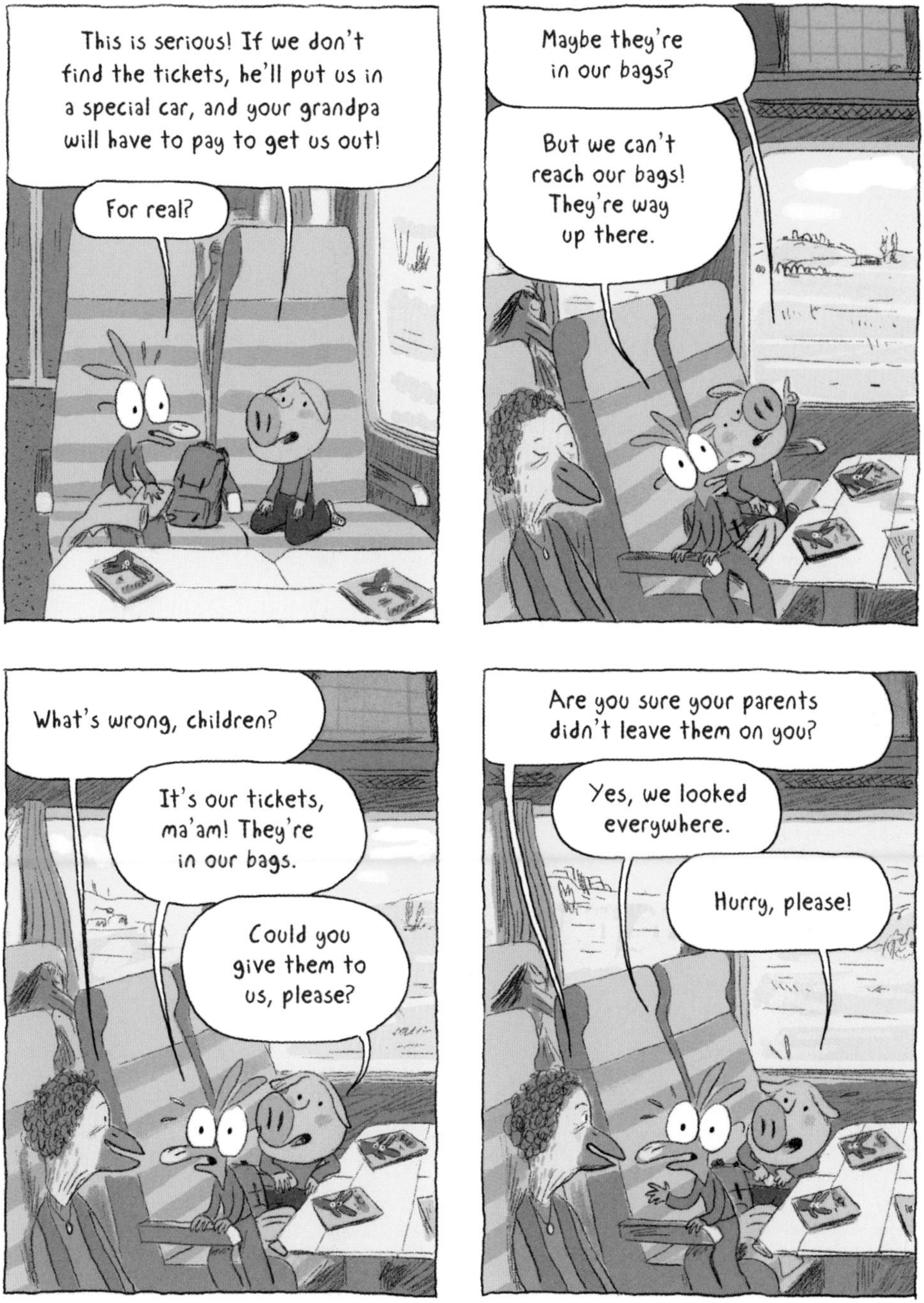
This is serious! If we don't find the tickets, he'll put us in a special car, and your grandpa will have to pay to get us out!
For real?
Maybe they're in our bags?
But we can't reach our bags! They're way up there.
What's wrong, children?
It's our tickets, ma'am! They're in our bags.
Could you give them to us, please?
Are you sure your parents didn't leave them on you?
Yes, we looked everywhere.
Hurry, please!

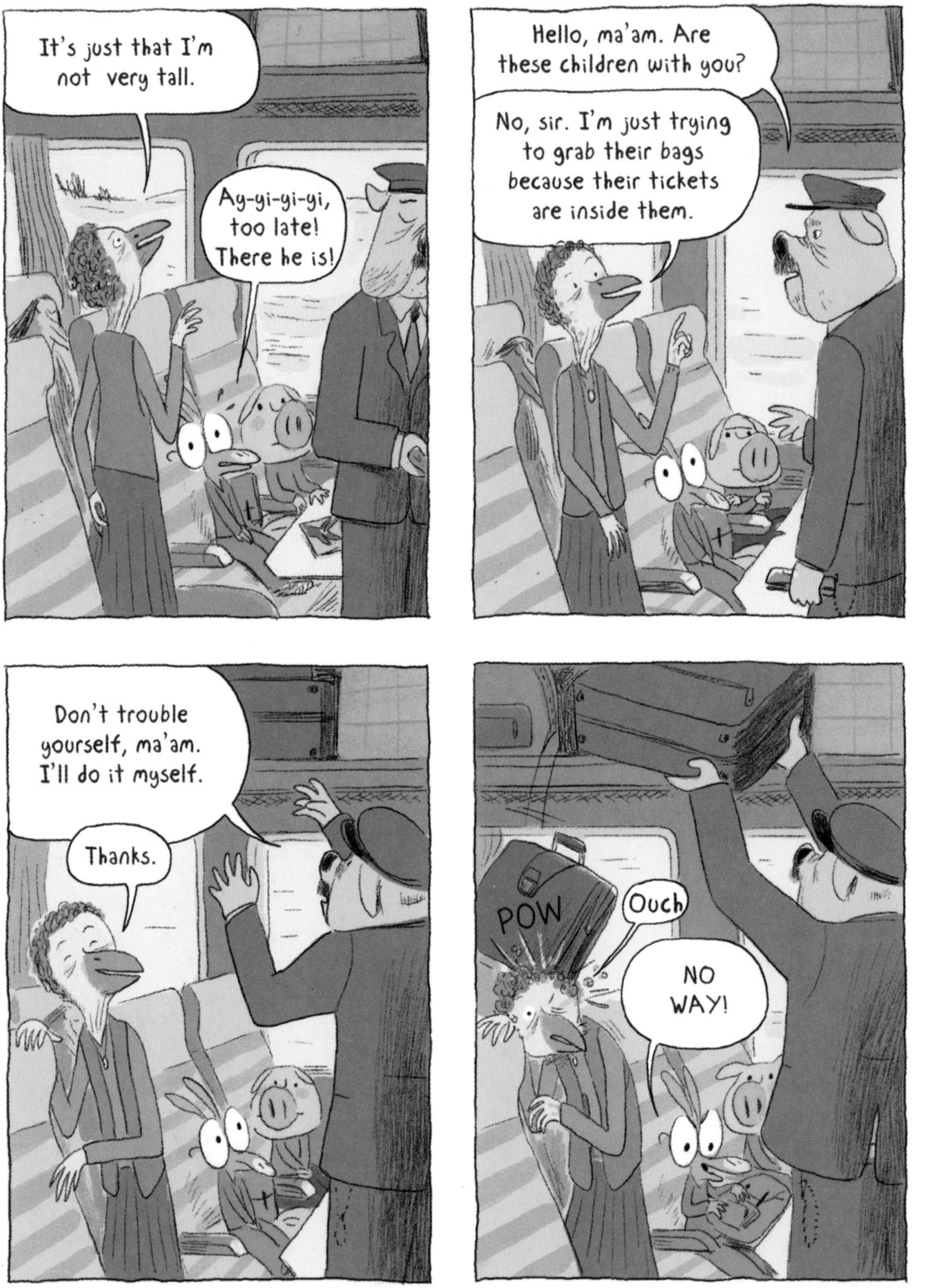
It's just that I'm not very tall.
Ay-yi-yi-yi, too late! There he is!
Hello, ma'am. Are these children with you?
No, sir. I'm just trying to grab their bags because their tickets are inside them.
Don't trouble yourself, ma'am. I'll do it myself.
Thanks.
POW
Ouch
NO WAY!

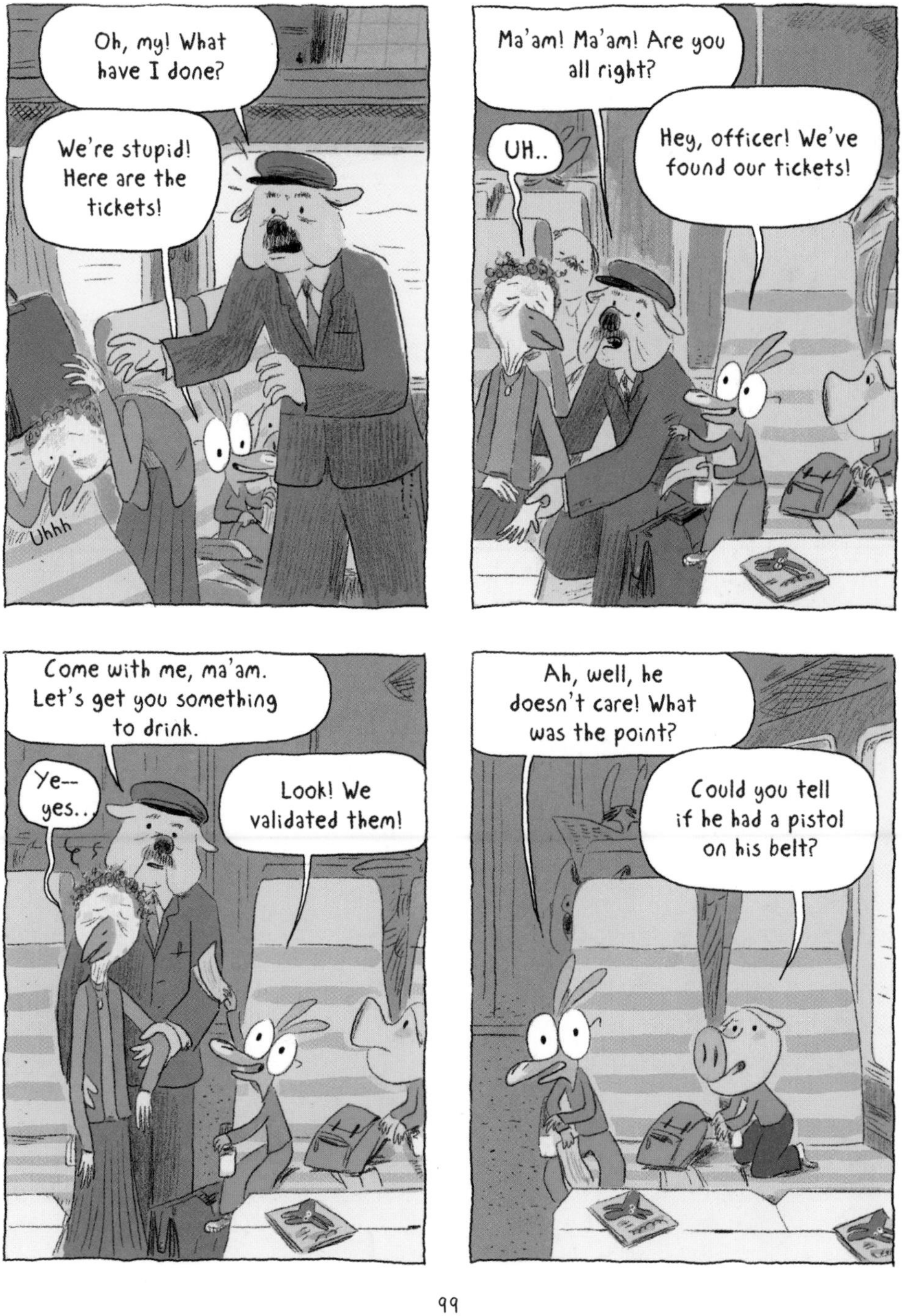

Oh, my! What have I done?
We're stupid! Here are the tickets!
Uhhh
Ma'am! Ma'am! Are you all right?
UH..
Hey, officer! We've found our tickets!
Come with me, ma'am. Let's get you something to drink.
Ye-- yes..
Look! We validated them!
Ah, well, he doesn't care! What was the point?
Could you tell if he had a pistol on his belt?

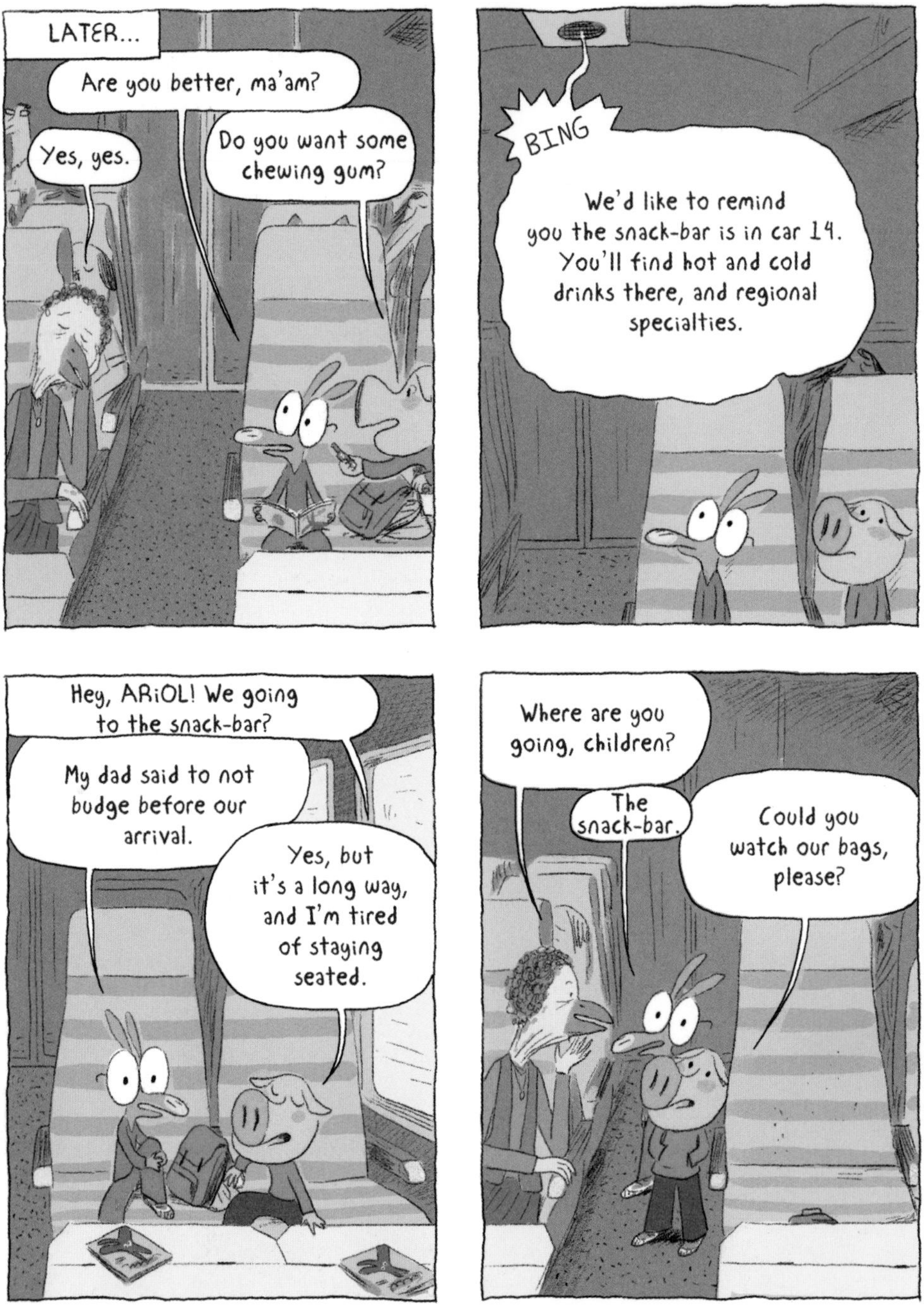
LATER...
Are you better, ma'am?
Yes, yes.
Do you want some chewing gum?
BING
We'd like to remind you the snack-bar is in car 14. You'll find hot and cold drinks there, and regional specialties.
Hey, ARiOL! We going to the snack-bar?
My dad said to not budge before our arrival.
Yes, but it's a long way, and I'm tired of staying seated.
Where are you going, children?
The snack-bar.
Could you watch our bags, please?

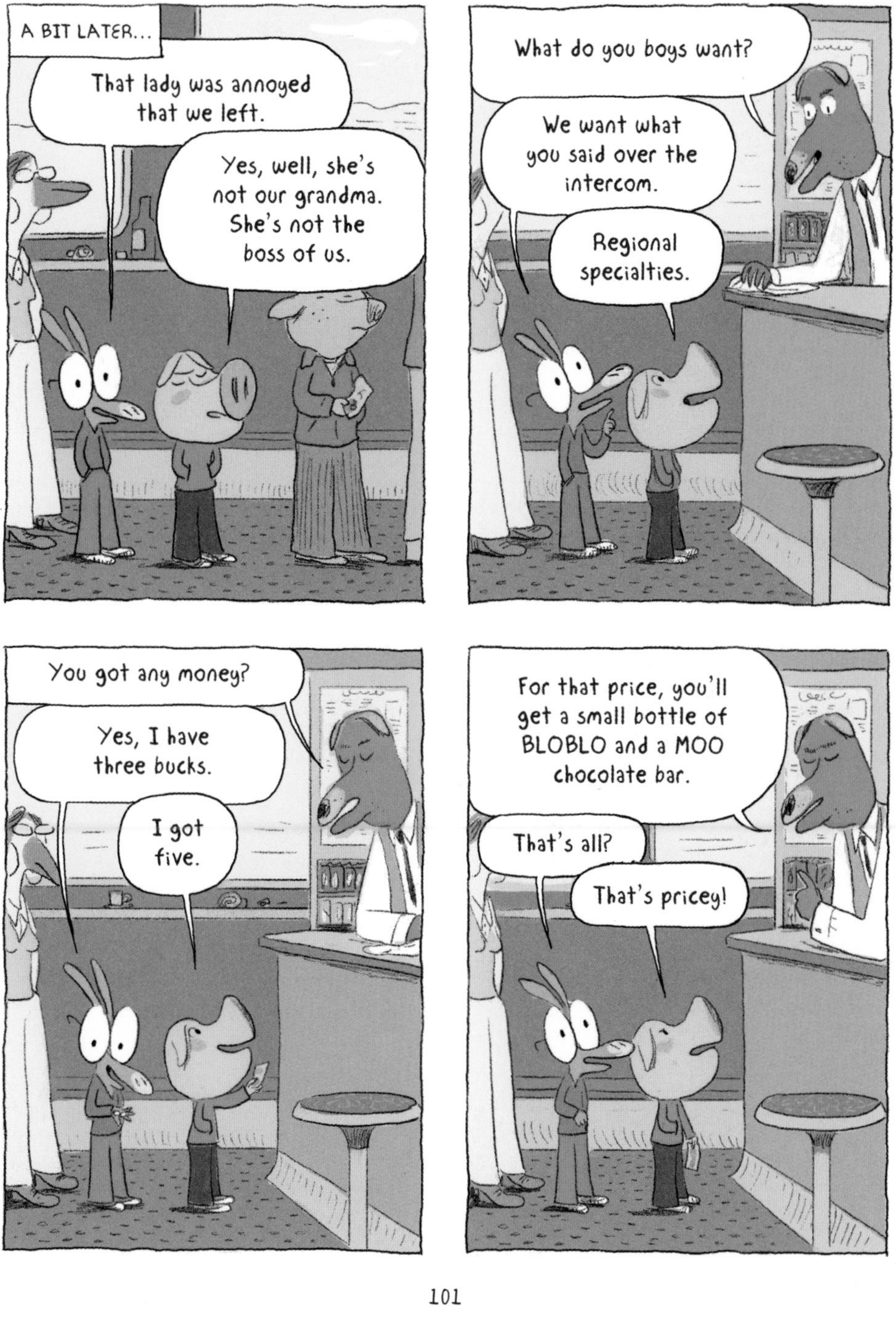
A BIT LATER...
That lady was annoyed that we left.
Yes, well, she's not our grandma. She's not the boss of us.
What do you boys want?
We want what you said over the intercom.
Regional specialties.
You got any money?
Yes, I have three bucks.
I got five.
For that price, you'll get a small bottle of BLOBLO and a MOO chocolate bar.
That's all?
That's pricey!

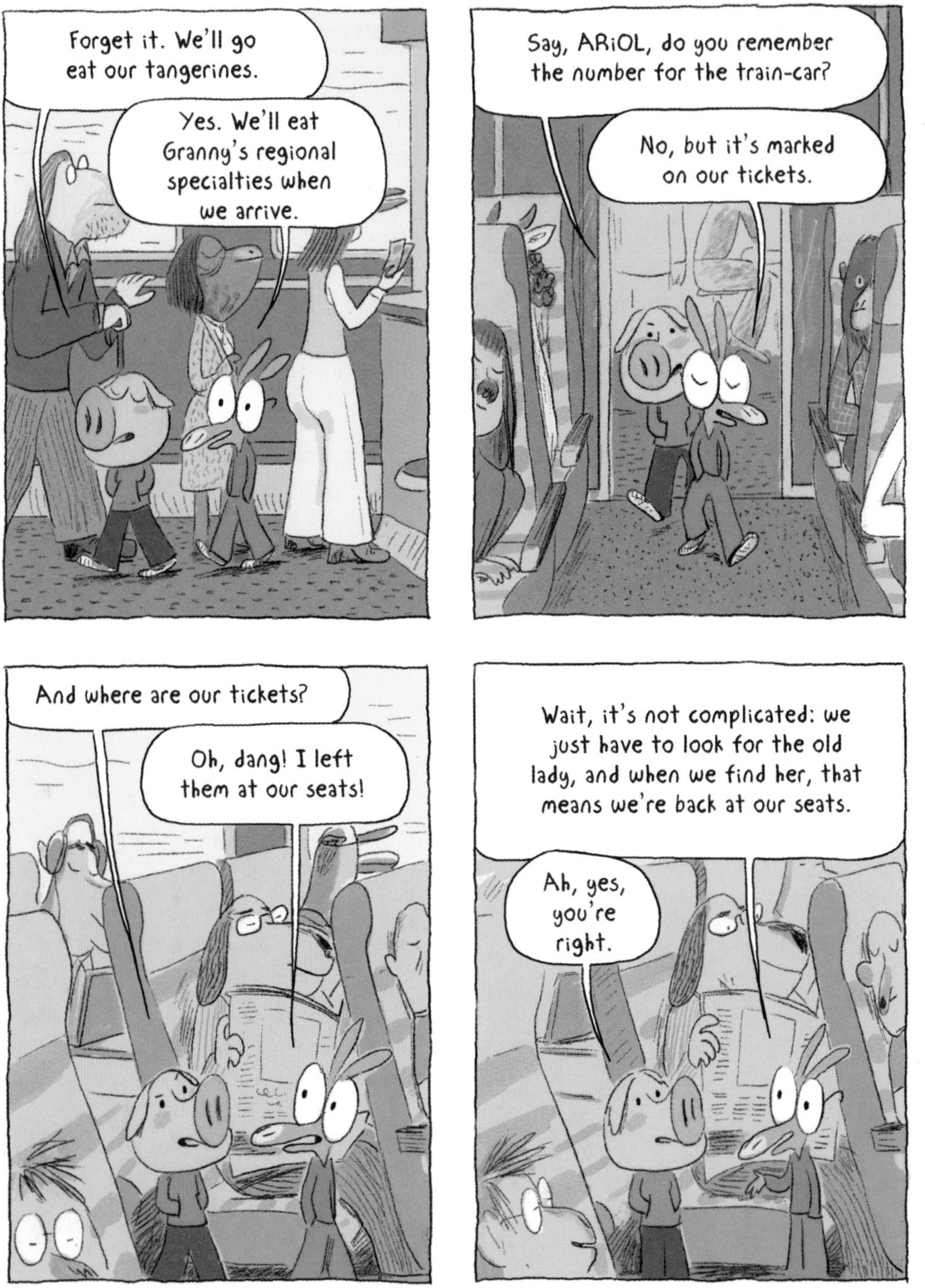
Forget it. We'll go eat our tangerines.
Yes. We'll eat Granny's regional specialties when we arrive.
Say, ARiOL, do you remember the number for the train-car?
No, but it's marked on our tickets.
And where are our tickets?
Oh, dang! I left them at our seats!
Wait, it's not complicated: we just have to look for the old lady, and when we find her, that means we're back at our seats.
Ah, yes, you're right.

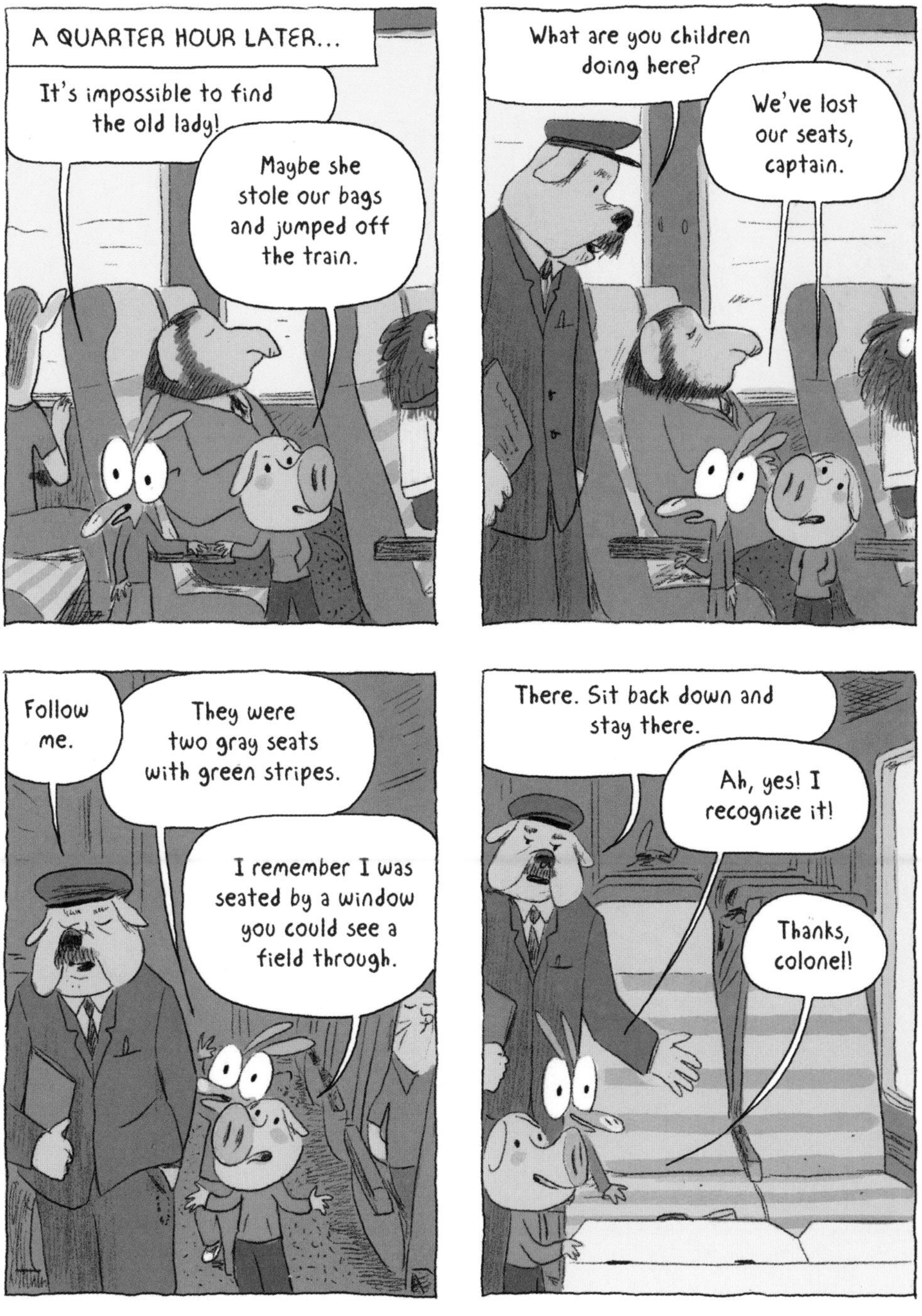
A QUARTER HOUR LATER...
It's impossible to find the old lady!
Maybe she stole our bags and jumped off the train.
What are you children doing here?
We've lost our seats, captain.
Follow me.
They were two gray seats with green stripes.
I remember I was seated by a window you could see a field through.
There. Sit back down and stay there.
Ah, yes! I recognize it!
Thanks, colonel!

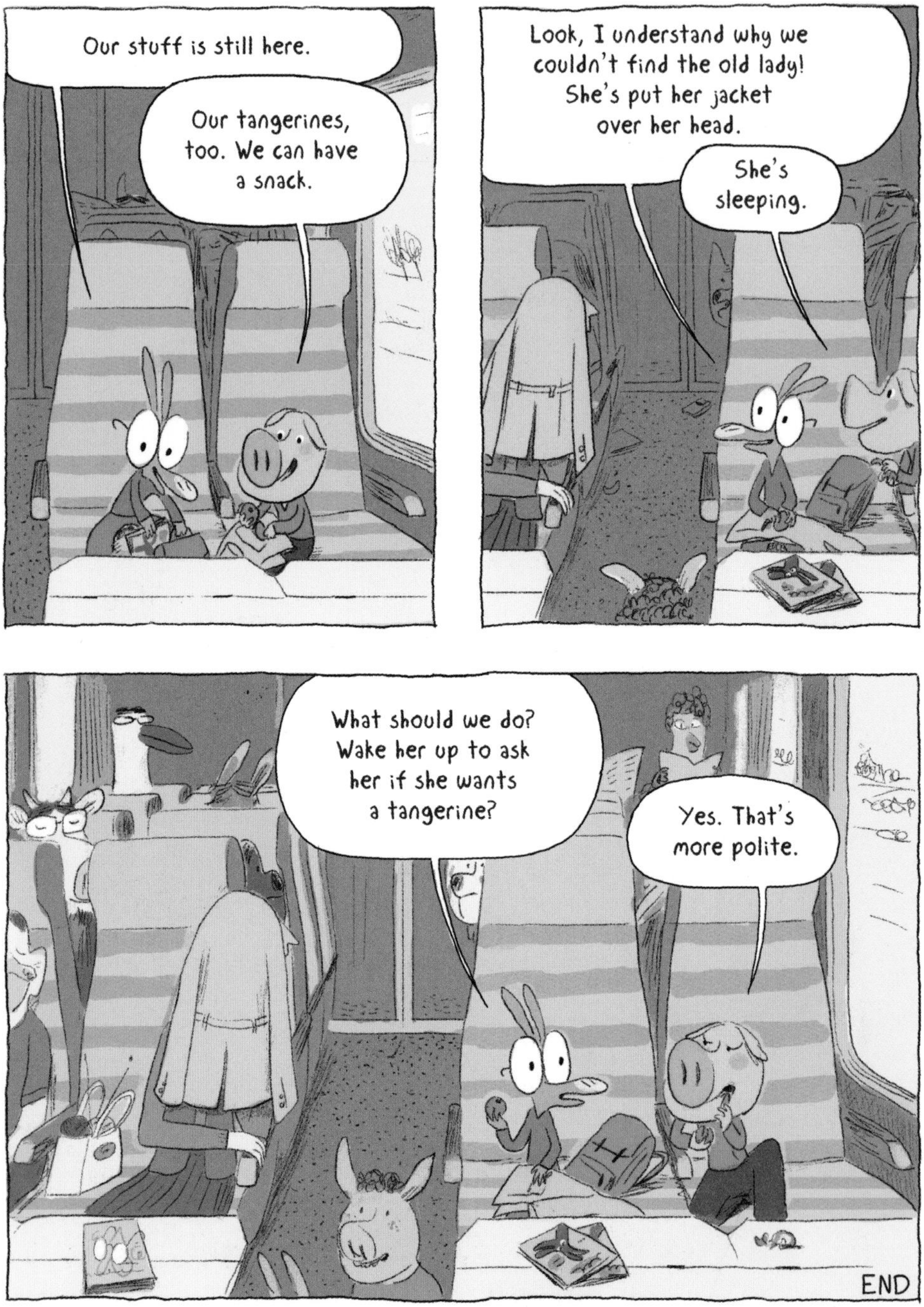
Our stuff is still here.
Our tangerines, too. We can have a snack.
Look, I understand why we couldn't find the old lady! She's put her jacket over her head.
She's sleeping.
What should we do? Wake her up to ask her if she wants a tangerine?
Yes. That's more polite.
END

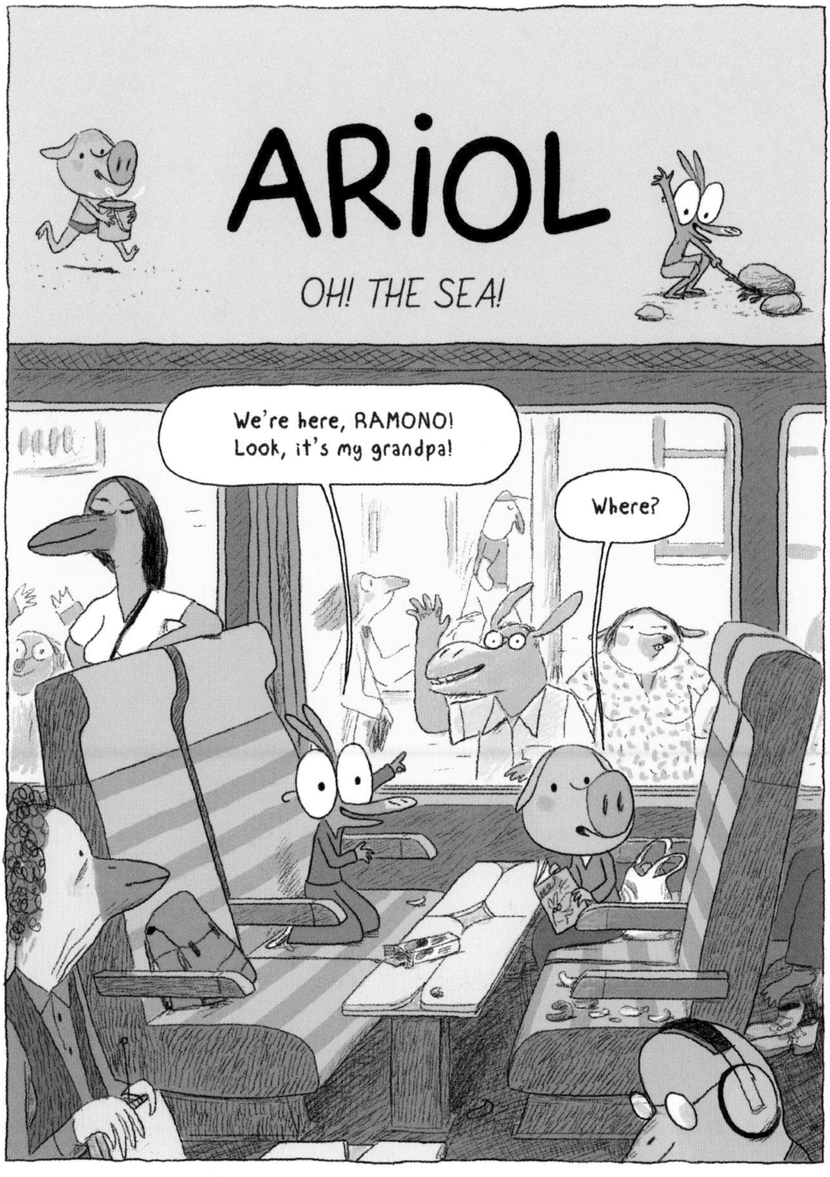
ARiOL
OH! THE SEA!
We're here, RAMONO! Look, it's my grandpa!
Where?

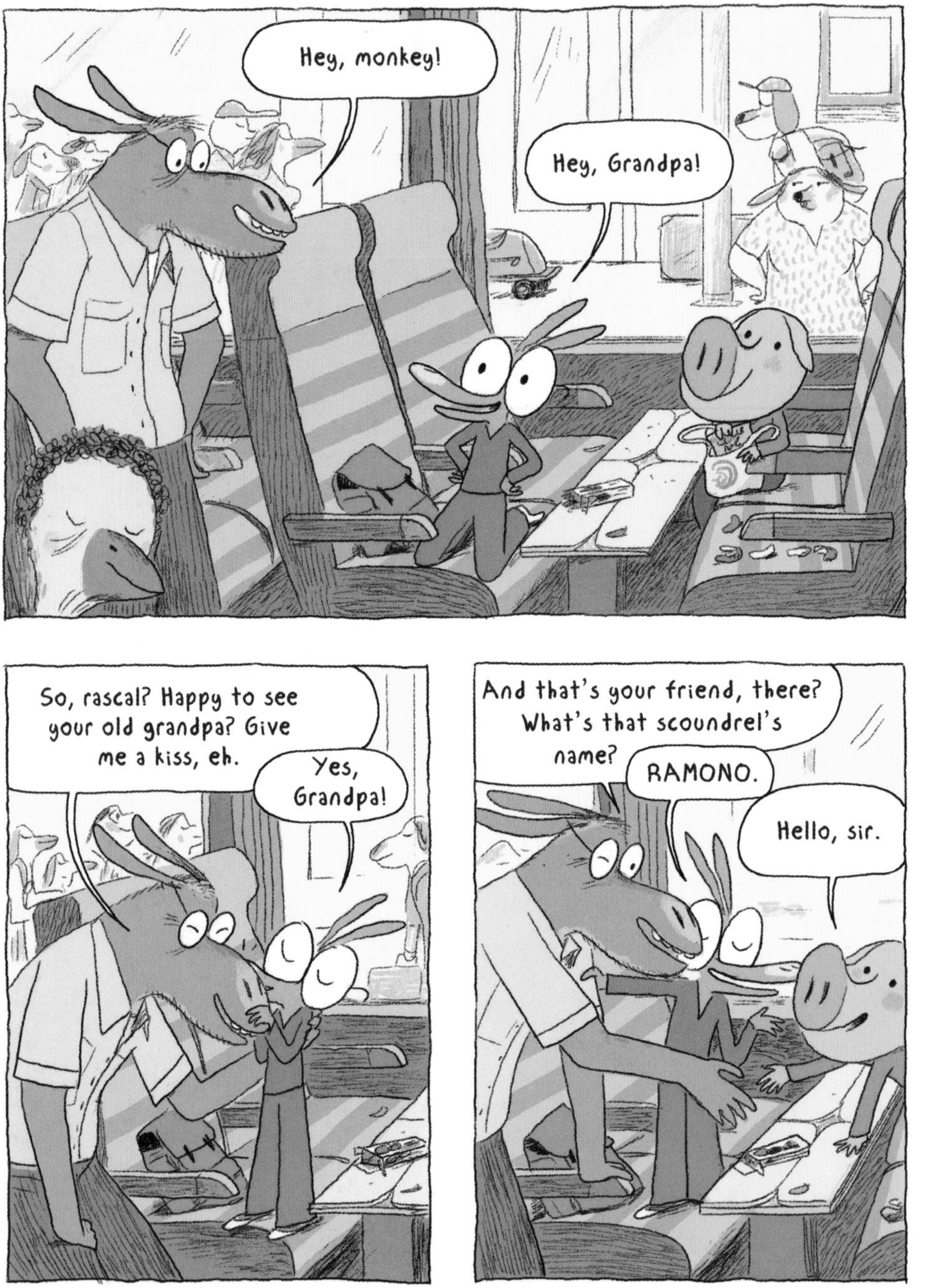
Hey, monkey!
Hey, Grandpa!
So, rascal? Happy to see your old grandpa? Give me a kiss, eh.
Yes, Grandpa!
And that's your friend, there? What's that scoundrel's name?
RAMONO.
Hello, sir.

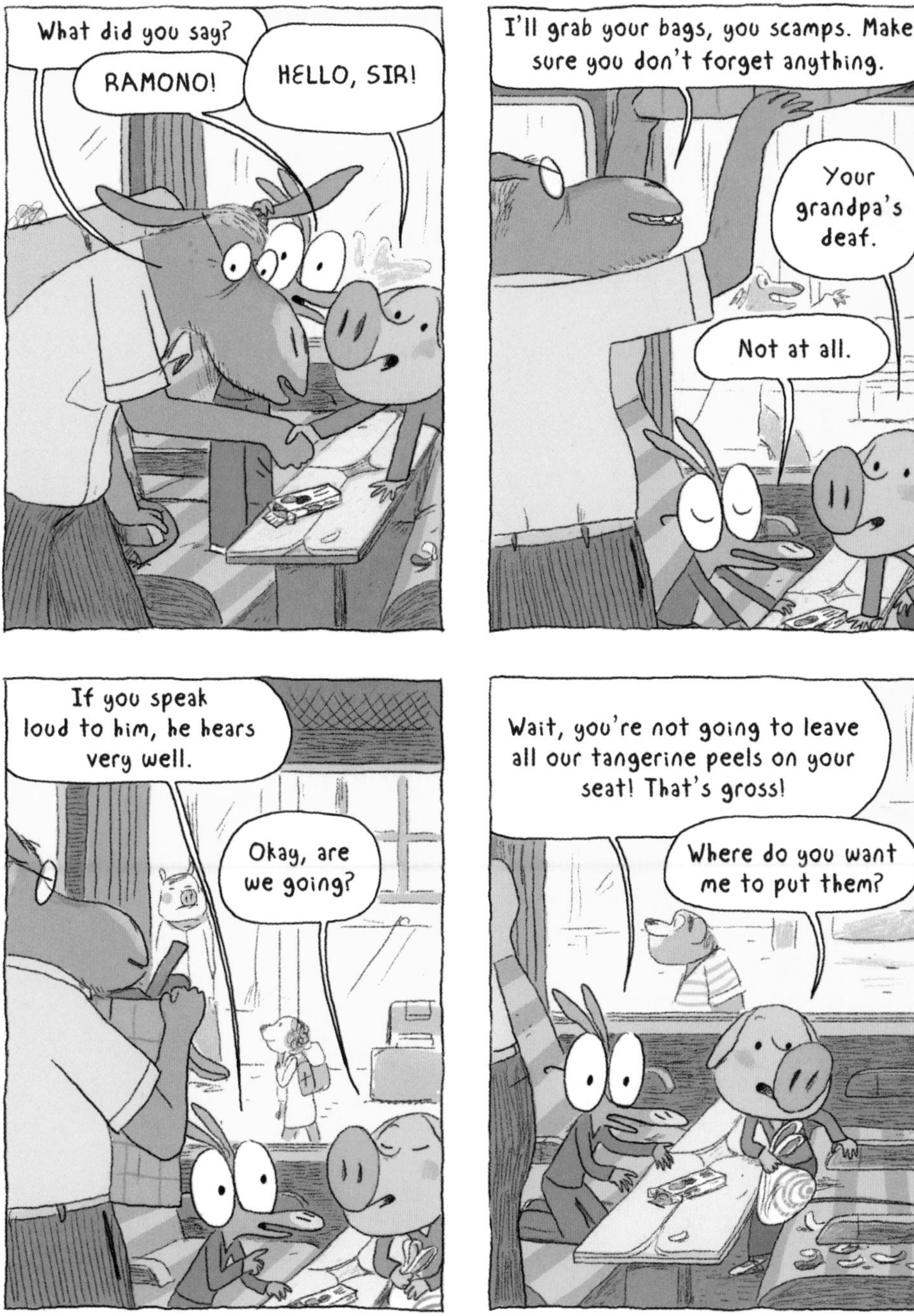
What did you say?
RAMONO!
HELLO, SIR!
I'll grab your bags, you scamps. Make sure you don't forget anything.
Your grandpa's deaf.
Not at all.
If you speak loud to him, he hears very well.
Okay, are we going?
Wait, you're not going to leave all our tangerine peels on your seat! That's gross!
Where do you want me to put them?

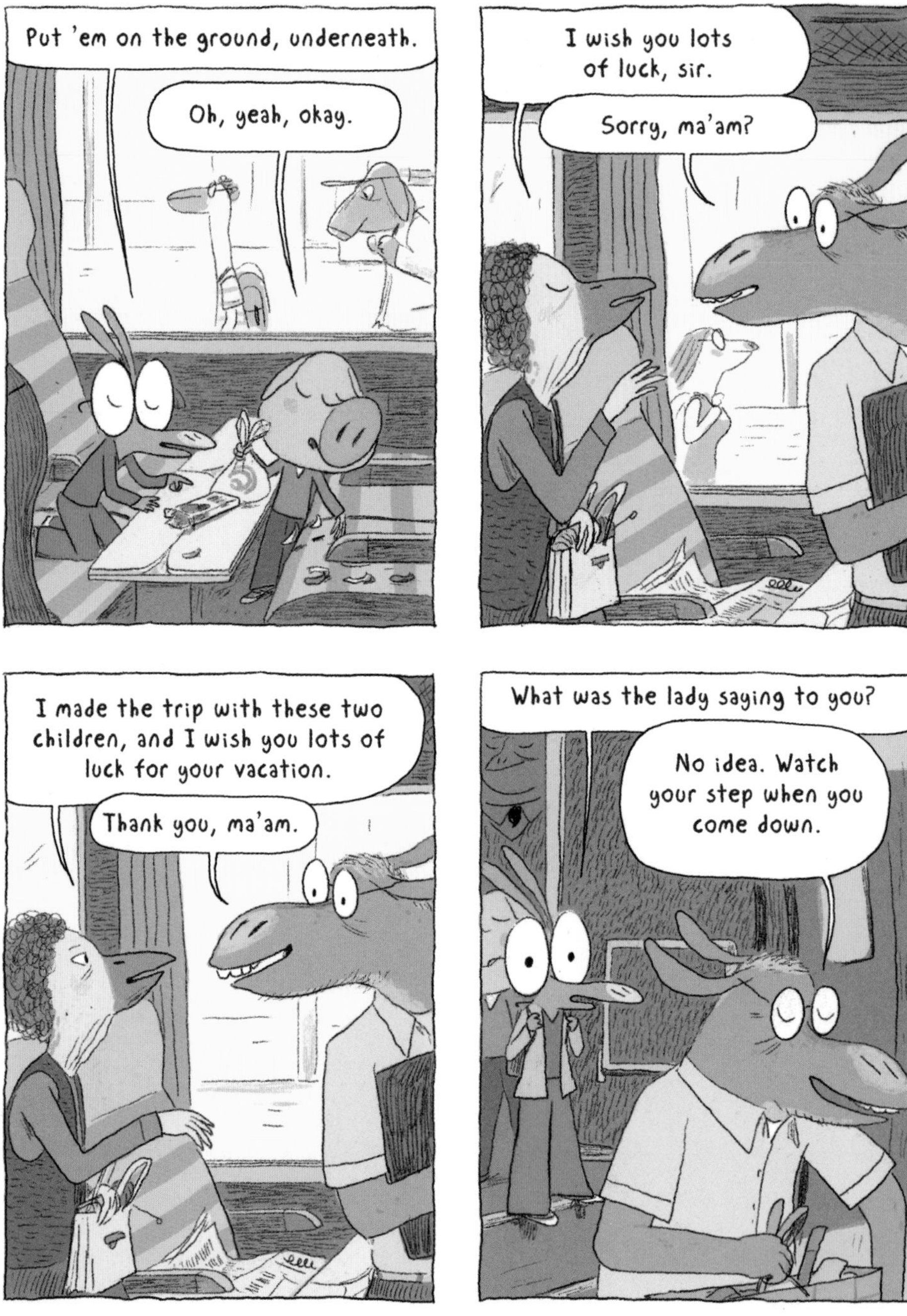
Put 'em on the ground, underneath.
Oh, yeah, okay.
I wish you lots of luck, sir.
Sorry, ma'am?
I made the trip with these two children, and I wish you lots of luck for your vacation.
Thank you, ma'am.
What was the lady saying to you?
No idea. Watch your step when you come down.

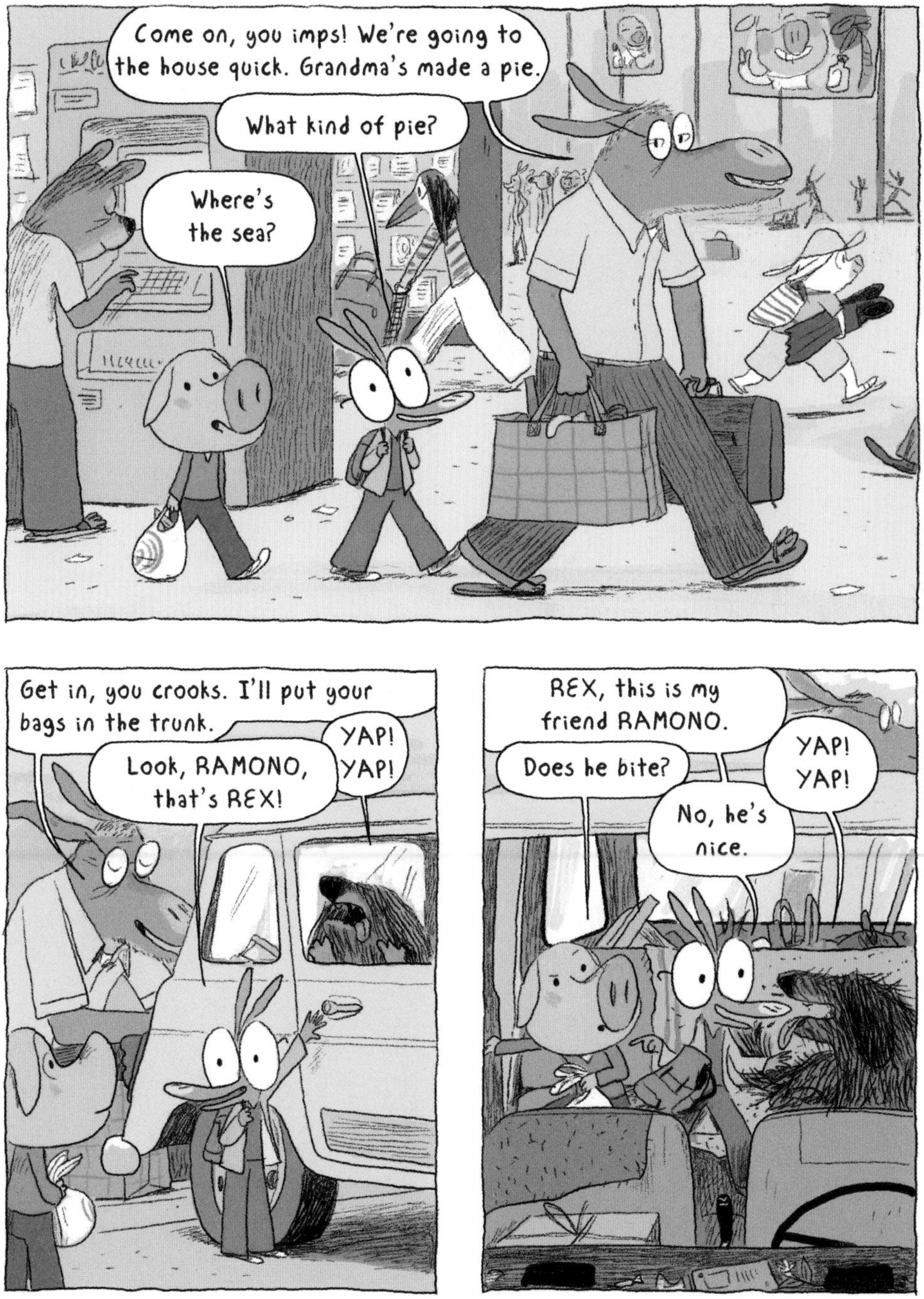
Come on, you imps! We're going to the house quick. Grandma's made a pie.
What kind of pie?
Where's the sea?
Get in, you crooks. I'll put your bags in the trunk.
Look, RAMONO, that's REX!
YAP! YAP!
REX, this is my friend RAMONO.
Does he bite?
YAP! YAP!
No, he's nice.

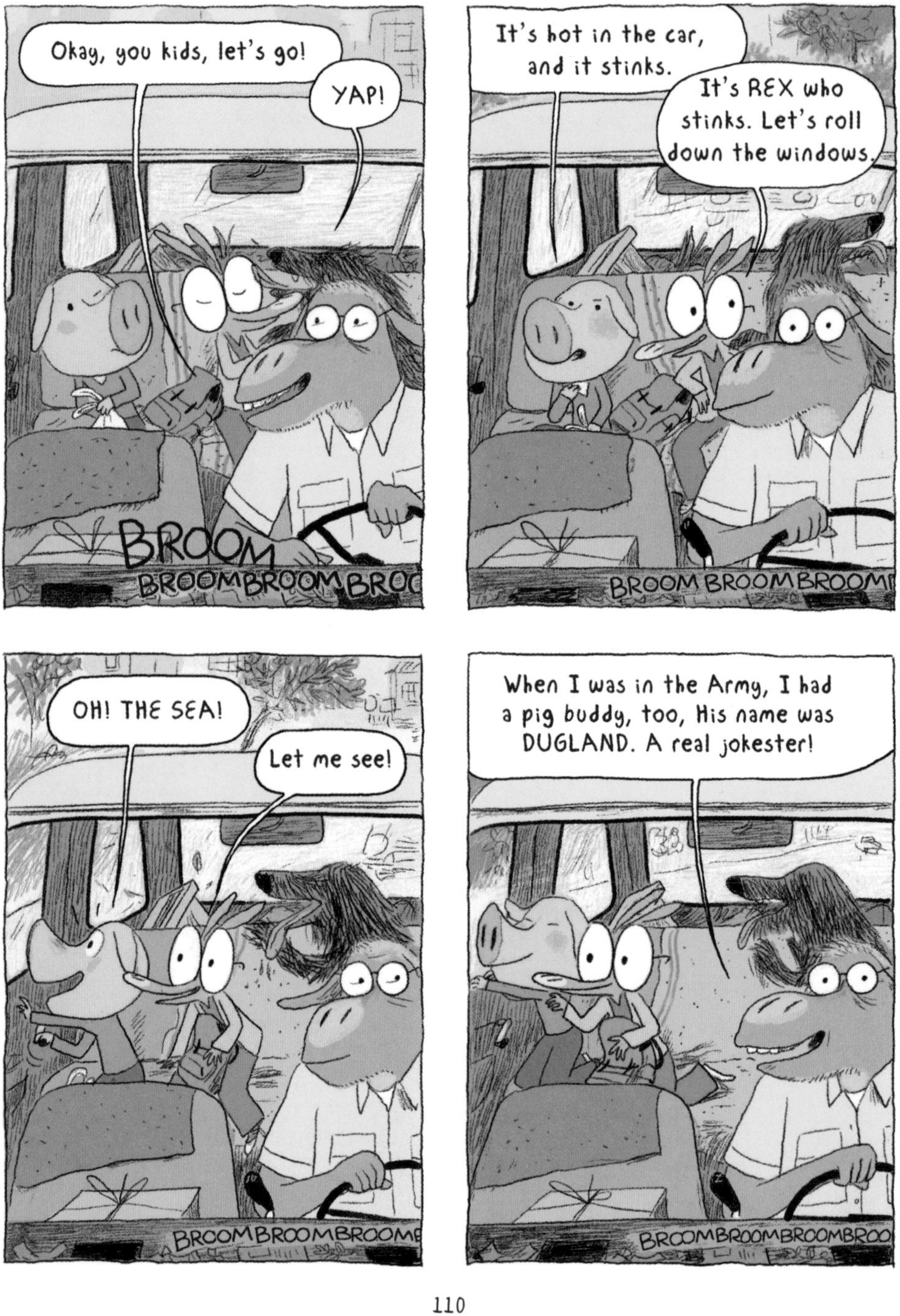
Okay, you kids, let's go!
YAP!
BROOM
BROOMBROOMBROO
It's hot in the car, and it stinks.
It's REX who stinks. Let's roll down the windows.
BROOM BROOMBROOM
OH! THE SEA!
Let me see!
BROOMBROOMBROOM
When I was in the Army, I had a pig buddy, too, His name was DUGLAND. A real jokester!
BROOMBROOMBROOMBROO

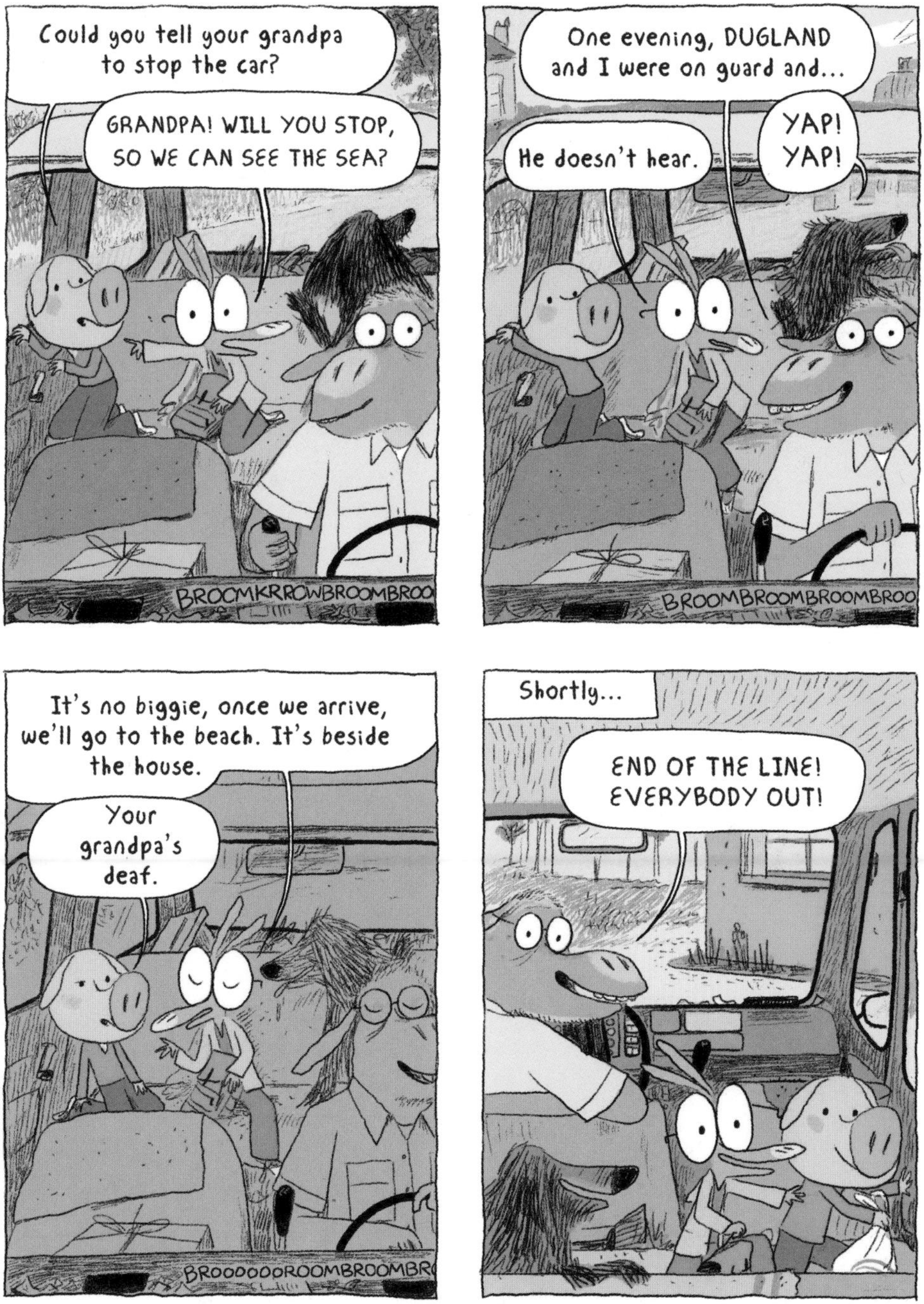
Could you tell your grandpa to stop the car?
GRANDPA! WILL YOU STOP, SO WE CAN SEE THE SEA?
BROOMKRROWBROOMBROO
One evening, DUGLAND and I were on guard and...
He doesn't hear.
YAP! YAP!
BROOMBROOMBROOMBROO
It's no biggie, once we arrive, we'll go to the beach. It's beside the house.
Your grandpa's deaf.
BROOOOOOROOMBROOMBR
Shortly...
END OF THE LINE! EVERYBODY OUT!

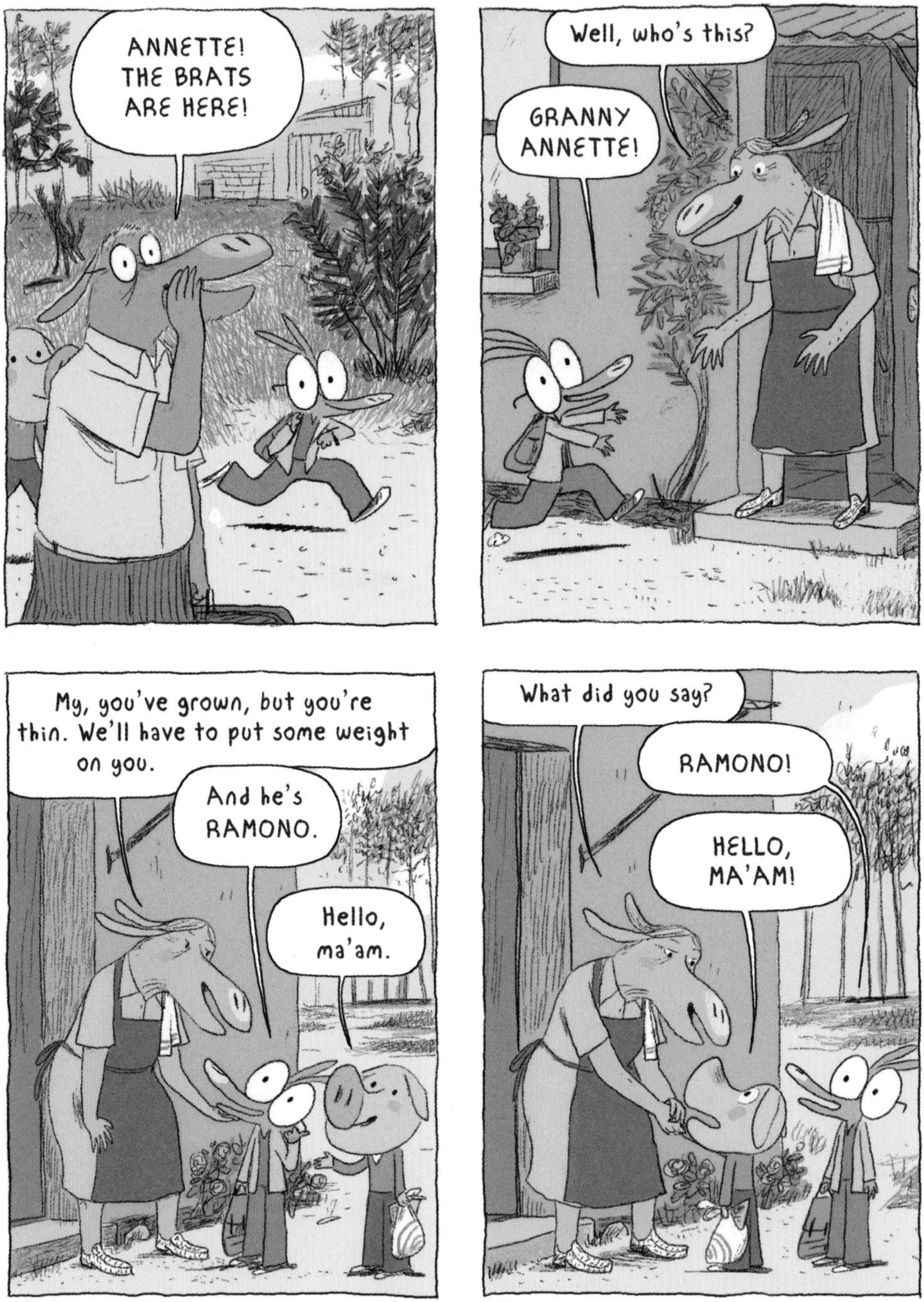
ANNETTE! THE BRATS ARE HERE!
Well, who's this?
GRANNY ANNETTE!
My, you've grown, but you're thin. We'll have to put some weight on you.
And he's RAMONO.
Hello, ma'am.
What did you say?
RAMONO!
HELLO, MA'AM!

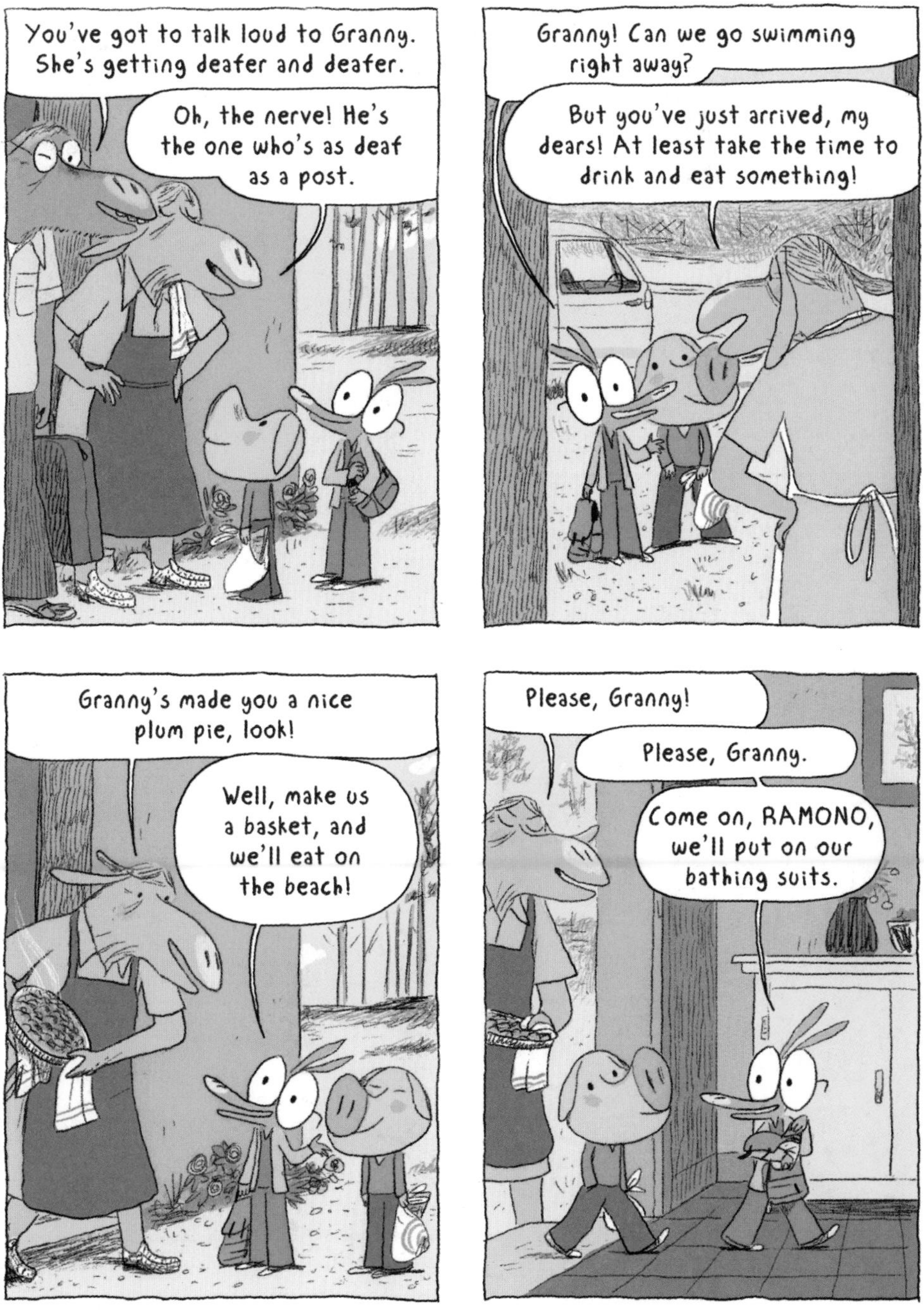
You've got to talk loud to Granny. She's getting deafer and deafer.
Oh, the nerve! He's the one who's as deaf as a post.
Granny! Can we go swimming right away?
But you've just arrived, my dears! At least take the time to drink and eat something!
Granny's made you a nice plum pie, look!
Well, make us a basket, and we'll eat on the beach!
Please, Granny!
Please, Granny.
Come on, RAMONO, we'll put on our bathing suits.

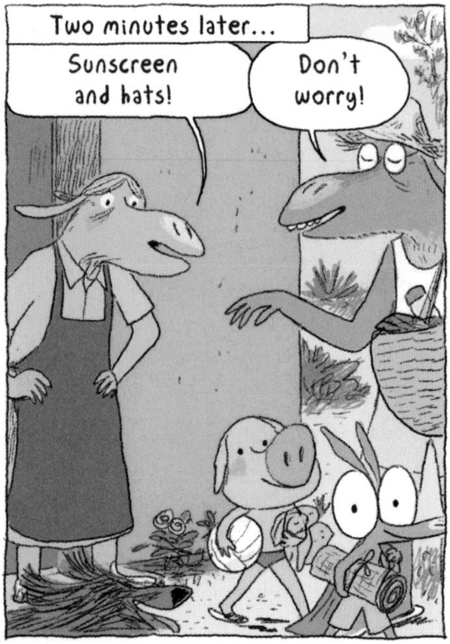
Two minutes later...
Sunscreen and hats!
Don't worry!

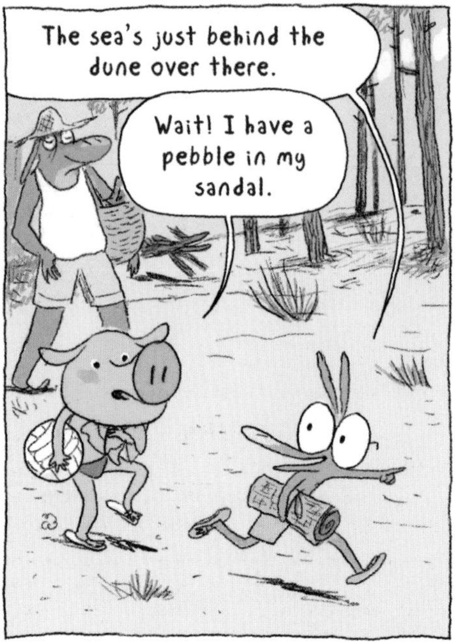
The sea's just behind the dune over there.
Wait! I have a pebble in my sandal.

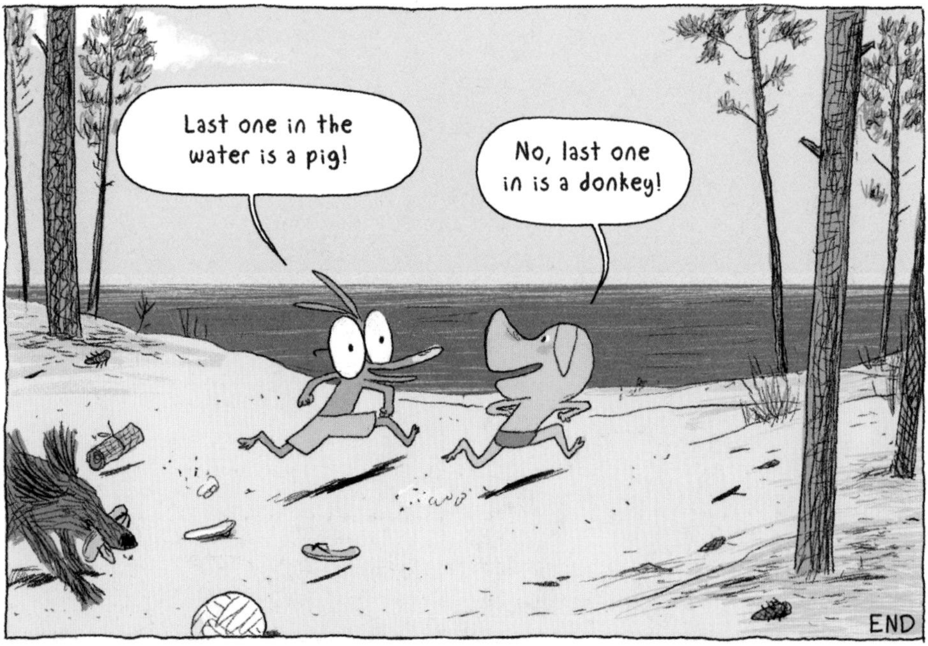
Last one in the water is a pig!
No, last one in is a donkey!
END

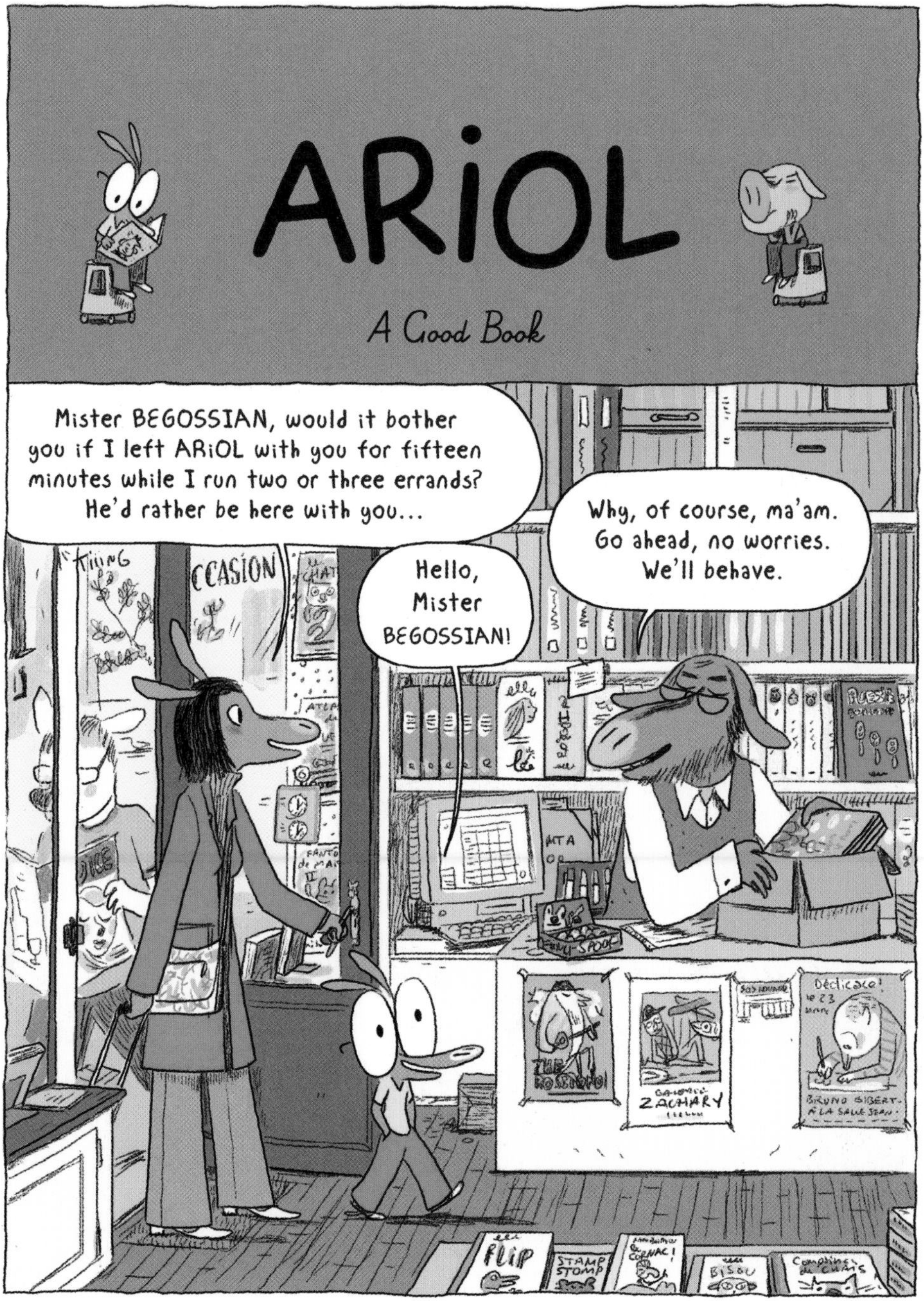
ARiOL
A Good Book
Mister BEGOSSIAN, would it bother you if I left ARiOL with you for fifteen minutes while I run two or three errands? He'd rather be here with you...
Hello, Mister BEGOSSIAN!
Why, of course, ma'am. Go ahead, no worries. We'll behave.
Tiiing
CCASION
ZACHARY
FLIP
STAMP STOMP
BISOU

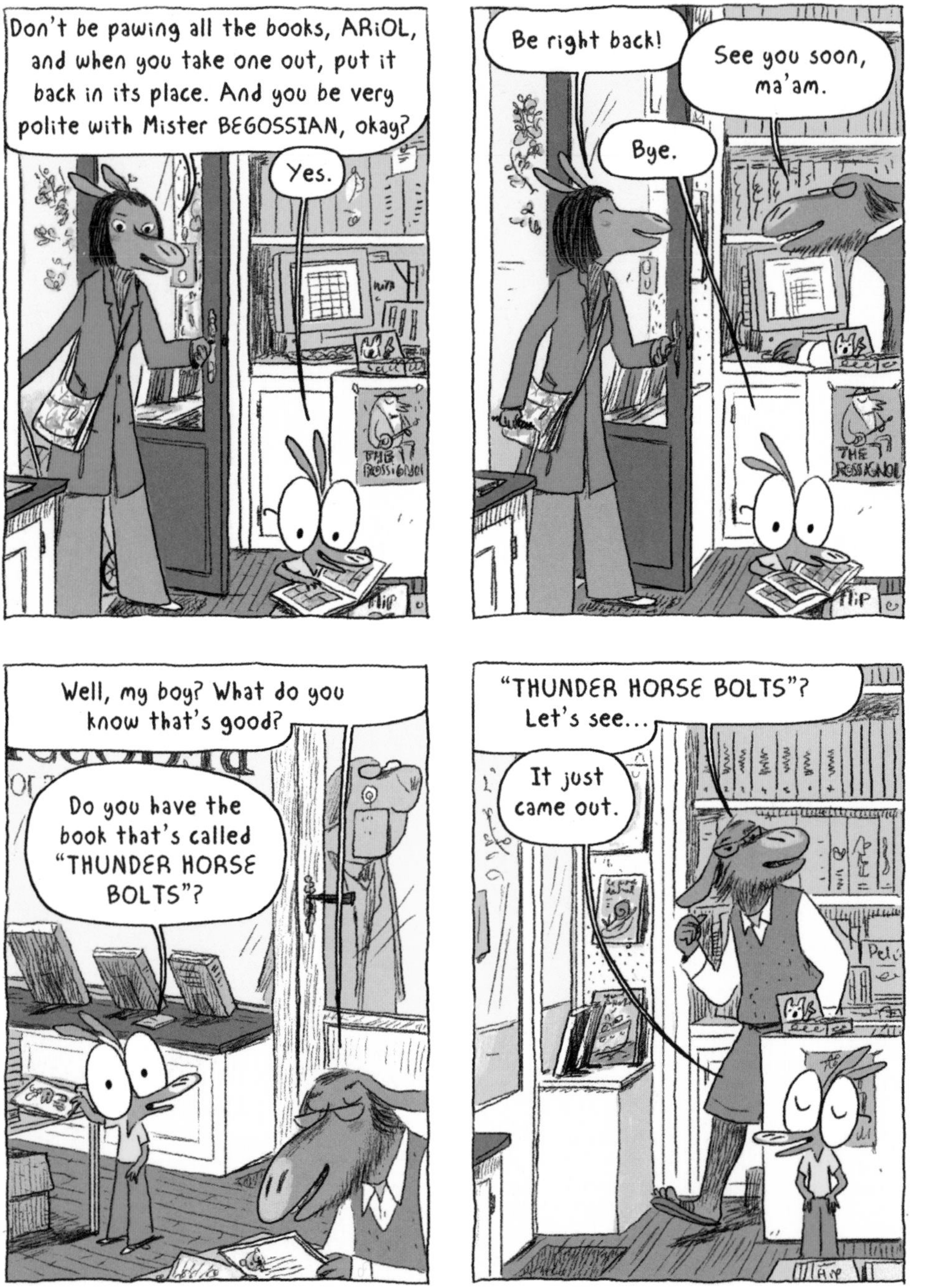
Don't be pawing all the books, ARiOL, and when you take one out, put it back in its place. And you be very polite with Mister BEGOSSIAN, okay?
Yes.
Be right back!
See you soon, ma'am.
Bye.
Well, my boy? What do you know that's good?
Do you have the book that's called "THUNDER HORSE BOLTS"?
"THUNDER HORSE BOLTS"? Let's see...
It just came out.

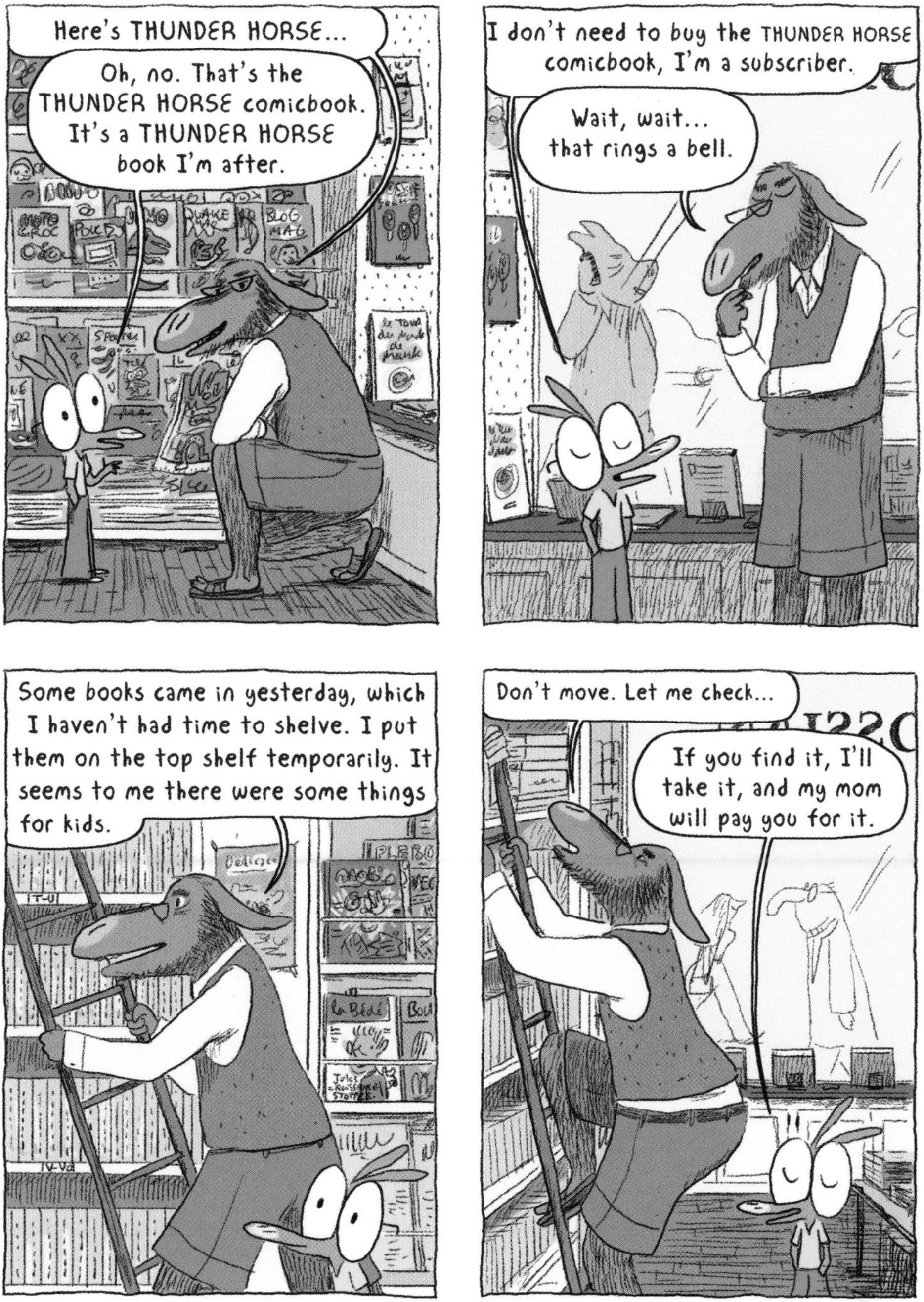
Here's THUNDER HORSE...
Oh, no. That's the THUNDER HORSE comicbook. It's a THUNDER HORSE book I'm after.
I don't need to buy the THUNDER HORSE comicbook, I'm a subscriber.
Wait, wait... that rings a bell.
Some books came in yesterday, which I haven't had time to shelve. I put them on the top shelf temporarily. It seems to me there were some things for kids.
Don't move. Let me check...
If you find it, I'll take it, and my mom will pay you for it.

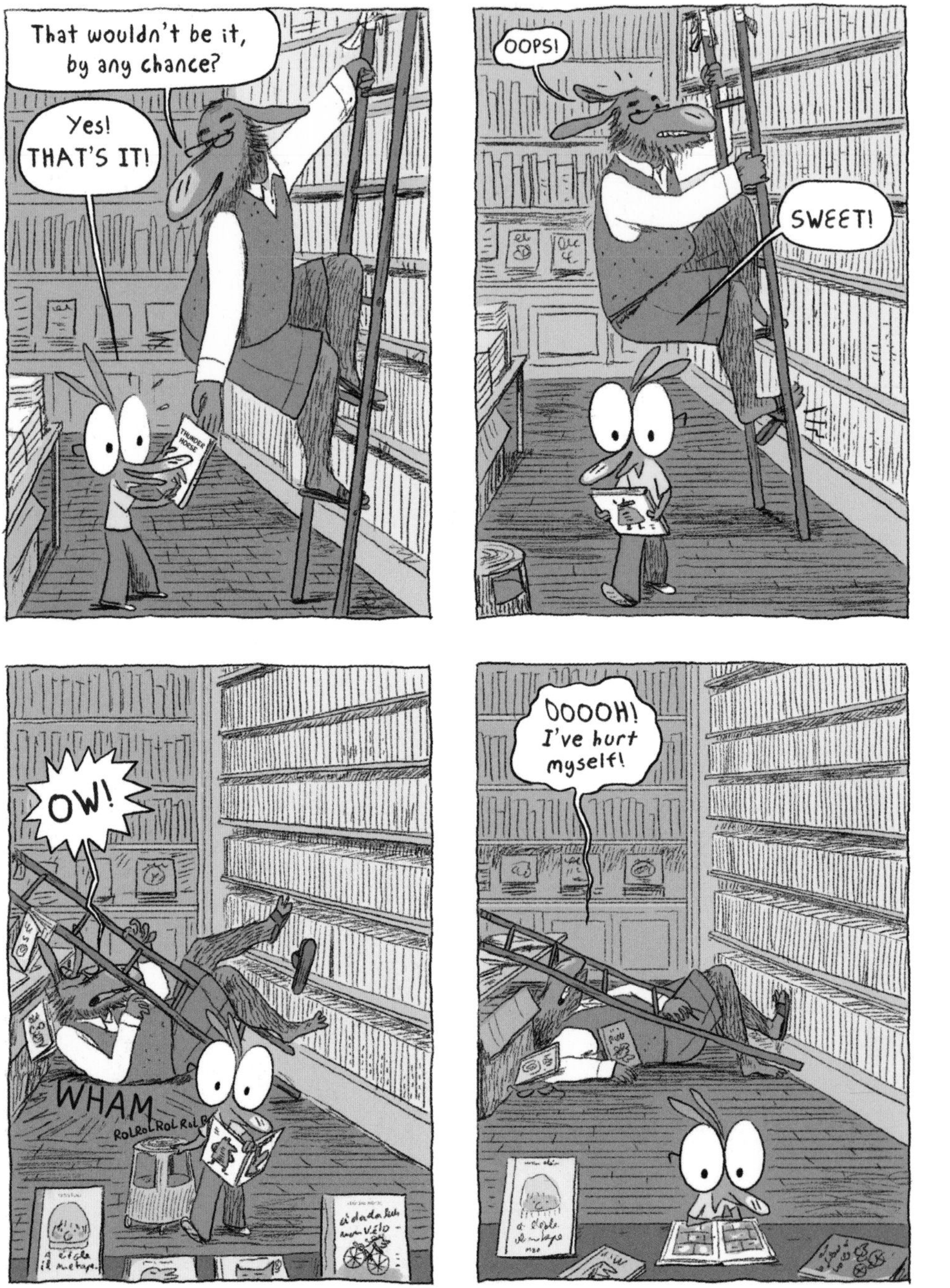
That wouldn't be it, by any chance?
Yes! THAT'S IT!
OOPS!
SWEET!
OW!
WHAM
OOOOH! I've hurt myself!

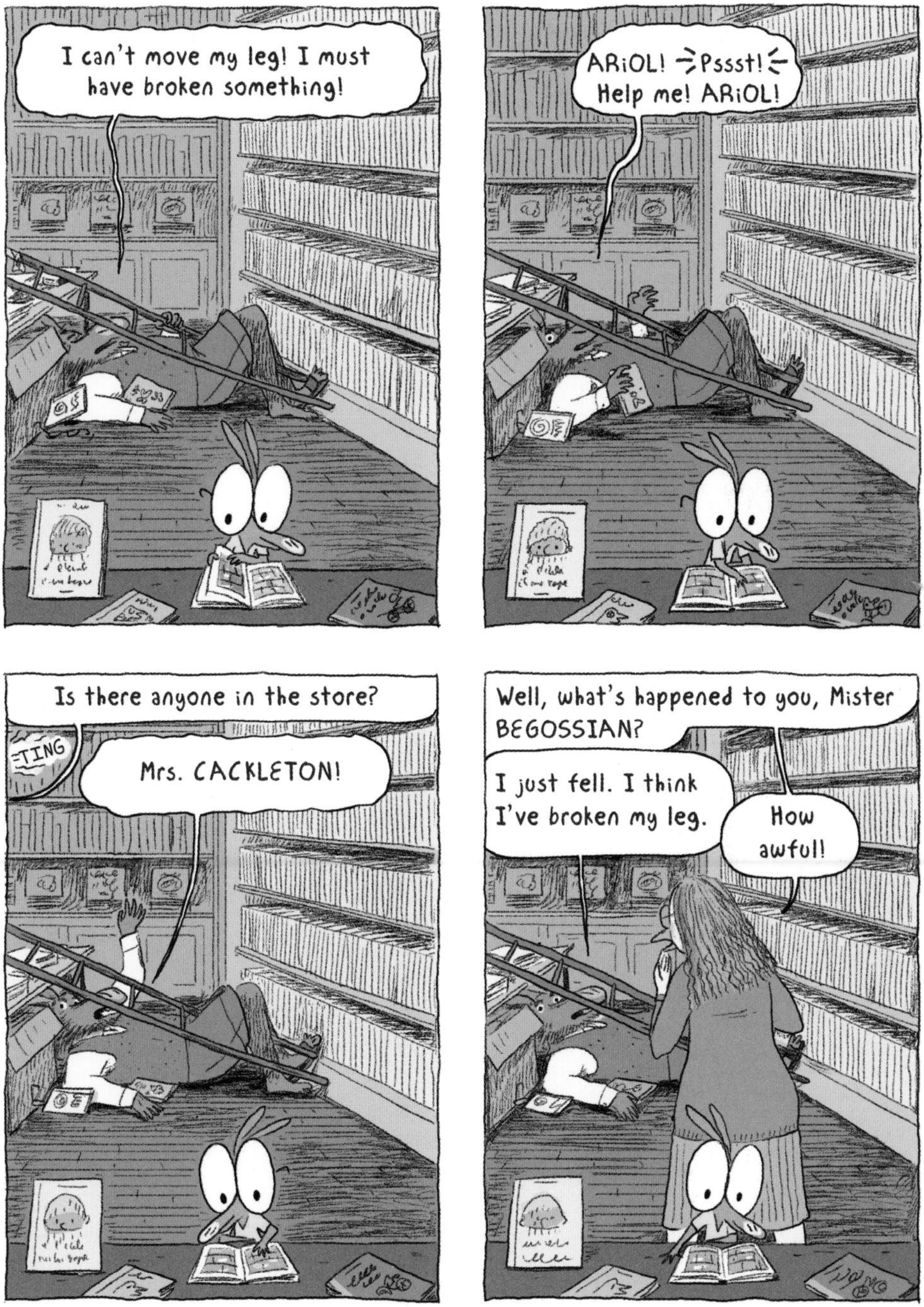
I can't move my leg! I must have broken something!
ARiOL! Pssst! Help me! ARiOL!
Is there anyone in the store?
TING
Mrs. CACKLETON!
Well, what's happened to you, Mister BEGOSSIAN?
I just fell. I think I've broken my leg.
How awful!

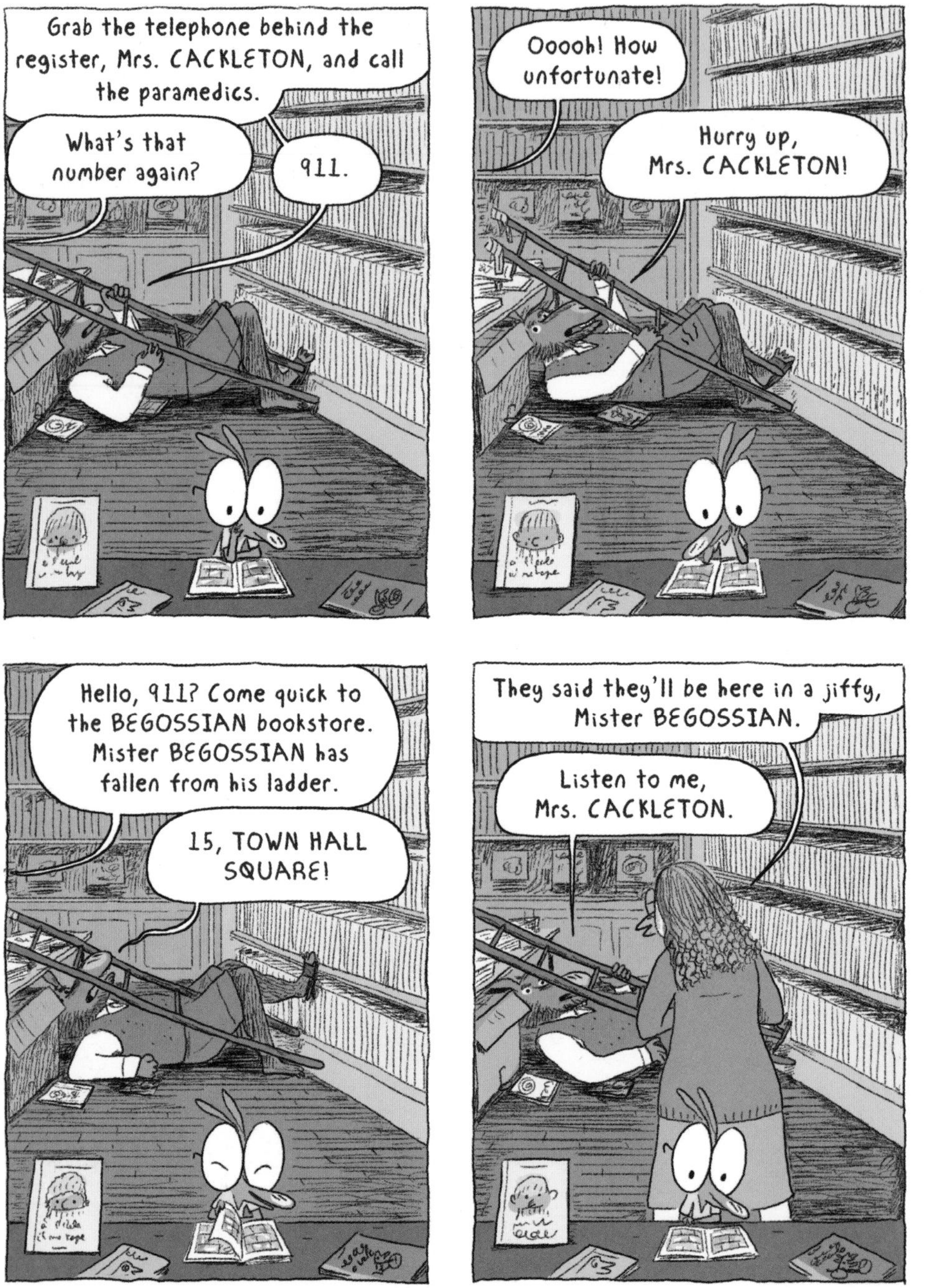
Grab the telephone behind the register, Mrs. CACKLETON, and call the paramedics.
What's that number again?
911.
Ooooh! How unfortunate!
Hurry up, Mrs. CACKLETON!
Hello, 911? Come quick to the BEGOSSIAN bookstore. Mister BEGOSSIAN has fallen from his ladder.
15, TOWN HALL SQUARE!
They said they'll be here in a jiffy, Mister BEGOSSIAN.
Listen to me, Mrs. CACKLETON.

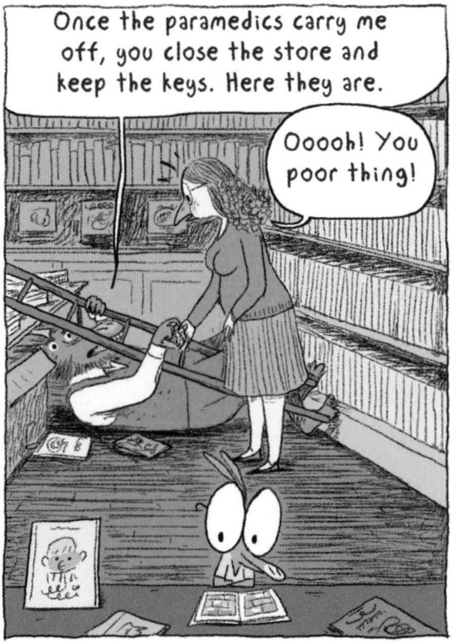
Once the paramedics carry me off, you close the store and keep the keys. Here they are.
Ooooh! You poor thing!

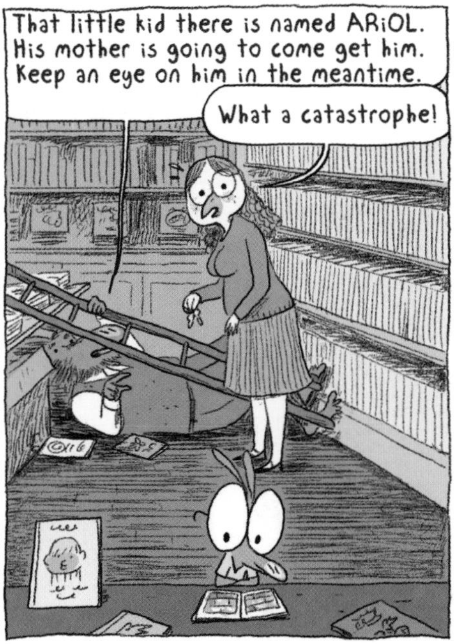
That little kid there is named ARiOL. His mother is going to come get him. Keep an eye on him in the meantime.
What a catastrophe!

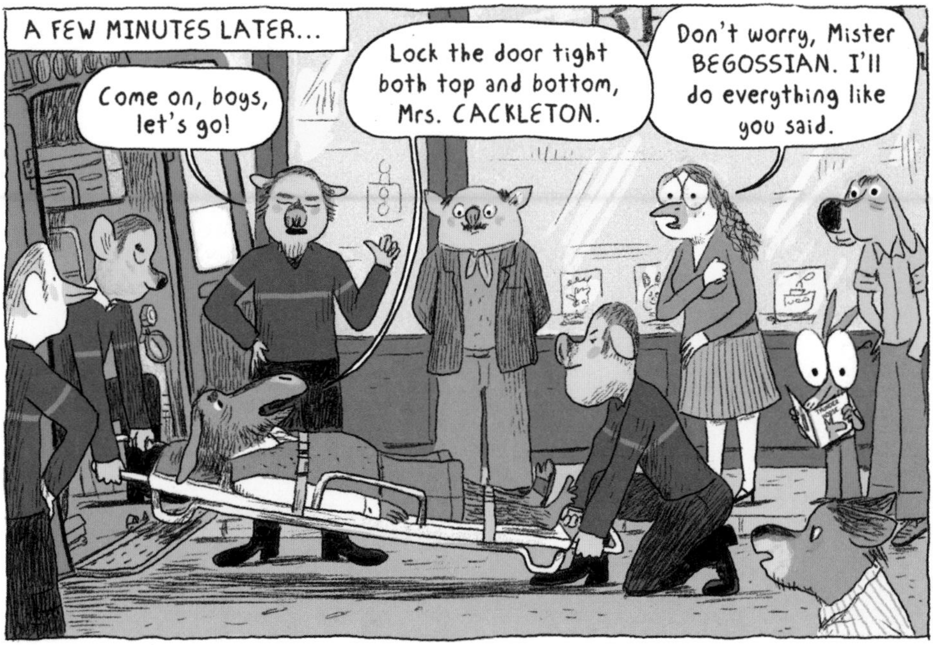
A FEW MINUTES LATER...
Come on, boys, let's go!
Lock the door tight both top and bottom, Mrs. CACKLETON.
Don't worry, Mister BEGOSSIAN. I'll do everything like you said.

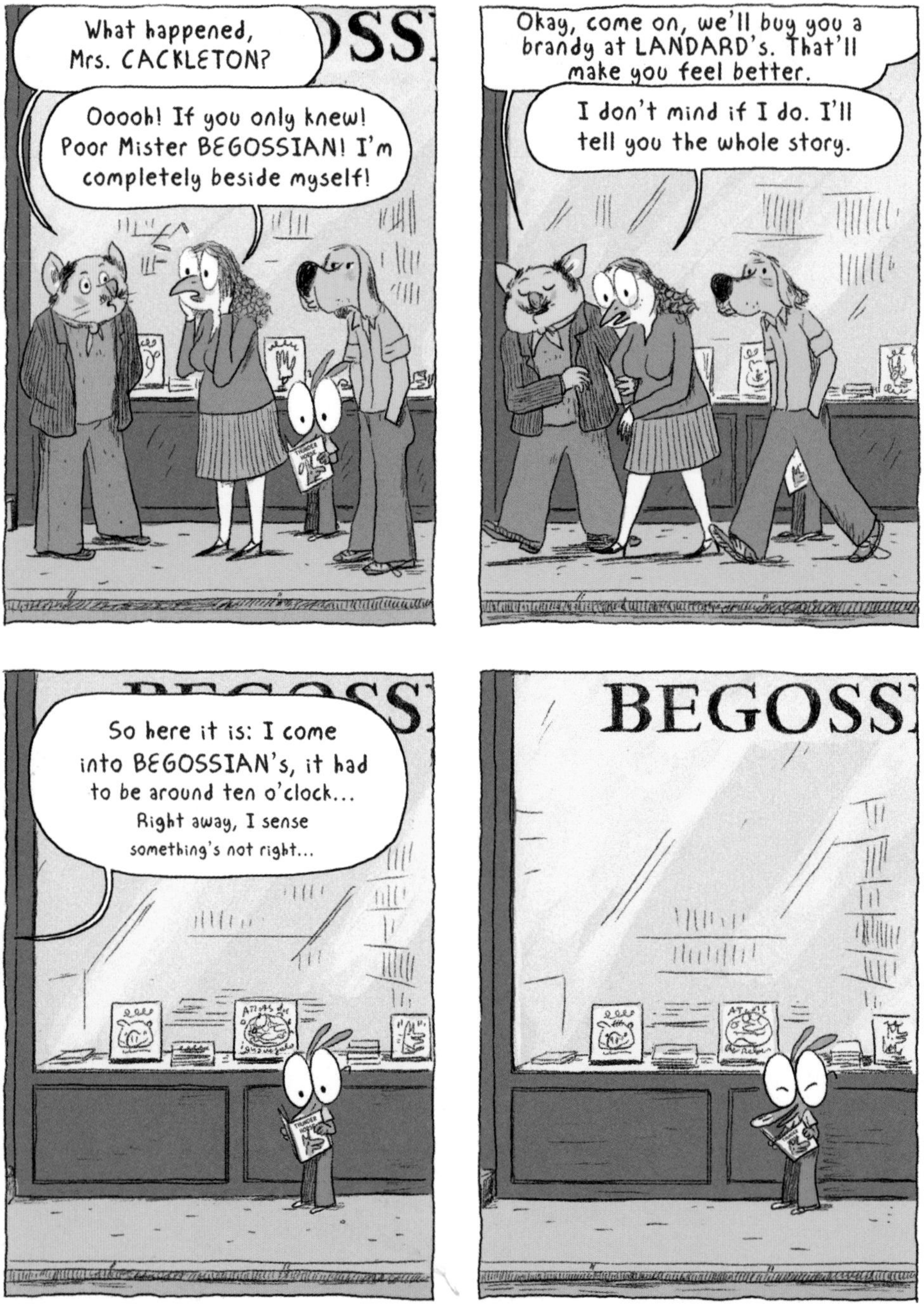
What happened, Mrs. CACKLETON?
Ooooh! If you only knew! Poor Mister BEGOSSIAN! I'm completely beside myself!
Okay, come on, we'll buy you a brandy at LANDARD's. That'll make you feel better.
I don't mind if I do. I'll tell you the whole story.
So here it is: I come into BEGOSSIAN's, it had to be around ten o'clock... Right away, I sense something's not right...
BEGOSS

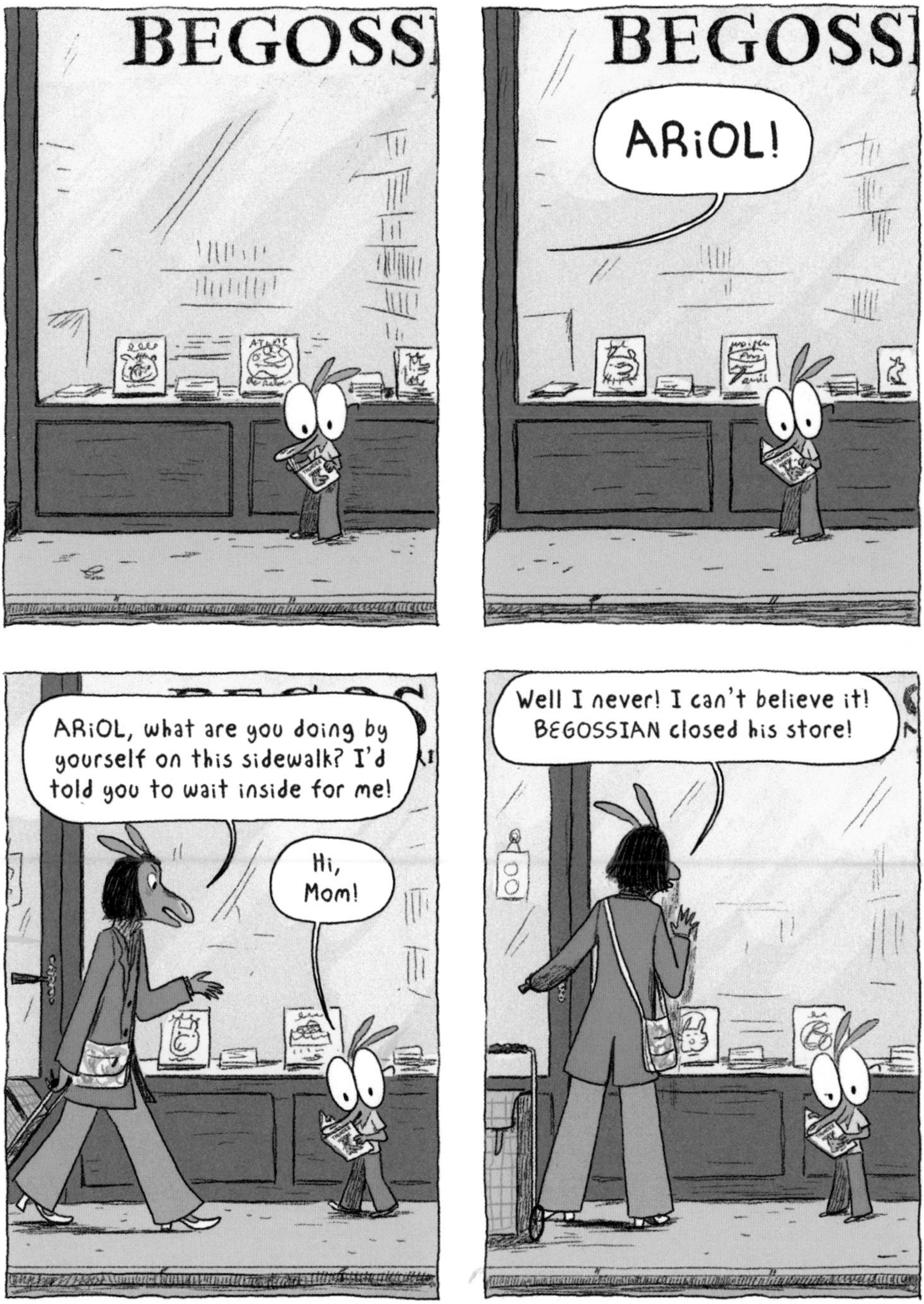
BEGOSS
BEGOSS
ARiOL!
ARiOL, what are you doing by yourself on this sidewalk? I'd told you to wait inside for me!
Hi, Mom!
Well I never! I can't believe it! BEGOSSIAN closed his store!

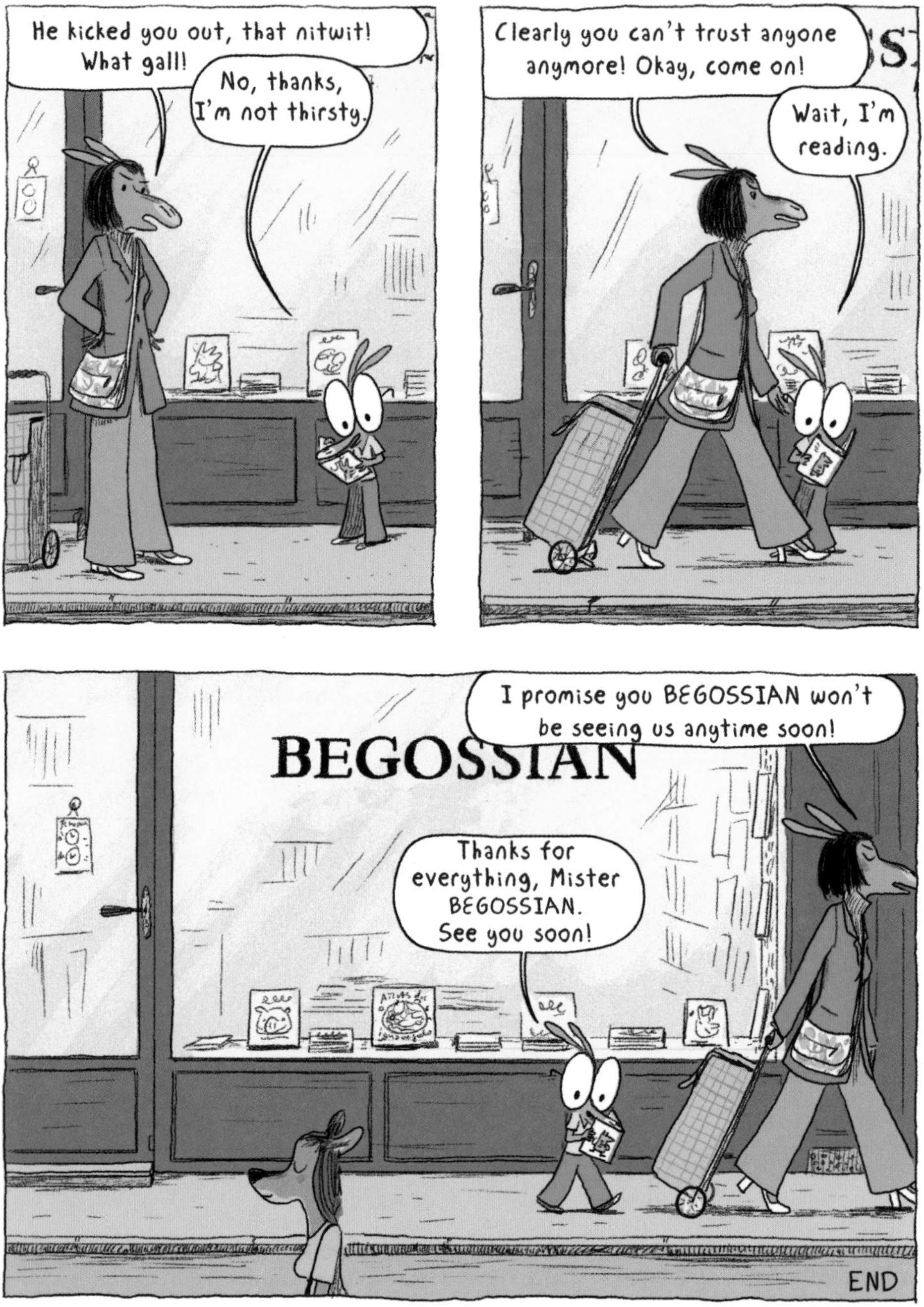
He kicked you out, that nitwit! What gall!
No, thanks, I'm not thirsty.
Clearly you can't trust anyone anymore! Okay, come on!
Wait, I'm reading.
BEGOSSIAN
I promise you BEGOSSIAN won't be seeing us anytime soon!
Thanks for everything, Mister BEGOSSIAN. See you soon!
END

WATCH OUT FOR PAPERCUT**Z**

Welcome to the second super-heroic ARiOL graphic novel by Emmanuel Guibert and Marc Boutavant from Papercutz, the folks dedicated to creating great graphic novels for all ages. I'm Jim Salicrup, your mild-mannered Editor-in-Chief and secret THUN- DER HORSE fan, here to share a few thoughts about "animals" in comics.

In the wacky world of comics there are all sorts of comics. Although if you visited your average comicbook store, you might think there were only super-hero comics. But over the years there have been Western comics, Romance comics, War comics, Teen comics, Humor comics, and many others, including something called "Funny Animal" comics.

So-called "Funny Animal" comics tend to usually feature very human-like animals-- for example: Mickey Mouse and Donald Duck. At Papercutz we've published the "Mon- ster" graphic novels by Lewis Trondheim, GERONIMO STILTON, THEA STILTON, and ARiOL by Emmanuel Guibert and Marc Boutavant. In Trondheim's "Monster" series, the main cast of characters are very human-like because they're based on Trond- heim's very own family! Now, having met Mr. Trondheim a few times, I can tell you, he doesn't have a beak. Nor does he exhibit any bird-like behavior. In ARiOL, the charac- ters do in some ways have aspects of the characters they're based on worked into their personalities, but they're still very much human.

I always thought that it was really strange that Mickey Mouse has a pet dog! Think about it-- how many mice have you seen that are bigger than dogs? And Mickey also has a friend, Goofy, who's also a dog. I was reminded of all this silliness, when on page 84, Ramono, known for his voracious appetite turns down a particular type of sandwich.

So, until someone explains to me what a metaphor is, remember that I'm just a donkey--like you!

Thanks,

JIM

STAY IN TOUCH!

EMAIL: papercutz@papercutz.com
WEB: www.papercutz.com
TWITTER: @papercutzgn
FACEBOOK: PAPERCUTZGRAPHICNOVELS
REGULAR MAIL: Papercutz, 160 Broadway, Suite 700, East Wing, New York, NY 10038

Other Great Titles From PAPERCUTZ™

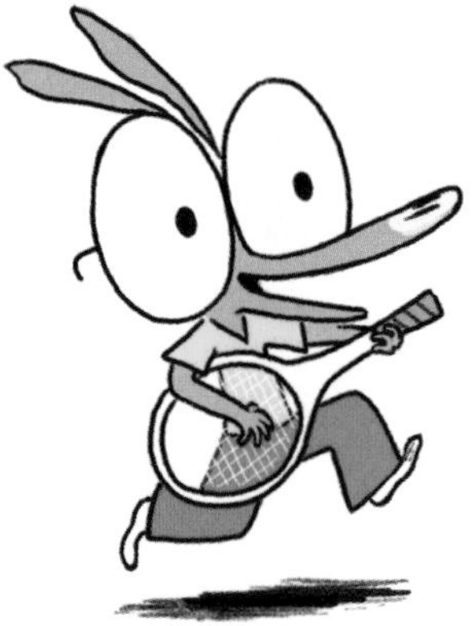

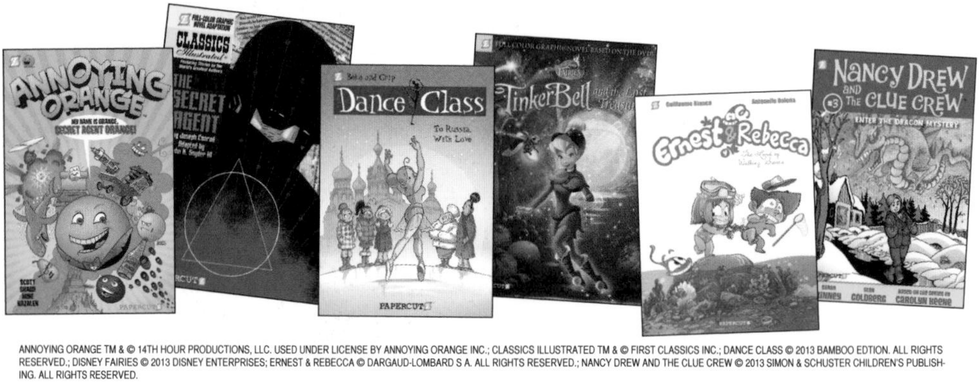
ANNOYING ORANGE
CLASSICS Illustrated
THE SECRET AGENT
Dance Class
To Russia, With Love
PAPERCUTZ
Tinker Bell
Ernest & Rebecca
Nancy Drew and the Clue Crew
#3
ENTER THE DRAGON MYSTERY

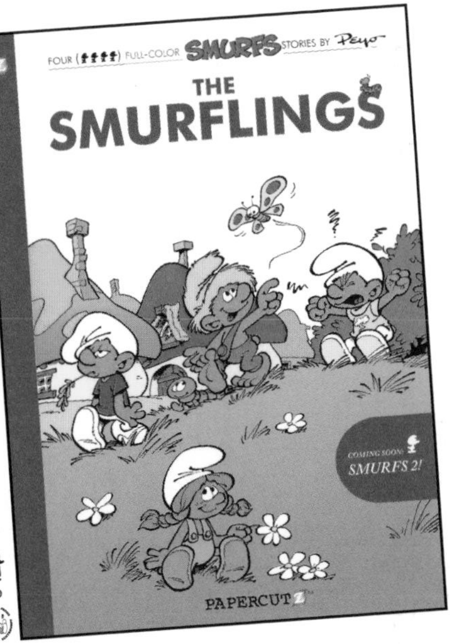
FOUR FULL-COLOR SMURFS STORIES BY Peyo
THE SMURFLINGS
COMING SOON: SMURFS 2!
PAPERCUT

And Don't Forget . . .

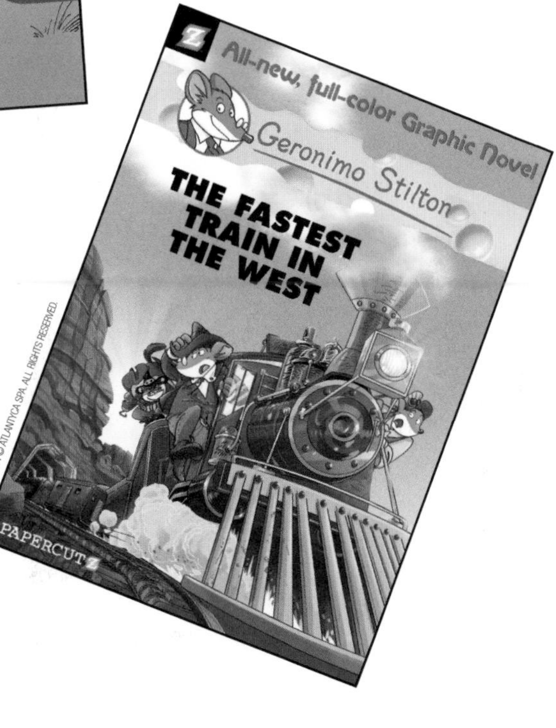
All-new, full-color Graphic Novel
Geronimo Stilton
THE FASTEST TRAIN IN THE WEST
PAPERCUT